The Ancient World

The Ancient World
The Eastern Empires, Greece, Rome

by

Albert Malet

PREFACE

I HAVE used *L'Antiquité*, by Albert Malet, as a work of reference in teaching the Middle Forms of the Park School, Preston, and the First year Freebel Students at the Maria Grey Training College.

I have known many history teachers deterred from the teaching of World History by the lack of suitable text-books, and I have made this translation of a book written to meet the requirements of French secondary schools, in the hope that it will fill a long-felt want, by providing a book for the first year's work.

I wish to express my thanks to Miss Alice M. Stoneman, Head Mistress of the Park School, Preston, who first brought the book to my notice, and who kindly allowed me to make use of the translation she had already begun, and to Mrs. Jehanne Russell, whose advice and encouragement have helped me throughout.

PHYLLIS WOODHAM SMITH.

Maria Grey Training College,
June 1920

Contents

PART I.

THE EASTERN EMPIRES

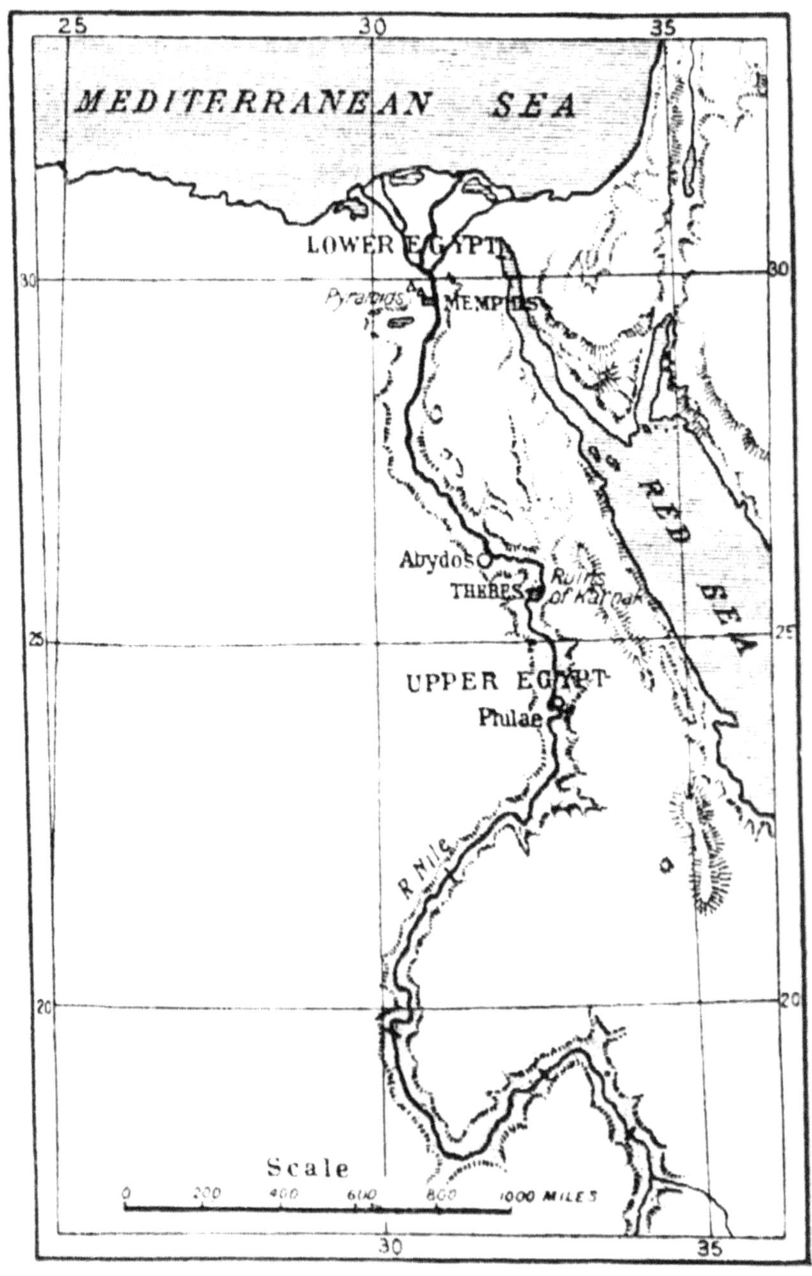

FIG. 1. - The Egypt of the Pharaohs.

CHAPTER I

EGYPT

EGYPT lies at the north-east corner of Africa, quite close to Asia, to which it is joined by the Isthmus of Suez. The Mediterranean and the Red Sea bound it on the north and east; on the south and west, it is surrounded by the desert. In these parts, rain seldom falls; the rainfall of a century is less than the rainfall of London for one year. So, for lack of water, Egypt would be nothing but a desert, a vast plain barren of all vegetation, if the Nile did not flow through it. In the middle of the plain is a long, narrow channel; its sides rise steeply and, seen from below, look like ranges of mountains; on the west rises the Libyan range, on the east the Arabian range. The Nile, coming from the Sahara, passes over six cataracts and then enters between these walls; its course is from south to north, carrying on average 13,000 cubic meters of water per second, which is five times as much as the Seine at flood. It overflows its banks each year from June to December; the soil becomes fertile wherever its waters spread. This led the ancients to say that "Egypt is the gift of the Nile." The river has made an oasis more than 500 miles in length, but of a width varying only from five to thirty miles. This valley is about as long as from the north of Scotland to the south of England.

Towards the north, near Cairo, the channel widens, and its walls divide into the form of a V. They outline an angle which was formerly a gulf of the Mediterranean. Here the Nile has deposited its alluvial soil, which has accumulated for thousands of years; it has made a piece of land that grows continually and advances yearly almost a yard into the sea.

In this land, the arms of the river and the coast form a triangle like the A of the Greek alphabet (a delta inverted): hence the land is called the Delta, which was the name given it by the ancients. The valley of the Nile forms Upper Egypt; the plain of the Delta is called Lower Egypt.

The rising of the Nile and the regularity with which this rising took place astonished the Egyptians, because they did not know the sources of the river—the Victoria and Albert Nyanza, immense equatorial lakes of which the Nile is the outlet—and because they did not know of the immense rainfall which occurs regularly in the upper part of its course and forms huge tributaries: on the left bank the Bahr-el-Ghazel, with its vast marshes; on the right, the Sobat, the Blue Nile, and the Atbara, rising in the volcanic rocks of Abyssinia. So the Egyptians regarded the river as a god, because it overflowed its banks although no rain had fallen on the land. This god descended from heaven and appeared to man between Elephantine and the island of Philae, near the cataract of Syene. He rose there from two bottomless abysses, and his overflow was due to the tears of Isis weeping for her husband, and from this came the fertilizing power of the water.

It was only in the nineteenth century that the 3,500 miles of the course of the Nile were entirely explored, and the phenomenon was fully explained.

In the month of June, the Nile is reduced to half its width; it flows, sky-blue in color, between banks of black mud. Vegetation is everywhere scorched by the desert wind blowing from the south. Then the Nile begins to rise; it loses its blue color and becomes green and brackish. The green color is due to the rubbish swept down from the marshes of Bahr-el-Ghazel. Some days pass, and the Nile still increases in volume and once more changes its color. Its waters are now full of red mud, which does not prevent them from being fresh and fit for drinking. The river seems to be made of blood. About July 15, the dams which hold in the river are opened, the water spreads over the fields, and deposits its fertile mud. The whole valley between the two ranges is now only a sheet of dirty water, which shimmers in the sun, and from the water rise like islands the villages, surrounded with palm trees, and the black causeways which connect village with village. Till the months of August and September, the flood is at its height; from then till December, the river returns little by little to its bed. Now is the moment to sow the seed, and four months later comes the harvest. These different phases in the life of the Nile and of Egypt were characterized by the Arabian conqueror Amru in these words: "Egypt," he said, "is in succession a mud field, a sea of fresh water, and a flower garden."

The rising of the Nile is the festival of the joy of Nature. The country revives, men and animals arouse themselves from their torpor, and life is reborn everywhere. An old hymn in honor of the god Nile celebrates this new birth in the following words: "Hail, O Nile, who hast appeared on this earth and cometh in peace to give life to Egypt. Thou waterest the earth everywhere, God of the Seeds, Lord of the Fishes, Creator of the Corn, Producer of the Barley. He rises, the earth is filled with joy, every belly rejoices, every living being has received its food, he creates all good things, Lord of all fair and dainty cates[1]. He makes the grass to sprout for the cattle, he prepares sacrifices for each god. He takes possession of the land that he may fill the marts and crowd the granaries and prepare abundance for the poor."

The entire area of land suitable for habitation is about equal to the area of Belgium, while the total area of Egypt is almost as large as that of France. On this little space live today nearly eleven million men, and in ancient times the number was not less.

So large a population can be supported by the extraordinary fertility of the mud deposited by the river. The seed is scattered broadcast onto this mud without any previous work, and the animals are driven into the fields to tread the grain into the earth.

In this way, the soil produces different crops: wheat, barley, dhura, millet; and leguminous plants such as lupines, beans, chickpeas, and lentils. Where water cannot naturally come, it is raised by hand, and so it is possible to cultivate gardens and

---

1   Delicacies or choice foods.

orchards planted with apricot and fig trees, on which vines also grow. Trees are rare: in some districts, sycamores are found; everywhere, the palm tree yields its dates and scanty shade.

Oxen, sheep, goats, and large flocks of geese are bred on the farms. The horse is a mark of wealth and is imported from Asia. The Nile feeds swarms of aquatic birds and fish. Its characteristic animals are the crocodile and the hippopotamus; its characteristic plants, the papyrus, whose bark was used for paper, and the lotus, whose fruit was edible and whose flower supplied to artists, architects, workers in jewels, and sculptors many suggestions for decoration and ornaments.

There is much discussion about the origin of the Egyptians. The most competent Egyptologists, including Maspero, regard them as a people of mixed nationality, with a predominating Semitic strain. In that case, the Egyptians would have come from Asia, although the Greeks thought they came from Africa, from the south or Ethiopia. The statues which have been found in the tombs, the men sculptured on the bas-reliefs or the monuments, show that the Egyptians of antiquity resemble the fellahs or peasants of today. When Mariette discovered one of the most celebrated Egyptian statues, his workmen thought they recognized one of their countrymen and called it Shekh-al-Balad, the Chief of the Village. The Egyptians were generally tall; the lower part of the body was thin, with narrow thighs and thin legs; but their shoulders were broad, high, and thick, their

Papyrus

Lotus

FIG. 2.

arms slim, while their feet and hands were long and fine. They had low foreheads, short noses, large eyes, and thick lips. The general expression of the face was gentle.

The gentleness of their face was reproduced in their character. Generally speaking, the Egyptians were patient, hard-working, obedient, improvident, and superstitious. They had strong natural affections. Woman, contrary to the general custom of the East, was held in high respect. She went out freely, with her face unveiled; she managed her house and was mistress in it. Respect and love for a man's mother were held as the first and most sacred of duties.

Their manners were simple. The common people lived sparsely, principally on cakes of millet, baked in the ashes. They lived in poor houses, square in shape and built of bricks, which were made of mud and chopped straw dried in the sun. The houses were low, with flat roofs made of palm leaves. The houses of the rich were more comfortable and were like modern Arabs' houses. The only openings were on the inner court.

The costume is known to us from wall paintings and bas-reliefs. Men of high rank wore a pleated petticoat called "calasiris" and a tunic with sleeves. The common people wore nothing but a piece of cloth tied around the waist and reaching as far as the middle of the leg. This was called a loincloth. The women wore a long, narrow dress supported by braces. The children wore no garments. The foot covering was generally a piece of leather attached to the foot by two thongs, one going around the ankle, the other passing between the toes. All the people painted the skin around the eyes with black antimony to soften the glare and to avoid ophthalmia. Rich people wore long, plaited wigs to protect them from the sun.

The Nile has determined the life of the Egyptians. Coming into Egypt in wandering tribes, they were obliged to defend themselves from the river floods by united effort. They grouped their houses on the higher ground and built dams. To get food, they began to sow the mud of the river. So they formed the habit of cultivating the earth and living in societies. Villages and towns grew

FIG. 3. - Peasant of modern Egypt.

up along the banks. Small states, called Nomes, were organized. The Nomes grouped themselves little by little into two large states, corresponding to the two natural divisions of Egypt: Lower Egypt in the north, near the sea, with a capital, Memphis, and Upper Egypt in the south, farther from the sea, with a capital, Thebes. In the end, the two states united, and the chiefs of the Nomes became the vassals of Pharaoh, the king of a united Egypt. According to tradition, this union was the work of Menes. He was the first king of the human race, but the kingship had a divine character: Pharaoh was the son of God.

From the time of Menes to the conquest of Egypt by the Persians, that is, from 5000–525 B.C., Egypt had twenty-six dynasties or families of kings. The first ten dynasties reigned at Memphis, the ten following at Thebes. The power then passed to the priest-kings of Napata in Ethiopia, still further south.

Then ensued a time of anarchy: Egypt was broken up into divisions, and unity was only restored by the princes of the 26th dynasty, who reigned at Sais. This long period was entirely concerned with internal events. The Egyptians only left their country to make sundry expeditions towards the Euphrates. In return, they experienced the invasion of the Hyksos, or shepherds, who came from the deserts beyond the Isthmus of Suez in the time of the Empire of Memphis, and the invasion of the Assyrians in the time of the Empire of Napata (671 B.C.). Finally, the Persians overthrew the 26th dynasty (525 B.C.).

The Egyptians were a hard-working and peaceful race and were naturally prone to worship. Herodotus says they were the most religious of men. They deified all the forces of Nature and all the mysteries of life. They had three forms of worship, namely, the worship of local deities, the worship of the Great Gods, and the worship of the dead.

(1) In every province, the Nile, the earth, the sky, and especially the sun, were regarded as persons and worshipped as gods. These gods were men, more perfect and more powerful than other men, but subject to the same needs, obliged to eat, to drink, to wear clothes. On the other hand, they were as eternal as the things they represented. Often they inhabited the bodies of animals; for example, the god Ptah at Memphis lived in the body of an ox, the Ox Apis. From this followed the worship of sacred animals. The Egyptians came to represent the gods as beings with the bodies of men and the heads of animals. Each god had a wife and a child, and these formed a trinity, such as Osiris, Isis, and Horus at Abydos.

(2) When the smaller princes became the vassals of Pharaoh, the gods of their towns became the vassals of the god of the capital city. So there arose the worship of the Great Gods. These Great Gods were personifications of the sun as he appears at different times of the day. The most famous were Horus, who was the rising sun, now regarded as a child, now as a youthful warrior, the conqueror of Set or Typhoon, the god of darkness; Osiris, the setting sun, who was slain by Set, lamented and restored to life by his wife Isis, the moon, and avenged by his son Horus (the fact of his death made him god of the dead); Ra, the father of Pharaoh, the sun in full strength; Amon, god of Thebes, the sun which rules Egypt; Hathor, the sun in its beauty, who was the goddess of the arts.

These gods, surrounded by inferior gods, wandered in their boats on the waters of heaven, which the Egyptians regarded as an immense river, a limitless Nile. They built temples, sumptuous homes on earth for these gods.

(3) There was another group of gods, the gods of the dead; these were Osiris, Thot, Anubis. The realm of the dead was a monarchy, as was that of heaven and earth, and Osiris was king of it. The dead, subjects of Osiris, became in their turn gods of a kind and received worship.

Like all primitive nations, the Egyptians spoke in symbols; they made the lotus the emblem of purity, because this plant grows in the middle of the stream, safe from defiling contact with the mud. The beetle was the image of God creating the world because each day it could be seen making the ball of earth out of which it fashioned its dwelling. The gods made their journeys in a golden boat, because the boat was the only means of conveyance in early times in a country where the Nile was the only line of communication between villages. The solar gods were represented with horns surrounding a disc and often draped as a mummy with the head of a cow. These signs represented the rising of the sun. As a matter of fact, the morning star shines between the slopes of the Arabian range like a globe between two horns.

The Egyptians had many Nature myths; the best known is that of Osiris. Osiris, who was married to his sister Isis, was king of

FIG. 4. - (1) Isis and the Cow, Hathor. (2) Isis Hathor. (3) Isis. (First Isis and the Cow; next Isis with the head of a Cow; lastly Isis with the horns of a Cow.)

the Nile Valley. After giving laws to his own country, he wished to travel all over the world to teach men the arts of peace. On his return, he was assassinated by his enemy, Typhoon or Set, who cut his body into pieces and scattered his limbs through the valley. Isis, in tears, began to search for her husband. She collected the limbs and embalmed them with the help of the gods Thot and Anubis, and this was the first mummy. Her son Horus attacked Typhoon, put him in chains, and sent him back to his mother, who pardoned him. Osiris was avenged, but Horus was obliged unceasingly to repeat the struggle against his enemy. Let us translate this myth: the sun (Osiris) rises on Egypt; he pursues his course; at the end of his course, he seems at first confined, and then destroyed, by the darkness of night (Typhoon). Another heavenly body appears and gives light to men — the moon (Isis). She seems to wander in the night until the moment when the rising sun (Horus) scatters the darkness. Later, this myth passed from the sphere of Nature to that of morals and became an allegory of the struggle between good and evil.

The Egyptians did not believe that a man's existence ended at death. When the last breath had been breathed, the Double, or soul, escaped from the body, and this continued to live as long as the body did not fall into decay. So they took great precautions to preserve the body, to embalm it, and transform it into a mummy. The soul had the same needs as the body of flesh and bones. It required a place to live in; so they built it a tomb and placed in it furniture and food. They also put by the side of the mummy portraits of the dead man and statues made in his likeness, so that the Double might have

FIG. 5. - Osiris, draped as a mummy.

a body in which to take up its abode. The mummy and the tomb were prepared to last forever, and the greatest care was taken to track down thieves who profaned the tombs.

Eventually, this life of the Double under the earth took on a purer meaning. The belief arose that the Double appeared before Osiris and underwent a solemn trial, in which the god Thot weighed the souls in the Balance of Truth. Souls which were pure rejoined Osiris in the Field of Peace, but only after certain transformations and purifications; the other souls were punished and destroyed.

The tombs were built above the line which marked the rising of the Nile, where the dryness of the earth has preserved them for long ages. The kingdom of the dead was supposed to begin where the valley of the Nile ended, for the Nile was called the River of Life. But the living, though separated from the dead in reality, were continually with them in thought. The Egyptians were most careful to render funeral honors to their ancestors and to assure the payment of such honors to themselves. A man would have his tomb built during his lifetime, and the Pyramids, which were royal tombs, are monumental examples of this practice.

Herodotus describes the way in which the Egyptians made the body into a mummy and assured its preservation, which was a necessary condition to secure the life of the Double. He says, "There are in every town professional embalmers. When the relatives of the dead man bring the corpse, they show the bearers various models of corpses, made in wood and painted so as to resemble Nature. The most perfect is said to be after the manner of the god Osiris. When the relations have agreed to the price, they depart; the embalmer works in his own house.

"The mode of embalming, according to the most perfect process, is the following: They take first a crooked piece of iron, and with it draw out the brain through the nostrils, thus getting rid of a portion, while the skull is cleared of the rest by rinsing with drugs. Next, they make a cut along the flank and take out the whole contents of the abdomen, which they then cleanse, washing it thoroughly with palm wine and again frequently with an infusion of pounded aromatics. After this, they fill the cavity with the purest bruised myrrh, with cassia, and every other sort of spicery except frankincense, and sew up the opening. Then the body is placed in natrum (subcarbonate of soda) for seventy days and covered entirely over."

At the end of seventy days, the parched body, almost reduced to skin and bones, was wrapped in linen bandages plastered with gum. It was then enclosed in three winding-sheets and in a red cloth fixed by bands running lengthwise and across. The mummy was then placed in a double wooden coffin, which almost reproduced the shape of the body, and at the head was carved the portrait of the dead man.

The respect of the Egyptians for their dead, their religious beliefs, and their care in preserving the body have made it possible for us to know accurately and in great detail the customs, occupations, art, and religion of the ancient Egyptians. In the past and in the present, scholars have only to remove the sand which has slowly covered their temples and their tombs. On the columns of the temples, covered with figures and hieroglyphics, can be deciphered the mysteries of their religion, the rites of worship, and the boastful dedications of the kings. Near each ancient town, and especially in the neighborhood of Memphis and Thebes, the numerous tombs form a veritable city of the dead. Today, we can enter these mortuary chambers, which are often hidden in a labyrinth of passages. Near the mummies, we find the ordinary possessions of the dead person — men's arms and tools, women's jewels, children's toys, the books of the learned, statues and portraits of the dead, the little models and images of the protecting gods — in short, the thousand objects which adorn the Egyptian galleries of our museums. On the walls of the tombs were painted the scenes of daily life: laborers in the fields, kings and priests and ceremonies, soldiers drilling and workmen at work, and so fresh are the paintings that the past ages live again before our eyes.

We can look also into the soul of this nation by reading the Book of the Dead, which lies near each mummy, ready for it to read in its defense on the Day of Judgment before Osiris, the great judge of souls. In it, we read: "I have not lied in the court of law. I have not been idle. I have not believed heresy. I have not committed sacrilege. I have not taken land by fraud. I have made no one weep. I have not killed. I have not stolen the wrappings nor the food of the dead. I have not opened a dyke. I have not taken the milk from the mouth of babes. I am pure. I am pure. I am pure."

CHAPTER II

EGYPTIAN SOCIETY

AMONG the Egyptians, the priests and warriors formed two privileged classes. The priests were charged with the performance of the rites and the administration of the possessions of the gods; they were also learned men and had magical powers.

They maintained their powerful position through their control of the temple treasures, the knowledge they possessed and kept secret, and the authority due to the respect and terror they inspired. They were bound by certain rules of life: they might not touch anything defiled, they must wear linen garments, have their heads shaved, and fast often.

The warriors consisted of families living on lands granted by the king. They were obliged, at risk of confiscation, to answer every summons to arms. Their children were specially educated in the camps. The backbone of the army was the infantry, divided into two classes: the one armed with a spear and a battle-axe, the other with a bow and a dagger. Their defensive armour consisted of a round helmet, a coat of mail, and a shield. There was also, but later in their history, a body of war chariots. Herodotus tells us that, in his time, the warrior class included 400,000 men. The later Pharaohs also employed foreign mercenaries.

The traders were like the Eastern traders of today: they sold in little shops the articles which they had made themselves with the help of their workmen. Their most famous merchandise consisted of glass, jewellery, fabrics, and embroidered skins.

The workmen practised all the crafts we know. They formed gilds according to their occupations, like those of the workmen of the Middle Ages. Clad only in a loincloth, they worked in workshops or yards under the direction of a foreman, who managed them with a rod in his hand. Some trades, like that of the weavers, were regulated by royal regulations. The workers were paid in kind, that is to say, in foodstuffs. When everything had been eaten too quickly, strikes occurred. Those who were employed in embalming the dead were treated as impure and were obliged to live in the suburbs.

The peasants ploughed their land with a wooden plough without wheels, such as a fellah uses today, and they cut the crops with a sickle. Methods of irrigation were known to them. They had great difficulty in paying their taxes, and the revenue collectors often had them beaten.

In Egyptian society, there was one class which had marked characteristics and played a most influential part: these were the scribes. The scribe was a man who had studied, who knew how to read, write, and keep accounts. Consequently, he was indispensable and acted as the eye and right hand of his master. It was the scribes who received the taxes, acted as foremen in the workyards, recruited soldiers, and supplied their weapons. The scribe was to be found everywhere: in the service of a rich individual, in the tradesman's shop, as well as in the farms and palaces of the Pharaohs. He was a foreman or an engineer, an architect or a tax collector, a priest or a general, according to his abilities, his success in examinations, or his good luck.

He went about accompanied by negroes carrying rods made from the palm trees to enforce his commands. He was generally puffed up with his own importance and convinced that no one could stand comparison with him: like the mandarin in modern China, he looked on the rest of the world as contemptible and far inferior to himself. He ridiculed the blacksmith, always at the door of his furnace; the stonemason, always bending his back till it ached; the barber, who asked for business from door to door; the weaver; the dyer, whose fingers smelt of rotten fish; and the shoemaker, with his poor stock of health. "I have considered all manual labour," said a scribe to his son, "and truly there is not

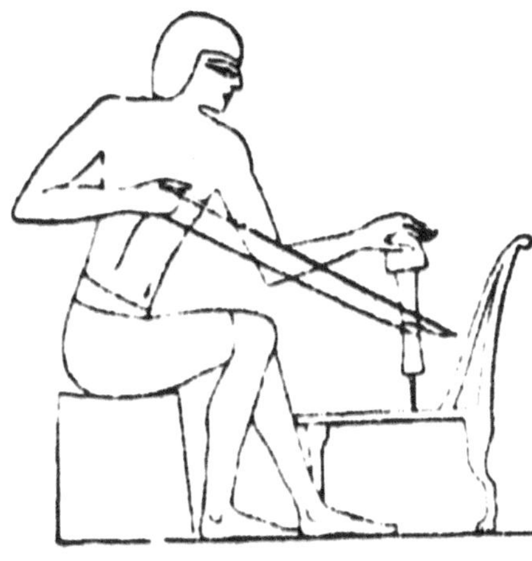

FIG. 6. - A carpenter.

one superior to literature. Therefore, I am making you love literature as your mother, and I am instilling its beauties in your head. Literature is more important than all the crafts. He who sets himself to draw profit from it from childhood is honoured." So the Egyptians, like the Chinese, made great sacrifices to enable their children to pass the examinations of the scribes.

The scribe was the chief agent of the king. The King of Egypt, or Pharaoh, was considered to be the son of Ra, the sun-god, and was himself a god. So he received worship, and temples were built in which his worship was performed, as was done afterwards at Rome to the emperors who reigned during the first centuries of our era. On the monuments, the image of the king was adorned with the attributes of the gods: the solar disc between the two horns and the sacred hawk, the symbol of the god Horus.

The royal emblem was a sphinx, which symbolised strength and wisdom. The royal headdress was a kind of mitre, symbolising the union of the two kingdoms of Upper and Lower Egypt; it was made by the union of two headdresses: one, red and low, was the crown of Lower Egypt; the other, white and like a cotton cap, was the crown of Upper Egypt. A golden serpent surrounded the lower part, with its head covering in front of the cap.

The king lived in his palace surrounded by his officers and crowds of servants — men to brush away flies and to carry umbrellas, guards of the royal treasure, commanders of the bodyguards, stewards of the palace, treasurers, equerries, librarians, musicians, stewards of his granaries, flocks, and so forth. When he went out,

FIG. 7. - Rameses II in his war chariot.

he was generally surrounded by a magnificent following. He was borne on a throne, supported on a dais carried by twelve men; his servants burnt incense before him and waved great fans. On the Nile, the royal galley was a blaze of gold.

This king, an absolute monarch because he was the son of God, lord of the land and life of his subjects, was himself a slave to etiquette, that is to say, to a rule of life which determined the employment of his time and fixed his occupations for the whole of the day. It was no idle life he led: he had to make himself acquainted each morning with all the reports sent to him by his governors.

Among the kings, there was one who was specially celebrated, Rameses II, who reigned at Thebes for sixty-seven years in the fourteenth century before Christ. The Greeks called him Sesestris, and they represented him as the wisest of the kings and assigned to him everything that was great in Egyptian history; for the Greeks were apt to summarise the history of a people in the history of one man. Rameses was not the mighty conqueror which legend described, but he was the typical Egyptian king, warrior,

Egyptian temples were remarkable for their size and solidity. They were of two kinds, for some were built in the open air, and others were excavated from the rock, but the internal arrangements were the same. The most celebrated are the ruined temples at Karnak and Luxor, on the site of ancient Thebes, the temples on the island of Philae, in almost complete preservation, and the underground temples at Abû-Simbel. The Labyrinth, which was so highly praised by the Greeks, was probably a temple built near Lake Moeris.

A temple was both the estate and the home of the god. It was surrounded by a great brick wall, which enclosed a whole population engaged in the service of the god. Within were dwellings for the priests and their servants, workshops, domestic offices, and gardens in which animals to be used for sacrifice were kept. The temple proper was in the center of the estate, within a second enclosing wall. The approach to it was by a flagged roadway adorned on each side by a row of sphinxes. The entrance was a huge building called a Pylon, composed of a massive doorway with a tower on each side, built like flat-topped pyramids, covered with carvings and inscriptions. In front of the Pylon, two obelisks or needle-shaped pillars of solid granite stood on a pedestal. Before the Pylon, colossal statues of the kings by whom the temple was built were arranged at intervals. Beyond the Pylon was an open court with a colonnade through which processions could pass; behind this court was a great hall where the public was admitted only on certain days. This was the Hypostyle or Hall of Columns. In this, there were three aisles; the central one, higher than the others, led to the Hall of Revelation. There, the priests, the kings, and certain other privileged persons could see the god when the priests bore him from the sanctuary in his sacred boat or ark.

The temple ended in a dark chamber called the Room of the Mystery or the Shrine, and it was there that the statue of the god was placed.

The halls were built on different levels so that the lighting became gradually dimmer. The roofs formed flat terraces. The

FIG. 9. – One of the Pylons of a temple at Philae.

FIG. 10. - The central aisle of the Hypostyle at Luxor.

walls and columns were covered with inscriptions and colored carvings, which represented, on the inside, the god and his ceremonies and offerings, and on the outside, the king and his battles.

The temples were of huge dimensions, especially that of Amen at Luxor. The Pylon was 147 feet high and 383 feet wide. The Hypostyle was 170 feet long and 329 feet wide. The columns

FIG. 11. – The original appearance of the interior of a Hypostyle.

of the central aisle are still standing, 62 feet high, 36 feet in circumference, and measuring 77 feet around the capitals. The solidity of the construction is wonderful, and even in ruins, this temple arouses the admiration of mankind.

From the Egyptians' belief in life continued in the tomb arose a special funerary architecture. This architecture included three principal types: the pyramids, the mastabas or flat-topped pyramids, and the rock-hewn tombs. In the rock-hewn tombs, the entrance to the tomb was marked by an opening cut in the solid rock, called a "false door." In all the tombs, the chamber where the bodies lay was far from the entrance, at the end of a succession of passages and pits constructed to baffle thieves. So, the monumental part was only the outside of the tomb.

When Memphis was the capital, the kings had pyramids of stone on a square base built for their tombs. The four angles of the base represented the four points of the compass, and the top of the pyramid was supposed to touch the sky. Three of these pyramids were remarkable for their size: they were built by the kings Cheops, Chephren, and Mycerinos, Pharaohs of the 4th dynasty. The largest pyramid, that of Cheops, was 480 feet high and is still one of the highest buildings in the world, being now 460 feet high.

The surface was covered with white blocks of stone, polished and placed cleverly on one another without any cement. The blocks of stone used in the building were brought by water from the quarries in the Arabian mountains. To raise these blocks, they built great inclined planes of earth, which they afterward removed. Inside, and hidden away, were the series of passages and rooms which form an Egyptian tomb. The pyramids were built by means of forced labor imposed on the subjects of the Pharaoh. So, the Egyptians long retained a hateful recollection of that epoch, and we can realize their sufferings when we think of the enormous mass of stone they had to handle. In the Great Pyramid alone, there are 960,000 cubic feet of stone.

Statues adorned the front of their buildings or decorated their temples and tombs. The forms of the statues were stiff, and the limbs were carved close to the body because the stone in which they worked was very hard and difficult to work with the bronze tools which they used. The larger the statue, the less free were the limbs, and some attempt to represent movement was only to be found in the little statues in the tombs, which were carved in soft stone. The statues can be divided into three classes: the colossi, the decorative, and the funereal statues.

FIG. 12. – The "Little Temple" at Philae with lotus-carved capitals.

Seated statues of the gods, about 70 feet high, were placed with their backs to the Pylons or doors of the temples. To this class belong the Colossi, called the Colossi of Memnon. Other colossi were the sphinxes, crouching lions with men's heads, emblems of the god Ra, which were placed in the roadways leading to the temples. The most ancient and most famous of the sphinxes, the Great Sphinx of Gizah, near the Pyramids, is a carved rock: it is 150 feet long and 70 feet high.

Our museums are full of decorative statues. They represent kings and gods in their sacred positions with their attributes. They differ widely in height and material; some are made of bronze.

The funereal statues are most interesting because they are portraits. They were put in the tomb for the Double of the dead man to dwell in and represent the man in familiar attitudes with life-like exactness. The finest is that of the seated scribe, now in the Louvre.

The walls and columns of the temples were adorned with carved pictures representing scenes in the life of the gods or the kings; these are called bas-reliefs. There were three kinds: in one kind, people were drawn in simple line on the stone; in others, the forms were stamped like letters of a seal; in others, they were carved in relief. All the details of feature and dress and all sorts of accessories were painted. The drawing was childish: while the body faced the spectator, the face was often in profile, and there was no perspective.

Painting was not a separate art. First of all, men painted walls, statues, and bas-reliefs. Later, they painted frescoes, that is, scenes from everyday life on a surface covered with plaster, which were like bas-reliefs without carving. The artists drew only the outlines and filled them in with flat and conventional coloring.

The colors were bright, and, as the artists had an eye for detail and carefully reproduced what they saw, these mural paintings, which are very common in the tombs, are among the most precious materials for picturing the life of ancient Egypt.

Writing seems to have been originally a decoration subordinate to architecture. The first signs were graven pictures. Then these pictures acquired the value of words, syllables, and letters. So the first system of writing arose, and the letters were called hieroglyphs, or sacred letters, being used for inscriptions on the monuments. In ordinary life, men used the hieroglyphic letters in forms which were more and more abbreviated, so that first there was hieroglyphic writing and then demotic or popular writing, and from this, the Phoenicians derived their alphabet. The key to the hieroglyphs was discovered in 1822 by Champollion, a Frenchman, and he was the founder of Egyptology, or the science of deciphering and translating the inscriptions on the Egyptian monuments.

During Napoleon's expedition into Egypt in 1798, an officer discovered on a stone near Rosetta an inscription engraved in three scripts: hieroglyphic, demotic, and

FIG. 13. - The seated scribe.

Greek. An Englishman, Thomas Young, recognized in the cartouches of the inscription the name of Ptolemy. Champollion did more. He saw that each of the signs of this sort of riddle had a value. He separated the name of Ptolemy.

Next, with the aid of these signs, he tried to decipher other cartouches, and he made out in succession the names of Berenice, Cleopatra, and Alexander. He obtained a sort of rudimentary alphabet. He finally proved that there was a likeness between the grammatical forms of the language of the hieroglyphs and those of Coptic or Modern Egyptian. So he was able, by the help of the alphabet he had made, not only to read the writings but also to translate them.

The Egyptians displayed their luxury especially in jewelry, which was remarkable for the fine quality of the workmanship, such as the breastplates which covered the breast and the necklaces which were literally collars of precious stones and metals. The common use of perfumes gave rise to many accessories, such as vases and spoons, which were often true works of art. To make these, the craftsmen drew ideas from the natural forms of plants, animals, and mankind. Numerous ideas in decoration were borrowed from the papyrus, the lotus, and the beetle. Our modern jewelers often try to reproduce the designs of the Egyptian craftsmen, and from this, we can judge the development of industrial art and the refinement of civilization in Egypt.

The position of foreigners in Egypt was like that of Europeans in China in the nineteenth century. The foreigner who insisted was allowed to enter the country, but he was treated with contempt as a barbarian. The Phoenicians were the first to come. They gained permission to trade freely, and they carried Egyptian trinkets all over the Mediterranean. Then, in their turn, the Greeks arrived, at first as pirates, then as soldiers. The Pharaohs of the Delta used them to strengthen their army, to remodel their equipment and methods, and with their help regained their prestige and authority. Henceforth, they gave their confidence to these foreigners, whom the common people regarded as impure; but they did not allow them to live among their people. In all important towns, they gave them separate districts in which they lived and carried on their business. In Memphis, there were Greek and Latin quarters. The Greeks had also their own separate ports, such as Naucratus. Their influence extended only over the upper classes, and even after the conquests of Alexander the Great, the common people, although they submitted to the conqueror, yet continued to show themselves hostile to all ideas and customs coming from the outer world.

As in ancient times, so today, Egypt continues to be the favorite country for traders, for travelers, and for conquerors. Lying as it were at the junction of Europe, Asia, and Africa, Egypt is the natural link between East and West. In commerce, Egypt is the road to India; from the military point of view, she is the key of the world; to the student and the historian, she offers traces of the oldest of our civilizations. Greek adventurers and Phoenician traders sought their fortune there, as successfully as European speculators of the nineteenth and twentieth centuries have sought theirs. Both Alexander and Napoleon tried to make themselves masters of the Nile before attempting the conquest of the East. The most famous wise men of Greece, Pythagoras and Herodotus, went to learn wisdom from the priests of Memphis and of Thebes. It was at Alexandria, after the Greek conquest, that the civilisations of the ancient East and of Greece became fused so as to give thereafter to the Romans, when masters of the world, a universal civilisation.

The value of modern Egypt seems to have been doubled by the cutting of the Suez Canal; but Pharaoh Necho of the 20th dynasty had already made a canal from the Nile to the Red Sea.

CHAPTER III

CHALDEA AND ASSYRIA

WHILE the Egyptians on the banks of the Nile were inventing architecture, government, and morality, the Chaldae-Assyrians on the banks of the Tigris and the Euphrates were originating methods of warfare and discovering the sciences which are based on calculation.

The Euphrates, about 1600 miles long, and the Tigris, 1100 miles long, both rise in narrow and deep gorges in the highlands of Armenia. After bending, the Euphrates towards the Mediterranean and Syria, and the Tigris towards Persia, they flow nearer one another and form a huge plain half the size of France, called Mesopotamia, a word meaning the part "between two rivers." Their streams unite and enter the Persian Gulf under the name of Shatt-el-Arab. In the time of the Chaldaeans, the mouths of the two rivers were separated by a marshy district. But the earth brought down by the rivers has filled the gulf to a distance of 120 miles.

The area watered by these rivers is altogether as large as that of France.

Mesopotamia, almost a desert today, in earlier times supported millions of men. The soil is very fertile, corn grows there naturally, and in well-watered places, three crops can be gathered in a year. There are few kinds of trees, but the palm tree grows everywhere and serves many purposes.

The climate is very warm in the summer but cold in the winter, owing to the northerly winds which come with icy blasts from the plateau of Armenia. The nature of the soil made the natives ingenious; the climate prevented enervation.

The first inhabitants of the country were the Chaldeans. They settled near the mouths of the two rivers and seem to have lived a peaceful life, digging canals for irrigation, and building towns where they formed governments and developed their religion and science. As the population increased, they moved north-wards along the Tigris and settled in the mountainous district which commands its left bank. Thus they formed the kingdom of Assyria, the Kurdistan of today. The Assyrians, settled now in a country rougher and less fertile, sought to live at the expense of their neighbours and became a nation of conquerors; war was their chief occupation. So, in the Chaldae-Assyrian civilisation, the arts of war were the work of the Assyrians, and the arts of peace were the work of the Chaldeans.

The history of Chaldaea and of Assyria can be divided into five periods: (1) the history of Lower Chaldaea; (2) that of the First Babylonian Empire; (3) that of Ashur; (4) that of Nineveh; (5) that of the Second or Great Babylonian Empire. It is noteworthy that the centre of the Chaldae-Assyrian power and civilisation moved continuously from south to north, following the course of the two rivers.

In the first period, Lower Chaldaea was peopled with a series of towns, of which the one best known to us is Lagash: here have been discovered the palace and statue of its King Gudea. It was by no means an important state, but Chaldaean civilisation spread far and wide and reached the borders of the Mediterranean, as is proved by the likeness between the Story of the Flood in the Chaldaean legends and the record in the Bible.

During the second period, the towns and states on the banks of the Euphrates grouped themselves round Babylon, which became the capital of the Chaldaeans. Its kings, the most famous of whom was Hammurabi, the author of the oldest known code of laws, undertook the construction of canals, and the plain between the two rivers became a veritable granary.

Then, during the third period, Assyria, colonised by the Chaldaeans, assumed in its turn the supremacy over all the valley of

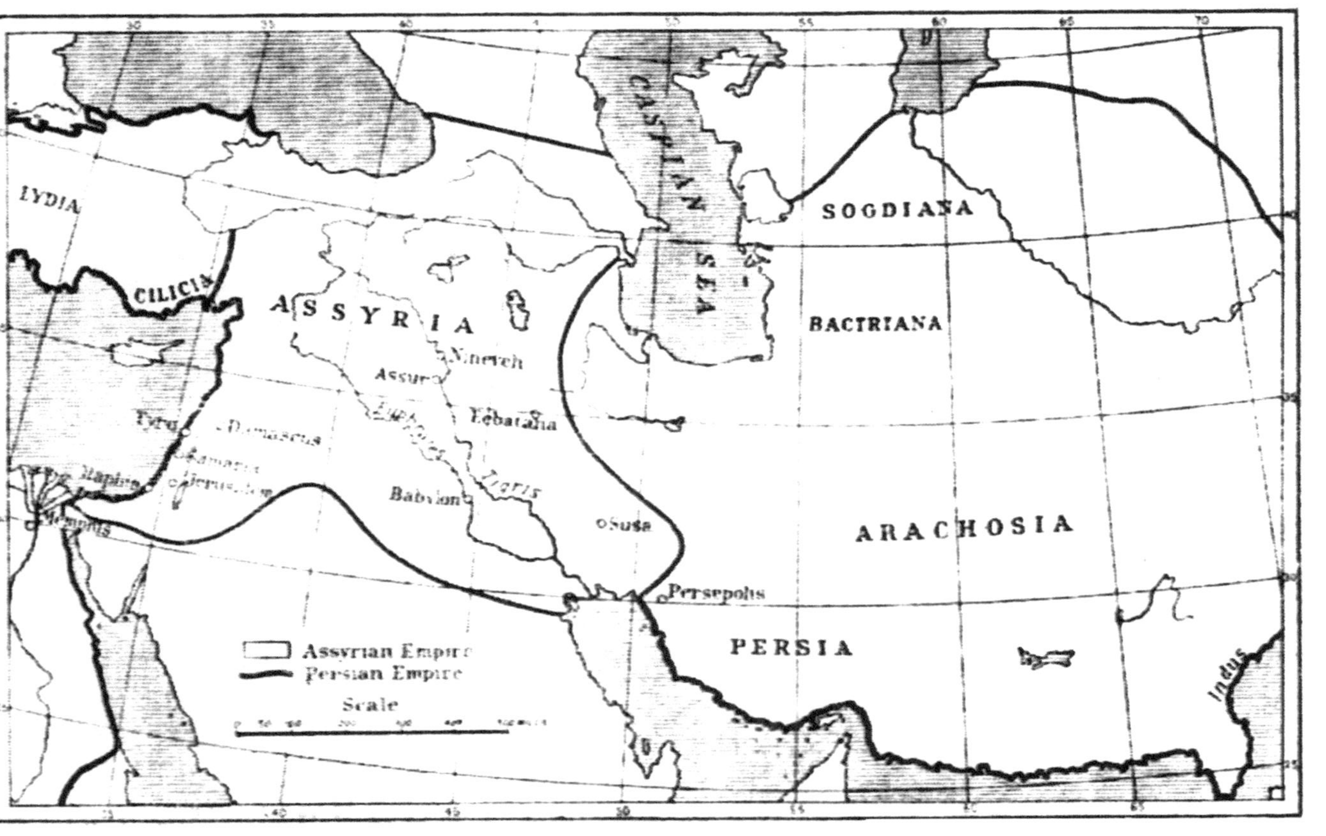

FIG. 14. - The Assyrian and Persian Empires.

the Tigris and the Euphrates. The kings who ruled at Ashur and Calah began to make themselves formidable to their neighbours by making war a regular system of plunder and conquest.

Assyria reached the zenith of its power during the fourth period, under the kings of Nineveh, chief of whom were Sargon, Sennacherib, and Ashur-bani-pal. They conquered all the country bordering on the Persian Gulf and Caspian Sea, as well as Armenia, Syria, Palestine, and Egypt. But Nineveh had roused deep feelings of hatred against herself in the minds of many races. An alliance of the Babylonians and the Medes overthrew the Assyrian Empire; its capital was taken and razed to the ground in 626 B.C..

The kings of Babylon during the fifth period inherited the Assyrian power, but their rule lasted but a little while. Babylon, extended and adorned by King Nebuchadnezzar, became a sort of fairy city, and kept this character even after the Persians took possession of it in 538 B.C..

The histories of the Greeks, the Bible, the inscriptions, and the carvings, all represent the Assyrians as a wild and cruel race, whose chief occupation was making war. The Assyrians had strong bodies, with marked muscles; their noses were hooked, their eyes large, and their lips thick. They had long hair and curly beards. The expression of their faces was strong, but animal. They considered their own god to be the master of the world, and foreigners were infidels and traitors. So they massacred them without pity. This fierceness survives today in the Kurds who inhabit the land of ancient Assyria, and the Armenian massacres have repeated in our own days the atrocities committed in olden times by the people of Nineveh and Babylon.

Their costume consisted sometimes of a large tunic with short sleeves, sometimes of long robes. Generally, these garments were embroidered and fringed. In addition, an Assyrian wrapped himself in a great woollen cloak, also fringed. In the town, he wore sandals; in war, high-laced boots. The usual headdress was a peaked felt hat. The use of jewels, perfumes, and paint was widely spread.

FIG. 15. - Kurds of to-day.

The houses were square buildings of baked bricks. They were covered with flat tops, on which were little square towers or cupolas. Windows were rare, and generally, daylight entered the houses by the doors.

Before the discoveries of the archaeologists who have given us the names and deeds of the Assyrian kings precisely, almost our only knowledge of their history came from the accounts in the Bible and the Greek histories. There we find mentioned as celebrated, Nimrod, the great hunter; Ninus, the conqueror; Semiramis, the queen who built such great structures; Sardana-palus, the voluptuary who devoted himself to self-indulgence.

These people of the legends include among them all the principal characteristics of the Assyrian monarchs.

The king, who was the servant of his god, was also at the same time his representative. For this reason, he was the absolute master of his subjects, and other kings had to pay homage to him in person and to his master, the god. Those who refused such homage were traitors worthy of every sort of punishment. The king made war on such and himself led the expedition. When he was victorious, he gave thanks to his god and dedicated monuments to him, on which he inscribed in pompous style the list of his victories.

The principal care of each Assyrian king was to build a town and a palace, just as each Pharaoh was careful to build a tomb. Often, the king was satisfied with transforming the town in which he lived. In this way, Nineveh was the work of Sennacherib, and Babylon that of Nebuchadnezzar. From Nineveh have been obtained a large number of objects exhibited in the Assyrian galleries of the British Museum. The king also superintended the

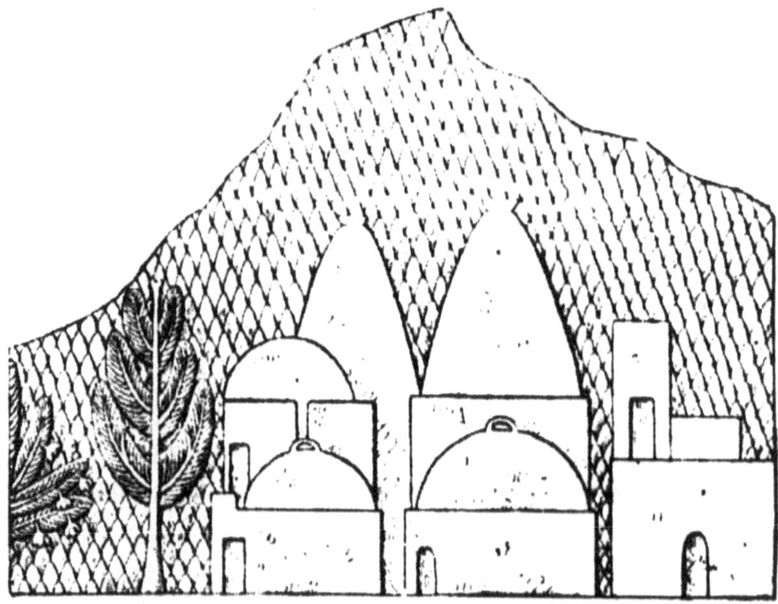

FIG. 16. - Early Assyrian houses (from a bas-relief).

making of canals and the keeping of them in good condition, and used in these works the captives he had taken in war.

The king practised a miniature warfare in his great hunts. In Assyria were found the wild bull or auroch, the lion, and the wild ass. These were the king's quarry, and he hunted with his pack of hounds, shooting them with arrows from his chariot. The hunting expedition was celebrated like a victory in war. "I, Ashur-bani-pal, king of armies, king of the land of Ashur," runs one inscription, "I have killed two lions; I have bent against them the mighty bow of Ishtar, goddess of battles; I have made over them an offering and libation of wine."

When the king was neither fighting nor hunting, he passed his time in feasts and festivals in his palace. It was the revel after the conflict. The carvings show him clad in an embroidered robe, wearing a tiara on his head and covered with jewels. Around him, his courtiers, his slaves, his wives are watching to anticipate his slightest wish. It is difficult to recognise the rude warrior in this idol which is shaded by a parasol. It often happened that the princes grew slack in this luxury, and their indulgence caused the loss of their empire.

In the spring of each year, the king of Assyria set out in battle

FIG. 17. - Modern Assyrian houses.

FIG. 18. - King Ashur-bani-pal at the hunt.

FIG. 19. - Ashur-bani-pal lion-hunting on foot.

array to exact tribute from his revolted subjects or to make new conquests. The soldiers were numerous, for all the Assyrians were obliged to serve in the army. The army was organised and equipped not only to fight in line but to take the enemy by surprise and to besiege the towns where they could take refuge.

FIG. 20. - Departure of Assyrian troops from the camp.

FIG. 21. - Assyrian archers and pikemen.

The Assyrians were the first to use cavalry and to know the art of besieging.

The infantry consisted of pikemen and archers, all armed with a short sword. The soldiers wore a long leather tunic covered with metal scales, closely fitting breeches, laced boots, and a pointed cap. They carried large shields. Each man had a leather skin which he inflated when necessary and used as a raft for crossing streams.

The horsemen were mounted on small strong horses and were divided into lancers and archers. Not only did they take part in battles, but they were used for scouting, for making long détours, cutting the enemy's lines of communication, destroying his crops, and sowing terror in advance of the main army. On these expeditions, they also took light-armed foot soldiers, who rode behind them on their saddles. They also invented cavalry operations at a great distance, which are called in modern warfare raids.

They had also a chariot corps; each chariot carried three men, and they were used to charge in line. To take the towns, they had corps of skilled engineers, who knew how to dig trenches and mines, to breach walls by means of the battering-ram, to raise siege towers, to riddle the walls, and to make an assault by ladders. The town of Tyre, being built on an island, was the only one which succeeded in resisting their science of the siege.

The inscriptions relate in horrible detail the long series of massacres and devastations of which Assyrian expeditions consisted and which form their history.

Sometimes the Assyrians ascended the Tigris and attacked the tribes of Armenia or of Media; sometimes they came down the Euphrates and conquered the Chaldeans and the kings of Elam and Susiana. Then they went by way of the valley of the

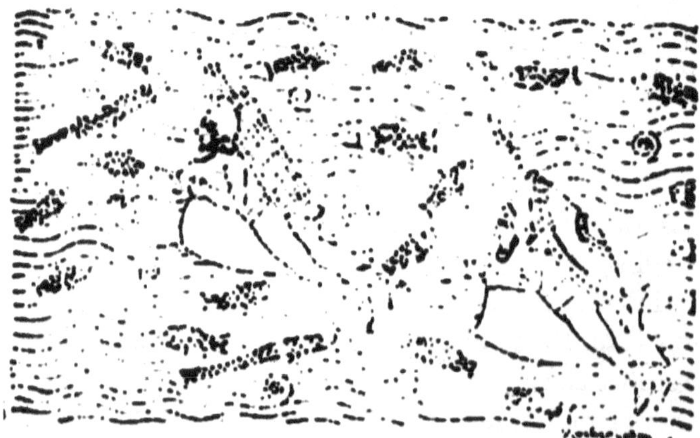

FIG. 22. - Assyrian soldiers crossing a river (from a bas-relief).

Euphrates to Syria, and, marching by the coast, reached Egypt. They penetrated even the deserts of Arabia. Weak nations yielded without a struggle. Others formed mutual alliances and they had to be overcome in battles and sieges. All were conquered by the dread Assyrian warriors.

It is noteworthy that each king, in his turn, undertook the same campaigns as his predecessors. The chronicles of the victories of Tiglath Pileser, king of Ashur, or those of Nebuchadnezzar, king of Babylon, contain the same names, and the reason for this is that the large majority of the wars were undertaken against revolting tributaries. After a victory, the Assyrians did not occupy the conquered country. They allowed the people to keep their organisation and their own kings; they only exacted a regular tribute. When the nations had forgotten the hardships of the conquest, or when the authority of the Assyrian king was weak, they tried to free themselves from his yoke by refusing the tribute. Then they had to be conquered afresh. Occasionally the royal princes, called governors

FIG. 23. Assyrian troops using a battering-ram.

of the large towns, took up arms against the king in order to win the throne for themselves; this was done by the brother of Ashur-bani-pal at Babylon. Finally, palace revolutions and assassinations of the kings were frequent, and always gave an opportunity for revolt.

The Assyrian Empire was then truly, to use the Biblical metaphor, "an image with feet of clay." It was always crumbling away and changing its masters, but always re-fashioning itself with surprising ease. It was the hand of the conqueror alone which produced unity.

The Assyrians showed no pity to those they conquered. They inflicted on them frightful tortures — they put out eyes, cut off noses, ears, and lips, and tore out beards and nails, or impaled and flayed their victims alive. They raised trophies composed of severed heads; they flung the corpses to the wild beasts. The kings made boast of their cruelty. "I slew one out of every two," said Ashur-bani-pal, "and I have led off those who survived as slaves. I built a pyramid before the gate of the town; I had some of the leaders of the revolt flayed alive and I stretched their skins on the pyramid. Others were bricked up alive, others were impaled along the ramparts. I had many flayed before my face; I carpeted the walls with their skins; I made crowns of their heads and garlands of

FIG. 24. - A siege (from a bas-relief).

their corpses. Over their ruins I smile; in the glutting of my wrath I find my satisfaction."

The country was systematically laid waste. Trees were cut down, crops destroyed, towns razed to the ground; the cattle were driven away by the conqueror. The gold, the silver, and all articles of value were divided between the king and his warriors. The inhabitants who had not been killed were carried off in a body to Assyria, where they were made to work at the king's buildings. The most celebrated of these transportations was that of the Jews. Settled by Nebuchadnezzar at Babylon, they remained there for seventy years, till the conquest of Cyrus.

The Assyrian towns, crammed with the spoils of the vanquished, were towns of luxury and pleasure. Early in their history, industry and commerce developed. Their methods of manufacture persist to-day in the pottery of the Persians, the arms of Damascus, and the embroideries and carpets of the East. Their fashion of building in brick made them excellent potters, and they discovered all the secrets of decorating and glazing bricks. Their embroidered stuffs, which the Greeks called "needle-paintings," were in demand throughout the whole of the ancient world. They were skilful engravers, making decorative panels of metal, arms and jewels, and goldsmith's work.

Assyrian merchants travelled far afield for their wares: iron and precious woods came from Armenia, purple from Phoenicia, woven stuffs and precious stones from India, glass and ornaments from Egypt. On the Euphrates and Tigris, the merchants had regular fleets which went far out in the Persian Gulf. A perfect network of caravan routes put them in touch with Central Asia and the Mediterranean.

It is no wonder that the wealth of these cities became a proverb. The warriors of Nineveh and Babylon refreshed themselves after their conquests with feasts and all sorts of enjoyment. They were as famous for their self-indulgence as for their cruelty.

Of all the Chaldaeo-Assyrian towns, Babylon was the most important and has the longest history. Founded in the early years of Chalda, Babylon survived all the sieges and attacks of the kings of Nineveh. Nebuchadnezzar made it the greatest city of Asia. The Persians, and later the Greeks, respected it. For long years, Babylon cast on the world the glamour of a civilisation refined to the point of corruption.

The great importance of Babylon and its long duration are due to its excellent position. It was built on the lower part of the Euphrates, at the heart of the most fertile lands of that time. It was the centre of the Chaldrean world and the home of its science. By the Euphrates, communication was open to the Persian Gulf and Syria. It commanded also the great trade route which passes from Eastern Europe and Asia Minor to India. It also dominated the roads to Egypt, to Armenia, and to Persia. All the international trade of the ancient world passed by its walls. When, under the Assyrian Empire, Babylon reached its supreme height, its political power increased its natural pre-eminence; its wealth, the fruit alike of war and science, knew no bounds.

The labour of its captive population resulted in making Baby-lon "the Queen of Asia." The Greeks never speak of the city without admiration. It was surrounded by a square wall twenty-seven miles in circumference, enclosing a space a little larger than that of Bradford. The brick wall, plastered with bitumen mortar, was about 320 feet high and eighty wide; there were ranged on the wall 150 square watch-towers, and there were 100 gates with folding doors of bronze. The Euphrates flowed through the city between two quays, built of brick, and united by a stone bridge. This immense enclosure was not entirely populated but contained gardens and fields, and formed a fortified camp where the inhab-itants could live in time of siege. The streets intersected at right angles and led up to the royal quarter or king's palace, whose ruins cover thirty-five acres. Near the palace rose the Hanging Gardens, one of the Seven Wonders of the World. They were high terraces built on piles of masonry, where were grown at great expense rare trees of huge dimensions. The city was adorned by eight temples magnificently rebuilt by Nebuchadnezzar. The wealth accumulated in this capital was so great that in order to ward off the invasions of the Medes, the king had the plain of the Euphrates barred off by a great wall. A motley crowd of soldiers, captives, pilgrims, and traders, collected from all the corners of the Asiatic world, filled the streets, above which rose the temple of the god Marduk, lord and protector of Nebuchadnezzar and his city.

The Chaldaeo-Assyrians owed their wealth to war, manufactures, and commerce, but not to these only. They were also skilful agriculturists. Chaldae, an alluvial plain like the Delta of the Nile, was very fertile, but subject to inundation from the rivers, while, on the other hand, Mesopotamia only yielded rich crops under irrigation. The Chaldeans knew how to make canals and construct irrigation works. The Tigris was united to the Euphrates by a canal, from which branched numerous smaller canals cutting one another at right angles. The plain was like an immense chessboard, and we can still trace the banks of earth. As in Egypt, the labourer was helped by the engineer and agriculture was a branch of science. It was a point of honour with the kings to maintain the canals and increase their number. One of them, Hammurabi, was able to say, "I have changed the desert plains to watered lands; I have given them fertility and abundance; I have made them a fair place of habitation."

Among the ancients, commerce, which dealt almost exclusively with luxuries, owing to the difficulties of transport, did not unite nations as it does to-day. On the whole, the normal form of intercourse between them was war. It was in a long succession of wars that the two civilisations of the Nile and of the Euphrates found their meeting-point. These wars fell into three periods.

In the first, the petty kingships of the Euphrates submitted to the sovereignty of the conquering Pharaohs of the 18th dynasty. The Egyptian invasion developed the war-like instincts of the Chaldeans.

Later in history, when the kings of Nineveh had become powerful, the Egyptians, panic-stricken, roused against them their allies of Syria and of Israel. These allies were defeated, and the fall of Damascus and of Samaria decided Sabaco, Pharaoh of Napata, to intervene in person; but his army was annihilated at Raphia by Sargon, in the eighth century B.C. The successors of Sargon penetrated Egypt, took Thebes, and drove back the Ethiopians.

After the fall of Nineveh, the Pharaoh of the Delta once more took the offensive in Asia. Necho invaded Palestine and Syria, but he was defeated by Nebuchadnezzar at Karkemish (604 B.C.), and Egypt lost all her influence in Asia. Then the two rival states were conquered by the Persians and together submitted to the yoke of Cambyses.

CHAPTER IV

CHALDEAN AND ASSYRIAN SOCIETY

CHALDEEA was a vast plain from which could be seen an immense expanse of sky. The contemplation of this sky inspired the inhabitants' religion and science. They deified the brightness of the stars, but instead of expressing their movements in poetical legends like the Egyptians, they expressed them in mathematical formulae. This was the origin of astronomy and mathematics. The Chaldeans showed their tendency to exactness and method in these respects, as in the art of war.

In everything, they desired to reach the realities of life. They judged everything by its utility and convenience: they worshipped a god in order to get his protection; they tried to divine the future to protect themselves from ill. The arts they invented were those which were useful for life. In place of ideals, they possessed a feeling for the practical, and their inventions were adopted by all the nations of antiquity.

The basis of the Chaldaeo-Assyrian religion was fear. Cruel and domineering themselves, the Chaldeans in their turn experienced the terror which they inspired in others. They feared the great powers of the sky, the influences of the stars, and the malignancy of demons. So among them, we find three principal forms of religion: worship of the great gods, astrology, and sorcery.

Originally in Chaldae, as in Egypt, each town had its presiding deity. When the great states were formed, these gods became common to all Chaldæo-Assyria, but the god of the chief city remained the king over the others. There was a religious hierarchy corresponding to the political hierarchy. The gods lived in the sky, having their homes in the sun or the moon or one of the five great planets. The chief gods were: Sin, the moon-god, the chief of the gods; Shamash, the sun-god, god of light; Nergal, god of the planet Mars, the lion-god; Nebo, god of the planet Mercury, the god of learning; Marduk, god of the planet Jupiter, the god of Babylon; Ninib, god of the planet Saturn, the god of strength, who could crush lions in his arms; Ishtar, goddess of the planet Venus, goddess of Nineveh, god of war and of love. We must add the good Ea, the fish-god, creator of Old Chalda; Ashur, the god of Assyria; Ramman, the god of the sky and of storms.

These gods were assisted by lesser gods and genii. These genii were the protectors of men, and the gates of the palaces were adorned with their images. These were great statues of men with four large wings, or of winged bulls with men's heads.

The Chaldæan or Assyrian god was in no respect a merciful god; he was a jealous master, exacting and bloodthirsty, and he demanded an absolute obedience. Ishtar at Nineveh or Marduk at Babylon were gods only of their own people, and all strangers were their enemies. They tolerated near them the gods of vassal tribes, but only in an inferior position. They rewarded their faithful worshippers with victory and booty, and they punished them with defeat. When the king set out for war, it was in the name of his god and to avenge him. An inscription of Ashurbani-pal contains these words: "Men who have plotted against Ashur and against me with their mouths, have had their tongues torn out. I have cast them into the ditch; I have cut off their limbs; I have given them to the dogs to eat. By so doing have I rejoiced the heart of the great gods, my masters." On his return from a campaign, the king had to offer to his god the spoils of the conquered.

Beyond these great gods, the Chaldeans worshipped the stars, which they regarded as mysterious powers. They called them the interpreters of the gods. Each star represented a god and was worshipped, and a special color was dedicated to it. By watching the stars, the will of the gods could be discovered, and their movements made it possible to divine what must happen on earth. So the priests or magicians were also diviners. They excelled especially in foretelling the future of men. According to them, the life of each man depended on the position of the stars at his birth, and everyone was born under a good or bad star. The Greeks called their prophecies horoscopes and their science astrology.

The Chaldeans believed in evil spirits or demons who persecuted mankind. Ghosts, misfortunes, and diseases they regarded as malignant demons who must be averted. They represented these demons as hideous creatures with the bodies of men and the heads and feet of animals. They lived in dread of sorcerers, or men who had the power of unchaining the demons. To protect themselves from the sorcerers, they had recourse to magicians. These magicians drove off the demons by their prayers, by sprinkling holy water, by brews of magic herbs or philtres, and by bands of linen worked with pious phrases. From the Chaldeans, we can trace the use of talismans, amulets, exorcism, and protective images, all of which are in use even to-day. We can notice also that Christian worship, rising as it did in the East, has preserved some of the practices of the magicians, but only as symbols and with changed meanings.

Chaldean art developed from very simple ideas. It consisted in building walls for their cities, strong castles for their kings, and lofty dwellings for their gods. The only originality it developed was in decoration.

One thing strikes the traveler in the ruins of Chalda and Assyria: the ruins are all in the form of hillocks of sand, which must be dug out, for nothing rises above the surface. We judge from this that all the buildings were built of brick. The Chaldeans used earth for building purposes because they had no stone in their country, and the Assyrians continued this tradition. It is for this reason that their architecture is solid, for they had no columns, and their buildings were always of geometrical design. The same style of building was employed for ramparts, palaces, and temples.

The ramparts were great walls of baked bricks held in place by bitumen. Their thickness, which was sometimes as much as eighty feet, made their solidity. Before them was a trench, the earth of which was used to make the bricks. The walls were adorned with battlements meeting them at a right angle and with square towers. Otherwise, the characteristic feature of the Assyrian style is the straight line. The city wall was rectangular, and the streets of the city ran either parallel to each other or at right angles, as in American towns to-day.

The palace of the king was a fortress in the center of the city. It formed a little city in itself inside the larger one, like the imperial city in the heart of Pekin or the Kremlin at Moscow. The palace stood on a lofty terrace built of bricks, approached by flights of steps. It was rectangular and formed by high walls with towers and lofty gates. There were no upper stories, and it must have looked like a mass of bricks in which courts had been, as it were, punched out. These courts were surrounded by rooms or halls, which had no windows, but only high doors. One part of the palace was assigned to the king, another to the nobles and guards, and another to the women. In its general outlines and internal arrangements, an Assyrian palace resembled the "Tatas" of certain negro chiefs in the Sudan to-day. A tower of several stories, partly a temple, partly an observatory, was reserved for the magicians.

The decoration of the palace was very rich: a pavement of precious marbles covered the ground; the walls were faced with painted earthenware, or with bas-reliefs carved on alabaster; the roofs of the halls were supported on lofty posts of cedar wood inlaid with gold, silver, or ivory; the doors were decorated with glazed bricks, and had at their approaches a double row of genii and of winged bulls; rare fabrics and growing plants completed the decoration.

The Chaldæan temple was a square tower, built of brick and rising to seven stories, each of which formed a terrace connected with the one below by a sloping way. On the highest level rose the chapel of the god, covered by a golden dome. Each story was

FIG. 25. - Chief gate in the palace of Sargon.

dedicated to one of the seven great stars and was painted the color of that star in the following order: white, black, purple, blue, vermilion, silver, and gold. The huge edifice contained only some rooms or chapels hidden in the thickness of the building. The height of the great temples at Babylon exceeded 300 feet, and the ruin which is called Birs Nimrud is still 250 feet in height.

To decorate their buildings, the Assyrians and the Chaldeans always employed the arts of brickwork and sculpture. In Chalda, we find neither stone nor metal of any sort; the place of these was taken in many ways by baked earth. It was used first in the form of building bricks. Of these, there were three kinds: the rough brick, dried in the sun; the fired brick; and the glazed brick. The rough brick was used on the inside of the walls, and the fired brick and glazed brick were used for facings. All bricks in the royal buildings bore the seal of the king who built them. On the making of these bricks were employed foreign captives, who were carried off into Assyria after the destruction of their own cities. Glazed bricks were sometimes glazed in one color and sometimes marked with patterns. Very often, a large picture was composed of a series of bricks, each of which bore a fragment of the complete design. The colors employed were very bright. With the plain-colored bricks, they beautified the lofty gateways and the walls of the storeys of the temples.

Glazed bricks were also used as ornaments. The Assyrians excelled in the highly effective art of brickwork. The employment of brickwork in modern building shows us how it can be used in decoration.

FIG. 26. - Assyrian seals.

Bricks were also used in what we may call the library. The leaves of Assyrian books were flat tiles engraved with a pointed instrument. After baking, these tiles could not be altered; so contracts of buying and selling, decrees of state, and treaties were preserved on these bricks. The storage of these must have been irksome and difficult, but it is a great gain to us to find these documents intact in the ruins.

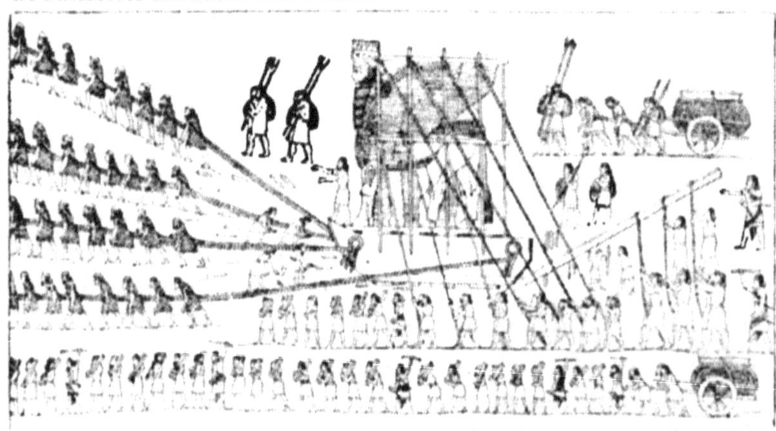

FIG. 27. - Moving an enormous winged bull, carved in alabaster, on wooden rollers.

Last, out of baked earth were fashioned the seals, which were used for signing documents. These seals were generally cylindrical, and on them were stamped inscriptions and pictures of gods or demons. These seals were used by rolling them on the soft clay.

The Assyrians obtained from their mountains a soft stone, of a chalky nature, called alabaster; out of this, they carved great figures and huge decorative panels for their buildings. The figures adorned the gates and corridors. They represented winged bulls, genii, and kings. The genii and the kings were placed with their backs to the walls; the winged bulls beautified the angles of the doors. They had five feet, in order to show two in front and three in profile. They were almost completely freed from the block of stone out of which they were carved, while the genii were only carved in shallow relief. Many of these can be seen at the British Museum, and the effect is colossal and striking.

The decorative panels carved in bas-relief were very realistic. The sculptors reproduced what they actually saw and did not draw on their imagination. With an extraordinary care for exactness and detail, they depicted scenes in the life of the king, religious

FIG. 28. - Ashur-bani-pal lion-hunting on horseback.

ceremonies, episodes of war, and the chase. So they have left us valuable documents, particularly in regard to costumes, types, and customs.

They were especially successful in representing animals, and in this respect, excelled even the Greeks. Certain bas-reliefs, in which are depicted wounded lions, dogs, horses, bulls, and wild asses, are remarkable for the correctness of the movements, the exactness of the proportions, and the play of the muscles. They were good at reproducing what they were good at seeing. Their art, like their science, was founded on observation.

While observing the stars to solve the mystery of the future, the Chaldean priests discovered the sciences of astronomy and mathematics.

In astronomy, they distinguished between the planets and the fixed stars, they determined the length of the year, they fixed the twelve signs of the zodiac, reckoned the eclipses of the moon, and invented the sundial.

In mathematics, they invented the measures of time, length, and weight, which were adopted by all the ancient world. These measures were:
1. The year, divided into months, days, hours, minutes, seconds.
2. The week, divided into seven days in honor of the seven planets.
3. The circle, divided into degrees, minutes, and seconds.
4. Length, divided into spans, cubits, perches, plethrons (100 English feet), and stades (600 English feet).
5. Weight, divided into minx, talents, and drachmas.

The principles of these sciences were recorded in the books which formed the libraries. The library of Ashur-bani-pal has been discovered. It consists of flat bricks covered with cuneiform writing. This writing was done with a stiletto before the brick was baked. These books contain scarcely any works of imagination; they are books of history, science, religion, or grammar.

FIG. 29. - An Assyrian letter.

Assyrian writing is called cuneiform because its characters consist of groups of strokes in the form of wedges.

They are very difficult to decipher, for the same signs represent both syllables and words. The Assyrians themselves found the same difficulty in reading them that we do, and they made regular dictionaries, which we find in their libraries. Scholars have deciphered them by comparing the proper names occurring in certain inscriptions in both Assyrian and Persian; in this way, they were able to construct an alphabet and read the Assyrian words. Assisted by the meaning of the Persian words, they recognized in Assyrian a language akin to Hebrew. This science of deciphering and translating the Assyrian writings is called Assyriology, and among Assyriologists, we must name Sir Henry Rawlinson in England and Professor Oppert in France.

CHAPTER V

PHOENICIA

ALTHOUGH the Phoenicians were a very small nation, they played an important part in the ancient world. They were sailors and merchants and acted as agents between other ancient nations. They had no characteristic civilization of their own, but they assisted powerfully in spreading that of other nations. Their vessels furrowed the Mediterranean and visited every port, and in this way, they became the first educators of the barbarians of Europe.

The character of the country they inhabited made them sailors — Phoenicia was merely a narrow strip of land shut in by the mountains of Lebanon, and so deprived of communication with the interior. Rocky spurs of the mountains ran out into the sea, dividing the coast into little bays, almost cut off from one another, and yet making fairly good harbors. From early times, the natives of this country formed the habit of communicating with one another by means of the sea. The cedar trees which cover Lebanon gave them abundant material for building boats.

The Phoenicians were a people of Semitic race, coming, like the Egyptians and the Hebrews, from the plains of Chalda. They had the ingenious and enterprising character of the Chaldeans. It was also their custom to build independent cities, no one of which was strong enough to dominate the others and make itself a great state. Their strength was not on the land; it was on the sea. Their towns were all ports: Arad, Byblos, Beyrouth, Sidon, Tyre, Acre. Each of these was built on a promontory or little island situated at the mouth of a fertile valley. Their fame was due to the vast extent of their navigation and their commerce. Two of

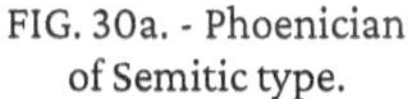

FIG. 30a. - Phoenician
of Semitic type.

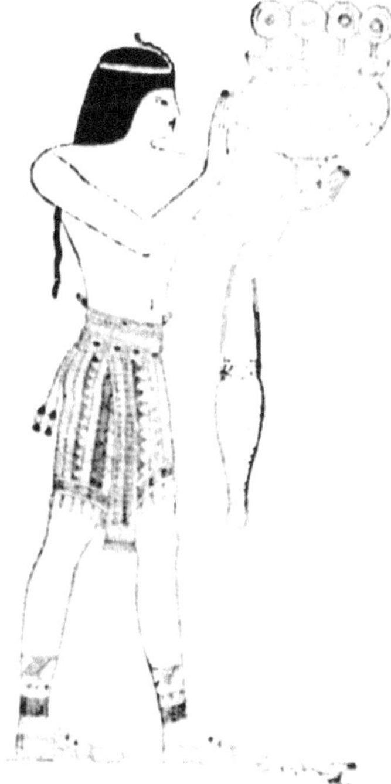

Fig. 30b. - Phoenician
of Assyrian type.

their cities, in successive periods, far surpassed the others in fame; these were Tyre and Sidon.

In Phoenicia, as in Chaldaea, each city had its own god, its lord and master, who was called Baal. Along with Baal, they worshipped a female deity called Astarte. The Baal of Byblos was called Adonis, that of Tyre, Melcarte. The Phoenician and Chaldaean gods had much in common.

Speaking generally, Baal represented the sun, the lord of sky and earth. He was capricious and fierce. His wrath could only be appeased by sacrifices, and occasionally human sacrifices were offered to him, especially the children of kings and nobles. These victims were burnt alive before the god to the sound of flutes and trumpets, while the mothers were present at the sacrifice, unmoved by the murder of their children. The god was represented by the image of a man or of a bull, sometimes of a man with the head of a bull. Melcarte was represented as a virtuous warrior. Distant conquests were attributed to him in the legends, and the Straits of Gibraltar were called the Columns of Melcarte, because it was there he had placed the bounds of his empire.

Astarte was the moon, the goddess of love and of the spring. Everything which dies and revives was under her sway; her worship combined loud demonstrations of grief with riotous feastings. She was represented as a woman with a dove in her hand and a crescent moon in her hair.

These gods had their dwelling place in the high trees, on the mountain, in the rough stones called Baitylor, or in columns, such as those which the Phoenicians put in Solomon's temple. This was the reason why, in addition to the temples, they had altars built on the tops of the mountains, called High Places.

The Phoenicians established their gods on all the coasts of the Mediterranean, and the Aphrodite of the Greeks was only a transformation of the Phoenician Astarte. In the same way, the legend of Hercules was borrowed in many respects from that of Melcarte.

Unrecorded by history, the Phoenician cities developed under the government of chiefs, who were called Suffetes. Busy with their commercial interests, the Phoenicians refrained from taking any part in the quarrels of their neighbours. They were unwilling to risk either the danger or the expense of resisting the great conquering nations, and they became in turn the tributaries of Egypt and of Assyria. As a matter of fact, Tyre did rebel against the Assyrians, but this was an exceptional event and brought about the fall of Tyre.

The internal history of the cities is practically unknown to us, except in the case of Tyre. Beyond the prosperous reign of Hiram, the friend of David and Solomon, the history of Tyre was one long succession of civil revolutions and struggles between the aristocracy and the people, and there grew up a class of men who were free though poor: sailors, mercenary soldiers, and workmen.

Certain pretenders to the throne obtained the support of this class to overthrow their rivals. The results were revolutions, often followed by the emigration of the defeated side. It was a defeat of the party of the nobility which brought about the foundation of Carthage about 814 B.C.

The true history of Carthage is that of her commerce and her trade. This history is divided into two periods: the period of the supremacy of Sidon and that of the supremacy of Tyre. Sidon, as the faithful subject of the Egyptians, reached in the fifteenth century B.C. a very high pitch of prosperity. The Pharaohs gave Sidonian sailors the right of carrying on all the foreign commerce of Egypt and allowed them to establish their depots in quarters reserved for them in various towns of the Delta, and even in Memphis, where they formed a regular town of their own.

The Sidonians were zealous in the discovery of new lands and precious merchandise throughout the eastern basin of the Mediterranean. Situated opposite Cyprus, they made themselves masters of that island rich in copper, and built certain towns there. From Cyprus, they passed along the seashore of Cilicia and Caria, and established flourishing trading stations. Next, they colonised Rhodes; then came the turn of the islands of the Aegean: Paros, which gave them marble; Melos, sulphur and alum; Thasos, gold; Cythera, purple from the murex. They also got purple from Crete, one side of which they occupied. Turning north, they made themselves masters of Lemnos, Samothrace, and Thasos, and they worked the mines of Thrace. They even dared to sail through the straits and enter the Black Sea towards the Caucasus and the unknown country near, whence they brought back tin, silver, gold, and slaves. They traded also with all the coasts of Greece, and legend has it that Thebes in Boeotia was founded by the Phoenician Cadmus.

The riches of Sidon aroused the greed of the Philistines, and they took the city and destroyed its supremacy in the thirteenth century B.C.

Tyre, where many Sidonians had taken refuge, now took

the place of Sidon. The Tyrians became masters of the sea, and deserved the name, given in later times to the Dutch, of "carriers of the sea." But while the Sidonians had displayed their energy in the western part of the Mediterranean, the Tyrians directed their business towards the eastern part, towards Africa and Spain.

Coasting along the shores of Greece, they reached Italy, Sicily, Malta, and Africa. They surrounded Sicily with a circle of colonies, which included Palermo. They discovered and developed Sardinia and the Balearic Isles and founded trading stations on the coast of Gaul, including Port Vendres. In Africa, they gained a firm footing on the coast of Tunis, and built there the cities of Utica, Hadrumetum, and at a later date Carthage. Coasting along Africa, they reached the Straits of Gibraltar, and beyond these they found the country of Tarshish, which was in reality Andalusia, a fertile land rich in minerals, supplying them with an abundance of corn, oil, wool, and silver. Gades, now known as Cadiz, built in an admirable position, became the centre of the Phoenician possessions in Spain. From Tyre to Gades, and from Gades to Tyre, there was as regular a communication as between Cyprus and Phoenicia.

The Tyrians dared to sail even into the Atlantic Ocean. They explored the coasts of Gaul and Britain, and discovered the islands on the west of Britain, now called the Scilly Isles, then called the Cassiterides; from there they obtained tin. Turning south of the straits by the coast of Africa, they seem to have gone as far south as Senegal.

On the shores of the Indian Ocean, recent discoveries made in South Africa, near the river Limpopo, lead us to suppose that the Phoenicians, in alliance with the Jews, worked the gold deposits of that country. Travellers have actually found ruins of fortresses of Phoenician construction containing a complete equipment of crucibles for melting gold.

Tyre can be taken as a typical Phoenician city. A Phoenician city was a depot protected by a god and fortified against the attacks of its neighbours. Safety had to be secured for the merchandise in the docks, the plant of the factories, and the merchants' wealth. For this reason, the city rose on rocks near the coast or on a promontory of land. There was no room for expansion; accordingly, the Eastern style of house, low and wide-spreading, was replaced by high buildings of many storeys.

At first, Tyre was divided into several little towns, separated from one another by shallow inlets of the sea. King Hiram filled up these shallows which divided the different parts of the town, and reclaimed from the sea a considerable amount of land by means of embankments and quays. In spite of this enlargement, the surface covered by houses was not large, and could scarcely have contained more than 35,000 persons. Afterwards, the city spread onto the mainland, and its merchants raised their villas on the slopes of Lebanon, and there the common people also must have had their streets and houses.

Tyre was full of extraordinary life. In the harbour, boats were constantly entering and departing, cargoes were being unloaded, and ships manoeuvred for good stations, while a picturesque mob crowded the narrow streets, dressed in the most diverse costumes; all the nationalities of the East elbowed their way. Tyre was a Venice with the activities of a Liverpool.

Tyre, in the pride of her wealth, revolted against Assyria. Her fall was due to the sieges which she underwent, - and she proved powerless to defend her empire against the Greeks and the Carthaginians. The heir to her sway in the Mediterranean proved to be her own colony, Carthage. Carthage in Africa rapidly became powerful enough to enter into rivalry with her mother country. Carthage drew into her power the Phoenicians of Africa, Sicily, and Spain, and from these formed the Punic Empire, which became the commercial enemy of Greece and the deadly rival of the Roman republic.

Phoenician colonies can be counted by the hundred, but under this name there are included three different types of settlement.

In Egypt and in civilized countries, the Phoenicians contented themselves with obtaining trading rights from the king, as nowadays Europeans obtain such rights in China. Such rights allowed them to form independent quarters in native towns, where they could build docks and bazaars. These quarters became of great importance in some towns, as, for instance, at Memphis, and they were centers of international trade.

In uncivilized countries, they founded trading stations. Choosing an island or a promontory which lent itself easily to defense, they would build there depots, storehouses, factories, and a temple, and they would add some fortifications. Just in this way, the Portuguese acted on the coasts of Africa and India in the sixteenth century. The neighboring peoples would come to these trading stations to barter, and regular fairs were held there. The Phoenicians did not make their homes in these trading stations, which had only a floating population of sailors and traders.

Some of their possessions were, however, regular colonies, in which the Phoenicians built towns, conquered the original inhabitants, and governed the country. Among such colonies must be placed Cyprus, Rhodes, Crete, the north of Africa, and the south of Spain.

The trade of the Phoenicians was enormous, for it embraced not only trade by sea but also trade by land. Phoenicians were to be found in all the cities of Asia. In these, they sold merchandise from Sidon and from Tyre, or articles they made themselves. Besides this, they had organized across all the ancient world a network of caravans which linked up the Caspian Sea and the Persian Gulf with the Mediterranean. By these means, their ships and their camels brought into Tyre in a steady stream the produce of the whole world.

From Arabia came incense, myrrh, and onyx; from India, precious stones, spices, ivory, scented woods; from Egypt, horses, flax, cotton; from Africa, gold, ebony, ivory, and ostrich feathers; from Spain, corn and gold; from the Isles of Greece, copper, tin, marble, and shellfish for dyes; from Assyria, rich stuffs, carpets, perfumes, dates, and from the Caucasus, minerals and slaves.

The slave trade was one of the greatest sources of Phoeni-

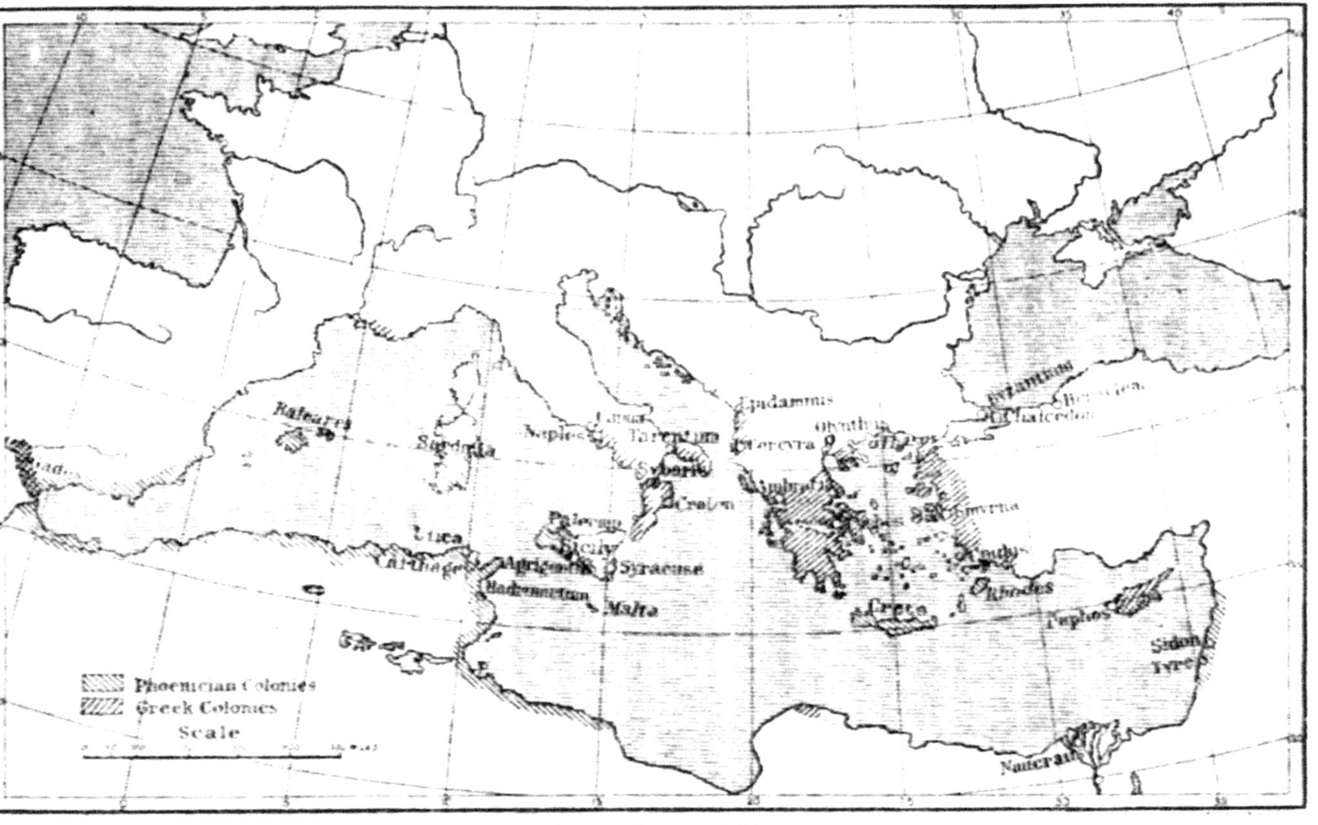

FIG. 31. – The colonies of Tyre and Sidon.

cian wealth. Slaves who were prisoners of war were not rare in countries which were victorious in battle; but elsewhere they were a costly article, and yet ancient luxury demanded a great number of servants. Tyre early filled her markets with negroes drawn from Ethiopia and white slaves brought from Greece or the Caucasus. The Tyrians knew where to get slaves sold after a victory and children bartered by their parents for tempting trifles.

Their other rare merchandise was tin. Tin was then a precious metal; because it was used in making bronze and was only found on the banks of the Nile and the Euphrates. The most daring maritime adventures of the Phoenicians were in search of this metal, and to obtain it they braved the storms of the Black Sea and the Atlantic Ocean.

The trade of the Phoenicians was not solely concerned with articles which they imported or exchanged. Many were manufactured at Tyre, and were exported for sale.

The originality of Phoenician trade lies in this very fact, that it was fed by a powerful industrial system. While other nations in the East had only individual artisans working with some assistance at their textiles or trinkets, the Tyrians collected together numbers of workmen into large workshops, and originated the factory. In this way, they manufactured articles for export in large quantities at a low price.

Their specialties were vases, jewels, images of the gods, and stuffs. They brought to perfection the weaving processes of the Egyptians, and supplied all the Mediterranean with materials of fine texture beautifully embroidered. Jewels, necklaces, bracelets, brooches, buckles, earrings, vases of silver or of bronze, statuettes of glass or of enamelled terra-cotta, which they sold to the Greeks and the Etruscans, became models for the first attempts at European art. They were scarcely works of art themselves; the same model was reproduced an infinite number of times, and the execution was careless. They were as commonplace as the things which are made today for cheap selling. Generally, they were imitations of Egyptian and Assyrian originals, and they were marked by the faults which belong to rapid and abundant production. It was not the object of the Phoenicians to create new forms: all they wished to do was to make money by reproducing or copying what was fashionable or in demand.

Their special manufactures were transparent glass and purple dye. The raw materials for these were found on the seashore: sand for the glass, the murex for the dye.

The murex is a shellfish which at the end of its shell has a reddish liquid called purple. There are several species. The Phoenician murex gave a violet red, much admired, which was called the royal purple. The murex of Greece gave a deeper violet hue; that of the Atlantic almost a black hue. Owing to the wools imported from Spain, there grew up at Tyre a great trade in purple stuffs. In ancient days, these stuffs were considered a mark of great luxury, for the murex was scarce and the stuff had to be dyed twice; the fame of this dye lasted right down to the last days of the Roman Empire.

To carry on trade successfully, it was necessary to be able to read, write, and reckon easily. The Phoenicians learned from the Assyrians the science of calculation, and they themselves invented the alphabet, or, rather, they adapted to their needs the alphabets of Egypt. The signs of the Egyptian writings, even of their cursive writings, had this grave fault: that some signs denoted syllables, others words, and some letters. Often several signs represented the same sound. With their practical genius, the Phoenicians simplified this complicated system. They chose twenty-two letters, drawn from the cursive and hieratic writings of Egypt, and by means of these letters, they were

FIG. 32. - The murex.

able to represent all the sounds of their language. In this way, they created an alphabet, which the Greeks, and later other nations, adopted. This alphabet was no longer composed of syllables or words, but of vowels and consonants, by means of which the words of all languages could be written.

The Phoenicians were so absorbed in voyaging and trading, their cities were so small and their government so poor and thrifty, that they had no original art.

The few Phoenician buildings which have escaped destruction reveal a slavish limitation of Egyptian architecture. The Phoenicians learnt from the Egyptians to build in stone, to use columns and set masonry in straight lines. Their tombs were hollowed out in the mountain-sides, like those at Thebes. The entrance had a portico of columns reminding us of the Egyptian style. The coffins, placed in these mortuary chambers, follow the forms of the Egyptian sarcophagi. Many of these came straight from Egypt, and the Phoenicians merely erased the hieroglyphs and put in their place a Phoenician inscription.

The art of navigation was, however, a Phoenician discovery. For long they were the only sailors on the Mediterranean. Their vessels were rowing-boats built with curved sides and with a keel. There were two banks of oars, and when the wind was suit-

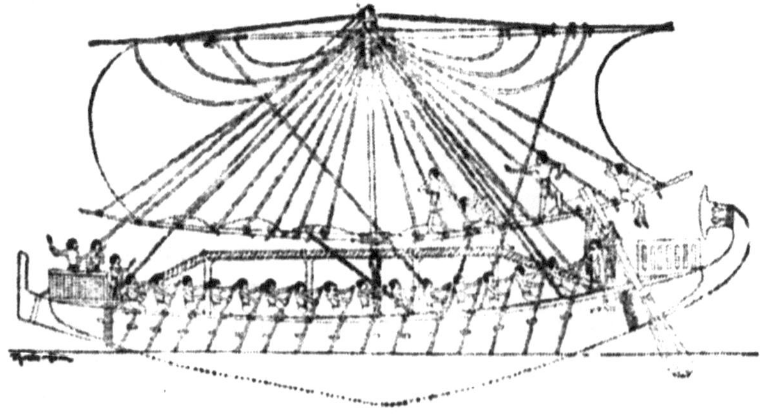

FIG. 33. - An Egyptian vessel.

able, they used a sail as well. There were two chief types in use: trading-ships, with rounded ends, and ships-of-war, with a ram at the prow. The Phoenicians, having no compasses, learnt to steer their ships by night by the North Star. But this they rarely did, for they sailed generally only in the daytime, hugging the shore. When evening fell, they cast anchor in some roadstead, or preferably they beached their ships on the sand and encamped on the shore. They made their way from point to point, always keeping the land in sight. In this way they explored the whole of the Mediterranean.

Phoenician traders would start with a cargo suitable to the country to which they were going. Landing, they would exchange their goods for the products of the district and then go further on to repeat these operations. Such voyages often took a very long time, and many a trader returned to Tyre only at the end of several years.

They did not scorn to join the profits of piracy to those of trade. They often raided uncivilised villages. At other times they would tempt on board ship women who were anxious to see their trinkets and jewels, and in the middle of the bartering, they would weigh anchor and be off. Many a Greek legend, dealing with the carrying off of women, was inspired by these acts of Phoenician piracy.

Each shipowner guarded with the greatest care the secret of his route. The Phoenicians never published abroad the places where they traded. Fear of rivals carried them even to feats of heroism, and a master would run his ship aground sooner than let another know where he was going.

Phoenician traders for the most part worked each man for himself; but sometimes they combined and formed regular companies for building or navigation. Foreign princes treated with them in constructing public buildings, or preparing fleets. In this way King Sennacherib obtained from Phoenicia engineers and sailors to build a fleet on the Euphrates and the Persian Gulf, and Solomon entrusted to Phoenician contractors the building of the temple at Jerusalem. With their help, he made the port of

Ezion-geber on the Red Sea, and sent his ships to explore the land of Ophir. It was from the Red Sea also that, in the pay of Pharaoh Necho, those Phoenicians started who in three years made the circuit of Africa. And last of all, we shall see the king of Persia calling in the Phoenicians to transport his troops to Greece.

The Phoenicians had the souls of sailors. They feared Baal, for he was lord of those elements which they faced day by day and, as we have seen, his worship was brutal as well as solemn. But they gave their love to Astarte, who embodied for them the good things of life, the joy of rest after storm, and they worshipped her with all the riotousness sailors exhibit on shore. All Phoenician festivals were characterised by this extravagance.

To live to get rich, to get rich in order to enjoy life, was the ideal of this strenuous nation. Engrossed in mercantile pursuits and only eager for gain, they left to others the disinterested glory of extending the conquests of the spirit. Still, without themselves desiring it, they helped to spread across the world with their bales of merchandise, arts, sciences, religions — all the fruit of the human mind.

CHAPTER VI

PERSIA

THE Medes and Persians belonged to the same race, coming from the plains of Bactriana and Sogdiana, the modern Turkestan (see Fig. 14). They had white skins, straight noses, oval faces, smooth hair, and thick beards.

The Medes lived near the Caspian Sea, and became the richer and more powerful of the two. One of their kings, Cyaxares, took part in the conquest of Nineveh. The Persians occupied the poorer regions on the edge of the Persian Gulf, and remained for a long time rough mountaineers, cultivating the soil and tending their flocks. This life of toil fitted them for the hard lives of soldiers. They became conquerors as soon as they had a leader.

Agriculture and fatherhood were held in the highest honour by the Persians. Family anniversaries were of the greatest importance and birthdays were celebrated by great feasts.

They were great eaters and drinkers, and frequently discussed their serious business at table. They were renowned for their politeness to one another. When they became conquerors, they soon gave up the customs of mountaineers and

FIG. 34. - A Persian.

easily adopted foreign customs. "They took," said Herodotus, "the Median dress, believing it to be more beautiful than their own." Their dress consisted of a long motley robe, often covered with patterns of flowers and animals, with a woollen cap called a tiara.

The aim of their education was to make their children upright men and good soldiers.

Until the age of five, the child was kept out of his father's way, and remained in the hands of women. Up to the age of twenty he learnt three things: to sit a horse, to shoot straight, and to speak the truth. The enemies of the intellectual movement in Greece praised Persian education, and Xenophon wrote the romance *The Education of Cyrus* to serve as a model.

The religion of the Medes and Persians was, according to tradition, revealed to them by a wise man of royal race named Zoroaster, who had passed his youth in a perpetual struggle with demons. One day he was caught up in ecstasy to heaven, and entrusted by God with the book of the law, the *Zend-Avesta*.

Returning to earth, he preached the Holy Word to the inhabitants of Iran.

According to Zoroaster, the world is the theatre of war between the principles of good and evil.

The Spirit of Good is the supreme and wise ruler, Ahura Mazda or Ormuzd. It was he, says an inscription, who created this earth, the sky above, and mankind. He is the god of life, purity, and truth — everything that is good and useful is his work, such as light, fire, water, harvest, fruits, and domestic animals. He is assisted by six chief genii, amongst them Mithra, the sun-god, and by thousands of petty genii.

The Spirit of Evil is the Spirit of Anguish, Ahriman; he had all the characteristics of Satan, and was sometimes represented with a serpent's body. All unhappiness, all vices, plagues, and misfortunes were due to him. He commanded an army of evil spirits and demons, and the struggle between these two armies, equally active and powerful, was to continue until the end of the world. The end would bring the triumph of Ormuzd, and then would begin the rule of light, life, and truth.

Ormuzd had neither images nor temples. He was worshipped under the form of a flame of fire, the symbol of purity. In this way, Zoroaster founded that fire worship which was the ancient national religion of the Persians, and which still survives to-day on the shores of the Caspian and on the Indus among the Parsees. Stone altars were built on which were burnt blocks of sweet-smelling woods.

On certain days in the year, the priests, or magi, clad in long white robes, with lofty tiaras on their heads, holding in their hands branches of tamarisk, used to go in procession to the altars. There they prepared the victim, pronounced over it the words of consecration, and poured out the drink offerings. Then they slew the victim, a horse, ox, goat, or sheep. The animal was cut in pieces, but the pieces were not burnt, for that would have defiled the purity of the fire. They were placed before the altar and were consumed at a solemn feast accompanied by sacred chants.

The magi formed a special caste and obtained great authority. They mingled with their own rites a certain number of Assyrian practices, and they professed to foretell the future. They taught that each man was protected by a guardian angel and that by doing what was right, a man could at any moment worship Ormuzd. Religion was thus combined with moral teaching, and the greatest stress was laid on purity.

To please Ormuzd, a man must work towards his triumph by tilling the soil, by founding a family, by protecting useful animals, especially the dog, and by cultivating good thoughts and performing good deeds.

To deserve the favours of Ormuzd, a man must keep himself pure in body and soul. If he fell from righteousness, he could not regain it by offerings and sacrifices; he could only regain it by repentance. Before all, he must be honest and loyal. "The Persians," says Herodotus, "consider nothing more shameful than to lie, and after lying to be in debt; for, say they, the man who is in debt is forced to lie."

They had also to keep the body pure, and not to touch such unclean things as corpses and lepers, and because anything dead was unclean, everything dead had to be avoided scrupulously.

From this idea of purity there arose a curious funeral custom. The corpse could not be burnt, nor buried, nor thrown into the water, for it would have defiled the fire, earth, or water. To avoid this, the Persians covered the corpse with wax before burying it, but more often they left the corpse to the birds of prey, putting it in a large round tower open to the sky.

This method of disposing of the dead is still practiced to-day in Bombay by the Parsees, the only surviving worshippers of Ormuzd. Three days after death, the soul left the body and came before the judgment seat of Ormuzd. Then the soul crossed the bridge Chinval; if it was pure, it passed easily; otherwise, it fell into the deep and was the prey of demons. If pure, the soul became a member of the household of Ormuzd and conferred benefits on its descendants.

The Persian people, strong and hardy, inspired by high ideals and quickly roused to enthusiasm, were for a time in subjection to the Medes; then one day they rose at the voice of King Cyrus.

The stories of Cyrus' childhood are purely legendary, but it is a fact that under the leadership of Cyrus, the Persians attacked the Medes and overthrew their king. Then, as king of both the Medes and Persians (549), Cyrus undertook the conquest of the Western Asiatic world.

He first attacked Croesus, the king of Lydia, who ruled over nearly all Asia Minor and was the most famous of ancient kings for his riches. During the summer, the war was indecisive, but, contrary to the customs of ancient warfare, the Persian mountaineers prolonged the campaign throughout the winter, took Croesus by surprise, and besieged him in Sardis. The city was taken by assault after four days' siege, and Asia Minor fell into the power of Cyrus (546). Then he turned his forces to the East and subdued Bactriana and Sogdiana, and took Arachosia, that is, Turkestan and Afghanistan, all the stretch of country from the Sea of Aral to the Persian Gulf (545-539). Then he attacked Chalda and took Babylon (538). All the countries of the Assyrian Empire submitted without a blow to this new master, and the Persian Empire extended from the Indus to the isthmus of Suez.

Cyrus did not invade Egypt; that was the work of his son Cambyses. He pushed northwards and perished in an expedition against the nomad races of southern Russia, called Scythians.

The victorious Persians were kind and merciful to the conquered peoples. There are well-established traditions of the goodness and generosity of Cyrus. He treated the Medes as a sister nation; he spared the life of Croesus and welcomed him to his Council; he spared the city of Babylon; he allowed the Jews to return to Jerusalem. This novel behaviour struck the imagination of the ancients, who regarded Cyrus as a hero of chivalry.

The Persians, in order to ennoble the hero who had gained their freedom for them, invented the fable that he was the son of the king of the Medes.

The story ran that Astyages, king of the Medes, had given his daughter Mandane to a Persian nobleman in marriage. Soon Astyages was warned by a dream that he would be dethroned by his grandson. When the child was born, he took him from his mother and gave orders to Harpagus, the chief of the guard, to destroy him. Harpagus, moved by pity, contented himself by exposing the child on a mountain, where he was found by shepherds. The boy grew up in the village, but soon showed his royal birth by exacting homage from the other children. This was reported to Astyages, and, struck by various coincidences, he discovered the truth. He inflicted a cruel punishment on the chief of the guard, but brought the child up to manhood and appointed him governor of Persia. Then Cyrus, spurred on by Harpagus, who yearned for vengeance, raised the standard of revolt among the citizens and overthrew Astyages, who had already been deserted by the army.

Cyrus founded the Persian Empire; fifteen years later, Darius extended it and organised it. He was a prince of the royal family, who ascended the throne after having delivered Persia from a usurper called Gaumata, who, after the death of Cambyses, pretended to be a son of Cyrus and persecuted the followers of Ormuzd. This usurper had caused numerous revolts. Then Darius appeared on the scene to restore at once the legitimate monarchy, the true religion, and the unity of the Empire.

The entire Empire was in revolt, for each province was trying to secure independence. With great promptness, Darius first subdued Chalda, Media, and Persia. The more distant countries were not slow in making their submission (521-519). Darius afterwards recorded his victories over the revolting people in the celebrated inscription at Behistun. These revolts being suppressed, he continued the conquests of Cyrus.

Two roads were open to him, the road to India and that to Europe. He turned first to India. He crossed the passes which lead to the valley of the Indus and marched down it. The Greeks who were serving in his army then sailed down the river and reached the ports of the Persian Gulf and the Red Sea.

On the western frontier, he marched against the Scythians of the Danube and the Don. The Asiatic Greeks gave him boats, which he used as bridges to cross the Bosphorus and the Danube. But the pursuit of the Scythians, who continued to flee from his approach, exhausted his army, which returned with broken ranks to Asia. He gained by this expedition the satrapy of Thrace, and the boundaries of his empire were the Indus, the Caspian, the Black Sea, the Sahara, the deserts of Arabia, and the Persian Gulf. This mighty power was broken, even in the lifetime of Darius, by a little Greek nation, who at Marathon inflicted on him his first check.

Darius originated in his empire the type of government we call a protectorate. The subject nations kept their own customs, languages, religions, and princes; but the whole empire was divided into twenty-three divisions, each of which had at its head a governor or satrap appointed by the king. This satrap, chosen from the Persian lords, had supreme authority in matters of justice and taxation. To him were attached a Royal Secretary, whose business it was to watch the actions of his chief, and a general who commanded the army of occupation. The rivalry of these three persons checked the misuse of power and prevented revolts.

Further, royal inspectors, called "the eyes and ears of the king," inspected the administration of the satrap each year, and, if necessary, suspended him from his office. A regular postal service kept the provinces in touch with the king and secured a prompt execution of orders.

The satrapies also formed a division of the financial administration. Each satrap had to assign, collect, and forward the taxes. The Persians alone were exempt from all taxation, but they were obliged to offer presents to the king whenever he travelled through their part of the country. This practice was like the right of requisition practised in the Middle Ages by kings on the lands of their vassals. The other satrapies paid tribute in silver or in kind. Lydia and Mysia paid 500 talents of silver; Syria and Phoenicia 850. The money tribute produced the equivalent of four million English pounds. Egypt furnished 120,000 measures of corn, Cilicia 350 horses; Media 100,000 sheep, 3,000 horses, 4,000 mules, etc. Beyond this, each satrapy had to support the satrap and his court. To make the payments and exchanges easier, Darius struck coins of gold and silver, bearing his likeness.

This organisation of the Empire put into the hands of Darius greater power and greater wealth than any ruler had possessed hitherto, and won him the title of "the Great King," and he set himself to deserve the title. He adopted the ceremonial of the Assyrian monarchs, and lived retired in his palace, surrounded by a court of several thousand servants, guards, and officers. No one could see him without permission. He was never seen, except seated on his throne of gold and silver, holding a golden sceptre in his hand. He wore the long Median robe with wide sleeves, and he wore on his head a tiara adorned with precious stones and jewels, round which ran a band of gold. Around him stood attendants holding a parasol over his head and waving fans before him. Men approached him on their knees, and an order from him was sufficient for the prompt execution of a guilty satrap or officer at the other end of the empire.

He lived in turn at Susa, Pasargada, and Persepolis, capitals in which he had built magnificent palaces.

His subjects imitated his luxurious mode of living, and so the Persians lost the great qualities of their race, and after their conquests became the most effeminate of men and were easily conquered by the Greeks.

Still, their army presented a formidable appearance. The historian Herodotus has given a detailed description of it. It was composed of native troops and foreign auxiliaries. The king's guard consisted of 10,000 men, called the Immortals. Their costume differed from that of the rest only in its richness. They wore woollen caps called tiaras, bright-colored tunics with sleeves, breastplates made of mail, and greaves. Their weapons were the lance, bow, and dagger. They held their lances in both hands and had on their arms large wicker shields.

The Assyrian auxiliaries had brazen helmets, clubs shod with iron, and breastplates made of many layers of stuff sewn together. The Saces were armed with an axe and a bow; the Indians and Caspians were also bowmen. The cavalry had the same costume and arms as the foot soldiers; they were assisted in the attack by chariots with scythes on the wheels. Finally, the transport service was secured by troops of camels, which took the peoples of Asia Minor by surprise.

The Persians, passing too quickly from obscurity to power, had no time to create a characteristic and original art. So they borrowed their architecture, sculpture, and decorations from the Assyrians; but they mingled these styles with those of Egyptian art, and even with those of Greek art. Temples they never built, as their religion did not allow it, but they built beautiful royal palaces. These palaces were built of worked stone, not of brick, like those of the Assyrians. They were one storey high, and stood on raised terraces. The lines of the building were slender; there were numerous halls of columns; the ceilings were of precious woods painted and inlaid with metal; the outside was decorated with enamelled brickwork. Such are the discoveries made known to us by the excavations of M. and Mme. Dieulafoy at Susa and Persepolis.

The grandeur of the Persian palaces can be imagined from the ruins of Persepolis. The terrace, the great flights of steps, several doors, including the principal one, and some of the columns of the throne-room, are still standing. The Persian column, which is sixty feet high, is very slender. It is remarkable for its enormous capitals, formed of several scrolls placed one upon another, and surmounted by the heads of two bulls placed back to back.

The decoration of the outer walls of the palace was very rich in color. The colors were formed by enamelled brick, an Assyrian invention, but while in Assyria the design on the brick is flat, in Persia it was in relief.

The sculpture of the Persians was entirely Assyrian. The gates of the palace were guarded by man-headed bulls and the exploits of the kings were depicted in bas-reliefs. The most remarkable of these bas-reliefs was found on the rock of Behistun, which overhangs the road to Ectatana. Beginning more than a hundred feet from the ground, it is covered with cuneiform inscriptions and carvings. The principal carving is the triumph of Darius over rebels. With his crown on his head and his bow in his hand, the king puts his foot on a man lying on the ground. Before him is a file of nine prisoners with hands bound together and a cord round their necks. Above flies the winged figure of Ormuzd.

The tombs were funeral chambers carved in the solid rock. The entrance represented the entrance of a palace, but there was neither a staircase nor a slope to reach it. The chamber was some distance above the level, and the body of the king was placed there by means of scaffolding and special apparatus. These buildings all reveal the Persians as people of taste who, while they invented little, knew how to borrow wisely from the inventions of others.

PART II.

GREECE

CHAPTER VII

THE EARLY GREEKS

IN studying the history of the Greeks, or the Hellenes, as they called themselves, we are studying the origins of modern civilisation. It is from them that we derive many of our ways of thinking and feeling.

Their works have been the models which have inspired through the centuries, and still inspire, artists, writers, and orators. We have learnt from them belief in human reason, love of country, and liberty. Their geographical position at one end of the Mediterranean made it possible for them to spread their culture, for by way of the sea they reached Asia, whence they learnt themselves; by the sea also they carried to Europe not only Asiatic civilisation, but the products of their own genius.

The Greeks lived on the coasts and isles of the Aegean Sea or Archipelago, which was absolutely a Greek lake. There was a Greece of the mainland and a Greece of the sea.

The Greece of the mainland, or Hellas, comprised the southern part of the Balkan peninsula, the most eastern and the most rugged of the three peninsulas which project from Europe into the Mediterranean.

The Peloponnesus, the modern Morea, is a small peninsula shaped like an open hand, or, according to an ancient comparison, a palm-leaf, attached to the mainland by the isthmus of Corinth.

Greece is bounded on the east by the Aegean Sea, which divides it from Asia, on the west by the Ionian Sea, which separates it from Sicily and the south of Italy. On the north, there is no natural boundary. According to the Greek geographer Strabo, the ancient boundary of Greece should be a line starting on the west from

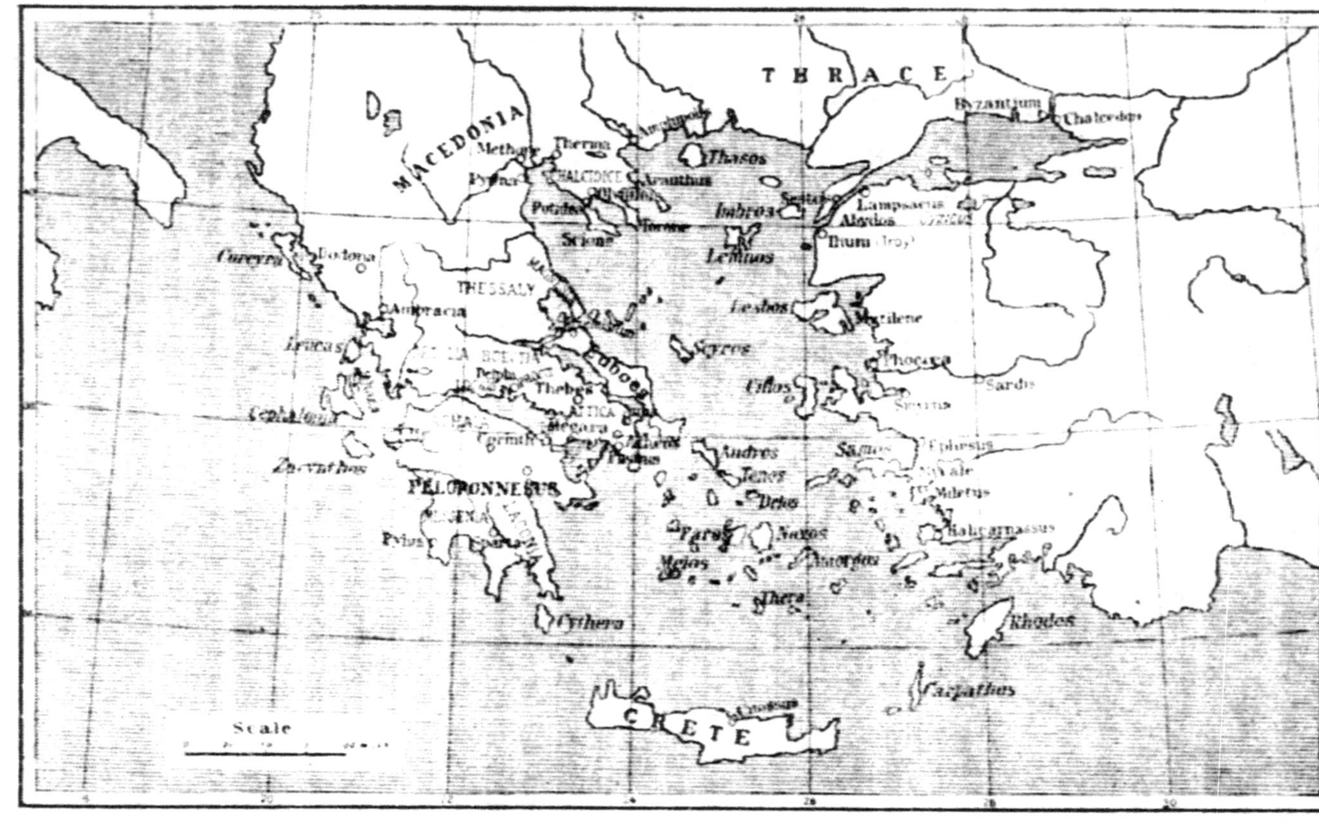

FIG. 35. - The Greek Empire.

the Gulf of Aeta, in ancient days called the Gulf of Ambracia, and ending on the east or the Gulf of Salonica, by the mountains of Olympus and the mouth of the Salambia, in ancient times called the Peneus. The greatest length from north to south is about 230 miles, the distance from London to Lancaster, and the greatest width is about 120 miles, the distance from London to Bristol. The country bristles with mountains, with steep slopes and hard ascents; they are for the most part of limestone formation, often denuded, and under a bright sun and in the clear air, they glitter with a snowy whiteness.

The mountain ranges show a fine irregularity sometimes separated by deep and narrow valleys, where the trees growing along the water-courses make verdant avenues; sometimes enclosing little plains, regular basins, sites of lakes now dry, where the soil is suitable for culture and where groves of olives are found. Of this nature are the plains of Thessaly, Thebes, Athens, Argos, and Sparta. The most famous mountains are Pindus, Olympus, the home of the gods, Ossa, Pelion, Parnassus, and Helicon, the home of Apollo and the Muses, Hymettus, famous for its honey, and Pentelicus, noted for its marble. In the Peloponnesus rises the lofty plateau of Arcadia, bounded on the south by the mighty chain of Taygetus.

The conformation of their country has played a very important part in the history of the Greeks. The land is divided into a large number of isolated districts, and each of these districts became the centre of a little state, none of them larger than an English county, but always passionately independent. So there were separate republics at Athens, Sparta, Thebes, etc., but never a single united Greek state.

Another fact has deeply influenced the history of the Greeks. While on all sides mountains hem them in and allow of no expansion, on all sides also the sea stretches before them. Their little country has the most indented coast in all the world. The Gulf of Corinth and the Gulf of Aegina, separated by a tongue of land only three miles in width, run right across the mainland. Nowhere do gulfs cut further into the land, nowhere are capes of greater length. The result is that Greece, which has an area only a tenth of that of France, has a sea coast of more than 1000 miles.

Further, Greece is almost surrounded with islands; some are so close to the mainland that they are like extensions of it, as, for instance, Euboea. Others, like the Cyclades, thrown across the Aegean like stepping-stones in a brook, link up Europe with the coast of Asia Minor, where other Greeks inhabited the large islands of Lesbos, Chios, Samos, and Rhodes. The Aegean is merely a Greek lake on which the traveller never for one moment loses sight of land. So the most timid took courage and dared to face the crossing, certain of finding a place of refuge close at hand in unforeseen danger, whether from a sharp gale or a sudden storm. The mountains bred in men a love of liberty, the sea made them sailors and traders. The sea brought Greece into touch with the nations of the East, and so she owed to it the first elements of civilisation. It was the sea which made it possible for states of very small area, consisting of little more than one city, to become rich, and then to become the centre of regular Mediterranean empires.

To the influence of the mountains and the sea must be added the influence of the climate. In the north grew the cereals and products of Central Europe, in the valleys of the south the vine, fig tree, olive, orange, citron, and even the palm tree. Nowhere has the climate that excessive cold which paralyses the energy and activity of man. The clear air and bright sky found their reflection in the keen and clear intellect of the Greek.

Finally, the Greeks themselves were industrious, shrewd, and enterprising. They asserted and believed that they were autoch-thonous — that is, sprung from the soil. As a matter of fact, they came from Asia. They were akin to the Medes and Persians, and with them belonged to the Aryan or Indo-European family. Their statues, designs, and vase paintings represent them as tall and well-developed, with finely-proportioned limbs. Their features were regular, and the beard was allowed to grow; the forehead was shaded by an abundance of hair, generally of light colour,

FIG. 36. - Type of Greek beauty.

sometimes short and curly, sometimes falling in long strands on the shoulders; the eyes were large and brilliant, the lips fine, and, last of all, as the characteristic mark of the Greek race, the nose was straight and in a straight line with the forehead. Such was the Greek type in perfection; it is rarely found today among the descendants of the ancient Hellenes; it is possible that it was exceptional even among the ancients.

The Greeks gave the name of Pelasgian to the first inhabitants of their country. The Pelasgians cultivated the soil and are credited with building the earliest cities.

After the Pelasgians came the Hellenes. There were four principal tribes, differing from one another in customs and dialect.

There were first the Achaeans and Aeolians, then the Dorians, a race of mountaineers and rude peasants, and lastly the Ionians, who were seamen and traders. The Dorians became masters of the Peloponnesus and continental Greece, the Ionians masters of the coasts of the Aegean and maritime Greece.

The Greeks, knowing nothing of the true history of their origin, satisfied themselves with legends.

The first man was moulded out of a little clay by the giant Prometheus. To give life to things he had created, Prometheus stole fire from Zeus. In revenge, Zeus nailed Prometheus to the summit of the Caucasus, where a vulture for ever devoured his liver. Then the wrath of Zeus fell on mankind and he destroyed them with a flood. But Deucalion, the son of Prometheus, escaped the flood on a boat and repeopled the earth when the waters had subsided. He threw stones over his shoulder, and from each of these stones a man was born. One of his sons was called Hellen, and he was the ancestor of the Hellenes or Greeks. Hellen in his turn had two sons, Dorus and Aeolus, and then two grandsons, Ion and Achaeus. From these four descendants of Hellen were born the four great families of the Greeks: the Dorians, the Aeolians, the Ionians, and the Achaeans.

In other legends we find traces of the establishment of foreign colonies in Greece, especially traces of the civilizing influence of the Phoenicians and Egyptians.

The first nations who occupied Greece built towns with walls constructed out of such enormous blocks of stone that they roused the admiration of the Greeks, and caused astonishment even today. Such towns were Pylos on the Alpheus, and Tiryns and Mycenae in Argolis.

The Greeks said these cities were built by the Cyclops, a race of giants endowed with more than human strength. The walls were generally built of irregularly shaped blocks of stones, placed upon one another without any mortar, and only kept in place by their own weight.

One of these stones in the Treasure House of Atreus at Mycenae is thirty feet long, twenty feet thick, and weighs about 120 tons.

The ruins of Mycenae were explored in 1876 by a German archaeologist called Schliemann. His excavations resulted in the discovery of a great number of things, including arms and jewelry of great richness, bearing witness to an advanced stage of civilization and showing the influence of the East.

There were two parts to the town of Mycenae, an upper town, the Acropolis or citadel, rising on a broad plateau about half a mile long, and a lower town spreading over the plain. The Acropolis was surrounded by a double fortification, the lower town by a single one. The walls were about thirty feet high and eighteen feet thick. The approach to the Acropolis was through the Lion Gate, so called because the door was surmounted by a pediment consisting of a great triangular stone, on which were carved in bas-relief two lions standing on their hind legs. The lions' heads were made of bronze. In the Acropolis were found six great tombs carved in the solid rock. These were apparently royal tombs, for the corpses were adorned with gold ornaments, crowns, rich jewels, and armor. One corpse had been embalmed and, like the Egyptian mummies, wore a mask, made in this case out of a sheet of gold.

In the lower town was found a domed building like a beehive, about fifty feet high, still bearing traces of beautiful decoration. This bears the name of the Treasure House of Atreus, but almost certainly it was a tomb.

Mycenae owed its wealth to its position. It commanded the mountain pass over which ran the shortest road from the Gulf of Argolis to the Gulf of Corinth. Numerous merchants used this road, and the inhabitants of Mycenae exacted toll from them or their caravans, as Solomon also did in Judah, and as today in the same Balkan peninsula certain Albanian tribes do on the roads from the Adriatic to Salonika. According to the poets, Mycenae had powerful kings. The most famous was Agamemnon, called in the Homeric poems the "King of kings." He acted as commander-in-chief of the great Greek expedition against the Asiatic city of Troy.

Troy was built almost at the entry of the Dardanelles or Hellespont, on a hill which commands the low-lying plain of the Scamander. Schliemann from 1870 to 1882 had this hill excavated; and he found there the ruins of six cities placed one above another. The ruins of the fifth showed signs of fire and were buried in ashes. From this, Schliemann concluded that he had discovered the city that had been destroyed by Agamemnon, and which, according to the poems, had been the capital of King Priam. The objects discovered among the ruins appear to be much more ancient than those which he discovered at Mycenae, but the fact remains that there was a Troy in Asia and that the town was a strong fortress.

It is extremely likely that the kings of Asia committed acts of piracy and that the Greeks joined forces to avenge these acts, and that the Trojan War had some such origin as this. The legend runs —

Paris, son of Priam, king of Troy, carried off Helen, the wife of

Menelaus, who was the king of Sparta and brother of Agamemnon, king of Mycenae.

In order to avenge the wrong done to his brother, Agamemnon called together the princes of Greece and was chosen chief of the allied fleet, which destroyed Troy after a siege of ten years' duration. The vicissitudes of the war and the adventures of the heroes concerned form the subject of the Homeric poems, and the subject has become as immortal as the poems themselves.

The Homeric poems were long stories in verse which the poets, who were called rhapsodists, used to recite to the accompaniment of music at the feasts or gatherings of the kings and chiefs. They were like the ballads which the troubadours sang in medieval castles, or like the poems of Serbian history of the nineteenth century which popular reciters today declaim at village feasts, accompanying themselves on a sort of violin.

All exploits are credited to great-souled heroes, aided by the gods, who personally interfere in the affairs of men. This form of historical poetry reaches great beauty through the truth of its descriptions, sentiments, and character-drawing, by the simple grandeur of expression and by the exactness of its detail.

Manners, language, costumes, beliefs — all are described with the greatest accuracy, and the Homeric poems are at the same time one of the greatest pieces of literature and one of the greatest authorities on Ancient Greece.

The Iliad and the Odyssey are the most famous of these poems.

The Iliad deals with war and the great battles, in which men and gods alike took part, during the ten years of the siege of Troy or Ilium.

The Odyssey, which was composed long after the Iliad, is a poem of the sea and the countryside. Ulysses (or Odysseus), the victim of the anger of some of the gods, was storm-tossed on his homeward voyage from Troy, and finally wrecked off the island of the Phaeacians. There he was welcomed by the king, to whom he told his marvelous adventures and from whom he borrowed a ship to take him home to Ithaca. He found his palace filled with chiefs who, believing him to be dead, were suitors for the hand of his wife, the faithful Penelope. She had cleverly kept them in suspense, until the day when Ulysses at last returned. He was recognized by his son, with whose assistance he massacred the suitors and made himself master of his own house again.

According to a recent authority, the Odyssey is a poetic rendering of very exact geographical records, which were collected by a seafaring nation to serve as a guide to seamen.

The Homeric poems describe the life of men who lived long after the heroes whose remains were found at Mycenae. The poems were probably composed in the ninth century, and it is Greek life of the ninth century that they describe.

In those distant times, the Greeks, who were then called Achaeans, were divided into petty kingdoms. In each of these, the land was owned by a small number of heads of families, who cultivated the soil by means of their servants, some of whom were freemen and some slaves. These nobles were true patriarchs, having absolute power over their property, their family, and their servants. They enjoyed the title of "king," which then meant head of a tribe, and in reality, they behaved like barbarous kings, working with their hands and eating with their servants. Occasionally, they met to form a Council, which was presided over by the real king.

The king was only the chief, whose authority was acknowledged by the other chiefs, who were his equals. He was not distinguished from them by his dress, but he carried a staff of office or sceptre as the sign of his pre-eminence. He commanded the armies in war, presided over religious ceremonies, and sat on the judgment-seat in the open air. He always belonged to a family which claimed descent from the gods, and this increased his influence.

The king lived in a palace; but this does not imply any special luxury or magnificence. The palace was only a house somewhat larger than the others. It consisted of two parts: the thalamos, or private apartments, built of stone, and the megaron, or great public hall, built of wood, where the men met for meals. Large courts and outhouses for the servants and for storing provisions completed the building. In the megaron, the king and the chiefs enjoyed great feasts, when they roasted whole carcasses of sheep, pig, or goat on the hearth, which was in the middle of the hall. The megaron was like a barn with a floor of beaten earth, without flooring or chimney, full of arms and articles of all sorts.

War, as described in the Iliad, was carried on in a very barbarous fashion. Each tribe fought separately, under the command of the king and the chiefs. The soldiers, who fought on foot, wore helmets and shields, as well as their national arms: the bow, sling, axe, javelin, or club, as the case might be. The chiefs wore complete armor and fought in chariots, armed with the lance

FIG. 37. - Early Greek soldiers.

and sword. In battle, the soldiers stood in line, while the chiefs, advancing in their chariots between the two armies, challenged the heroes of the opposing forces to battle, by heaping insults on them, and then proceeded to fight in single combat, their prowess being celebrated by the songs of the poets. Often, the two armies stayed the battle to watch as spectators one of these duels. As yet, there was no scientific sieging of cities. Before Troy, the Greeks constructed neither siege towers nor trenches. They sheltered in a fortified camp, near where their ships were beached side by side like houses. The only method they knew of taking a city was by using scaling-ladders.

In the Odyssey, we have a picture of the simplicity of life during times of peace. The heroes, so proud in battle, were peaceful rulers in their palace, farm, or castle, good countrymen, personally superintending the cooking of food, treating their slaves well, and working with them in the fields. In his own house, Ulysses worked as a mason and made his own furniture; he built the walls of his room and made his bed out of olive wood inlaid with gold, silver, and ivory. Nausicaa, a king's daughter, went with the maidens of the house to wash the family linen. Woman was respected as the mother of the family and as housekeeper, doing everything in the house, but she could not mingle in the gatherings of men. "Return to your rooms," says Telemachus to his mother, Queen Penelope, "employ yourself on your own tasks, spinning and weaving. Order your maids to finish their appointed tasks. War is for men, and especially for me, who am master in the palace."

The stranger received a warm welcome of great dignity and courtesy. He was considered, as was also the beggar, to be the messenger of Zeus; his arrival was the signal for feasts, at which he was begged to relate his adventures, and on his departure, he was laden with gifts.

Costume was very simple, and is known to us from the advice which the poet Hesiod gave for the winter. They were shod with strong pieces of leather lined with slippers of wool. They wore a long tunic. Goatskins stitched together with ox sinews formed a covering for the shoulders and a protection from the rain. "Get also," says the poet, "a woollen cap, to wrap up your head and keep the damp from your ears."

This costume recalls that worn today by peasants in the Balkan mountains. The same simplicity of life, combined with dignified politeness, may still be found there. One can easily picture the primitive Greek chiefs, when one has seen a Serbian noble driving the plough, going down to the cellar, and superintending the cooking, and all with the air of a king entertaining another king.

NOTES ON CRETAN CIVILIZATION

By P. Woodham Smith

Recent excavations on the island of Crete and the islands of the Aegean Sea have revealed a civilization as old as that of Egypt, and prior to the Mycenaean. They suggest the probability of a maritime empire which included the isles and coasts of the Aegean, and had its seat of government at Cnossus in Crete. Some archaeologists have thought that the strength of the Philistines in the time of the Jewish kings Saul and David was due to the fact that they were a part of this great empire.

At Cnossus, there has been discovered a great palace with innumerable rooms and passages, which may account for the well-known Greek legend of the Labyrinth; whilst there is evidence from mural paintings and the decorations on golden cups that the bullfight was a national pastime, perhaps a religious observance, and this may account for the story of the Minotaur.

The Cretan people possessed considerable artistic skill in the making of cups, vases, and personal ornaments, which they may have learned originally from Egypt. There is evidence that they traded in these things, but the presence of vast oil vats in the royal palace shows what was their chief article of trade, and the manner in which the kings received their tribute.

The Cretans could read, write, and cast accounts, but as yet no one has found the key to their language.

CHAPTER VIII

GODS AND HEROES

THE Greeks had the souls of artists. Intoxicated by the beauty of Nature, they made Nature an object of worship, and their religion remains an embodiment of the most beautiful poetry.

The forces of Nature appeared to the Greeks as great mysterious beings endowed with wills and feelings like those of mankind.

On the other hand, the love which children feel for their parents made it impossible for them to believe that death could separate them forever. They believed that even in the tomb, the dead continued to live and remember their families, and that if honor were paid to them, they would become their family's protector. So there existed two religions and two worships: the public religion and worship of the gods, and a private religion and worship of ancestors.

All that man admires or dreads in Nature, the thunderbolt, the tempest, the light of day, the coolness of the mountains, or the murmur of the deep, appeared to the Greeks as manifestations of divine powers. They believed that they were surrounded by a crowd of invisible beings, and they worshipped these beings, thinking of them as persons, and giving them names. This worship of more than one god is called, from two Greek words, polytheism.

The gods, the Greeks imagined, were men, women, or youths whose strength, intelligence, and beauty could never alter nor perish. They were all superior to human nature: in their bodily development, the majesty of their faces, the greatness of their thoughts, and the violence of their passions. They were immortal and their features glowed with eternal youth. They lived like Greek chiefs in a palace on the top of Mount Olympus. There they held their councils, under the presidency of Zeus, or took part in feasts where Ganymede or Hebe, servants of the gods, offered them nectar and ambrosia. This fashion of representing the gods under human form is called anthropomorphism.

The popular imagination credited the gods with customs like those of men. Among them, there were relationships, marriages, rivalries, and alliances. They mingled with mortals, and their adventures were the subject of a mass of stories or myths.

On the other hand, the worship of the gods was local. Although they might have the same name, the god of one city was not the same as the god of the next city. There were many Zeus and Apollos, and these were often distinguished by a surname. Zeus was especially worshipped at Olympia, Hera at Argos, Athena at Athens. Speaking generally, the Greek expected protection only from the god of his own city.

The Latins, moulded by the literature and art of Greece, attempted to identify their national gods with the gods of Greece. They have bequeathed to us the custom of calling Greek gods by Latin names. In the following list, we give the gods their two names: -

All forces of the sky are personified in Zeus (Jupiter), who turns the thunderbolt, and at his nod collects or disperses the clouds. He represents also order in Nature, and accordingly is the master of the universe, the almighty father of gods and men.

The clear sky is Hera (Juno), the wife of Zeus, and the rain which falls from the sky and enters the earth is Hermes (Mercury), who is the messenger of Zeus and guides souls to Hades. The rainbow is Iris, also the messenger of the gods. The sun is the young and radiant Apollo (Phoebus), the divine archer with his golden arrows, a kindly god when he dries up the swamps, a dreadful god when he deals sunstroke. The moon is the white Artemis (Diana), the virgin huntress whose silver bow deals death to the wild animals of the mountains. The very winds had names: Boreas, the north wind; Notus, the south wind; Eurus, the east wind; and Zephyrus, the west wind. They obey their master Aeolus, who holds them imprisoned in the caverns of Etna.

The Greeks worshipped as gods all the aspects of the sea, which was to them a second fatherland. The sea, sometimes peaceful, sometimes raging, is Poseidon (Neptune), who raises and calms the storms with his trident. The coastal waters are Amphitrite, his wife. The calm sea is represented by the aged Nereus.

In the hollows of the waves lives the goddess Thetis of the silver feet; in the tumult of the waves, the Greeks heard the horn of Triton blowing, and in the rhythm of the waves, they saw the grace of the Nereids. The sea gods were generally represented with a human body and a fish's tail.

The fertility of the soil is represented by Demeter (Ceres), the Earth mother, who is the support both of crops and of cities.

Her daughter Persephone (Proserpine), goddess of the growing seed, returns to her mother every spring after spending the winter with her husband Pluto. The vine has its own god, Dionysius (Bacchus), coming from Asia, and represented sometimes as a bearded man, sometimes as a fair youth with clustering locks. Around him are grouped Silenus, the god of drunkenness; the Maenads, who are frenzied dancers; and the Satyrs, coarse and cowardly creatures with goat's feet and tails, symbols of the brute forces of Nature.

Vegetation is the work of Pan, god of shepherds. Fair maidens called Nymphs express the charm of Nature; these are Oreads in the mountains, Dryads among the oak trees, and Naiads in the streams.

The pale Hades (Pluto), god of the kingdom of the dead, rules in the underworld; he has a three-headed dog, Cerberus. Near him are the three Fates: Clotho, Lachesis, and Atropes, who spin and cut the thread of human destiny.

The fire of the volcano is Hephaestus (Vulcan), the blacksmith god, who, assisted by his workmen, the Cabires and the Cyclopes, causes the flames to pour out of the top of Etna.

The energies of man were also personified. Ares (Mars) is the god of war. Aphrodite (Venus) is the goddess of beauty and of love. Her son is Eros (Cupid), that is, desire, and her attendants are the Three Graces.

Athene (Minerva), emerging fully armed from the brains of Zeus, is the goddess of reason, and of science applied both to peace and war.

Asklepios (Esculapius), the son of Apollo, is the god of medicine. Apollo himself, god of the light, is equally the god of gymnastics and music; he leads across the mountains his choir of nine muses, the goddesses who are the incarnation of the Greek genius: Clio (history), Melpomene (tragedy), Terpsichore (dancing), Erato (elegiac poetry), Calliope (epic poetry), Urania (astronomy), and Polymnia (oratory). Moral forces also had their divine representatives. Zeus is majesty; Artemis and Athene are purity; Themis is justice; Nemesis is punishment; and Hestia the domestic virtues.

Twelve of these gods were considered the chief, and they formed the Assembly of Olympus. Eventually, all represented simultaneously a natural force and a moral idea, and artists gave them certain attributes in their statues to render this clear. They are: -

Greek Name	Latin	Force or Idea Represented		Attributes
Zeus	Jupiter	Air	Omnipotence	Eagle Thunderbolt Sceptre Peacock
Hera	Juno	Sky	Marriage	Peacock
Athena	Minerva	Brightness	Wisdom	Owl, AEgis Olive tree
Artemis	Diana	Moon	Purity	Stag, Crescent
Aphrodite	Venus	Love	Beauty	Dove
Demeter	Ceres	Earth	Fertility	Sheaf, Sickle
Apollo	Phoebus	Sun	Arts and Letters	Bow, Lyre
Hermes	Mercury	Rain	Eloquence	Wings, Caduceus
Ares	Mars	Storm	War	Helmet, Lance.
Hephaestus	Vulcan	Subterranean fire	Labour	Hammer, Anvil
Poseidon	Neptune	Sea	Anger	Trident, Horse
Hestia	Vesta	Hearth	The domestic Virtues	Sacred Fire

The early Greeks believed that the dead lived in their tombs, and that it was a duty to offer them food at definite times. Each family had a family altar, where the head of the family made his offering. In return, ancestors who were thus worshipped watched over their descendants.

In the next stage, the ancestors of the royal line became the divine guardians of nations and cities and were called Heroes. Each city had its national hero, to whom a temple was built, and worship was offered. Such heroes were also called demi-gods, because they were supposed to be the offspring of a marriage between a god and a princess. In fact, they were kings or warriors whose valour or benefactions had struck men's imaginations. Often they were confused with a divine person who was an incarnation of a natural force.

The worship paid to the gods and the heroes was entirely external. The ceremonies consisted of songs and sacrifices, whose rites had to be observed scrupulously at the risk of offending the god. Sacrifices were offered at an altar in front of the temple, for the Greek temple was only a kind of small chapel containing the god's statue.

The houses of the priests and the storehouse for offerings were placed around the temple.

The priests did not form a separate class, as among the Egyptians and Persians; they were merely official sacrificers and temple stewards. They knew the rites and formulas, but they did not give, as in modern religions, any moral teaching.

Great importance was attached to knowing the will of the god, which they believed could be discovered by omens, drawn from the flight of birds and the entrails of the victims. Sometimes they wished to learn the future. For this purpose, they applied to the oracles of the gods, of which the most famous was that of Apollo at Delphi, and that of Zeus at Dodona. At Delphi, Apollo communicated with men by means of an inspired priestess called the Pythian.

On the days for consulting the oracle, the Pythian seated

herself on a tripod placed over a crevice, from which there rose fumes that threw her into a state of nervous excitement, when she uttered inarticulate sounds, which the priests translated to the worshippers. The oracles were always expressed in phrases with a double meaning, and the word of the god was difficult to interpret exactly.

As religion consisted only of external acts, moral ideas were taught by the philosophers and poets, instead of the priests.

Thanks to them, the idea was generally accepted that man, although subject to Destiny or Moira, which was above the gods themselves, yet was responsible for his actions. When the dead arrived at the realm of Pluto, they appeared before the three judges, Minos, Aeacus, and Rhadamanthus. The good enjoyed perfect happiness in the Fields of the Blessed, while the wicked were punished with eternal torment in Tartarus, the river of Hades.

The Greeks loved to hear and tell stories of marvellous adventures. For this reason, disturbances of sky or sea, movements of the stars, migrations of nations, conquests, and voyages all appeared to them as extraordinary adventures happening to people superior to human nature. Such personages they made the heroes of the fabulous stories called legends. All heroes, gods, or demigods had three features in common: (1) they had a mysterious birth; (2) their unconquerable might overthrew the monsters who filled the earth; (3) they endured trials and were the sport of a blind fate which dogged their footsteps. At bottom, the legends represented the struggle of mankind against the elements and against fate; that is why they were an inexhaustible mine for poets and artists, whence they drew suggestions for songs, drama, pictures, and statues.

CHAPTER IX

SPARTA

ATHENS and Sparta have always played the leading part among Greek cities, and their rivalry determined the course of Greek history.

Sparta, or Lacedemon, the capital of Laconia, was a sort of garrison town. It was a group of five towns built on the marshy borders of the Erotas, a stream that descends swiftly from the plateau of Arcadia, and then flows more gently across Laconia. Sparta was never enclosed in walls and never needed them, for Laconia, of which she was the centre, was entirely surrounded by lofty, snow-clad mountains crossed by a few narrow, easily defensible passes.

The valley of the Erotas was fertile and could support the population. Thus, Sparta was a naturally fortified camp, inhabited by a race of soldiers.

The Spartans had formed part of a Doric invasion — Greeks from the north, who, after being driven from their own lands by the Thessalians, flung themselves into the Peloponnesus and conquered the Achaean towns.

They took the name of Spartans, and, being fewer in number than their conquered foes, could only retain their conquest by remaining always under arms in the middle of the subject peoples. So they were unable either to till the soil or engage in trade; they were an army of occupation, living on the produce of the soil worked by the conquered.

The Spartans were the best-trained and bravest soldiers in Greece, but they despised comfort and intellectual culture, which, in their eyes, debased the military virtues.

Their ideal was that of a military community in which each member was proud to sacrifice, through discipline, his liberty and his life to the supreme interest of the State.

The land of Laconia was divided into lots, which the owner could neither part with nor sell, and these lots were shared by the conquerors.

The dwellers on the plain continued to live on their ancient soil, in a condition not far removed from slavery. The dwellers in the mountains and the coasts, who were the last to be conquered, were treated less harshly.

Thus, there were three classes in Laconia: the Spartans (about 9,000), the Perioeci (about 30,000), and the Helots (about 200,000). Of these, only the Spartans were citizens.

The Perioeci — that is, "the people dwelling around" — lived on the frontiers of Laconia. They seem to have been the descendants of the old owners of the country. They were scattered in a hundred villages, which they governed themselves. They were allowed to own their own lands and enjoy the fruit of their toil. They devoted themselves to agriculture, commerce, industry, and navigation, all of which were occupations forbidden to the Spartans. They had to pay taxes and render military service, but they had no political rights.

The Helots were the former Laconians of the valley, whom the Spartans had made serfs. They did not live in villages, but in isolated huts built on the lands they cultivated. These lands did not belong to them; on the contrary, they themselves belonged to the lands and were part of the property. Each year, they had to give the owner a portion of their crops, but they retained the rest. Their only right was that they could not be sold.

The Spartans overwhelmed these unhappy Helots with cruelty. In war, they used them as light infantry, and in times of peace, they forced them to wear special clothes and forbade them ever to sing a martial song. They often forced them to drink until they were drunk, that the sight of their degradation might disgust the Spartan youth with the vice of drunkenness.

Their numbers formed a great danger to their masters, who killed them on the least excuse. Death was the punishment for a Helot who owned a weapon or who was found abroad after nightfall. Each year, on the election of new magistrates, the youth of Sparta had the privilege of a Helot hunt. This rule of terror kept hatred and the spirit of revolt alive among the Helots. "As soon as one speaks to them of the Spartans," says the Greek historian Xenophon, "not one of them can hide the delight he would have in devouring them alive."

This military state could no more allow powerful neighbours than rebel subjects. The two neighbouring peninsulas, Argolis and Messenia, were inhabited by other Dorian conquerors, who were a menace to Sparta. This resulted in a series of wars against the Argives and Messenians, at the end of which the Spartans possessed all the south and east of the Peloponnesus. The fiercest wars were those against Messenia in the seventh century, which lasted nearly twenty-four years.

The Spartan army, first in Greece for organization and discipline, was the instrument of these conquests. In the other cities, a man only became a soldier in case of need; the Spartans were professional soldiers. Accustomed from childhood to the chase and violent exercises, they remained in the ranks of the army until the age of sixty. Twice a day, they had exercise or maneuvers, and peace, with them, was only a preparation for war.

FIG. 38. - Hoplites on the march.

The Spartans fought on foot and formed a band of hoplites. They wore red coats, bronze breastplates, helmets to protect their faces and heads, shields of leather covered with brass, and leg guards of metal, or greaves, running from the knee to the ankle.

Their arms were a short sword, like a hunting knife, and a lance about six feet long. In battle, they formed ranks eight deep; the shields, touching one another, formed a regular wall before them.

So, formed in a phalanx, they marched against the foe, crowned with flowers and with the sound of the flute and a war song they called a paean. They never attacked before sacrificing a goat and seeking omens in its entrails. They were regarded as invincible, so great was their reputation for strength and bravery.

The phalanx was divided into battalions and squadrons. This division was useful for small expeditions and military exercises, and the precision of their movements filled the other Greeks with admiration.

In reality, the Spartan army was unrivaled as a school of soldiery and comradeship. As for the art of attack, it was all summed up in the charge. The force of the phalanx was due to the habits of obedience, honor, and sacrifice which were inspired in the Spartans by their laws, which they called the laws of Lycurgus.

Lycurgus is said to have lived in the ninth century. He was evidently a man of honor, for he refused to accept the title of king at the expense of his nephew, whose guardian he had been. He was a sage, that is to say, an educated man, who had traveled in Crete, Egypt, and Asia. The Spartans, rent by civil strife, asked him to give them laws. Lycurgus first of all consulted the oracle at Delphi, which encouraged him by calling him "the friend of the gods." He then prepared the constitution which bears his name, and after making the Spartans swear to keep it till his return, he went away, never to return again.

Doubtless, all this is legend, and possibly Lycurgus himself never existed, but the so-called laws of Lycurgus were nonetheless the constitution of Sparta.

The laws of Lycurgus were a collection of detailed regulations, which settled not only the government and administration of the state but even the life of private citizens and the education of the young. The aims of these laws were: (1) to establish the authority of the aristocracy in Sparta; (2) to assure to the Spartans the possession of their conquests by imposing upon them an exclusively military mode of life.

Before the time of Lycurgus, Sparta was governed by two kings, who had all the power in their hands. Lycurgus reduced them to figureheads, with no real authority. The two kings were chief priests and commanders-in-chief. They celebrated sacrifices and led the army in battle; but although they ruled, they did not govern.

The government was in the hands of the Gerousia, a council of twenty-eight members, all of whom were over sixty years of age. The Gerousia initiated and drew up the laws, then submitted them to the Assembly of the People, which met once a month. There was no discussion, and the people expressed their views by shouting. Later, the people appointed each year five Ephors, or overseers, whose function it was to control the actions of the kings and other magistrates, whom they could suspend or condemn. They also accompanied the armies in the field. Thus, in Sparta, the power was in the hands of the aristocracy, not with the kings or the people.

Lycurgus desired that there should be neither rich nor poor in Sparta. He divided the soil among the citizens in lots, which they were forbidden to sell.

The produce of the lands cultivated by Helots was to suffice for their wants, and every trade was forbidden them. In this way, the Spartans, freed from the anxiety of obtaining their own livelihood, were able to devote themselves entirely to their military duties. To prevent them from growing rich, they were only allowed to use bronze money of great weight and low value. Yet, in spite of these precautions, there grew up an inequality of fortune.

The child, destined to be a soldier, belonged rather to the state than to his family. At his birth, he was examined by the old men of the tribe, who gave him back to his mother if he were a healthy specimen. If not, they had him thrown down a chasm of the Taygetus. All the mothers reared their children in the same way. They did not wrap them in swaddling clothes, and they trained them to eat anything and to be afraid of nothing. When seven years old, the boy was returned to the state. He became a member of a troop of boys and formed one of a class which was commanded by the boy who showed himself superior to the rest in intelligence and strength.

Study had a small place in this education. The boys were taught to sing and to express themselves exactly, but the great aim was to make their bodies supple and strong. By a series of graduated exercises, they learned to run, leap, and throw the disk or javelin. Then, they were practiced in the use of weapons and the war dance, which they called the Pyrrhic. They learned also how to bear cold and heat, hunger and thirst, fatigue and pain, without complaint.

They wore the same costume all year round and slept on the rushes which they gathered themselves in the Eurotas. They washed and anointed themselves only on great festival days.

They were badly fed and were forced to steal to appease their hunger; but the boy who was caught stealing was severely punished. One of them, who had hidden a live fox under his tunic, let it devour his flesh rather than acknowledge his theft. There were also competitions to test their physical endurance. Each year, they were whipped before the altar of Artemis, and the one who was the last to cry out was the winner. The result was that boys died before complaining.

The boys had a grave demeanor and restrained movements; they walked with downcast eyes and only spoke in answer to questions. This iron education fitted them for military discipline.

At seventeen, the youth became part of the army; at thirty, he was a citizen and had to marry, but the employment of his time was still fixed by rules. He wore a uniform and had to take part in exercises every day, either running, leaping, or weapon practice.

The most remarkable institution was that of the public meals, which were obligatory on all Spartans, even on the kings. At these meals, which were not held every day, the men were grouped in companies of fifteen; in war, they shared one tent. These companies were close clubs to which a man was only admitted by vote. They ate black broth, a stew celebrated throughout all Greece, which was composed of small pieces of meat, fat pork, vinegar, and salt; but the menu might be increased by the products of the chase or part of the flesh of the victims after a sacrifice.

This stern life gave the Spartans a character full of grandeur and dignity. They appeared to adopt the heroic attitude of cynics who pretended to despise whatever other men loved or feared. They bowed only to older men, whom they respected as their

Fig. 39. - Artemis, the huntress, dressed as a Spartan girl.

fathers. Their language was intentionally rough and simple; their fashion of replying, in a phrase at once short and bitter, is still known under the name of Laconic.

The girls were educated no less sternly than the boys. They underwent the same exercises as the boys, and they were present at their competitions; their tunics reached scarcely as far as the knee, leaving their movements free. Their athletic life was an object of rude jests to the other Greeks, who kept their girls carefully shut up. Once married, they became the wives and mothers of soldiers. They were noted for their energy and self-sacrifice, for with them love of country had precedence over maternal love.

One of them, learning simultaneously of the death of her five sons and the victory of Sparta, cried: "So much the better; let us thank the gods." Another killed with her own hand her son who had fled from the field of battle.

As long as Sparta existed, she remained faithful to this mode of education and these customs. Many changes were made in the political and civil laws of Lycurgus, but the rule of life which he had imposed on the Spartans was maintained and rendered them the best soldiers in Greece and the true masters of human heroism.

CHAPTER X

ATHENS

THE history of the Athenians is the history of a nation as different from the Spartans as can be imagined, for Athens was a maritime state, a city of commercial enterprises, and of intellectual culture.

The foundation of her maritime empire was closely related to her democratic government, for her seaborne commerce gave rise to a class of rich and energetic citizens. These refused to be governed by the nobles who owned the land and accordingly wrested their power from them. So the prosperity of Athens and her political constitution were equally the work of the sea.

Attica, the land of which Athens was the capital, is destined by its geographical position and the nature of its soil to be the home of a nation of traders and seamen, for it is a peninsula, a rocky triangle, which, projecting from the mainland of Greece, runs into the Archipelago between the island of Euboea and the Isthmus of Corinth. This peninsula terminates in Cape Sunium, which commands all the sea routes to Crete, Asia, and Thrace.

The land is scarcely suitable for agriculture, for there is little good soil; the three small plains of Eleusis, Marathon, and Athens merely scar a block of rock.

Yet the original Athenians made their living from this barren soil. In the small valleys between the mountains and the sea, they raised barley and wheat, and on the hills, they cultivated the olive tree, the vine, and the fig tree. When the population became larger, they had to depend on countries overseas for their food supplies, and so necessity made them sailors. Their capital city, Athens, which was originally two towns, exhibited these two phases of their history.

Athens stands in the valley of the Cephissus. In this valley, which is the most fertile in Attica, living is pleasant because the valley is open to the south wind, which, blowing from the sea, brings warmth in winter and coolness in summer. In addition to these advantages, the formation of the land gives two benefits. In the middle of the plain rises a steep rock, about three hundred feet high, flat at the top and suitable for the construction of a national sanctuary and a strong fort: this was the Acropolis, where the Athenians built the temple of Athena and the palaces of their first kings. On the west, where the land is naturally low-lying and flat, there is a rocky peninsula full of creeks and harbours, of which the most important became the port of Peiraeus. So the town on the mainland was united to a town on the sea, and by its position, Athens was mistress of Attica and of the sea.

Athens was too poor to tempt invading armies and too far from the great highways of the world to be overrun by nations migrating from one part to another.

The Athenians, however, were a very mixed race, for many fugitives settled in Attica and intermarried with the Pelasgians who lived there, and settlers from foreign parts came by sea. In this mixture of races, the Ionians proved themselves masters, and Attica took from them the name of Ionia. In their mixed origin, we may perhaps seek an explanation of the extraordinary aptitude of Athenians for different pursuits, for they were at one and the same time a nation of traders and a nation of scholars and artists.

The Athenians were the first to give to the world the example of a people governing themselves by their votes. Their early history is a chronicle of the revolutions by which the power passed from the kings to the nobles and from the nobles to the people.

Thus, there arose among them a form of free government, which they called Democracy, and its final establishment coincided with the splendour of Athens.

Originally in Attica, as in all countries, the people lived under patriarchal rule. Each family was governed by the father, who acted as priest, judge, and leader in war. Then these families were grouped into twelve tribes. One of these, of which Athens was the centre, imposed its authority on the others. In this way, the kingdom of Attica was created, and its first king was Theseus.

The original heads of families, whom they called the Eupatridae or Well-born, formed an aristocracy which alone was able to own land. These nobles refused to tolerate the authority of a king. They abolished kingship, and Attica was governed by magistrates chosen yearly by the Eupatridae, and called Archons.

But the Eupatridae ruled the people with great harshness. The peasants and workmen, having no means of livelihood, borrowed money from the nobles, who threw them into prison, took them as slaves, and sometimes sold them when they were unable to pay back the money they had borrowed. Then came risings and revolts, and to check these in the future, there was established a code of laws attributed to Draco, the severity of which has become proverbial. However, in spite of the tradition to that effect, it is not true that the penalty of death was pronounced in every line. The laws of Draco only succeeded in increasing the sufferings of the people, and to avoid civil war, the nobles and people agreed to entrust a wise man named Solon with the task of giving Attica a new political constitution.

There is no such doubt of the existence of Solon as there is in the case of Lycurgus. Solon belonged to the royal race and had the highest reputation for benevolence and kindness. He had travelled and made a fortune in trade; he had been a pupil of the philosophers of Asia; he was a poet, and his poems had kindled the patriotism of the Athenians, whom he had led in person to victory against the island of Aegina. He could have made himself master of Athens, but he was content to be her benefactor.

Solon began to re-establish order by setting at liberty all who were enslaved for debt and forbade, in the future, any creditor to take possession of the person of the debtor. Next, he gave to the peasants part of the land which formerly belonged exclusively to the nobles, and he set a limit to the amount of land which each citizen could hold. After that, he gave them a constitution.

The Athenians were divided into four classes according to their fortune. Privileges and duties were proportional to their property; and these went on growing smaller from the first to the fourth class, which at first had only the right to vote but paid no taxes and was not subject to military service.

Considerations of birth were not, therefore, of any political importance; property alone, which a man could acquire by work and individual merit, decided the rank of the citizens in the State.

The most important result was that from this time forward nothing could be done in Athens but by the will of all as expressed in the Assembly of the People.

The Assembly consisted of all the citizens collected in the public square or Agora. It elected the magistrates or Archons and afterwards also the members of the Council of the Four Hundred or Boule. Finally, the Assembly passed the laws prepared and proposed by the Boule. The administration of justice was in the hands of the Areopagus, which was composed of those who had served as Archons.

Later, after the tyranny of Peisistratus, this constitution was completed by Cleisthenes, who established "ostracism." When a citizen threatened to become too powerful or was a disturbing element in the city, the Assembly of the People could, as a measure of prudence, decide that for ten years he should be banished from Athens. This banishment, which carried with it no dishonour, was pronounced after a vote, each citizen inscribing his verdict on an oyster-shell; hence the name of ostracism, or vote of the oyster-shells, in distinction from other votes, which were signified by raising the hands.

The laws of Solon, which regulated all the details of Athenian life, show us a people who at first depended entirely upon agriculture.

The majority of the Athenians lived in the country on their estates. The town was especially a center for religious and political purposes. This is the reason why the laws had for their first object the organization of the ownership and cultivation of the land. Solon endeavored to increase the number of landowners in order to encourage the energy of each man and make him produce more from the soil, which was far from fertile. In fear of famine, he forbade the export of any produce except oil. Cattle were scarce, and it was forbidden to kill the plow-oxen and lambs. The horse was regarded as a luxury, and those who owned horses formed the second class of citizens, and were called knights.

The idea of supplementing the scantiness of the resources of the land by favoring the development of crafts was due to Solon.

For this reason, the town, which was at first small and poor, became exceedingly prosperous. The inhabitants obtained from Laurium, a mountain near Athens, great quantities of silver, and this made it possible for them to create manufactures, establish commerce, and build a fleet. They sought by these new methods a prosperity which they could not obtain from their barren soil. Foreigners could become citizens on the condition that they brought to Attica a craft that was unknown there. Everywhere furniture, weapons of war, textiles, and especially pottery were made. From this time, Athens became a manufacturing town, famous for the good taste and beauty of her products.

The constitution of Solon did not put an end to political crises in Athens, for the men of the fourth class thought that he had not done enough for them.

Even in the lifetime of Solon, an ambitious man called Peisistratus used this discontent for his own purposes and posed as the spokesman of the popular demands. One day he presented himself in the Assembly covered with blood; his wounds were self-inflicted, but he pretended that the enemies of the people had tried to assassinate him. He was granted an armed bodyguard, and with it, he gained possession of the citadel. His rule was called a tyranny, a word that did not at first stand for cruel government, for the Greeks used it for all power that was usurped, and for kingship exercised by a man who was not a king by birth.

Peisistratus kept the constitution of Solon, governed with kindness, made many roads, beautified Athens, made a library there, and caused the various poems which compose the Iliad and Odyssey to be collected for the first time.

He was succeeded by his sons Hippias and Hipparchus, but the Athenians now found the weight of the tyranny oppressive. Two young men, Harmodius and Aristogeiton, took an opportunity at a feast to stab Hipparchus; they failed to touch Hippias, who afterward, however, was forced to flee from Athens.

CHAPTER XI

THE GREEK COLONIES

THERE never existed a Greek state, but in spite of the division into republics, which were often bitter rivals, there was a Greek people who had the same language and common customs and interests. The Greek world consisted not only of the Greek cities in Europe but also of all the Greek cities founded overseas.

The sea naturally tempted the activity of the Greeks. But in the early period of their history, individual men scarcely dared, in their little boats, to face the storms and the pirates. Only great disturbances, such as invasions or revolutions, forced them to cross the sea. There were actually two such great movements, the first caused by the invasions of the twelfth century, the second caused by the revolutions and wars of the eighth and seventh centuries.

We saw that originally Greece was inhabited by Aeolians and Dorians in the north, Achaeans and Ionians in the Peloponnesus. This division was overthrown in the twelfth century by the invasion, which was called the return of the Heraclidae. According to the legend, the sons of Hercules (the Heraclidae) were driven from Mycenae, but after being welcomed by the people of the north, they returned at their head and conquered the Peloponnesus. This legend was founded on the following facts: The northern races were driven out of their country by an invasion of Thessalians. The Aeolians migrated to Asia, but the Dorians retired into the Peloponnesus, where they overcame the Achaeans. As for the Ionians, they made their way into Attica or crossed over to Asia (see Fig. 31).

The Aeolians, starting from Aulis in Boeotia, established themselves in Lesbos, the largest island off the coast of Asia, and on the Asiatic coast from the Hellespont to the Gulf of Smyrna. This territory was called by the name of Aeolis and comprised twelve cities, of which the chief were Mitylene and Smyrna, which, however, were soon conquered by the Ionians.

Further south, the Ionians first colonized the islands of Chios and Samos, then all the coast between the Gulf of Smyrna and the Meander. This formed Ionia, a country renowned for its prosperity. Its chief towns, Smyrna, taken from the Aeolians, Phocaea, Ephesus, and Miletus, were renowned for their luxury, literature, and art.

The Dorians were not content with the conquest of the Peloponnesus. They colonized the chain of islands forming the southernmost limit of the Archipelago of the Cyclades, from Cythera to Rhodes; then on the coast of Asia, they founded Halicarnassus and Cnidus. This country, called Doris, continued to the south of Ionia, the belt of Greek territory and cities which bordered Asia Minor.

In the eighth and seventh centuries, the Greek cities were rent by civil wars, brought about by the struggles between the people and the nobles. At Athens and at Sparta, these struggles were settled by the constitutions of Solon and Lycurgus, but in other cities, the conquered party was obliged to leave the country. This resulted in a new movement of colonial expansion. Nowhere did they follow the same direction as the first. The emigrants moved in three directions: (1) on the north, to the coasts of Thrace and Chalcidice; (2) on the west, to southern Italy, Sicily, and the western lands of the Mediterranean; (3) on the south, to Cyprus, Egypt, and Africa.

The Ionians from the island of Euboea settled in the peninsula of Chalcidice and founded, amongst others, the town of Olynthus, on the borders of the Gulf of Salonika.

The Dorians of Megara settled in the district of the Bosphorus, on the Asiatic side, founding the city of Chalcedon, on the European side Byzantium, and Heraclea Pontica on the Asiatic coast of the Black Sea.

The Dorians of Corinth settled in the islands of the Ionian Sea, at Leucas and at Corcyra, at Ambracia in Epirus, at Apollonia, and at Epidamnus on the coast of Illyria.

The Euboeans of Chalcis had already a settlement in Italy, and they had colonized the rock of Cumae, celebrated for its prophetess, the Sibyl. Cumae, in its turn, had founded Naples.

In the eighth century, the south of Italy and Sicily were covered with Greek colonies. The most famous were Tarentum, in the great southern bay of Italy; in the south, Calabria, Croton, and Sybaris; and in Sicily, Syracuse and Agrigentum.

Most of these colonies were originally Dorian, and they became extremely prosperous. The tyrants of Sicily were famed in history, and the luxury of the Sybarites has passed into a proverb.

The Ionians of Asia were not long in entering the island of Cyprus and in passing from thence to Egypt, where they played an important part under the 26th dynasty. They founded the city of Naucratis. At the same period, the Dorians founded in Africa the colony of Cyrene. The Phoceans entered Gaul and founded Marseilles, whilst other Greeks discovered Spain and exploited the riches of the country of Tarsis.

All these settlements made Greek commerce possible. The colonists exploited countries that were richer than Greece, and they exported their surplus products. Wines and stuffs from Asia, metals and cattle from Italy, corn from Thrace, fish from the islands, works of art from the East, first circulated in the Greek seas, then through all the Mediterranean lands. The Greeks became the lucky rivals of the Phoenicians, and the trade of the Mediterranean was divided between the two races, the Greek race being on the European, the Phoenician on the African shores.

All Greeks, whether on the mainland or in the colonies, felt that there was a strong bond of kinship between them. Each of them was passionately attached to his own little country, but he realized that across the blue sea there were other white towns like his own, where they spoke his language, and where he would not feel an exile. This feeling of community of race created the unity of the Greek world, and this unity manifested itself in religion. The Greek of Sicily or of Asia was the brother of the Greek of Athens or of Sparta because they worshipped the same gods. Colonial expansion, far from weakening the religious bond, did much to strengthen it.

The foundation of a colony was a religious act. The founder or chief of the colonists, with great ceremony, took from the Acropolis, the citadel and sanctuary of his native city, some of the sacred fire and the images of the protecting deities. The place chosen for the new town always included a harbour and a hill, which should be the new Acropolis. As soon as they landed, the gods were put in their places; a hearth was built, where the fire brought from their country was placed. So the city was founded. If there were not enough inhabitants, they accepted as citizens all Greeks who would sacrifice to the gods of the city and confess their allegiance to them. The natives were kept quite apart.

One proof of the religious character of the colonies is the part played in their foundation by the Delphic oracle. The priests of Apollo at Delphi were well-informed on the subject of the countries overseas. Pilgrims coming from foreign lands to the temple supplied them with a great deal of information on foreign countries and their products, from which they drew their own conclusions. Accordingly, when the oracle was asked in which direction the colonists ought to go, the Pythian priestess rarely failed to point out a suitable locality, and it is worthy of remark that cities thus founded exist for the most part to this day.

A Greek colony was in no sense a possession of the mother country, and was neither administered by her nor submissive to her laws. A colony was a completely independent state, only attached to the mother country by customs and religion. Certainly, the citizens of the motherland were received with special kindness; certainly, they borrowed from her their priests, and even the chiefs of the state; certainly, they continued to take part in her feasts, embassies, sacrifices, and offerings. But this fidelity to ancient religious customs, these marks of respect, did not subordinate the colony in any sense; she was not a dependent of the mother country; she was her equal.

These family relations between the Greeks of the colonies and those of the mainland brought about the result that all profited in the progress of each.

The Greek colonial movement was a great advance in civilization. The colonists, men of energy and enterprise, were in no way affected by the prejudices which hampered the inhabitants of the older cities. They formed small commercial republics, aiming at wealth, not conquest. These colonies acted as intermediaries between East and West. The first Greek masterpieces saw the light of day on the soil of Asia. It was in Ionia that the Homeric poems were composed, and where the philosophers and wise men, such as Thales of Miletus and Pythagoras of Samos, lived. In fact, the Ionians came into close contact with the civilizations of Chalda, Phoenicia, and Egypt in all their splendour, and the result was that the sciences of the Chaldeans, the arts of the Egyptians, the alphabet of the Phoenicians, and their art of navigation, and the religious ideas of all the East, mingled in one single civilization, which was the Greek civilization.

All the Greeks acknowledged as the supreme god, Zeus, whom they called Panhellenic, that is to say, lord of all the Hellenes or Greeks. In fact, all Greeks came to worship him in his principal shrine at Olympia in the Peloponnesus. In the same way, all the Greeks had a great devotion to Apollo and came to consult his oracle at Delphi, at the foot of Mount Parnassus.

So there grew up among the peoples most closely united by the same worship, regular religious associations, which sometimes became political associations. These were called Amphictyonic Councils, and the most famous were those connected with the worship of Apollo at Delphi and at Delos.

In honour of certain gods, great athletic festivals or games were held, in which all Greece took part and which were followed with

FIG. 40. - The disc-thrower; carved by the Athenian sculptor Miron, a contemporary of Pheidias.

intense interest. In spite of the Greek taste for physical exercises, these games were not simply spectacles but religious feasts, during which wars were suspended. In the games, the triumph of human beauty and strength was consecrated to the gods.

The chief events were the foot race, with or without arms, the four-horse chariot race, the race on horseback, in which the conqueror leaped to the ground to touch the goal, the long jump, disc-throwing, wrestling, boxing, and the Pancratium (boxing and wrestling combined).

The competitors were called athletes, and they underwent a long training before competing. The victors received a palm, or a simple crown of olive or laurel, and sometimes a tripod, as a prize. But in their own cities, they became great personages, to whom the greatest honours were given. They had a triumphal reception; statues were raised to them, and poets sang their fame in their poetry.

The principal games were: (1) the Olympic games at Elis, in honour of Zeus; (2) the Pythian games at Delphi, in honour of Apollo; (3) the Isthmian games at Corinth, in honour of Poseidon; (4) the Nemean games in Argolis, in honour of Hercules.

The Olympic games, which were held every four years, were the most famous. This interval of four years was called the Olym-

FIG. 41. - A Greek pugilist in bronze.

piad, and this name was used to mark Greek chronology. They said: Such and such an event took place in the first or second year of such and such an Olympiad.

Literature and art were also a bond of union between the Greeks. Recitals of poems, singing of songs, and exhibitions of pictures and statues were often held at the Great Games. Artists and poets were known and loved throughout the Greek world. There was a proverb to the effect that a man could die happy when he had seen at Olympia the beautiful statue of Zeus, the work of the sculptor Pheidias.

Such was the Greek world, whose intelligence and bravery won for it the victory over the dreadful power of the Persians.

CHAPTER XII

WARS WITH THE MEDES AND PERSIANS

For half a century (500–449 B.C.), the Greeks engaged in war against the kings of the Medes and Persians. The wars are related in great detail by the Greek historian Herodotus, who was contemporary with the events he describes.

It was the triumph of Europe over Asia, of liberty over despotism, but not, as used frequently to be said, the triumph of civilization over barbarism.

In every war, there are obvious causes which are the occasion for the war, and also deep underlying causes. The real cause of the Persian wars was the necessity under which the Persian kings found themselves for expansion toward the west. In Africa and in Asia, Darius had reached the desert, the sea, or inaccessible mountains. So he dreamt of new conquests. Europe, separated from Asia only by an arm of the sea, tempted his ambition. He had already invaded Scythia and conquered Thrace; there only remained the Greek world.

This was a splendid prey, and he thought it would be an easy matter to seize it. He knew of the activity and industry of the Greek race from the Greek cities in his territory on the coast of Asia Minor. He hated the Greeks because they yielded obedience to no despots, and he hoped to impose upon them tyrants who would be his vassals.

Exiled Greeks, including Hippias, the former tyrant of Athens, urged him on to war. The position of Greece at this time encouraged his hopes. Sparta was the only formidable city; Athens was as yet only a large town, limited to its own area, and with no external power. Moreover, the Greek cities were divided by rivalry. Many of them were rent by struggles between the aristocrats and the democrats, and the aristocrats of their own accord asked aid from the Great King, as the Greeks called him. It looked as though an expedition to Greece would be a military promenade. At the first excuse, Darius declared war.

The war can be divided into three periods: (1) the period of Darius, (2) the period of Xerxes, (3) the period of the Confederacy of Delos.

War began in 500 B.C. by the revolt of Miletus, an Ionian city in Asia; the Athenians supported the revolt. The Ionians and Athenians, penetrating into the interior of Asia Minor, took and burnt Sardis, the residence of the Persian satrap. All the cities on the Greek coast of Asia rose in revolt, but the Ionians, unused to war and exertions, were reduced in six years, one city after another, by Darius, assisted by the Phoenicians.

Darius, to avenge himself on the Athenians, sent in 492 B.C. an expeditionary force, but his fleet was destroyed in a storm near Mount Athos.

Two years later, Darius sent a demand "for earth and water," the signs of submission, from the Greek cities. Some, in terror, consented. In Athens and Sparta, the ambassadors of the Great King were slain. Soon a fleet of six hundred ships landed an army in Attica, on the plain of Marathon, five miles from Athens. The terrified Athenians asked help from the Spartans, but a religious festival made it impossible for them to come. So the Athenians had to depend solely upon their own forces, but they had a great general in the person of Miltiades. Thanks to his skillful disposition of his forces, the Persians, slightly superior in numbers, were conquered and forced to re-embark. On that day, Athens saved Greece (490 B.C.).

In 455 B.C., Darius died, without having avenged his defeat. His son Xerxes inherited his power and his designs. He not only wished to punish the Athenians; he wished to destroy the strength of the Greek world, and he prepared a formidable expedition. He massed together all the armed forces of his empire in order to turn them on Greece. According to the Greek historians, this multitude amounted to five million men, of whom 2,600,000 were combatants. The rest formed the transport and service corps. All the ports of Asia, Phoenicia, and Egypt were forced to contribute to the fleet of 1,200 ships and 3,000 transports. The Phoenicians were in command of these, and they rejoiced in their opportunity of destroying the Greek naval power. Finally, Xerxes added bribery to force of arms, and by distributing money, tried to obtain surrenders and treachery.

Sparta and Athens summoned to Corinth a congress of all the Greek cities, to form a league under the direction of the Spartans. Several cities refused to join through jealousy, and it was a very small number who decided to fight for liberty to the death. The Athenians, realising from the Battle of Marathon the greatness of the peril, on the advice of the orator Themistocles, had dedicated all their resources to equipping a fleet of 200 ships. This fleet was to save Greece.

In the spring of the year 480 B.C., Xerxes' army, having taken seven days and seven nights to cross the Hellespont on two bridges of boats, marched down into Greece, while the fleet moved in a line parallel to them along the coasts of Thrace and Macedonia. The Greeks, whose numbers were too few for a battle on the plain, waited for the enemy in the pass of Thermopylae.

This pass, between Mount Æta and the sea, was so narrow that two chariots could scarcely enter it abreast. But because of the celebration of the Olympic Games, they could only leave in this pass 7,000 men, three hundred of whom were Spartan Hoplites, commanded by King Leonidas. This handful of men held up the Persian hordes until a traitor showed Xerxes a way of turning the pass. Then Leonidas, in obedience to the Spartan laws, which forbade retreat, resolved to perish with his men. He sent back the other troops and, remaining there with his heroic comrades, showed the Persians and the world how men can die for duty, liberty, and fatherland.

The Greek fleet, comprising about 400 ships, followed the same tactics as the army on land. They took up their position in the Straits of Artemisium, between Euboea and the mainland, and there they sank some of the enemy's ships. Then, while Xerxes invaded Attica and burnt Athens, they waited for the Persians opposite the coast of Attica, in front of the island of Salamis, where the Athenian women and children had taken refuge. The allied forces were just going to disband when they were surrounded by Xerxes' fleet. Then they thought of nothing but fighting, and thanks to the Athenian triremes, they defeated the Persian fleet. Xerxes, who had watched the battle seated on a golden throne on the shore, fled back to Asia.

The pick of the Persian army, 300,000 men, wintered in Greece under the generalship of Mardonius. But the Greeks had regained confidence; they rallied around the Spartans and, to the number of 120,000, advanced to attack Mardonius near Plataea in Boeotia. After several maneuvers, whose object was to guard the water supply and repel the enemy's cavalry, the battle became a rear-guard action, which ended in a general engagement in which the Persians were defeated (479 B.C.).

Meanwhile, the Greeks in Asia had risen, and, assisted by a Greek fleet, defeated the Persians at Mycale. The parts were now reversed — the Greek world was attacking the Persian.

As the Persians could only be attacked by sea, Sparta surrendered the command of the fleet to Athens. Then Athens and the principal Ionian cities formed a confederacy, whose seat was the temple of Apollo at Delos. Each member of the confederacy had to furnish men, money, and ships, according to an assessment made by Aristides the Athenian, who was surnamed the Just.

At the head of the confederate forces was Cimon, the son of Miltiades. He drove the Persians from Thrace, from the islands of the Aegean Sea, and from the coasts of Asia Minor.

These successes brought Athens both fame and territory. But

as the allies grew weary of the war, Athens suggested that they should substitute for their contingents of men and ships a larger contribution in money. This suggestion was accepted, and they became, as it were, the tributaries of Athens, who assumed the sole direction of the war and became the capital of a sort of empire.

Ancient historians asserted that in 449 B.C. the Great King decided to sign peace. By a treaty, called the Treaty of Cimon, he acknowledged the Aegean Sea to be a Greek sea, and he undertook never to send a warship there nor advance within three days' march of the coast. As a matter of fact, there was no formal treaty marking the end of the Persian wars.

Athens, rising from her ruins and enriched by the war, now became the rival of Sparta, and it was clear that a war to the death must soon break out between the two cities.

The Greeks, who were inferior in number to the Persians, owed their successes to the quality of their soldiers and the superiority of their arms. From his earliest years, the Greek was trained for bodily exercise — games of strength and skill were the basis of his education. He easily supported the heavy bronze armor, the cuirass covering his chest, and the helmet with a visor almost completely enveloping his head. He was completely master of the use of the sword and the lance, which were his usual weapons.

The Greek army was composed of Hoplites, trained, like those of Sparta, to charge the enemy in line. Their method of fighting was something like our bayonet charges. They left the use of the bow to the auxiliary forces, and they made small use of cavalry, which indeed was almost useless in their mountainous country. Their strength always lay in their discipline and their science of maneuvers, and this strength was doubled by the feelings of honor and love of country which inspired free citizens.

The Persian army consisted chiefly of archers and cavalry; they shot their arrows from a distance, and they failed to withstand the shock of the enemy's charge, while they knew nothing about attacking in close order. Their defensive armor was poor; for example, their shields were made of osiers and proved of

FIG. 42. - A Greek soldier.   FIG. 43. - A Persian soldier.

little use in hand-to-hand fighting. Their lances were shorter than those of the Greeks. They fell in little groups advancing against the Greek phalanx. When the center of their line, where the Immortals, their picked regiment, were placed, came to grief, the wings were immediately broken.

Their cavalry was formidable, but they could make little use of it on the narrow plains of Greece. Lastly, their soldiers were not citizens fighting for hearth and home, but subjects, who were almost slaves, fighting for the glory of a master, whom they always feared and often hated. Even their numbers were a source of weakness; for, in the first place, it was difficult to maintain discipline in such a crowd, where men came from all countries — Persia, India, Assyria, the Caucasus, Arabia, Egypt, Nubia, and Abyssinia — and did not even use the same language; and secondly, it was extremely difficult to supply so many millions of men with ammunition, food, and shelter.

At Marathon, the Athenians put into the field about 31,000 men: 10,000 Athenian Hoplites, 1,000 Plateans, and almost

20,000 auxiliary troops, consisting of aliens permitted to live in Athens and armed slaves. The Persians had not more than 40,000 men. The Battle of Marathon was a heroic charge, lance in hand, and it was at once a skillful piece of tactics and a victory of the sword over the bow.

Miltiades, having seen the army of Darius in Thrace, knew that the Persians themselves were in the center and the subject peoples in the wings. He intended to smash the wings in order to turn the center. With this object, he placed his Hoplites along a front equal to that of the enemy but strengthened his own wings. Then he gave orders to charge at a run in order to avoid casualties from the barbarians' arrows.

"The Persians," says Herodotus, "seeing their adversaries charging at a run, awaited the shock. From their small numbers and their manner of attacking, they judged them to be hit with folly that would cause their defeat in a twinkling of an eye, all the more as they had neither cavalry nor archers. The Athenians engaged in the struggle and acquitted themselves with memorable bravery. They were the first Greeks, as far as I know, to attack their enemy at a run, the first men also to look without terror on the Median dress and the men it contained."

The plan succeeded. The Athenians, victorious on the wings, wheeled round on the Persian center, which had so far had the best of it, and cut them in pieces. The Persian arrows slew 192 Athenians; the Greek lances laid low 6,400 barbarians.

Xerxes, as well as the Greeks, realized that the war would be decided on the sea. For by sea, the Greeks could cut his communications with Asia and draw reinforcements and food supplies from the islands. Accordingly, Xerxes collected a fleet of 1,200 vessels from his maritime provinces, which he thought would prove invincible. He left the native oarsmen in these ships and entrusted the conduct of operations to Phoenician seamen, while the Persian soldiers were to act as marines.

The vessels, being of different sorts and sizes, failed to maneuver together, and this proved a source of weakness, for the fleet, made up of different units, could not perform mass movements. The Phoenicians in command had been excellent captains of a mercantile marine, but they had never had occasion to fit themselves for maritime warfare.

In Greece, on the other hand, a far-seeing statesman called Themistocles had persuaded the Athenians to build a war fleet in preparation for a fresh invasion. "By land," said he, "we are not in a position to offer resistance, even to our neighbors; while with a fleet, we could repel the barbarian and dominate Greece." Themistocles was the leader of the democrats; his opponent was Aristides, the leader of the aristocracy, who, while celebrated for his virtue and justice, was a man of narrow ideas and an enemy of innovations. He suspected the transformation of Athens into a maritime state, the decay and ruin of agriculture, and the presence in the city of sailors and foreign traders. The Athenians put an end to this rivalry by banishing Aristides by a vote of ostracism. Then Themistocles used the public funds to build 200 triremes.

Until this time, the Athenians had only built galleys of fifty oars, called penticonters. They were light enough to be beached every night and were fitted for coasting and not for the high seas. On the other hand, the trireme combined two qualities: it was a long ship finished by a metal beak projecting in front of the ship; it

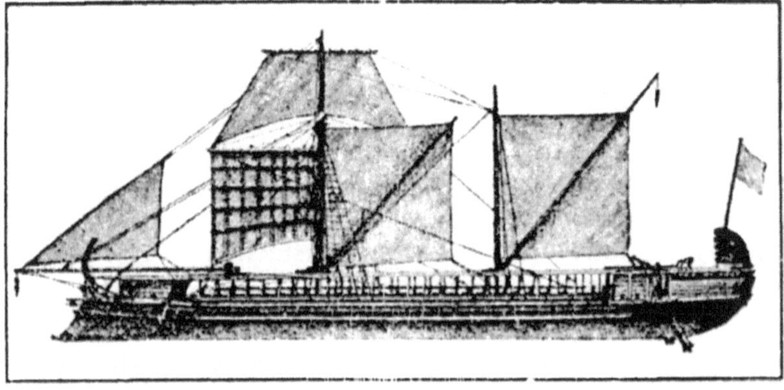

FIG. 44. - A triremo.

was rowed by 150 oarsmen arranged in three stages of twenty-five men on each side. The ship was also furnished with square sails.

It could reach a speed of nine to ten knots an hour, and its slender lines made it very easy to maneuver. Its height out of the water made it dangerous in times of storm, but the Greeks did not put to sea in bad weather.

The trireme carried about 200 men, divided into three classes: the rowers, the sailors, and the boarding force. The last-named were drawn up on deck and scanned the faces of the enemy as they waited for the moment to board their ships.

The 200 triremes of Athens were entirely manned by Athenians, for the oarsmen were recruited from among the citizens of the fourth class, who could not serve in the army because they were too poor to buy their equipment. The captains of the triremes, or trierarchs, had their ships well in hand, and this fleet, which was practiced in maneuvers en masse under the intelligent discipline which marked the Athenians, had great offensive strength. To this, Athenians owed the glorious victory of Salamis.

The Greeks, to defend the Athenians' families who had taken refuge in Salamis, had anchored their fleet in the strait which separates this island from the mainland, and which was scarcely 2,000 yards wide.

In this narrow space, they could face the Persian fleet, which had come to seek them there, in spite of their disproportionate numbers. But when they saw Athens in flames and the Persian hordes, most of the Greeks wished to abandon their boats and hasten to defend their homes. Themistocles, thinking that Athens and Greece would be lost if they disbanded the fleet, and feeling confidence in the strength and courage of the fleet, used a trick to force a battle. He sent a secret message to Xerxes that the Greeks were going to depart and said that his best course was to surround them. Xerxes, always ready to trust a traitor, took the advice of Themistocles and prepared to surround the Greek fleet.

The Greeks fought desperately and carried the day. They owed their success to the excellence of the Athenian triremes and the

FIG. 45. - A naval fight: from a vase painting.

tactics of Themistocles. Taking advantage of the mobility of his fleet, he attacked the Persian lines on the wings, as Miltiades had done at Marathon.

In the narrow space, the Persians could not escape the rams of the Athenians; they crowded together and fouled one another, smashing their oars. Then, unable to be steered, they were easily destroyed. Of the 500 ships engaged by Xerxes, 200 were sunk. At the last, it was a massacre, in which the Persians were stunned with blows from the oars "like tunnies caught in a net."

The salvation of Greece was the work of Sparta and Athens. Sparta, on account of her army, stood for the first power in Greece and held supreme control over the confederate forces. Her soldiers were true heroes; at Thermopylae, as elsewhere, they allowed themselves to be killed rather than desert their post. But while they were brave, they showed little enterprise. At Marathon, they arrived too late; at Plataea, they had to wait for the Athenians before they could face Mardonius' entrenchments. They left the merit of intelligence to the Athenians, and Athens owed her greatness quite as much to the routine of the Spartans as to the intelligence and strength of her own citizens.

Athens played the leading part throughout the war. National liberty was saved by three of her citizens: Miltiades, who invented the tactics of Marathon; Themistocles, who created and directed the war fleet; and Aristides, who, returning from exile and converted to new ideas, founded the Delian confederacy.

On every field of battle, Athens was the incarnation of intelligence over brute force. Alone among Greek cities, she grasped what was her real danger and what her real duty. "If the Athenians," says Herodotus, "by fear of the danger which threatened them, had abandoned their country, or if, remaining in their city, they had submitted to Xerxes, no one would have dared to resist the Great King at sea, and Greece would have perished." As a result, Athens became the queen of the Greek seas and the true capital of the Greek world.

CHAPTER XIII

ATHENIAN CIVILISATION

THE period immediately succeeding the Persian wars was a time of extraordinary brilliance for Athens, whose citizens were proud of her fame and enriched by her conquests. We see then in her the most finished picture of Greek life, widely different from our own. The comforts and pleasures of the home had little hold on a Greek. Like most southerners, he passed his days out-of-doors, occupied with business, sport, politics, or ceremonies. He lived not for his family, but for his city. The magnificence of his city was a source of pride to him, and he was contented with a very simple and modest home life, provided that the public buildings and festivals of his gods awoke universal admiration.

Athens was by no means a city of fine houses and broad streets. The houses were huddled on the side of the Acropolis, according

FIG. 46. - Athens: the side of the Acropolis.

to the whim of the owners, forming a regular labyrinth of lanes. When Athens was rebuilt, after the burning of the city by the Persians, new districts planted with trees were made, where the houses were placed in line and had plenty of space around them; but these were only the dwellings of the rich. The trading classes remained in their hovels in the old town.

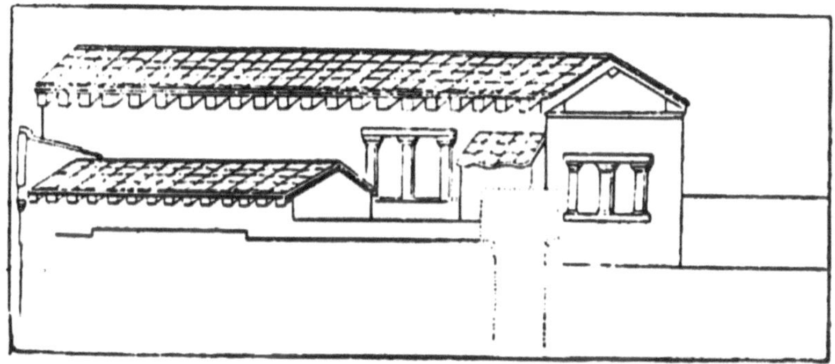

FIG. 47. - Plan of a rich man's house, as drawn on a bas-relief.

Ordinary houses consisted of a ground floor divided into two small rooms, and one upper storey, to which approach was gained by an outside stairway. The lower part was carved out of the rock, and the walls were made of wood, brick, or clay. Instead of forcing locks, thieves were able to make holes in the walls! Inside, the walls were whitened with lime; there was no chimney; warmth was obtained from a brazier. Rich men's houses were like the Homeric palaces. They were in three parts: an entrance, guarded by a porter; the men's side of the house, where the halls and rooms opened onto a courtyard surrounded by a portico, that is, a covered gallery supported on columns; and the women's apartments, or gynaeceum, which opened onto a garden. The chief pieces of furniture were couches, chairs, tripods, stools, beds for sleeping, and beds for meals (for the Greeks always ate in a recumbent attitude) and chests to hold clothes. The walls were decorated with paintings, and the floors were covered with rugs and cushions.

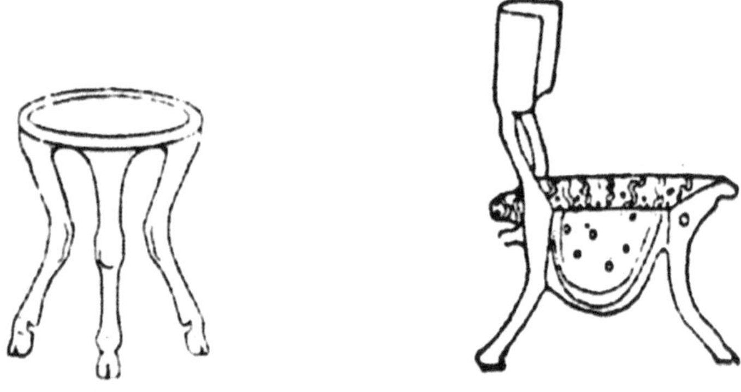

FIG. 48. - Table and chair.

FIG. 49. - A Greek chest: from a vase painting.

The essential parts of the dress of the men and women were the same and were called the chiton and the himation. Chiton can be translated by tunic and himation by cloak. They seem to have formed the complete dress of the men, at any rate when in the town or dressed for ceremony. But vase paintings represent warriors wearing drawers, and men clad in tight-fitting coats with short sleeves and high necks like our jerseys. There is a statuette of Hermes in which he is represented in a sort of pleated petticoat, like the kilt of the modern Greek. At the time of the Persian wars, civil dress became simplified. The chiton was a long, sleeveless tunic with a girdle at the waist. It reached as far as the knee and

FIG. 50. - A kilted Greek
of modern Thessaly.

FIG. 51. - Clytemnestra,
from a painted vase.

often as far as the feet. The himation was a large wrap, made of a single piece of stuff wrapped right around the body, like a Spaniard's cloak. Younger men preferred to wear the chlamys, which was a kind of cape fastened around the neck. Headwear sometimes took the form of a felt cap, called the pileus, sometimes of a broad-brimmed hat, the petasus, which was thrown back off the head right onto the shoulders.

Women's dress was not more uniform or less changeable than it is today, for fashion was capricious even in Athens. Greek women had worn complicated dresses, tight-fitting bodices with puffed sleeves, and skirts with narrow pleatings or box pleats, even with flounces, and these were ornamented with designs and embroidery. But at the time of the Persian wars, the chiton was the chief article of dress for women as well as for men.

The woman's chiton was so long and full that it was a flowing

FIG. 52. - Group of women at a fountain: from a vase.

robe, bound only by a girdle. Sometimes it was made of wool and fell in heavy folds, sometimes of linen and beautifully ironed. Out-of-doors a woman wrapped herself in a himation, which was fuller, richer, and softer than that of a man. Clothes were of all colours and designs, but the most usual were those of white woollen material with a band of colour. Real luxury was shown in the women's jewels. The fashions of hairdressing varied greatly. Women used combs and coronets, even hair dyes and false hair.

Men and women were shod with sandals, bound to the foot by thongs, and they were very fond of coloured leather. With such houses and clothes, Athens must have had a strong likeness to a modern Arab city.

The Athenian had two sides to his life. He went to the market-place, the law courts, the temple, the gymnasium, the baths, or his shop; but when he returned home, he said nothing to his wife about what he had been doing. She was not associated with his life. She was his wife and the mother of his children. Still, she was not a kind of slave, as in the East. She was legally married, and she had a dowry which gave her independence. She managed the house and directed the work of the servants. She could leave her house and could receive friends of her own sex. She took part in religious sacrifices, and certain forms of worship, such as the worship of Demeter, were exclusively reserved for women. These were her only distractions; she never took part in the men's gatherings, and her interests were limited to her home and her toilet.

The young girl was strictly confined to the women's quarters. She received little education and knew only a little about singing, cooking, embroidery, and sewing. At the right age, her father married her to the man of his choice, without consulting her wishes.

Boys left their mothers when they were six years old and were taken to school by slaves, who were called pedagogues. Education was compulsory in Athens, but it was given in the houses of private masters. Education had two sides: music and gymnastics. Music included not only the art of playing on an instrument, the lyre, harp, or flute, but also reading, writing, arithmetic, and the recitation of poetry, especially Homer — in fact, all the elements of a general education.

Gymnastics played a great part in education, especially after fourteen years of age. The Athenians, like all Greeks, worshipped the beauty of the human form and sought its development by well-planned exercises. The boys practised these exercises naked, in the gymnasia or palaestra, under the direction of special masters. They included wrestling, running, jumping, and throwing the disc and the javelin. A youth whose moral and physical education had been complete deserved to be called "beautiful and good." His muscles were strong and controlled by a well-trained mind.

At the age of eighteen, the young Athenian entered the class of Ephebi. This was at the same time a period of study and of military training. The Ephebi attended gymnasia built outside the city, such as the Academy or the Lyceum. When they became Ephebi, they were given arms, they took an oath and were counted as citizens. They had all the rights of citizenship, but they could not always be chosen for public offices. The training lasted two years, and the second year was passed in military exercises in a frontier fortress.

Athenian citizens had time to attend to all their various

occupations, because all disagreeable work was done by slaves. So indispensable was the slave to the ancients that they never doubted their right to reduce other men to the position of human beasts of burden. There were three sorts of slaves: children born of slave parents, prisoners of war and slaves bought in the market. Rich houses had large numbers of slaves; poorer citizens had one or two in their service, for the price of a slave was seldom more than £10. They were the property of their master, who could punish them or sell them, but could not kill them, for their lives were protected by law.

The Athenians, as a rule, treated them with kindness: they often used them to work in their workshops, and sometimes paid them small wages. The very prosperous trade of Athens owed its existence to the slaves' manual labour. Many of them worked in artistic trades and won from their masters the boon of freedom.

Banquets were the only entertainments the Athenians offered their friends in their own houses. They were held by invitation of a single host, or by clubs, and only men were present at them. The guests took their places on couches provided with coverlets and cushions, and before them were placed tables fully laid. They ate with their fingers, leaning on the left elbow. After the first course, acrobats and musicians came in; after their performance,

FIG. 53. - Greeks at table: from a vase painting.

the guests continued to eat and drink, discussing at the same time politics or philosophy.

Funeral rites were domestic solemnities in which women played the principal parts. The women dressed the corpse for burial. Then the body was placed on a bed of state, where it remained a whole day, watched and lamented by all the family. Before sunrise, the procession was formed. The corpse, carried on the shoulders of men dressed in black, or put on a hearse, was followed by all near relatives, dressed in mourning attire. Behind them walked the flute-players, who accompanied the songs of lamentation sung by the family. The tomb was hollowed out in the mountain and closed by a slab of marble or rock called a stele, which was carved and placed upright. Here the corpse was put, and a sacrifice was offered in its honour. Some time later, the mourners came and offered it the funeral feast of cakes and wine, a custom still existing among Christian peasants in the Balkan States. It was the pious custom of the family to renew these offerings to win the goodwill of the dead person, who was living, as they thought, the mysterious life of the tomb. In this respect, their beliefs resembled those of the Egyptians. By observing these burial rites, they thought they could ensure the happiness and repose of the dead man's soul, which without such rites would be wandering about in an unhappy state. To neglect such rites

FIG. 54. - A funeral: from a brick carving.

was sacrilege and a crime punishable by law. Victorious generals were sometimes condemned to death for having neglected to pay funeral honours to soldiers killed in battle.

PUBLIC LIFE

The life of an Athenian citizen was that of a man who, in ordinary times, would be at once a merchant and a member of Parliament, but who, in certain circumstances, would be called by election or by lot to become a magistrate, a minister of state or a general. All citizens had equal rights, and took part in the government and administration of the city. "Our constitution," said Pericles, "has been called a democracy, for its aim is the benefit of the largest number of citizens, not the benefit of a minority." Aristotle has summed up a little more exactly the working of a democracy in these words: "The magistrates must either be chosen by all the citizens or be chosen by lot; positions of honour must not be distributed according to men's income; tenure of office must not be long; all the citizens must be summoned to sit in the law courts; lastly, the decision on all matters must rest with the General Assembly of the citizens."

This was how matters stood at Athens. Every citizen, whatever his birth or his fortune, could reach office; for the Archons, the judges and the members of the Boûle were chosen by lot yearly. Every citizen had his share in the government, for by his lot he decided on all the laws which governed Athens and her empire. Moreover, he had a right to the public funds, for in order to make it possible for the poorest to fill any office, they conceived the idea of paying fees for public services, even for attending the Assembly. The result was that the fulfilment of his duties as a citizen became a regular profession for the Athenian.

This democracy was really an aristocracy. The electors were few in number, about 15,000, and the Assembly was a public gathering where everyone knew each other. They had slaves to do their work and subjects to pay money to the city. Living was cheap, and the easy distribution of money assured a high standard of comfort for all. Each year, 6,000 citizens were chosen by lot to be magistrates, with the result that half the city managed the other half.

This bears no resemblance to modern democracies, in which the people consist of millions of electors and are obliged to entrust to representatives the tasks of government while the people work for their livelihood.

The real master of Athens was the public speaker or orator. This part was played with particular brilliance by Pericles, the leader of the popular party. By birth, he belonged to the family of Peisistratus, and to that of the ancient kings of Athens. To this advantage of birth, he united the charm of a highly cultivated mind. He had had as masters several celebrated philosophers. He had acquired all the accomplishments necessary for a statesman. On all matters, he took large views; his character was straightforward and open, and the breath of slander never dared touch his disinterestedness. He inspired confidence by his modesty, and finally his eloquence made him a true master of the people. Without having held any public office, without having been even an Archon, he was the real governor of Athens.

His speeches had the greatest influence on the course of events. This influence was directed to increasing the rights and powers of the people, to extending the Athenian Empire, and to helping on the

FIG. 55. - A Scythian policeman.

development of art and letters. That is why this period, the most glorious in the history of Athens, is called the Age of Pericles.

The Assembly of the People, which was dominated by Pericles, met on a hill facing the Acropolis, the Pnyx, or even on the very slopes of the Acropolis in the theatre of Dionysius, or most generally in the agora or market-place. All the citizens in the town or countryside had a right to be present. The Assembly met three times a month, and there were extraordinary meetings as well.

The Athenians, an extremely witty people, loved to amuse themselves while waiting for the hour to begin. So Scythian policemen, whose business it was to keep order in the city, stretched a cord covered with red powder across the agora, and by means of it urged everyone to the place of meeting. Those in the rear got a red mark on their backs and had to pay a fine.

The sitting was presided over by a division of the Boûle, and began with a sacrifice. Then a herald read the proposed law, which had been prepared by the Boûle, and asked: Who wishes to speak? Orators arose and took turns in speaking, ascending a platform of stone where they could be seen and heard by all. The people were deeply appreciative of eloquence, and listened eagerly to the discussion; then a vote was taken by show of hands. From this decision there was no appeal.

There had developed alongside the aristocratic tribunal, the Areopagus, a system of tribunals composed of citizen-judges or jury. Each year, 6000 citizens were empanelled, of whom 5000 were divided into ten sections of 500 members. One of these sections was called for each case, and it heard and pronounced judgment on the same morning under the presidency of an Archon. The whole 6000 citizens were called the Heliaia. The accused were obliged to defend themselves without the help of barristers; those who were not able to do so, learnt by heart a defense prepared by professionals called logographers. The time of the defense was limited and marked by an hour-glass filled with water, the clepsydra. The sentence was pronounced, after a vote had been taken, by means of pebbles, black for condemnation, white for

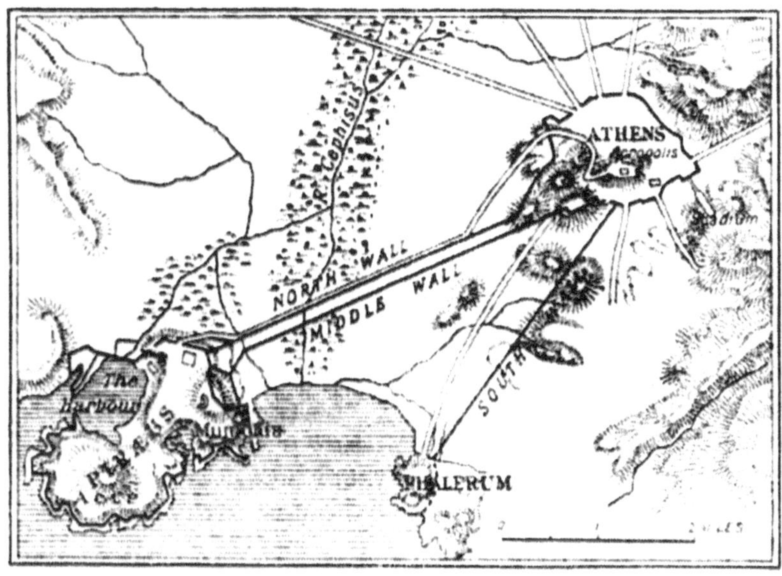

FIG. 56. - Plan of Athens and the Pirmus.

acquittal. Thus, the Athenian people were their own governors, administrators, and judges.

The State required great resources in order to exist; for Attica, like England today, could not produce enough to feed all her inhabitants, and the bread which the Athenians ate was made from corn brought by sea from Thrace. They were obliged to seek abroad for fresh supplies, either from their colonies or by trading with foreigners; consequently, they made themselves masters of the sea. The Piraeus was the center of their trade and maritime power; there were the docks, the dockyards, the arsenal, and the two naval bases, Zea and Munichia. The whole was enclosed by walls and connected with Athens by two long walls, between which there was a road protected by forts the whole way.

The Piraeus became the center of an important commerce. It was the market for Thracian and Egyptian corn, for fish from the Euxine, metals from the north, Eastern carpets and fabrics, purple dyes, and cut glass from Phoenicia, wines and fruits from the islands.

It became the home of a cosmopolitan society; Levantines of every conceivable race might be met there. These foreigners who made their homes in Athens were called Metics, and they had not the rights of citizens, although they were subject to some of the responsibilities, and extra taxes were often levied on them.

Cleruchies, military colonies of a new character, were established by Pericles to ensure the free passage of Athenian ships. The cleruchies consolidated the power of Athens and enabled her to utilize her poor population by employing them to furnish the garrisons of these citadels. They were established at all points of approach in Euboea, Naxos, Macedonia, and Thrace. These colonies were not independent towns, like the ancient Greek colonies; they formed part of the Athenian domain, and the colonists remained Athenian citizens and retained their civic rights.

In order to maintain her supremacy, Athens had to make war on the Persians, put down revolts, and conquer fresh lands. For this purpose, she increased the number of her ships and altered the character of the army. The corps of Hoplites had been the nucleus of the army; now she added cavalry and light infantry, armed according to the necessities of each campaign. These auxiliary forces were composed almost entirely of mercenary soldiers.

One characteristic of the Athenian army was that the generals or strategoi were elected. Thus, the people controlled even the conduct of war. The maintenance of these forces and the expenses of democratic government required large sums of money. There were three sources of revenue: (1) the silver mines at Laurium and the Thracian gold mines; (2) the tribute of the allies; (3) impositions. The ordinary impositions were the custom duties, the town tolls, the tax on foreigners, and, in time of war, an income tax.

There were also extraordinary burdens called liturgies, which were paid only by wealthy citizens. The principal liturgies were the trierarchy or equipment of a trireme, and the choregos or equipment of a drama.

The age of Pericles was that of the greatness of Athens. He set aside large sums of money for the embellishment of the city

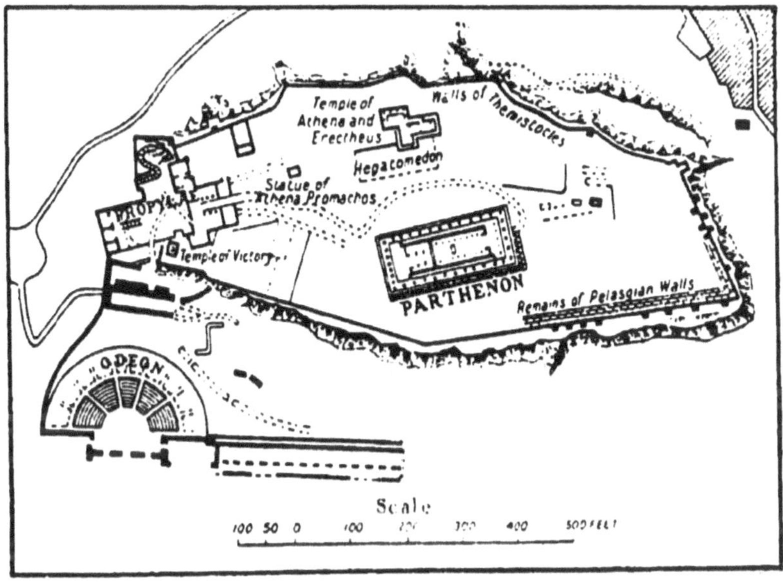

FIG. 57. - Plan of the Acropolis.

and gave his country monuments of which even the ruins excite universal admiration. Under his impetus arose a new city, with temples and monuments replacing the monuments destroyed by the Persians.

At the foot of the Acropolis were the Odeum, the theatre of Dionysius, the Theseum, and the Portico or Poikile, which was decorated with paintings of scenes from the national history. On the Acropolis, in place of the ancient destroyed monuments, arose the sanctuaries of the city, masterpieces of Greek architecture. A wide staircase led to the sacred rock; the entrance was decorated by a monumental gateway, the Propylaea. On the paved summit was the temple of Athena, the Parthenon, which, ruined and mutilated, still astonishes visitors by the perfection of its proportions. Further on were the temple of the ancient king Erectheus, with a pulpit, where the statues of maidens took the place of columns, and the shrine of Victory. A colossal statue of Athena dominated everything; another statue in gold and ivory, made by the sculptor Pheidias, occupied the interior of the Parthenon.

FIG. 58. - Section of the temple of Zeus.

A crowd of statues and other monuments covered the summit and slopes of the Acropolis. The marble came from Pentelicus, and the allies' tribute paid the artists.

These buildings, the result of many years' labor, enabled Greek architects to fix the rules of their art. It is possible to distinguish three styles, characterized by the dimensions of the pillars and the shape of the capitals. All Greek buildings were supported and decorated by pillars; some were employed in the masonry and called pilasters, others were replaced by statues and called caryatids. There were three kinds of pillars: the Doric, Ionic, and Corinthian. The Doric columns stood on the floor of the building. The capital was composed of a simple tablet of stone; the Theseum and the Parthenon were in this style. The Ionic column stood on a kind of pedestal, called a base; the capital was decorated with two volutes in the form of a ram's horns, with an egg beading on the upper part; the Erectheum and the temple of Victory were in this style. The Corinthian pillar was later than the other two; the capital was much richer and represented a bunch of acanthus leaves.

The Parthenon was a typical Greek temple. It was built in the form of an oblong and was of small dimensions, for it was not intended to accommodate crowds, like our churches, but only the statue of the goddess. It was surrounded by pillars supporting the roof and forming a colonnade. Along the outer walls of the temple and within the colonnade was a wonderful frieze, the work of Pheidias, which represented the Panatheniac procession in bas-relief.

FIG. 59. - Plan of the Parthenon.
A. Peristyle; B. Vestibule; C. Naos; D. Statue; E. Treasure.

The temple was raised from the ground by three stone steps, from the top of which sprang the pillars. They supported a further support, called the architrave, above which were the metopes, each containing a pair of fighting figures, centaurs and giants. At each end, hiding the roof, was a triangular pediment framed in by a cornice. On the eastern pediment, Pheidias had sculptured the birth of Athena, on the western her struggle with Poseidon for the possession of the city.

Inside, the temple was divided into three parts: the vestibule, the chamber of the goddess, and the inner chamber, where the treasure of Athens was kept. Bronze ornaments completed the decoration, and colors were also employed, but although some traces remain, we know little about them.

Greek sculpture played an important part in the decoration of the temples, but it was also an independent art. The statues of this period are considered among the most beautiful which have ever been made; Pheidias and his rivals united Egyptian dignity and Assyrian realism in an art in which they expressed perfect beauty. The statues were in marble, in bronze, sometimes in gold and ivory. We see them nowadays weathered by age, quite white and with blank eyes. Then they had eyes put in with enamel; the bodies were painted

FIG. 60. - North-west
corner of the Parthenon.

flesh color, and the draperies were rich with colors. The gods and heroes were supermen, but they were none the less men.

The Greeks, like the Egyptians, painted pictures on the sides of walls. They only understood painting in fresco; they employed also painting in warm wax or encaustic, but they used that only for the decoration of vases and little statues, which they manufactured in great numbers. The mythological or domestic scenes which they painted on their black, red, or white earthenware have given us the most valuable information about Greek civilization.

The making of earthenware was an Athenian art par excellence. Their vases and statuettes were celebrated for elegance of shape and beauty of design, and they formed the principal objects of Athenian commerce.

The religious festivals of Athens were the most celebrated in Greece, and gave great impetus to the arts. At least eighty days in the year were given up to them, and the poorer citizens were given money in order that they might take part. The most celebrated were the feast of Athena, the Panatheniac, those of Dionysius, the Dionysia, and of Demeter, the Eleusian mysteries.

The Panatheniac festival, held once in four years, was the most beautiful. It began with public games, dramatic representations at the Odeon, athletic competitions at the Stadium, and boat races off the Piraeus. The games were ended by a solemn procession, in which all the citizens took part, climbing to the Acropolis to offer to the goddess a robe which was carried in a galley mounted on wheels.

The festivals of Dionysius were celebrated by dramatic representations open to public competition. The competing authors received from the Archons a troupe of actors and a chorus, for Greek plays were a mixture of speaking and singing.

This is to be explained by their religious origin. They began in the custom of singing songs round the altar of Dionysius on his festival. Little by little, monologues were introduced amid the singing, then dialogues. Then, instead of celebrating the adventures of Dionysius, the stories of other gods and goddesses were introduced, and finally, serious pieces or tragedies, and lighter pieces or comedies, were played by actors and a chorus. The poets Aeschylus, Sophocles, and Euripides in tragedy, and Aristophanes in comedy, increased the number of the actors, varied the subjects, and created dramatic art.

The plays were given in a huge theatre open to the air, which would seat 30,000 persons; women might only attend tragedies. The theatre was divided into three parts: the tiers of seats, or amphitheatre, for the audience; the stage for the actors; the orchestra, or wide space between the seats and the stage, for the chorus. The decorations were simple, but mechani-

FIG. 61. - A Greek tragedian.

cal art was very far advanced. The actors, who were all men, wore masks representing traditional persons and designed to make the voice carry; thus, they could not rely on facial expression. Tragedians had high head-dresses, gorgeous clothes, and very high boots or stilts; comedians wore only low-heeled shoes. The clothes and the masks were designed to add to the height of the actors; the dimensions of the theatre rendered this necessary. In early days, the audience proclaimed the victor by acclamation, and the plays so honored still appear to us to be masterpieces. So great was the taste of this wonderful nation.

An enumeration of the great names which adorned the age of Pericles will show the artistic and literary splendor of Athens.

Then lived the tragic poets Aeschylus, Sophocles, and Euripides, the historians Herodotus, Thucydides, and Xenophon. The architect Ictinus built the Parthenon, Callimachus the Erectheum, Pheidias made the statue of Athena and the Zeus at Olympus; Polykleitos painted the Poikile, and Myron, the sculptor of the Discobolus, followed Praxiteles, the sculptor of the Hermes. A number of philosophers attracted pupils. Masters of rhetoric, called Sophists, trained orators by teaching their pupils to speak on any subject.

In the midst of them all shone the great mind of Socrates. Pericles could say with truth that Athens was the school of Greece.

CHAPTER XIV

THE DECAY OF ATHENS

THE victories of Athens, her rapid recovery after destruction, and the success of the Delian Confederacy, made her a town of the first rank. Her neighbours, Thebes and Corinth, alarmed at her ambition, united with Sparta to check her schemes for aggrandisement. Greece became divided into two confederacies, the States of the Peloponnesus and Central Greece, under the direction of Sparta, and the islands and coastal cities of the Aegean Sea under the guidance of Athens.

The cities were opposed to one another through a triple rivalry: (1) the rivalry of ambition and interests; (2) rivalry of race between the Dorians and Ionians; (3) political rivalry between an aristocracy and a democracy.

This situation brought about a war between Greeks less than eighteen years after the end of the Persian wars. But the war was not solely a struggle for supremacy between two states. The whole Greek world took part in it: all the Dorians of Greece, Asia, and Italy were the allies of Sparta, whilst Athens rallied round her all the Ionians. In every city, political divisions between aristocracies and democracies turned to civil war, the first aided by Sparta, the second by Athens.

The immediate cause of war was the revolt of Corcyra against her mother-city Corinth. Athens aided Corcyra, and the Corinthians appealed to their Peloponnesian allies, who declared war against Athens.

The war lasted for twenty-seven years (431-404 B.C.), and is known as the Peloponnesian War. Two contemporary historians, Thucydides and Xenophon, have written about it.

The war can be divided into three periods: (1) the ten years' war; (2) the Sicilian expedition; (3) the Decelian war.

1. At first, the Spartans' objective was to invade and ravage Attica, and that of the Athenians was to pillage the coasts of the Peloponnesus.

This was Pericles' plan; he wished the Athenians to neglect land conquests and remain mistress of the sea. There broke out a terrible plague among the country people who had flocked into Athens to escape the enemy's raids. It decimated the population and carried off Pericles (429 B.C.).

A new man, the tanner Cleon, succeeded him in the popular favour, and decided on a coup de main, which resulted in the capture of 300 Spartans on the island of Sphacteria, on the western coast of the Peloponnesus.

Sparta then attempted to starve Athens by occupying Thrace, from which she obtained her corn. The Spartan general Brasidas took Amphipolis; Cleon set out to retake the city and perished under the walls, as did also Brasidas. Then the peace of Nicias was signed (421 B.C.), by which the two states restored their conquests.

2. The Athenians became infatuated with a nephew of Pericles, Alcibiades, a rich and handsome young man, who was rendered popular by his eccentricities even more than by his abilities. His ambition dreamed of great projects. He persuaded the Athenians to try to make an end of Sparta by conquering the Dorian cities of Sicily, and thus holding the sea on all sides.

The subjects of Syracuse, the most powerful of these cities, were in revolt. The Athenians resolved to help them, and an expedition of 134 ships and 10,000 men departed in the midst of delirious enthusiasm (415 B.C.). Alcibiades did not go far; accused of treason, he took refuge with the Spartans. His colleague Nicias conducted the siege with slackness; Syracuse was able to receive help and a good general, Gyllipus, from Sparta. Gyllipus was able to enclose the Athenians in their trenches and turn the besiegers into the besieged.

In spite of receiving help, the Athenians failed in attack, their fleet, blocked in the roadstead, was destroyed, and they raised the siege by making a retreat which was a complete disaster. Everyone perished or was taken prisoner (414 B.C.).

3. Athens seemed lost; her fleet, as well as her army, was destroyed; Sparta had put a garrison into the fortress of Decelea, which commanded the whole of Attica, and opened negotiations with the aristocratic party. In the courage born of despair, she rebuilt her fleet. The principal war zone was the north-east of the Aegean Sea, because the Athenians obtained corn from Thrace and the shores of the Hellespont. Alcibiades, pardoned, reconquered the coasts of Asia and Thrace; exiled afresh, his place was taken by Conon, who defeated the Spartans near the islets which lie between Lesbos and the Asiatic coast.

The Athenians regained confidence to the length of despising the fleet that the Spartan general Lysander had raised with Persian money, the Persians having become the allies of Sparta. Lysander surprised the Athenian fleet at Agospotami, on the Hellespont, and destroyed it. Then he laid siege to Athens, which, decimated by famine and betrayed by the aristocratic party, surrendered (404 B.C.).

The conquerors imposed hard terms: the destruction of the Long Walls and the fortifications of the Piraeus, the surrender of the remainder of the fleet, the recall of the banished citizens, and alliance with Sparta.

The victory of Sparta was the end of Athenian supremacy. Her old allies of the Confederacy of Delos, to whom she had promised liberty, had only a change of mistress: all Greece seemed to be part of a Spartan empire. Each city had an oligarchic government appointed by Sparta, and backed by a Spartan garrison. The Persians continued to furnish the money needed for this domination. But the cruelty of the conquerors led to many revolts, beginning with Athens.

Athens was governed by an aristocratic council of thirty members, known as "The Thirty Tyrants." They exiled or caused to perish more than 1500 members of the democratic party. Their rule became so odious that a band of exiles, commanded by Thrasybulus, returned to Athens with the connivance of the people, drove out the tyrants and re-established the democracy. To put an end to civil war, they decided on an amnesty, that is to say, the forgetting of all injuries, and Athens might have become once again a great city.

The Athenians agreed upon an amnesty, but popular rage showed itself for a long time against the oligarchs and their friends. Socrates, unjustly counted in their number, was an innocent victim of this reaction.

This philosopher, all through his life, appeared to be an extraordinary person to his fellow-citizens. An upright man and a brave soldier, he refused to meddle with politics. Poor, he would not take fees for his lectures like other philosophers. Then he was ugly, and this was a serious fault among the Athenians. He did not teach in a school, but walked up and down, surrounded by a circle of admirers and pupils, to whom he put philosophical problems which he discussed in informal conversations. Some philosophers tried to explain the laws of Nature, others, called Sophists, taught the science of reasoning and remained indifferent to all opinions. Socrates' philosophy was founded on ethics. The first of all his precepts was "Know thyself." With great breadth of view, he showed the distinction between good and evil, the immortality of the soul, and the existence of a Providence over and above all the individual gods. He had a great influence on all the cultivated minds of his time, among them Pericles and Alcibiades, and his teaching has been transmitted to us by two of his pupils, in the *Memorabilia* of Xenophon and the *Dialogues* of Plato, the founder of the school called the Academy.

Misunderstood by the people because he had criticised certain aspects of the Athenian constitution, he was accused of having favoured the Thirty, of corrupting the youth, and teaching doctrines contrary to the religion of the city. In spite of his accusation, it had been resolved not to condemn him to death, but Socrates irritated his judges by saying: "In order that I may consecrate myself to the service of my country by working to make my fellow-citizens virtuous, I propose that I be fed in the Prytaneum at the public expense."

Condemned prisoners had to drink poison prepared from hemlock; Socrates drank the poison in the midst of his weeping friends, and died at seventy years of age with the serenity of a great man.

After the Peloponnesian War, Athens, thanks to her remarkable vitality, recovered sufficiently to take an honourable place again in Greece. She remained the centre of Greek civilisation, but she was deposed from her maritime empire. Three causes brought about this decadence: a proud reliance on her forces, a too great care for particular interests, the changeableness of democratic feeling unable to take long views. In point of fact, she treated her allies with great haughtiness, she exacted heavy tribute from them by force and did not attempt to gain their affection. Further, the citizens lost in prosperity some of the qualities of their ancestors. They thought less of the greatness of the State and more of their private fortunes. They made war or peace as it suited their commercial interests. Then this people, who decided everything by their own votes, showed an incredible lethargy. When the great voice of Pericles ceased to arouse them, they listened only to those who flattered their passions, passed their time in changing councillors and policy, and exhausted themselves in foolish quarrels which rendered the Spartan victory easier.

The Demagogues, who led the people, were orators who cared less for the greatness of the State than for popularity and the profits it assured them. They followed public opinion, pandered to the hatreds and enthusiasms of the electors, flattered their passions, and by these means obtained votes, power and honour. Such was the rôle of Cleon and Alcibiades, during the Peloponnesian War.

Cleon, a tanner by trade, pleased the people by the lowness of his origin, his hatred of the aristocratic party, his rough and violent eloquence and the ruthlessness of his propositions. He was the first citizen of low origin to exercise power in Athens. He had not the knowledge, nor had he had the political education Pericles had enjoyed, but he was enterprising and brave. He was killed at the siege of Amphipolis, for which he had voted.

Alcibiades was a demagogue of good birth. He pretended to carry on the policy of his uncle Pericles, and his talents justified such a pretension. Nature had endowed him with many gifts: he was the most handsome, as well as the richest man in Athens, and at the same time he was a good soldier and an easy orator. He was the spoilt child of the city, for he was loved for himself, his speeches, his gifts and even his extravagances. But he was absurdly vain, and incapable of controlling his temper when he was crossed. He forced Athens into the expedition against Sicily, then, driven into exile, he had the infamy to excite the Spartans and Persians against his own state. Discontented with Sparta, he entered the Athenian service again, for the Athenians, with astonishing indulgence, received him like a prodigal son, and when he had repented publicly pardoned him. But he was driven into exile afresh, for his noisy ambition made him a danger to the republic.

In spite of the faults of the Athenians, Sparta was not able

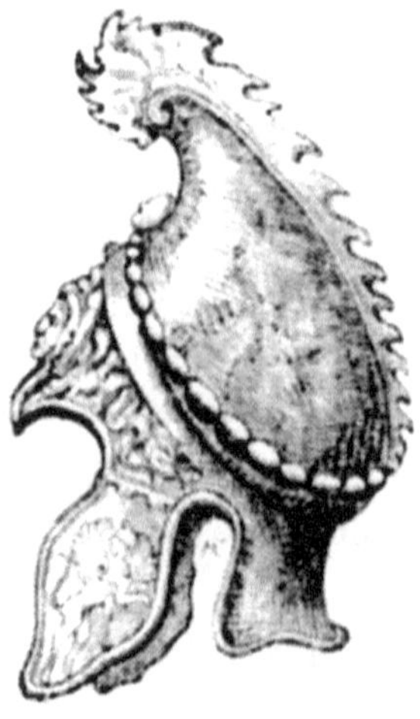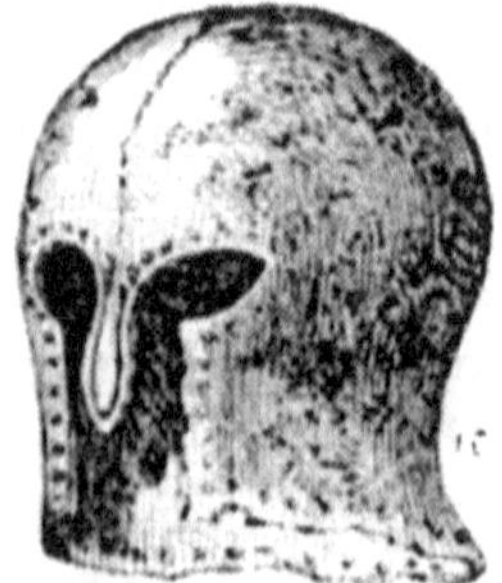

FIG. 62. - Two Greek helmets.

alone to make an end of her rival. Sparta was only powerful on land, whilst the Athenians held command of the sea. It was necessary to destroy the Athenian fleet to prevent them receiving corn from Thrace and money from the Ionian cities. This was Lysander's plan, and in order to execute it he did not hesitate to ally himself with the Persians. They found the occasion favourable for revenging their old losses, and they furnished him with gold and ships with which he gained the battle of Agospotami.

Thus Persian gold became master of Greece by playing a part in its quarrels. The Athenians and Thebans received some in order to revolt against Sparta. The Spartans received it in order to dominate Greece. Soon the Great King exacted the price of his services and obtained from Sparta the treaty of Antalcidas, which reversed Cimon's treaty and placed the Greeks of Asia Minor under the Persian yoke. This disgrace inflicted by Sparta on Greece was the Persian revenge for the Persian wars (387 B.C.).

CHAPTER XV

MACEDONIA

BY 360 B.C., forty years after the end of the Peloponnesian War, Sparta had lost her supremacy; Athens had regained part of her maritime empire; Thebes, thanks to her two great soldiers, Pelopidas and Epaminondas, had experienced six brief years of glory. At the battles of Leuctra (371 B.C.) and Mantinea (362 B.C.), Epaminondas, the organiser of the Theban army and the inventor of new tactics, had shown that the Spartans were not invincible; but when her two generals died, Thebes fell into the rank of a second-rate power. There were three states in Greece of about equal strength: Sparta, Athens and Thebes. All three aimed at domination, and no one of them was strong enough to conquer if the other two united against her.

During this time the barbarians of the north had organised themselves into states resembling the Greeks; one of these states, Macedonia, under an enterprising prince, triumphed over the Greeks, and Philip II was able to accomplish by conquest the unity of Greece.

Macedonia was a country of high mountains covered with forests, which to-day are to a great extent denuded, enclosing extremely fertile circular plains, the bottoms of ancient lakes, the well-watered regions yielding three crops a year. The Macedonians were hardy peasants of a warlike character, great hunters and drinkers, half barbarians, half Greeks. They spoke a language derived from Greek, and their kings were of Greek race and had the right of taking part in the Olympic Games.

The Macedonians were isolated from the sea by the colonies the Athenians had planted on their coasts; therefore they neglected

FIG. 63. - A peasant of Macedonia.

commerce and remained agricultural labourers until the day when they became conquerors. But the kings and nobles who came in contact with Greece developed a desire to pass for Greeks.

They adopted the religion and manners of their neighbours and founded a new capital, Pella, nearer to the Hellenic world than the old one. When they had beaten back their barbarian neighbours, they tried to imitate Greek arts and even to mix in Greek quarrels.

It was in this fashion that Philip, when a child, was carried away to Thebes as a hostage by Pelopidas. There he was brought up as a Greek. He learnt the art of eloquence and military science, with all the innovations the Thebans had made. He learnt also to understand Greeks and Greek things. He realised that there was no real strength in these little cities, which had to make war with mercenary soldiers and foreign money; he saw also that many men were tired of these useless wars, and that the taste for luxury had killed the old spirit of sacrifice for the city. Every one desired a lasting peace, and was ready to submit to the domination of whoever imposed it, provided that he spared their vanity. Philip resolved to be that man. He had the energy of a barbarian and the methodical spirit of a Greek. Possessing all the resources of a new country, and knowing clearly what he wanted, he carried out with patience and energy a plan which seems to have been as follows: (1) The civilisation of Macedonia and the formation of it into a Greek state with the sea as its natural boundary; (2) the assertion of his supremacy over all the Balkan colonies; (3) to profit by the Greek divisions to impose his dominion, and to pacify them by uniting them against Persia. In order to succeed, Philip employed force, strategy, and money. He first of all created an army, modelling it on the Greek armies but making it superior in organisation and armament. In the first place, it was a permanent army, whereas the Greek armies, with the exception of the Spartan, were only militia, called up in time of war. The Macedonian peasants made good soldiers, and the nobles good officers.

He made everyone undergo a course of severe discipline, forced marches, and frequent manoeuvres.

The nucleus of this army, which was always ready to take the field, was the phalanx, analogous to the Spartan phalanx but of much deeper proportions. The simple phalanx was a mass of 4,096 hoplites presenting a front of 256 men, sixteen ranks deep. Each man was armed with a sword and a long lance, called a sarissa. The six front rows held their lances at such an angle that those of the sixth rank protruded about a yard beyond the men of the first rank. The phalanx was thus a veritable moving fortress bristling with six rows of iron points and sweeping all before it on level ground. Four simple phalanxes formed the great phalanx, a mass of more than 16,000 men. Behind and on the two wings were columns of light infantry or peltastes resembling the Athenians.

The advance of the phalanx was preceded by a curtain of skirmishers, archers, and slingers called psilistes. Philip also organised a strong detachment of cavalry for fighting in the plains of the north. This was a corps of picked men, "cataphractes," who were covered in armour from head to foot like the knights of the Middle Ages. To attack the Greek towns on the coast, he prepared all kinds of besieging machines until then unknown to the Greeks, although the Assyrians had used them for a very long time. These enabled him to wage a war by sieges which surprised and terrified the Greeks. He had the sinews of war, thanks to the gold mines of Thrace, and his famous pieces of gold decided hesitating minds in his favour.

In the realisation of his projects, Philip came up against the Athenians. He was their enemy because he wanted to reach the coast, and their old-established colonies covered the Chalcidice. They were able to resist him, for their fleet was powerful again, and they still cherished the ambition of restoring the maritime empire of the time of Pericles.

But although the Athenians had great dreams, they were little inclined for action, and they were very much divided in opinion.

There were Aeschines, whom they accused of having been bought by the Macedonians; Isocrates, who hoped that Macedonian supremacy would lead to the unity of Greece; Phocion, who did not consider his country to be in a state to bear a war. Others, on the contrary, faithful to the ideals of their ancestors, would not admit that their country ought to become the province of a great Greek empire. They remained attached to the old policy of independent cities, rivals one to the other; and their proud but rather narrow patriotism was represented by, and immortalised in, the person of Demosthenes, the greatest orator of ancient times.

Demosthenes' tongue was eloquent, and he had great tenacity of character. Orphaned young, ruined by his guardians, impeded by a stammer, rough in speech, yet he triumphed through force of character over all his enemies and became the orator who held best the public ear. He saw in Philip the enemy of Athenian power and Greek liberty, and never ceased to exhort his fellow citizens to make war on him. This was the subject of his famous orations, the Philippics and the Olynthiacs.

Philip took twenty-one years to realise his ambitions. He did not attack the Greeks directly, but he cleverly exploited their rivalries and interfered in their quarrels. He pretended to sympathise with all those who applied to him for help and always allied himself to some city at war against another. Thus, he helped Olynthus against Athens, which enabled him to take Potidaea,

Amphipolis, and Methone from the Athenians. After that, he helped Athens against Olynthus, which he took in its turn. Too late, Athens perceived her error and tried in vain to help her old enemy.

A religious war against the Phocians, who were accused of sacrilege on the charge of ploughing up land belonging to the oracle of Delphi, gave Philip the chance of leading his army into Greece for the first time.

He profited by this war to occupy Thessaly. But the Athenians armed themselves and resisted him for a time (352 B.C.).

A similar act of sacrilege, thirteen years later, and this time by the Locrians, furnished him with a new pretext for intervention. But instead of marching against the Locrians, he marched into Boeotia.

The Athenians armed themselves at the command of Demosthenes and came to the Thebans' aid; the Spartans, always selfish, refused to help. The allies were completely defeated at Chaeronea (339 B.C.), and this was the end of the independence of the Greek states.

Demosthenes, whose task it was to pronounce the funeral eulogy of the citizens who had died on the field of battle, tried several weeks later to comfort the conquered in phrases which move even posterity. "No, Athenians!" he cried. "We have not erred in resisting to the point of death for the health and freedom of Greece. I swear it by your ancestors' graves at Marathon, Salamis, and Plataea."

Philip treated the Thebans without mercy but accorded the Athenians an honourable peace. From that time, he occupied himself in uniting the Greek states in a confederacy of which he was the elected head. He called the representatives of the cities to Corinth, expounded his projects against Asia, and nominated himself commander-in-chief against the Persians. The preparations for the great campaign to revenge the Persian wars were completed in 336 B.C., and Philip was preparing to start when he was murdered.

Alexander, Philip's son, was twenty years old at the time of his father's death. He was already celebrated for his beauty, horsemanship, and intelligence. He boasted a good deal of having trained an untameable horse, the famous Bucephalus; he was also famous as the pupil of the great philosopher Aristotle. Men talked of his passion for literature, which made him carry the Iliad on his campaigns.

He had shown marked military ability at the battle of Chaeronea, and his education had prepared his mind for great projects; he was capable both of making great plans and of carrying them out.

He began by showing everyone that he was master in his own house. His father's second wife wanted to be regent — he had her and her son killed. Directly the Macedonians had recognised him as king, he descended into Greece to have his supremacy acknowledged there. The Athenians hastened to send an ambassador.

Satisfied, he marched against the people who bordered Macedonia to the north and extended his empire as far as the Danube. While he was in these remote districts, a rumour of his death spread. The Greeks at once rose, formed a coalition under Thebes, and prepared for war.

Alexander marched from Thrace in seven days and completely defeated the rebels. The town was razed to the ground, and the inhabitants were sold as slaves. As for Athens, whose citizens had favoured the movement, he wished to humiliate her by demanding the surrender of Demosthenes; but he was appeased by the petition of Phocion and respected Athens as the home of Greek civilisation.

The Greeks were definitely beaten, and Alexander could now satisfy his ambition and flatter their conceit by putting before them again his father's plans against Asia. The representatives of the Greek cities, meeting once more at Corinth, proclaimed him head of a united Greece (333 B.C.), and the Greeks came and enlisted in large numbers in the army which he was to lead against the Persian empire.

CHAPTER XVI

THE CONQUEST OF ASIA

ALEXANDER realised the project, which the Greeks had played with for so long, of conquering Asia and her treasures. To revenge the Persian wars had always been a popular idea in Greece, which Philip and Alexander could easily exploit to hide their own ambition. The moment was well chosen; the march of the Ten Thousand had revealed the weakness of the Persian Empire. This was an expedition carried out by a band of mercenaries whom Cyrus, satrap of Asia Minor, had hired and paid to try to dethrone his brother, the Great King. At Cunaxa, near the Euphrates, where he attacked, Cyrus was killed, but the 10,000 Greeks remained masters of the battlefield. Then began an extraordinary retreat from the Euphrates to the Black Sea, led by Xenophon, who afterwards wrote an account of it.

They marched nearly 4,000 miles in fifteen months, encountering many difficulties in an unknown country in the midst of a hostile population, but everywhere they were victorious. Returning to Greece, these heroic adventurers were able to say that their most redoubtable enemies had been hunger, thirst, cold, and the mountains. Alexander took his best troops with him: 40,000 foot soldiers and 5,000 knights. Both soldiers and officers were accustomed to war, greedy for glory and pillage, ready to conquer or die. The army was strong in organization and courage; Alexander owed his victories to the irresistible power of his personality, for he does not seem to have invented a new way of fighting. Darius II opposed him with the old Persian army, which had learned nothing since the Persian wars and could not even await the encounter with its old courage. The huge empire

FIG. 64. - The Empire of Alexander.

was dislocated; each satrap dreamed of making himself independent and was ready to betray the Great King. The peoples only demanded a change of masters. The true difficulties of the enterprise were the vastness of the country to be conquered and the hesitation of the European troops, frightened of going too far from their own country. Alexander overcame these obstacles by the force of an intelligent boldness and a tenacious will.

Alexander disembarked near Troy and offered a sacrifice in honour of Achilles. This was the symbol of the unity of the Greeks against the Asiatics.

The Persians advanced to meet him. A Greek in the service of Darius, Memnon of Rhodes, advised him to place the desert between his forces and Alexander's, and thus wear out the latter's army. The satraps preferred to wait beside the river Granicus. They were cut to pieces. Sardis and all the coast towns surrendered without the intervention of the Persian fleet (324 B.C.).

The following year, Alexander went into the interior of Asia Minor to attack Phrygia and concentrated his army against Gordium. There was a chariot there, the yoke of which was fixed by a very complicated knot of cords. An oracle promised the empire of Asia to the man who could untie it. Alexander cut the knot with his sword. He marched then towards Taurus. At the point where Asia Minor is joined to Asia, Darius, at the head of 300,000 men, tried to bar his passage near the Issus. The Persian army was overthrown, and Darius retired beyond the Euphrates (333 B.C.).

Instead of following him, Alexander marched towards Egypt. On his way, Damascus surrendered without conditions. Tyre refused to surrender; she was taken by assault after a siege of seven months. Jerusalem received him as a conqueror. Egypt accepted him as a liberator and gave him the title of son of Ammon, like the ancient Pharaohs. Alexander accepted this title, although it was ridiculous in the eyes of the Greeks, for it inaugurated a new policy which consisted of reconciling the conquered people and respecting their traditions. He built Alexandria in order to unite in the same city Greek and Egyptian civilization.

Darius, frightened, tried to treat, but Alexander wished to be the sole master of Asia. He retraced his steps, crossed the Tigris, and attacked Darius' formidable army near Arbela. The Persians, thanks to their numbers, counted on surrounding the Macedonians, but Alexander spoilt their plan by breaking their centre (331 B.C.). Abandoning the pursuit of the conquered, he entered Babylon, took Susa, and then, forcing the mountain passes, he occupied Persepolis and Pasargadae.

Having conquered all Darius' capitals, he took to the pursuit of the fugitive king and marched against Ecbatana. There he learned that Darius had been assassinated by a satrap who counted on conciliating himself with Alexander; but he had the assassin executed and gave the corpse a royal burial. He was then proclaimed king of Persia and set to work to gain the affection of his new subjects. He treated Darius' family kindly, married a Persian princess, sacrificed to the gods of the country, and introduced Persians into his army. But at the same time, he lived the life of a satrap, giving himself to luxury and debauchery. He became vain and irritable and caused many of his officers to perish, guilty only of being critical. The army, covered with glory and riches, murmured a little, but it pardoned a victorious king who had given silver shields to the soldiers of his guard.

His victories had only excited Alexander's ambition. He dreamed of making Persia the bridge of union between Europe and the people of China and India. With this object, he marched towards Arachosia (Afghanistan), which commanded the passes of the Indus. He founded cities which still exist under the names of Mesched, Herat, Kandahar, and Kabul. Then he turned towards Bactriana (Turkestan). He took two years and three campaigns to establish himself firmly in this country, which he wished to make the boundary of his empire and a point of contact with the yellow race, that is to say, with the Russians of today. After having founded the cities now known as Samarkand and Khojend, he left a strong army in Bactriana, where it was able to preserve Greek civilization for seven centuries (330–328 B.C.).

FIG. 65. - Fight between Greeks and Asiatics: from a bas-relief.

Then he turned towards India, and in 327 B.C. crossed the defiles which form the basin of the Indus with 100,000 men. He met with no more resistance than that of the Rajah Porus, with whom, after defeating him, he made friends. His army refused to go further; therefore, he descended the Indus in a fleet of 800 ships, sometimes being received like a god, sometimes having to force his passage. Again, he founded cities, which were not lasting because the conquerors' stay was too short (325 B.C.).

The Macedonian army returned to Babylon in three divisions: by Afghanistan, Gedrosia (Baluchistan), and the Persian Gulf. Alexander commanded the Gedrosia division, which suffered a good deal from thirst in the desert.

Back at Babylon, where he received divine honours, Alexander reorganized his empire in the midst of festivals of all kinds. He undertook great works and the construction of a port, which was to put Greek Asia into communication with India through the Persian Gulf. He was preparing an expedition against Arabia when he was stricken down by an attack of fever at thirty-three years of age (323 B.C.).

Alexander's empire extended from the Adriatic to the Indus, and from the cataracts of the Nile to the Caucasus. The conqueror did not leave an heir, and he had not nominated a successor. His generals disputed the succession and divided the empire among themselves. This resulted in a long series of wars, which were ended by the Battle of Ipsus (301 B.C.). Three great Greek kingdoms were established: (1) the kingdom of Egypt, under the dynasty of the Ptolemies; (2) the kingdom of Syria, under the dynasty of Seleucus; (3) the kingdom of Macedonia, under the dynasty of Cassander.

Alexander had conquered the world in order to unite it. He had taken with him to Asia artists, philosophers, and engineers, who helped to found Greek cities all along his triumphal progress. The ancient writers well understood the importance of his work. "He did not listen," said Plutarch, "to those who advised him to behave like a prince among the Greeks, a master among the barbarians. Believing that he was sent by God to arbitrate and to unite, he reduced by force those whom he could not make submit by strength of will." This policy prepared the way for the later coming of the Roman Empire and the Christian religion. Its immediate results were: (1) The putting into circulation of the riches of Asia; (2) The development of commercial relations between Europe and the East; (3) The diffusion of Greek language, art, and thought from the steppes of Siberia to India.

The true capital of this new world was Alexandria in Egypt, the home of the Ptolemies. The meeting place of the routes from Europe, Asia, and Africa, it became rapidly the mart of the world, and it is still a great port today. It was also the intellectual capital, the place where the ideas of the West met those of the East, and where ideas, like merchandise, could circulate through the whole world.

The Ptolemies built a curious monument dedicated to the Muses. It was at the same time a library, an academy, and a university. For the first time, instruction was organized. In their masterpieces, the Greeks had reached perfect beauty; the Alexandrians explained it to the rest of the world. Thanks to them, Greek thought became universal thought.

PART III.

ROME

CHAPTER XVII

PRIMITIVE ITALY

ROME is in the center of Italy, and Italy was the center of the ancient world. This central position explains why Roman rule extended throughout the Mediterranean basin.

Italy is a peninsula divided into two distinct regions: continental Italy in the north, and peninsular Italy.

Continental Italy consists of the plain of the River Po, lying between the Alps and the Apennines. Early in history, this fertile region was invaded by the Gauls, who came from central Europe through the Alpine passes. Peninsular Italy, which is often compared to a boot, is the land surrounding the different ranges of the Apennines, which stretch from the north to the south.

The slopes of these mountains fall nearly into the sea on the Adriatic side, leaving room only for narrow coastal plains and valleys badly irrigated by torrents. On the Tyrrhenian coast, the slope is more gradual. There are the plains of Etruria, Latium, and Campania, through which run rivers with courses of a fair length, such as the Tiber and the Arno. Between Vesuvius and the Arno is a volcanic region, studded with lakes and high rocks, such as the hills of Rome, which show the existence of ancient craters.

These plains have made Italian history; for powerful peoples, first the Etruscans, then the Latins, cultivated them and built cities upon the heights. The Tyrrhenian Sea, which is not closed like the Adriatic, made intercourse with other ancient peoples easy.

The southern portion of the peninsula, Calabria and Lucania, is a land apart. It is a mass of granite divided into two parts: one nearly touching Sicily at Messina, the other sloping towards Greece. Between the two stretches is the Gulf of Tarentum, a

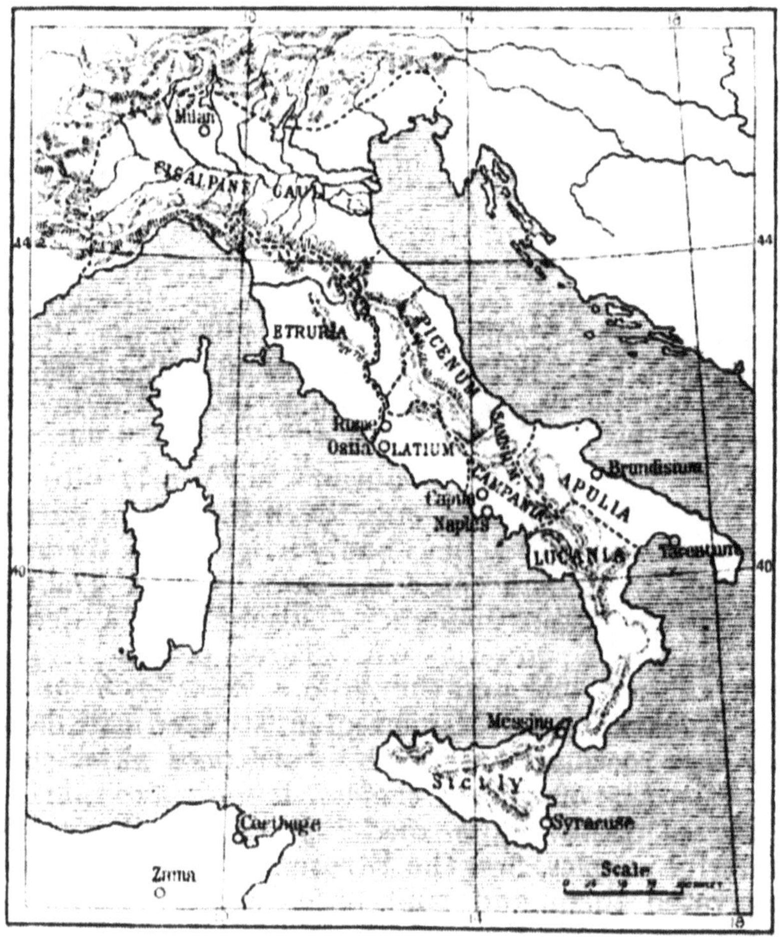

FIG. 66. - Ancient Italy.

landing point for the Greeks who peopled this region, strangers to the rest of Italy.

The climate is mild and humid, with severe but short winters, dry and sunny summers, and wet autumns. This climate made Italy a land of corn, wine, and oil, and the inhabitants were, above all, agriculturists, who only took late to industry and navigation.

Italy, in spite of the extent of her seaboard, is not like Greece — a jagged peninsula where the sea invites men to meet one another. It is a compact mass with a nearly straight coastline, except in the south, where there are some inlets like the Gulf of Naples. A circle of sandbanks, lagoons, and marshes imprisons the inhabitants inland, and malaria, especially in the region of Rome, drives them from the seaboard. One coast is washed by the Adriatic, famous for its storms, the other by the Tyrrhenian, a wider expanse; but both are bad seas for the frail ships of primitive peoples.

The peninsula divides the Mediterranean into two basins, which in ancient times represented the civilized world of the East and the barbarian world of the West. When one powerful people occupied the whole of it, they became masters of both worlds. But the mountainous nature of the country favored, as in Greece, the existence of little independent states.

This was the primitive state of Italy. Unity was not realized, and consequently, expansion beyond the peninsula was not possible until the Roman conquest. The country seems to have been peopled by invaders from the north, for the many passes through the Alps have often been routes of invasion.

FIG. 67. - Two Etruscan aged men from a tomb painting.

At the threshold of history, four races — the Gauls, Etruscans, Greeks, and Italians — divided the land. The Etruscans, a mysterious people, of whom we know neither the race nor the language, lived to the south of the Cisalpine country. Nearly two million of their inscriptions remain, of which only about twenty words have been deciphered. They resembled neither the Greeks nor the Latins, and we do not know from whence they came.

They have been described as men "squat, short, fat and vigorous, with prominent faces, curved noses, large and tapering foreheads, dark color, and depressed craniums covered with curly hair."

They first lived in the valley of the Po, but, hunted by the Gauls, they established themselves between the Tiber, Arno, and the Apennines in a fertile region, which is today called Tuscany. Then they spread beyond the Tiber and occupied Campania as far as the Gulf of Naples.

Etruria and Campania each consisted of twelve federated cities united by a common culture. The leading cities were Volsinii in Etruria and Capua in Campania. A rich and powerful aristocracy lived in each city, called the *lucumos*, who appointed the magistrates each year. The signs of magisterial office were, as we shall find later in Rome, purple cloaks and seats of ivory, or curule chairs.

The Etruscans reached a state of advanced civilization, and in many ways resembled the Phoenicians. Like them, they did not form a highly organized state, and again like them, they were a very flourishing, agricultural, seafaring, industrial, and commercial people. They were able to obtain full value from the damp plains of Tuscany and obtained rich harvests, thanks to their careful drainage of land, which has today relapsed into marshes. They worked the iron mines in the island of Elba, and in their workshops wrought in gold, iron, copper, and bronze with very great care to detail.

Their navy was renowned in the time of the Homeric poems, which mention "The Tyrrhenian pirates." They had the monopoly of trade in the northern Mediterranean and traded with Gaul, Carthage, and the Greek colonies, and through them with Greece. In the last-named case, the Etruscans employed a method very common in ancient times: in order to spare their ships the dangers of the straits between Sicily and the mainland, they unloaded their merchandise—timber, lamps, mirrors—in Lucania and took it by land to the port of Sybaris, where the goods were shipped to Greece. In return, the Greeks sent vases and jewels, which

FIG. 68. - An Etruscan tomb.

served as models for Etruscan workmanship. They copied the Greek objects of art in great numbers, especially the little statues in red and black pottery, and they sold them broadcast to the neighboring peoples.

They were also good architects. They built towns enclosed with solid ramparts and constructed arched sewers. Their houses were built around an atrium, an inner court open to the sky, which later became the origin of the Roman house. Their tombs also had a distinct character. They were great subterranean vaults; a set of cabins decorated with pictures were built into the walls. There were funeral chambers, in which the corpse reposed on a bed, surrounded by furniture. Etruscan vases and jewels have been taken from these tombs.

The Etruscans, like all ancient people, had a twofold religion: that of the gods and that of the dead. Their practices were of a strange character. They lived in terror of the unknown, both in this world and the next. The gods of evil, particularly the god of the dead, had the chief place among the gods. Mantus, who held the torch; Charun, armed with a hammer; and Tuculcha, a monster with an eagle's beak who brandished serpents, were represented with horrible characteristics. The Etruscans worshipped the souls of the dead because they feared they might do them harm. To appease them, they used to offer human sacrifices; this was the origin of gladiator fights. Their timid spirits feared the anger of the gods. To understand their wishes, they had a body of priests, called augurers, who tried to discover signs in the flight of birds, the entrails of victims, and celestial phenomena. These superstitions, as well as many Etruscan customs and inventions, passed to Rome. The Romans adopted the costumes and ideas of the Greek colonies, as well as their alphabet. Roman civilization originated from this adoption.

Between the Etruscans and the civilised and civilising Greeks of the south, there lived in central Italy a race of shepherds and

FIG. 69. - Peasants of the Roman plain.

labourers generally called the Latins, but who formed four distinct groups: the Umbrians, Sabines, Samnites, and Latins. They lived in the plain of the Tiber or Latium and on the Abruzzian hills, which surrounded Latium like a wall of rock. The isolated hill peoples retained their primitive culture for a long time. They were small tribes of poor but fierce warriors, renowned for their courage and fine armour, who hired themselves as soldiers to neighbouring peoples. Sometimes the tribes united for pillaging expeditions, but they never formed a nation.

On the contrary, the people of the plain, occupying the land between the Greek colonies and Etruria, came more often into contact with strangers. They learned their type of culture, the art of building cities, and adopted their political and religious institutions. That is why they formed a single state more quickly than their brothers in the mountains. This state was the Roman state.

In the early days of Rome, all the people of similar race and language had the same organisation. They lived in independent groups or cities. A city consisted of a tiny fortified town, an acropolis, at the same time temple and citadel, built on a hill, and called both *civitas* and *res publica*. This was the religious centre and a refuge in times of danger for the inhabitants, who were all farmers scattered in the neighbouring country. Such were the ancient towns of Alba, Lanuvium, Tusculum, and the Rome of Romulus. In times of exceptional peril, many cities of the same race formed a confederation of a religious character. The Latins of the plains consecrated this religious meeting with an annual sacrifice, celebrated on Mount Alba in the sanctuary of the Latin Jupiter.

In the lower part of Latium, not far from the mouth of the Tiber, in the midst of a marshy plain often inundated by river floods, there were seven hills, of which the highest was the Palatine. These hills were natural fortresses commanding the routes north and south. According to Roman traditions — traditions which recent discoveries hardly permit us to accept — it was on the Palatine that Romulus founded, on April 21, 753 B.C., a town which he called Rome. He founded his city with Etruscan rites.

After observing the flight of birds, he celebrated a sacrifice and purified himself and his companions by jumping across a lighted brazier. This done, he dug a ditch into which each companion threw a clod of earth brought from his own land. Over this ditch, he built an altar and dedicated it to his ancestors and to the protecting deities of the new city.

Then, garbed as a priest with a veiled head, he traced an enclosing furrow with a brass plough to which a white heifer and a white bull were harnessed. At the locations for the gates, he lifted the plough and carried it. The space thus marked out was the sanctuary of the national gods; the gates alone could be leaped over without sacrilege. It is said that Romulus did not hesitate to punish his brother Remus by death for jumping the sacred furrow in scorn.

The city thus traced was a little four-sided enclosure, the *Urbs quadrata*, defended by stone ramparts and furnished with four gates. The anniversary of its foundation became an annual Roman feast.

CHAPTER XVIII

THE BEGINNING OF ROME

THE history of the beginnings of Rome is uncertain. We only know of them from the writings of the historian Livy, who lived in the time of Augustus and who has distorted and embellished facts for patriotic reasons. However, his stories are probably not entirely legendary, and the discovery of the tomb of Romulus in the Roman Forum seems to confirm this opinion. It is possible to distinguish between two periods in these traditions: (1) the kings and (2) the Republic.

Romulus was the founder and first king of Rome; he was the son of Mars and descended from Venus through his mother, Rhea Sylvia, daughter of Numitor, king of Alba. The Trojan Aeneas, son of Venus, took refuge in Italy after the fall of Troy and founded the city of Alba.

FIG. 70. - Romulus and Remus, with the wolf, their foster-mother.

The gods had favoured this land even before that time, for Saturn, driven from heaven by Jupiter, had come and cultivated Latium, and Hercules had killed the brigand Cacus there.

Numitor was dethroned by his brother Amulius, who, in order to cut off his line, imprisoned his daughter Rhea in the college of Vestal Virgins. Mars gave her twin sons, Romulus and Remus. Then Amulius threw the children into the Tiber in a basket; but it was flood time, and when the waters abated, the twins were left at the foot of the Palatine. They were miraculously tended by a wolf and discovered by a shepherd, who brought them up secretly. Having grown tall and being celebrated for their strength, they were recognised by their grandfather Numitor, whom they set on his throne again. Romulus established himself on the Palatine and founded Rome. To people the city, he opened it to all the adventurers in the neighbourhood. They came in great numbers, but they had no wives, and the surrounding peoples refused to mate with them. So, they planned to raid the great Sabine games and to carry off the maidens during the spectacle. This was the cause of a war during which the Sabines penetrated into the centre of Rome. But the newly wedded wives threw themselves between their husbands and their fathers and stopped the fighting.

The two peoples soon united, with Romulus as their king.

He then organised the kingdom and created the Senate. Some time afterwards, he disappeared in a storm in front of the assembly of the whole people. They believed he had ascended to the sky and worshipped him by the name of Quirinus.

Numa Pompilius, his successor, was a Sabine. He was a king-priest who, it was said, was inspired by the nymph Egeria. He regulated most of the ceremonies of the Roman religion, reformed the calendar, and built the temple of Janus, which was open during times of war and closed during peace.

Tullius Hostilius, a Roman by birth, was a warlike king, who took part in the war against Alba. This war was ended by a fight between three Romans, the Horatii, and three Albans, the Curiatii. In the first engagement, two of the Horatii were killed, and the three Curiatii were wounded. The surviving Horatius, who was unwounded, pretended to flee in order to separate his opponents and kill them one by one. In the full flush of triumph, he met his sister Camilla, who mourned for her betrothed, one of the Curiatii. This sight angered him so that he committed a crime: he killed her. Alba was destroyed, and its inhabitants were transported to Rome, which inherited its ancient supremacy. After this, the Capitol replaced Mons Alba as the religious centre of the Latins.

Ancus Martius was a Sabine and a religious king like Numa. He extended the Roman lands to the sea, founded the port of Ostia, built a fortress on the Janiculum, on the other side of the Tiber, and united it to Rome by a bridge of boats. Then he constructed the Mamertine prison, which still exists.

Tarquinius Priscus, who succeeded him, came from Etruria. He was the son of a Corinthian Greek who had emigrated to Tarquinii. He introduced into Rome the cult of augurers, Etruscan architecture, and the costumes and insignia of Etruscan kings: the purple robe, the crown, the throne, and the sceptre. He was a builder-king; he improved the city, constructed docks, a circus, and a great drain, the Cloaca Maxima, so well that it has lasted to our own day. He was assassinated.

Servius Tullius, according to some authorities, was of the race of Tarquin. According to the Emperor Claudius, an antiquarian of some merit, he was an adventurer named Mastarna, son of an Etruscan lord. His reign saw an important reform: the population of Rome was divided into four tribes according to region and into seven classes according to wealth. This reform, similar to that of Solon in Athens, had for its object military organisation; the first six classes furnished the contingents for the army, divided into corps called centuries. Servius also constructed a new wall, which enclosed the seven hills of Rome. It was a double wall, the space between being filled by a great mound of earth. It is said that Servius was assassinated by his daughter and her husband.

Tarquinius Superbus, the son-in-law of Servius, was the last king of Rome. He established her supremacy over all Latium and conquered the Volscian country. But he was a cruel tyrant and was hated by his nobles. His son outraged his cousin, the virtuous Lucretia, who killed herself. This crime caused universal indignation; Brutus, the king's nephew, and Collatinus, Lucretia's husband, called together the army and revolted. The Tarquins were driven out, and a republic was formed (509 B.C.).

In this jumble of early traditions, it is difficult to distinguish between truth and legend. All we know for certain is the manner in which the Romans lived at this period. Rome was formed by the union of three Latin tribes: the Ramnes, Tities, and the Luceres. The inhabitants were divided into two classes: those who were citizens and those who were not, the patricians and the plebeians.

The patricians alone formed the Roman people, *populus*. They only had rights; only they administered the State. A patrician had to be a member of a noble family or *gens*. The organisation of Rome was aristocratic, founded on the cult of ancestors.

The gens consisted of all the branches of the same family having a common ancestor. All the members of the gens bore the same name, no matter how many there were, and they honoured as chief the eldest son of the eldest branch, who was the priest of the ancestor worship. He who by birth was the nearest relation to the ancestor was called father, pater.

The other members of the gens were called patricians. In name and character, they corresponded to the Athenian Eupatrids. The father was at the same time the religious, civil, and military chief. He was priest and king in his family and had power of life and death over them.

The patricians possessed nearly everything: lands, herds, and many freemen possessed nothing or scarcely anything. The patricians gave them protection, and they were called clients in their protectors' families. They owed obedience to the patricians and called them patrons. In return, the patron gave a client his assistance, and in many cases, he lived with him. A family was thus a miniature state containing several hundreds of people; it had its chief, its religion, and its peculiar practices.

The *gentes*, grouped in tens, constituted the *curia*. The curia was a great family having its priest and its temple. There were in all thirty curia, which, joined together, formed the Assembly of the People. It decided everything by its vote. With it worked a council, the Senate, composed of the heads of the gentes, for which reason the members were named *patres* (fathers).

Beneath the citizens, there were a crowd of people, whose number continually increased, who did not form part of any family. They were refugees, the conquered, adventurers, clients of extinct families, freed men. In this state with a religious foundation, as they were not members of a cult, they had no rights. They were almost all foreigners and constituted what was called the multitude, plebs. Not being able to be either citizens or magistrates, they were not able to unite with the patricians. In the name of religion, marriage was forbidden between the two orders.

However, the plebeians were the more numerous; some were rich; they were able to furnish good material for the army. King Servius was the first to think of utilizing this force, and in classifying Romans according to fortune, he gave some of the plebeians a place in the army.

The army decided the question of peace or war. It formed an assembly of its own, called *comitia centuriata*, from the name of the centuries of which it was composed. The plebeians acquired at the same time the right to fight and the right to vote with the army. But although they had the right to vote, they had not the right to be elected; by virtue of ancient religious right, the patricians alone could exercise this function.

When the kings were driven out in 509 B.C., the Roman people exercised the sovereign power. The people being composed only of patricians, the revolution only benefited these. As the kings had shown a tendency to favor the plebeians, they were replaced by two consuls, who had to be patricians. The government was in the hands of the Senate, composed only of patricians. The consuls and the Senate were only the organs of government, the executors of the will of the people, that is to say, the patrician assembly.

The two consuls were elected for a year. They commanded the army, presided over the Senate and the Assembly of the People, proposed the laws, and presided over sacrifices for the city. They had to render an account of their acts after they laid down their offices. The signs of their dignity were: the border of purple, *protexta*, on the toga, the curule chair, and the lictors. This was the name of the bodyguard, twelve in number, who walked in front of the consul, carrying bundles of faggots, in which in time of war was placed an axe to signify the consul's right over the life and death of citizens.

In times of special danger, the consuls chose a special magistrate, the dictator, who was invested with absolute power, greater than that of the kings. He chose himself a special magistrate, called the master of the horse. He acted as an absolute monarch, took action as he wished without consulting either Senate or people, and had a guard of twenty-four lictors; but his office only lasted for six months.

Beside these temporary magistrates, there existed a permanent element, the Senate, composed of 300 members chosen by the consuls from the ranks of the patricians. They settled by their decrees the administration of the republic and its foreign policy. This honorable body showed great dignity and great perseverance in its policy, and Rome owed part of her success to its greatness.

When the majority of the plebeians were numbered in the centuries of the army, they were no longer content to be of no account in the State. There were among them both rich and poor. The latter were obliged to run into debt in order to serve in the army and to borrow from the patricians at interest, which varied from 12 to 25 percent. Moreover, the creditors' rights were terrible: they could imprison the insolvent debtor and even reduce him to slavery.

As a result, the poor plebeians were exasperated by their misery and the avarice of the patricians. The rich plebeians aspired to political rights and honors. As they bore the same burdens as the patricians, they wished to have the same rights, to become their equals and unite with them in marriage. Rich and poor joined together in the same attack against the ancient patrician order. They obtained the victory after a struggle lasting two hundred years because they were soldiers, and Rome had need of them for her conquests.

Their first weapon was the military strike. They had recourse to it several times to force the patricians to alter the debtors' laws. Tired of promises which were never kept, the plebeians retired armed to the Mons Sacra to found a new city. The frightened Senate dispatched Menenius Agrippa, who told them the fable of the Members and the Belly and brought them concessions from the patricians.

Those enslaved for debt were granted their freedom, and the plebeians were given for their protection two special magistrates called tribunes because they were elected by the tribes (493 B.C.).

The tribunes were not, strictly speaking, magistrates. They were plebeians, and they had not a religious character. They did not celebrate any sacrifice nor carry any badge of office, but their persons were inviolable, sacrosanct. They had the right of defending plebeians, thanks to the *ius auxilii*, but they had no control over what took place outside their own immediate surroundings. They defended the plebeian interests by the veto, that is to say, the right of opposing any decision of the consuls or the Senate which they considered injurious to the people.

Their first move was to demand an agrarian law, that is to say, the division between rich and poor of the land taken in war, which the patricians had monopolized. Then they demanded written laws to remove the exclusive knowledge of the laws from the patricians, who alone knew the old formula of the ancient religious code.

After ten years' struggle, they obtained the nomination of ten magistrates, *decemviri*, with full powers to draw up laws; this resulted in the code called the Twelve Tables (449 B.C.).

After that, they claimed freedom of marriage between patricians and plebeians, and participation in the consulate. The

Senate gave them the right to marry but abolished the consulate by dividing it into three distinct offices: the military tribune, the censor, and the questor.

After the Gallic invasion (390 B.C.), the consuls were re-established and plebeians began again their struggle to be admitted to the offices. They gained their end in 366 B.C. At the same time, the Senate created two new magistracies reserved for patricians, the *praetor* and the *curule aedile*.

These were in their turn opened to the plebeians, and by 300 B.C. their victory was complete when they had gained religious equality and obtained the right of being elected to the priesthood.

During the struggle for civil, political, and religious equality, the tribunes had organized a new Assembly, *comitia tributa*, which met in the Forum without religious formalities. The voting was by tribes, and the decision was called a *plebiscite*. In the beginning, only laws affecting the plebeians were voted upon, but in the end, their decisions were obligatory even upon the patricians. Then there was in Rome one people instead of two. There were no longer patricians and plebeians, but only rich and poor. They were equal before the law.

This situation created a new nobility. Since all Romans had the right to all honours, the Senate was no longer filled only from the ranks of the patricians but from all retired magistrates, whatever their rank, and they no longer had the religious character of ancient times. The members kept the name of *patres*, but their power and dignity were entirely civil.

CHAPTER XIX

THE RELIGION OF ROME

W ERE one to judge the religious spirit of a nation by the number of that nation's gods, one might truly say of the Romans, as Herodotus said of the Egyptians, that "they were the most religious of men." The Roman Pantheon contained at one time more than 30,000 gods, demi-gods, and genii — so many, indeed, that the sceptic Petronius wrote: "Our country is so thickly populated with gods that it is far easier to meet a god than a man." The early Romans, being an agricultural people, invoked many gods to protect the crops, constantly in danger from many possible disasters. In general, they, like the Greeks, worshipped the sacred fire, their ancestors, and the forces of nature. So, we have again a cult of the domestic hearth and a cult of the gods.

Family religion, the worship of ancestors, was more important in Rome than in other countries. Each house had its cult and its sacred hearth, and the head of the family was high priest. They worshipped the spirits of their ancestors: first in importance, the god *Lars*, the spirit of the founder of the family; then the spirits of other dead ancestors. These were the *Manes* and were benevolent gods when honoured by regular sacrifices but malevolent if neglected. In this case, they were called *Lares*. The Romans used to scatter black beans during the nights of May to propitiate wandering spirits.

In every house, there was a domestic altar, before which burnt a lamp. Around it stood the *penates*, statuettes representing the protective genii of the family. Before every meal, the father sprinkled on this altar a few drops of wine and a few crumbs of food. These offerings were the *libation* and the *premices*. Besides this, for any event in the family, such as birth, death, or coming of age, there was a feast in honour of the Lares.

The State, as one great family, had its Lares — Romulus and Remus — and its sacred hearth, the temple of Vesta; but the cult was celebrated by the official priests (see p. 97).

In addition to the gods common also to the Greeks, the Romans had a number of familiar gods, who presided over the ordinary acts of life, the seasons, the crops, and the livestock. One book of the priests contains the names, sacrifices, and invocations for 160 of these gods.

The early Romans were simple and matter-of-fact men, without much imagination. They worshipped the gods without feeling any need for concrete images of them. Jupiter was for a long time simply represented by a stone and Mars by a sword. The first image of Jupiter was introduced from Etruria by Tarquin, and later the Romans introduced the Greek mythology.

With the Romans, religion was largely a matter of ritual and practice. Sacrifices played an important part and were accompanied by formal prayers. The animals sacrificed were of two kinds: large cattle and smaller beasts. Each god had his own peculiar victim: white animals were sacrificed to the great gods, particularly Jupiter; black animals to the gods of the lower regions; and to the others, animals of colour. Ceres demanded a hog, Liber a goat. First of all, the priest burnt incense on the altar and then sprinkled the people with lustral water. This water was spring water that had been purified either with salt or with a hot iron. The victim had to be without blemish and acceptable to the priests. It was led to the altar with a garland on its brow; on its head was placed a ball of salted dough, and then it was slaughtered either by bleeding or with a blow. After death, the entrails were examined to see if the gods accepted the sacrifice. The fat and the bones were burnt on the altar, the blood poured in libations, and the flesh shared among the priests and the worshippers. These latter had to stand veiled in gala dress by the sacrificing priests, repeating word by word after the priests the necessary prayers. One sacrifice was said to be specially agreeable to the gods, i.e., the *suovetaurile*, a simultaneous sacrifice of a bull, a sheep, and a pig.

The aim of the sacrifices was to please the gods, but it was also necessary to find out the will of the gods. This was a special science, practised by special priests, the augurs, who carried, as a sign of their profession, a staff in the form of a crook. Before battles, public events, or even private undertakings, the augurs were consulted to see if the gods were favourable. The augurs observed signs of three kinds only: (1) the flight and cry of birds; (2) the heavenly bodies; (3) the appetite of the sacred fowls.

Besides the augurs, there were other diviners, the *haruspices*, who undertook to prophesy the future. They observed the heavens and examined the entrails of the sacrifices but were not State priests. They had numerous supporters, as the Romans were superstitious and were constantly on the lookout for good and bad omens.

The priests were united in orders or colleges, of which these are the principal: -

FIG. 71. - The chief Vestal: a statue found in Rome.

The *Pontifexes*, or bridge-builders, in memory of the Sublician bridge, were the most important. They were twelve in number, presided over by the Pontifex Maximus, the head of Roman religion. He nominated the Chief Priest, selected the Vestals, and was in particular the priest of Janus. He had supreme authority over all the priestly caste and was the judge and arbiter of things human and divine.

The *Flamines* (those who light the fire) were the

priests of the great gods. They wore a pointed headdress, ending in a woollen tassel. There were three great flamines: the flamine of Jupiter, who was subject to certain strict rules (for instance, he might not leave Rome, ride a horse, or go out bareheaded), and the flamines of Mars and Quirinus.

The *Fecials* were in charge of the ceremonials relating to the making of war and peace.

The *Lupercales* were the priests of Faunus or Pan. At the feast of the god, they marched in procession around the Palatine, striking the passers-by with straps cut from the skins of the sacrificial beasts.

The *Arvales* celebrated in the month of May a festival similar to Rogation day, in honour of a goddess of the fields, the Divine Dea Dia. They invoked her protection on the crops, singing an ancient hymn that has come down to us but was no longer understood in the Augustan age.

The *Salienes*, instituted by Numa, had the care of the twelve sacred shields, one of which it was said had fallen from heaven. Eleven replicas had been made to prevent its being stolen, for it was said that if it were lost, Rome would lose her greatness.

FIG. 72. - A Graco Roman temple.

The *Vestals* were the priestesses of Vesta and kept alive the sacred fire. There were six of them, chosen by the High Priest from amongst the daughters of the best families. They entered the college of the Vestals between the ages of six and ten, and were compelled to stay for thirty years. They took a double vow: to remain virgins and never to let the sacred fire of Vesta out. They cut their hair short and wore white garments. They were respected everywhere and treated with great honour, but if they broke their vows, they were punished by being buried alive.

The Roman temples were modelled from the Greek, generally rectangular, but in some cases round with a domed roof. Essentially, the temple was a sacred enclosure containing the statue of the god; before the temple stood the altar.

The chief temple in Rome was the temple of Jupiter, built on the Capitol, and containing the statues of Jupiter and Minerva. It was many times destroyed and built up again in increasing luxury, but always on the same plan. Here were celebrated the

FIG. 73. - The temple of Vesta.

great festivals, and here great generals were crowned. The Capitol was to Rome what the Acropolis was to Athens, the centre of religious life, covered with statues and monuments.

The Romans introduced foreign gods and honoured them, so as to bind the conquered races more closely to Rome, and they had their statues in the Pantheon. But this had a marked effect on the old national religion.

First came the Greek gods. Tarquin introduced the Sibylline books, the oracles of the priestess of Cumae. Then followed the cults of Apollo, Bacchus, Castor, and Pollux. Little by little, the Greek gods became Roman gods, and under their influence, the character of the deities changed. Instead of representing vague, abstract ideas, they became merged with the new gods and took more definite form. But the Romans never gave up their old names. Demeter became Ceres; Poseidon, Neptune; Hera, Juno, etc.

After the conquest of the East, more gods appeared in Rome. The worship of Isis and Serapis came from Egypt, the worship of the sun-god Mithra from Phrygia, the worship of Cybele from Asia Minor. This latter was a very popular religion, and on certain days, the priests of Cybele collected money in the street, playing music and dancing sacred dances.

CHAPTER XX

THE ROMAN ARMY

R ome conquered the world by arms, but the Roman army underwent many transformations before it became the excellent instrument of conquest it was under Caesar.

In the beginning, everyone was not a soldier; the poor who were unable to buy arms were excluded from the army. The soldiers were not enrolled or provided with barracks by the State. On the day of assembly, the men called up grouped themselves by *gentes*, that is to say, by families, armed as they liked; the rich fought on horseback.

They even fed themselves, equipped themselves at their own charge, and they did not receive payment. The citizens left their families and their fields for a time; the war over, they returned to work. The wars were of short duration; they were in the neighbourhood of Rome and resembled raids. The army was a citizen army, that is to say, "A nation of small proprietors trained to fight."

Servius' reform, in increasing the number of soldiers, put order into the fitting out of the army. As we have seen, he divided the people into seven classes according to wealth. The lowest class, *proletarii*, continued to be outside the army. The first class, the knights, formed the cavalry. The other classes served as infantry, but each class had its distinctive armour. The second was completely armed — helmet and round shield of bronze (*clipeus*), cuirass, greaves, lance, and sword. The third and fourth had a long wooden shield covered with skin and iron (*scuturi*). The fifth had pikes and arrows without armour, and the sixth had only slings. The order of battle array was the phalanx, as with the Spartans and Macedonians, that is to say, a compact mass, of which the first ranks were composed of the best-armed men. The soldier continued to equip and feed himself.

The army was completely altered by Camillus during the Gallic war. The length of the campaigns did not permit of the soldiers returning to their fields, and they were given pay, which by the time of Caesar amounted to the equivalent of £4 16s. a year. Moreover, the soldiers were no longer divided into classes according to fortune, but in distinctive arms according to their bravery and length of service. Thus, there were the cavalry, where the rich always served, the heavy and the light infantry. The light infantry formed four legions, which replaced the phalanx. Each legion consisted of three lines of soldiers, called *hastati, principes, triarii*. They were divided into thirty companies, called *manipules*. They were still soldier-proprietors, who were called up by tribes at the command of the Senate and consuls.

Marius changed this state of things. He enrolled the poorest class, and moreover, instead of an army of citizen-soldiers returning to civilian life as soon as the expedition ended, Rome had an army of professional soldiers having no other manner of life, no other industry than war. The army was unified, and the cavalry ceased to be the monopoly of the rich. This was the definite organisation of the legion.

So long as the army was composed of citizen-soldiers, the calling up of the soldiers was a civil act analogous to the calling up of voters for an election. The Senate fixed the number. The consuls announced by edict the day the people were to assemble at the Capitol in tribes. There were four tribes, which had to furnish four legions, two for each consul. They drew by lot the first tribe from which men were to be taken. Then they proceeded to call the roll of names. Four by four, the citizens, as they were named, marched before the magistrates; they were examined as they passed and divided into the four legions, whose officers had been nominated in advance. The consuls gave exemptions in certain cases and punished the absent by fines, floggings, imprisonment, and even slavery. The proceedings ended when the numbers of the legions were complete.

The Roman soldier was the Latin peasant in arms. As a rule, he was a short man, bronzed, thick-set, and strong, whom the work in the fields had hardened to fatigue. Only men of proved health were permitted to stay in the army, and the committee of inspection, which followed the calling up, was very strict. Roman soldiers showed remarkable qualities of endurance. Each man carried during the march most of his arms, various tools, an axe, shovel, pickaxe, and a fortnight's provisions. When they arrived at the end of the day's march, the soldiers had to fortify a camp before resting. They also built roads. They carried the shovel and

FIG. 74. - A legionary.

FIG. 75. - A centurion.

pickaxe, as well as the pike and sword. Moreover, they were very sober, indefatigable marchers, and good sappers.

The Roman soldier had faith in his officers, showed tenacity, and was ready for any sacrifice to add to the greatness of his country. Reverses did not discourage him, and his energetic patriotism was always the admiration of his enemies. Moreover, he was bound by a religious oath. On entering the army, he swore to obey his general, to follow wherever he was led, and to remain under the flag until he was freed from his oath. The oath was taken solemnly in front of the consul by officers, tribunes, and centurions. Then it was read to the troops, followed by the reading of the roll, to which each soldier replied, "Idem in me." Rome owed her greatness to the exceptional qualities of her first soldiers.

A Roman army was composed of many legions, and each legion was a little army in itself. It had its heavy and its light infantry, its cavalry, and its artillery. The legion, properly speaking, consisted of the infantry of the line, from 4200 to 6000 men, who were subdivided into ten battalions or cohorts, each consisting of three companies or *manipules* of two centuries. The cavalry was composed of 300 men, divided into ten *turmes* of thirty men.

The light infantry formed the corps of *velites*, the number of whom was not fixed, and who fought between the ranks of the legion. To the legion was added a company of sappers, *fabri*.

In battle, the ten cohorts were ranged in three lines, and arranged in a quincunx like the squares of a draughtboard. Each cohort was separated from its neighbour by a space the size of its front; in this way, the cohorts of the second line were able to fill the gaps in the first.

An army was commanded by the general, *dux*, who had under his command *legates*, the commanders of the legions. Each legion was commanded and managed by six military tribunes. Each century was commanded by a centurion; the non-commissioned officers were called *decurions*. The officers had a double origin: the legates and tribunes were nominated by the consuls or the

Assembly of the People; the centurions were old soldiers risen from the ranks, and never rose to any high rank.

Alongside of the legion served a varying number of auxiliary infantry and cavalry. They were divided into *cohortes* and *turmes*, and commanded by Roman officers called *profecti sociorum*.

The legionaries had for defensive arms the helmet, cuirass, shield, and greaves; for offensive, the javelin and sword.

FIG. 76. - Roman helmets.

In early times, the helmet was of leather, *galea*, but it lost its shape in rain and sunshine, so it was replaced by the bronze helmet, cassis, fitted with a pugaree, a chin-piece, a visor, and instead of a crest, a ring. A cord could be passed through this ring, so that the helmet could be slung on the back during marches. The cuirass, *lorica*, was at first a leather cloak scaled with plates of iron. Later it was composed of jointed pieces of worked steel, some of which covered the chest, others the shoulders like long braces. They were often extended by a skirt of mail to the knees. The shield, *scutum*, was a long, convex *rectangle* made of wood covered with leather and rimmed with iron. In the centre was the boss, umbo, which served to make projectiles slip off. The *pilum*, the national weapon of the Roman infantry, was a javelin seven feet in length, over two pounds

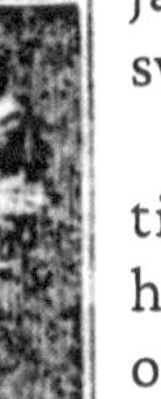
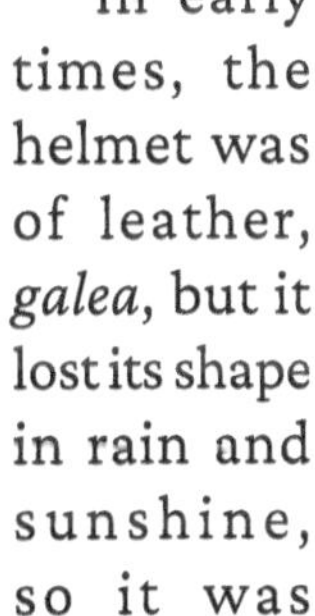

FIG. 77. - The pilum.

in weight, with an average flight of eighty-one to ninety-seven feet, which, with the assistance of a lance and a leather strap, could be extended to over 200 feet. It also served as a lance. The sword, *gladius*, was the short Spanish sword with two blades; the officers carried it on the left in a sword-belt. The soldiers were clothed in tunics, short drawers, and a great cloak of brown cloth called *sagum*. They were shod in *caliga*, a half-boot made with thick, hob-nailed soles and leather thongs which reached above the ankle.

The cavalry wore, beside the helmet, cuirasses of ring-mail, leather greaves, a round shield, *clipeus*, a lance, and a long sword. The horse's harness consisted of a saddle-cloth, a leather saddle fixed by strap, a bridle, but not stirrups.

The light-armed troops had a light cuirass, clipeus, javelins or bows, but not greaves.

The artillery was composed of engines to throw stones and bolts. There were two chief types, the catapult and the ballistra. The ballistra or onager was a scoop fastened to two stands by stretched cords. It was forced back by a sudden discharge which caused a detonation, which threw big stones five or six hundred yards.

The catapult or scorpion had a smaller projection. It was a great

FIG. 78. - Ensigns.

fixed cross-bow, for use in a trench or for bolts or small projectiles, which were thrown by pulling a cord. Certain very powerful machines threw their projectiles more than 800 yards; they were only used in sieges or in the defence of fortified places. There existed lighter engines which were used in battle, and which were placed in front of the legion.

The legion had for its ensign a staff with the figure of an animal at the top, which in the end came always to be an eagle. The cavalry had a red standard called *vexillum*.

The legions went into battle side by side in the order we have indicated. This arrangement had two advantages: it offered a more extended front against the more numerous barbarian armies, and it permitted of an attack in echelon, with some troops always fresh.

The action opened with the manoeuvres of the velites, who, placed as skirmishers before the line of battle, annoyed the enemy with bows and arrows. Then the legion charged; the first ranks threw their javelins at the same moment at the enemy's line in order to break it. After this assault, they took to the sword. When

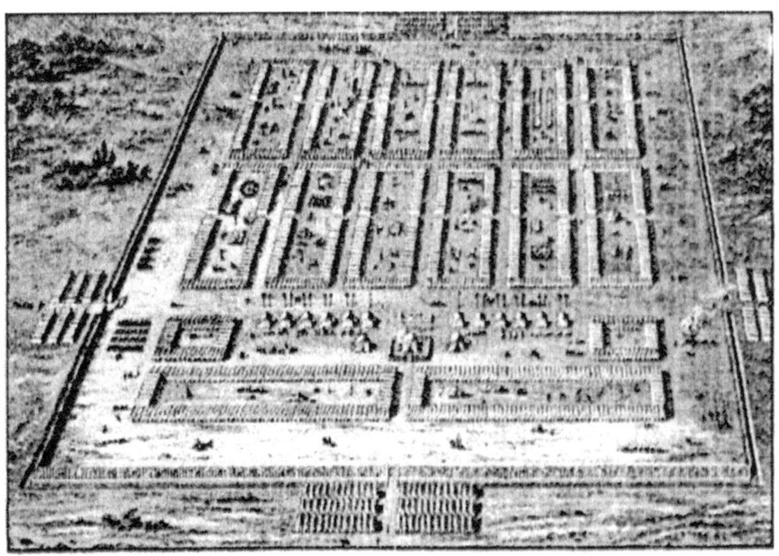

FIG. 79. - A camp for four legions.

the enemy turned their backs, the cavalry and the light-armed troops continued the pursuit.

This kind of fighting required of the soldiers great skill in fencing. So exercises were frequent. They fenced against dummies or posts with weapons twice as heavy as the regulation arms. These fencing exercises took place once a day. Also, the soldiers were trained to manoeuvre by century, manipule, or cohort, for the mobility of these units was one of the great advantages of the legion and the principal reason for success.

Each day an army on the march camped, that is to say, it built a temporary fortress. The camp was a great rectangle cut by two roads which ended in four gates. At the crossing of the two roads were erected an altar for sacred fire, the general's tent or *pretorium*, and the tribunal. A public place, the forum, was arranged at the side. The camp was therefore a miniature city, with its gods, courts of justice, and assemblies.

The rest of the rectangle was filled by lines of tents made of skin, each of which contained ten men. Each company had its own fixed place. A trench was dug outside the camp, with a pointed bottom, an average width of four yards, and a depth of three and a third yards. The earth thrown up from the inside of the trench served to raise a parapet more than a yard in width,

FIG. 80. - A circumvallation.

which was crowned by a parapet of stakes of equal height. If the camp became permanent, these works were carried out in stone. The protection of the camp was assured by relays of cavalry, and by sentinels who occupied posts placed near the gates outside the entrenchment.

Thanks to the division of work, the building of a camp was as rapid as it was useful. The camp was a shelter from surprises, a retreat in case of failure, a depot for convoys and baggage. (This was very important, for the Roman soldier had to unload himself before fighting.)

The Romans excelled in siege-craft. In every siege there were three movements: investment, the work of approach, and assault. The investment consisted of surrounding the besieged place with a *circumvallation*, that is to say, trenches and palisades studded with forts to drive back any assault from the city, as well as attack from outside. The preliminary works were numerous. They built rows of little fortified huts or *manteletes*, which were perpendicular to the wall, to allow of cutting the foundations after filling the trench. Then they erected round towers higher than the ramparts, which they could sweep with the assistance of machines. Parallel to the wall, they built a high mound, *agger*, also furnished with machines.

They then endeavoured to make a breach by means of battering-rams, heavy beams furnished with iron, which they worked from the inside of armoured sheds, called *testudos*. Sometimes they tried to mine the ramparts, or to enter underneath by means of an underground passage.

The breach ready, they made the assault by means of the *testudo*. This was a method in which the men in the first rank locked their shields together, whilst the others held them horizontally above their heads. The attacking column looked like a tortoise in its shell.

The strength of the army did not lie only in its armament and tactics; it lay also in its discipline.

The generals imposed long marches, hard work, and many

privations on the soldiers when their obedience flagged. The discipline was very severe. Any failure to obey orders was punished by death; the condemned man was executed by the lictors, who beat him with rods and then cut off his head. Thus perished, in spite of his father's defence of him, the son of the consul Manlius for fighting a single combat against a Gaul. Lighter faults were punished with the bastinado, and the centurions always commanded with a stick made from a vine plant.

In grave cases, the legion was decimated. A name in every ten or twenty was called out, and the men thus called were struck down with the axe. Such was the lot of the two legions of Fabius Rullus, which fled before the enemy. Even the Senate refused to redeem 8000 prisoners taken by the Carthaginians.

Rewards were numerous; they consisted of special armour, decorations, and crowns, sometimes gifts of money.

The conquering general received the title of *Imperator*. Then the Senate granted him the right of celebrating a *triumph*. This was the name given to the solemn sacrifice which the general offered on the Capitol in the presence of his whole army. He entered Rome in a chariot drawn by four horses, seated on an ivory chair, his face painted red like the old statues of the gods, and his head crowned with laurels. In front of the triumphal car marched the captives and cars containing booty taken from the enemy.

The procession was sometimes very long. The triumph of P. Amilius, the conqueror of Macedonia, lasted three days. The general was escorted by his soldiers, who sang pæans of victory and carried branches of laurel. They did not spare coarse jokes to remind the triumphant general that he was still a man. The conquered chiefs were carried away to the Marmertine prison and strangled in their dungeon.

Besides the triumph, there was a lesser reward, the *ovation*, when the conqueror made his entry on horseback.

After victories, pillage was carried on methodically. The booty was held in common, and sold for the good of the State, which deducted the greater part. Thus the public treasury was enriched by war, which became a profitable undertaking. The conquest of Macedonia alone brought in a hundred and twenty million sesterces. The citizens were able therefore to live free from taxes; they had an interest in the conquests, no less than the soldiers, and it has been justly said of Rome that "she conquered the world not for glory, but for profit."

The Romans completely occupied the lands they conquered; that was why they kept them. Their establishment was assured by two original inventions: the military colonies, and the roads.

All the conquered countries were guarded by colonies, which were neither colonies for an overflow population nor for trade. They were permanent camps, a little portion of the army stationed in a strange land, and called *sentinelles*. A strategic position was chosen, the crossing of routes, the ford of a river, the meeting-place of two rivers. They began by building a fortified enclosure; there they installed themselves with their families, for they were veterans who had been given portions of land. They remained Roman citizens and had an internal organisation resembling that of Rome. Gradually these fortified posts absorbed the neighbouring peoples and maintained them in obedience. In case of invasion, as in the time of Pyrrhus or Hannibal, they stopped the invader and dissipated his efforts. The enemy chased away, the Roman dominions remained intact.

To reach the colonies, the Romans constructed roads. This was an innovation in the ancient world, for the Greeks had only had tracks. The Roman road, on which the legions and their war machines could easily move, had the same importance as modern railways in conquered countries. They prevented risings, and enabled troops to move quickly to dangerous points. The solidity of their roads has become proverbial. The sub-soil was built up, and the surface was paved with great unequal flagstones laid out in mosaics. The first and most celebrated was the Via Appia, which was built from Rome to Capua in 312 B.C. Nothing shows better the methodical mind of the Romans.

CHAPTER XXI

THE ROMAN CONQUESTS

THE Romans conquered the whole of the Mediterranean basin, following a course laid out for them by their geographical position.

Rome is at the center of Italy, and Italy commands the whole of the Mediterranean, for it divides it nearly equally into two basins. There resulted three periods of war which gave the Romans the empire of the ancient world.

They were in order: -

(1) The conquest of Italy.

(2) The conquest of the western Mediterranean basin.

(3) The conquest of the eastern Mediterranean basin.

From the foundation of Rome until the year 266 B.C., the history of Rome presents a double interest. At home, there were the struggles between the patricians and plebeians, abroad, the conquest of Italy from the Apennines to Sicily. This double series of events occurred side by side during five centuries, and it was in the course of these wars that the plebeians, the principal part of the army, obtained equal rights with the patricians.

Rome's first wars were sudden movements and raids which the kings led against their neighbors to increase their territory. Tullius Hostilius wrested from the Albains their political and religious supremacy over Latium. Ancus Martius extended Roman lands as far as the mouth of the Tiber, where he founded Ostia. Servius Tullius enlarged the city and enclosed the seven hills within one wall. At the time of the fall of the kings, Rome was at the head of the Latin Confederation, which included thirty cities.

The Etruscans hoped to profit by the troubles which followed the downfall of the kings and to conquer this powerful rival. They invaded the Roman lands, and one of their chiefs, Porsenna, took the city. The Romans submitted to the hard conditions imposed on them — of not allowing them iron tools, as the Philistines treated the Jews. The Latin Confederation was dissolved, but the Greek colonies, disturbed at the near approach of the Etruscans, united against them and delivered Rome at the battle of Arica (506 B.C.).

The Romans invented legends of heroic combats to hide their defeats: Horatius Cocles, who alone stopped the enemy army at the head of the Pons Sublicius, while they cut down the bridge behind him; another hero, Mucius Scaevola, who had sworn to kill Porsenna, entered his camp, but, deceived by his clothes, killed the secretary instead of the king. Then Porsenna, frightened by this energy, concluded peace. A young girl, Cloelia, retained as a hostage by the Etruscans, escaped from the enemy's camp, and Porsenna, struck with admiration, gave all the child prisoners their freedom.

Rome, once delivered, made war against all her neighbors, the Latins, Volscians, Aquians, and Etruscans. It was at this time that the incident of the Fabian gens took place. They perished to the number of 306 patricians and 3000 clients in an ambuscade led by the citizens of Veii.

The Aquian War shows us in the dictator Cincinnatus the kind of man who was then a Roman leader. After having defeated the enemy and ended the war in a fortnight, Cincinnatus returned modestly to his fields and his plough (458 B.C.).

The campaign against Veii was the hardest. It was ended by the taking of Veii after a siege of ten years directed by the dictator Camillus (395 B.C.). It was on this occasion that payment was instituted. This was important, for it made it possible to retain citizens in the army and to undertake longer wars.

Roman success was interrupted by the incursion of the Gauls, which caused her fall. Having become overpopulated in the valley of the Po, they had overflowed into Etruria. The Etruscans appealed to the Romans; then the irritated Gauls marched on Rome to revenge themselves for this intervention. It was not an invasion, but a genuine military expedition, for the Gauls did not drag behind them their baggage-wagons and families, as did the later barbarian invaders. They cut the Roman army to pieces near the river Allia, July 18, 390 B.C., a date always to be considered unlucky by the Romans, who feared this brave and adventurous people. The city of Rome was taken without a blow, and the senators remaining in their houses were massacred. The soldiers took refuge in the citadel of the Capitol, where they sustained a siege of seven months.

The Gauls climbed up during the night, but the Roman leader, Manlius, was awakened by the sacred geese in the temple of Juno; he ran to the ramparts with his men and beat back his assailants head over heels. The Romans were, nonetheless, reduced to capitulation. They had to pay a thousand pounds of gold, and to promise to keep a city gate open. The Gallic chief was again able to humiliate them by throwing his sword into the balance and crying, "Woe to the conquered."

Rome, delivered from the Gauls and recovered from her reverses, again undertook the conquest of Italy. She first conquered central Italy, where her principal enemies were the Samnites (343-280 B.C.). Then she conquered southern Italy, and triumphed over King Pyrrhus (280-274 B.C.).

The Samnites, mountaineers of Abruzzia, did not form a true people. They were a little tribe of brave and half-savage warriors who often descended from their mountains to pillage the towns of Campania and Magna Graecia. Because of their disunion, their courage did not prevent them from being conquered by the Romans. But there were three wars in succession, and the Romans suffered more than one check.

The most important was in the course of the second war, about 328 B.C.. A Roman army was surprised in the Candium valley and forced to surrender. The Romans were made to pass under the yoke, that is to say, under a pole supported between two lances, which was a sign of slavery.

The Samnites united for the third war with the Latins, Etruscans, and Gauls, who were jealous or discontented with Rome. It was a general rising of Italy (311 B.C.). But the allies attacked separately; they were conquered one after another, and the Samnites were crushed at Aquilonia and were obliged to become the allies of Rome. It was during these wars that the devotion of Decius was shown. To assure the victory of his hesitating troops, the Roman general vowed the enemy to the gods of the lower regions and threw himself into the midst of their army that he might be the expiatory victim.

The cities of Magna Graecia, rich from commerce and industry, accepted the supremacy of Rome; only Tarentum, proud of her riches and her fleet, dared to resist the Romans. A Roman fleet was insulted in time of peace in its port, and the Senate declared war. As the Tarentines had no soldiers, they called Pyrrhus, King of Epirus, to their assistance.

Pyrrhus claimed to be descended from Achilles, and was related to Alexander. His kingdom was the modern country of the Albanians, who have always been, and are still, a fierce people devoted to war and pillage. He himself was a robber prince, the head of an army ready to sell itself to the highest bidder. He possessed a good army. The Tarentines believed they had found a docile servant, but he became their master (294 B.C.).

He landed in Italy with 25,000 men and twenty elephants. Thanks to these animals, which the Romans did not know how to fight, he won at Heraclea and Asculum. The Romans defended themselves valiantly, and the name of "Pyrrhic victories" has remained for combats in which the conquerors suffer more than the conquered. Frightened, Pyrrhus sent an ambassador to Rome, but the Senate refused to treat with him as long as he camped in Italy. Pyrrhus crossed over to Sicily and conquered it. When he returned to Italy, the Romans knew how to fight elephants. He was defeated at Beneventum, and returned to Epirus (275 B.C.). He died obscurely while besieging Argos, killed by a tile which an old woman threw from the top of a roof. Tarentum then submitted, and with her fell the last resistance in Italy.

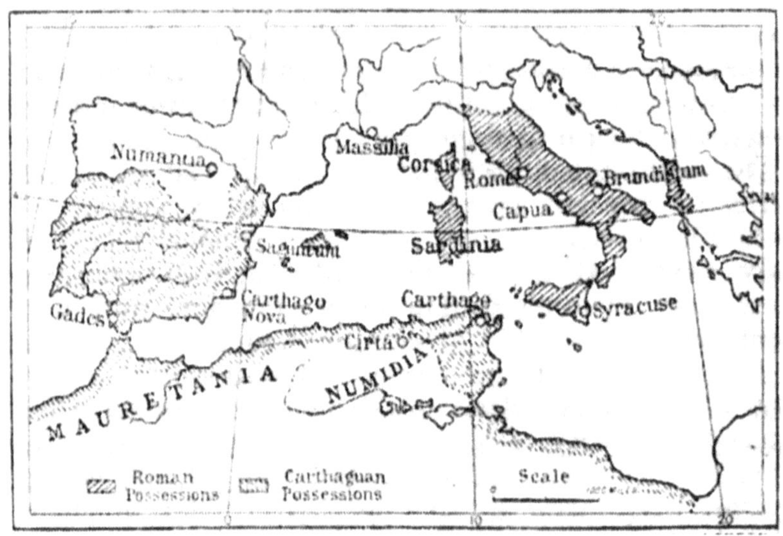

FIG. 81. - Rome and Carthage.

Rome had become the greatest power in Italy, but she was faced by a still greater power, the Carthaginian Empire, which was an obstacle to her growth. The two states engaged in a long series of wars which gave to victorious Rome the possession of the western Mediterranean. These wars divide themselves into three periods and are called the Punic Wars, because the Latin name of the Carthaginians was Poni (264-146 B.C.).

We have already seen how Carthage, a colony of Tyre, was founded on the northern coast of Africa, and developed until it became the mistress of the seas. It occupied an admirable situation, commanding the narrow passage which separated the two basins of the Mediterranean. The Carthaginians retained their Phoenician customs and the cruel worship of Baal-Moloch, represented by a colossal figure of bronze, the interior of which was a furnace. There they burnt alive in days of distress children offered in sacrifice.

They were like the Tyrians, a trading, industrial, and maritime people. Their caravans penetrated as far as the centre of Africa, crossing the Sahara. They covered the north of Africa, Sicily, and Spain with their trading-stations. By means of the Straits of

Gibraltar, they travelled as far as Britain to the north, and Senegal to the south. They disputed the trade of the Mediterranean with the Greeks, and their wealth was immense.

But if they had the force of money, they had neither moral nor military force. They were governed by an oligarchy of rich merchants, jealous of preserving fortune and power for their families. The citizens did not take part in public life. They had no national sentiment; they had no national army — their soldiers were mercenaries, Spaniards, Gauls, or Numidians who only knew their general. Their demands were a peril to the Carthaginians; also, they were on their guard against these soldiers, who had to be paid before they would obey, and against their leaders, who had to be prevented from becoming powerful. The interests of individuals were put before those of the State, and everywhere there was jealousy, disunion, and weakness.

Rome, on the other hand, was strong in its unity. The internal struggle over, all Romans, equal in rights, formed one people, having law for their master, and devotion to country for an ideal. The Senate, the guardian of the laws, made the plans, and the army which carried them out was composed of citizens ready to die for the greatness of Rome.

It did not seem as if two peoples so different from one another ought to have been rivals. Rome was a European and continental power; Carthage, a maritime and African power. Rome had no fleet, Carthage no army. It would seem that they ought to have been good neighbours, and this was the case at first: there were between the two cities amicable relations, and a commercial treaty; Rome even received help from Carthage against Pyrrhus. But when Rome possessed Magna Gracia, she saw near her, as a good prey to be seized, rich and fertile Sicily. She wished to own it; the Carthaginians, who possessed numerous trading-stations there, opposed her. Pyrrhus foresaw the conflict, and when departing from Sicily, he cried, "What a fine field of battle we leave to the Carthaginians and Romans!"

The occasion of war was a quarrel between Syracuse and

the Mamertines of Messina. The last-named sought the help of Rome, so Carthage aided Syracuse. The Romans then undertook to drive the Carthaginians from Sicily; but they had no fleet to defeat them at sea, so the story goes that they built in two months 300 ships from a Carthaginian model. They manned them with crews exercised on dry land, and furnished them with grapnels, called corons, and swinging bridges to facilitate boarding. With this fleet, the consul Duilius defeated the Punic fleet near Mylee (260 B.C.).

Encouraged by success, the Romans threw an army into Africa, which besieged Carthage. But it was enfeebled by the recall of part of the troops, and Xantippus, a Spartan chief in the service of Carthage, defeated the consul Regulus, who was taken and tortured (255 B.C.).

The war continued in Sicily, where Hamilcar Barca held the country, receiving help from the sea. The naval victory of the Agates Insulae forced the Carthaginians to surrender (241 B.C.).

The rivals were both exhausted by war. Carthage, fearing the ruin of her trade, demanded peace. She gave up Sicily, which became a Roman province, and undertook to pay 3200 talents in twenty years. This peace was in reality a twenty-two years' truce, during which the two enemy powers did not cease to extend, although each ran a great danger — Rome from the Gauls, Carthage from her mercenary troops.

Rome profited by the Carthaginian difficulties, and took in time of peace, in spite of the treaty, Corsica and Sardinia. She sent a fleet into the Adriatic and subdued its shores. Then she was attacked by a coalition of Cisalpine Gauls. The panic in Rome was immense; the *Tumultus*, that is to say, the levy at the same time of all able-bodied men, was proclaimed. Superiority of arms assured the Romans the victory over the Gauls at the battle of Telamon, for they only had bad sabres (225 B.C.). The Romans, following up their successes, crossed the Po, took Milan, and annexed Cisalpine Gaul (222 B.C.).

At Carthage, the mercenaries, who had remained for a long

time unpaid, demanded their wages, and as the money was not forthcoming, they revolted. This was an atrocious war, which lasted three years. Thanks to Hamilcar's ability, the greater number of the mercenaries, hemmed in the valley of the Axe, perished of famine. The others were massacred in Tunis, which they had fortified. Forty thousand perished, and this revolt was called the Truceless War (241-237 B.C.).

The General Hamilcar, the saviour of Carthage, soon became an object of suspicion to the aristocracy. He was the head of a new party, who wished Carthage to have, like Rome, a democratic government and a national army to resist the threats of Rome. The aristocracy feared war, which disturbed their trade. They rid themselves of Hamilcar by sending him to command an expedition in Spain.

Hamilcar conquered Spain as far as the Ebro, and founded a Carthaginian kingdom of which he was the head; he called his capital New Carthage, and had a well-exercised, well-disciplined army with which he could do what he liked. After his death, his son Hannibal inherited his command and his army at the age of twenty-seven (220 B.C.).

At the head of this army, Hannibal showed himself to be the most terrible adversary Rome had ever known. He had at heart an oath of hatred against the Romans, and the ambition to regenerate Carthage.

The Romans themselves regarded him as an extraordinary man. The historian Livy said of him, "He was the leader in whom the soldiers had most confidence. He had great boldness in attack, prudence in peril. No amount of work tired his body or his mind. He could endure equally heat and cold. He was temperate, and only gave to sleep the time he could spare from business. He had no need of a soft bed for rest; for he was seen many times to wrap himself in a soldier's cloak and go to sleep on the ground among the sentinels or outposts. His clothes were no different from those of his companions; only his armour and his horses distinguished him. He was much the first among foot-soldiers and among knights. He was the first to march into battle, the last to retreat. This remarkable soldier was endowed with marvellous intelligence. He was successful because before he acted he could anticipate events and make preparations."

Hannibal endeavoured to provoke a quarrel between Rome and Carthage by attacking the town of Saguntum, which was under Roman protection. A Roman ambassador left for Carthage and demanded a reparation, giving the choice between peace and war. "Choose yourselves," replied the Carthaginians. The Romans chose war. Hannibal, pleased at this opportunity of satiating his hate, wished to knock the power of Rome on the head, and concocted the difficult plan of attacking Italy by land and raising against Rome all the peoples still shuddering at their recent defeats. To carry out this plan, he had to cross the Ebro, the Pyrenees, the Rhone, and the Alps, and this was only possible for an army certain of its leader and a leader certain of his army. But Hannibal commanded an excellent army of veterans, broken to war and hardened to endurance and absolute fidelity. They were agile Iberian foot-soldiers, Numidian cavalry, whose horses charged without bridles, and Balearic slingers. Hannibal, preferring quality to quantity, led only 5,000 men determined to conquer or die with him. There was bound to be a war to the death between him and the Romans. This was the war. He went by land because he did not wish to expose his army to the caprices of the sea and risk his fortunes in a naval battle; also, because he did not ask of Carthage the co-operation of its fleets, he escaped from all control.

The journey through Gaul was undertaken easily, and the Rhone crossed on rafts. In order to cross the Alps, Hannibal entered the valley of the Isère. The passage took a fortnight; the principal crest was crossed at the Clapier hill, to the south of Mont Cénis. The march was very trying on account of the cold and the snow. He had to cross fields of ice, to cut in the rock a road for his elephants and convoys. Hannibal lost the greater part of his army (218 B.C.).

To reinforce it, he counted on the Gauls of Cisalpine Gaul, but, protected by the Romans, they would not stir.

Hannibal, however, broke up the legions of the consul Scipio, which tried to bar his road, first on the Ticinus, then on the Trebia. After that, the Gauls were his. He wintered in Cisalpine Gaul; then, during the spring, he crossed the Apennines and passed into Etruria with a reinforced army. At this season, the snows melted and the country was in flood; some of his troops perished in the marshes. With the remainder, he surprised the consul Flaminius near the Trasimene lake and killed 30,000 men (217 B.C.).

Hannibal did not march on Rome, because he had no siege engines. He conquered Apulia, and he sought to raise the Latins. The Romans, during this time, refused to give battle and raised new armies. Fabius, called the Lingerer (*cunctator*), schemed to worry Hannibal without ever attacking him in a pitched battle, and thus to exhaust him. But many did not understand his tactics and demanded a battle; to please them, the consul Varro gave battle at Cannae (216 B.C.).

Cannae was a plain well known to Hannibal. He arranged his troops in such a way that the wind, the dust, and the sunshine hit the Romans in the face. He placed his best troops in the wings, forming the horns of a crescent. He let the centre be driven in, which permitted an enveloping manœuvre in which 50,000 men surrounded 80,000. Towards the end of the action, the Numidian and Spanish cavalry charged the Roman cavalry. The latter did not know how to fight at a gallop; they dismounted and were cut to pieces. As Hannibal's cavalry attacked the remains of the Roman army again and again, the battle became merely a massacre, in which 70,000 legionaries were killed.

Rome prepared herself to meet an attack; Maharbal, the commander of the cavalry, begged Hannibal to advance. "Let me go," he said, "with my knights, and in three days you shall sup in the Capitol." But Hannibal did not think his army was strong enough to take a city so powerful and so resolute. He penetrated into the south.

In these battles, the Romans fought with discipline and courage worthy of their reputation, but they were defeated by trained troops, better arms, and better commanders. They were not prepared for the strategy of a great army. The legions, formed from recruits levied in haste, were heavy infantry who only knew how to fight in line and at close quarters. They lacked lightly-armed troops to attack at a distance and to protect them from the enemy's cavalry. Their lack of mobility aggravated the fact that the Roman cavalry was less numerous and did not yet know how to scout or charge. Then the leaders were not great generals. They were content, except Fabius, to follow or await the enemy without having any well-thought-out plan of action. They were consuls who commanded for one year, often without any preparation, and who did not even know their soldiers.

Hannibal, on the contrary, commanded tried soldiers who had been for a long time used to military tactics. His army contained a number of archers and slingers, by whom he decimated the legions from a distance. It consisted largely of Spanish and Numidian horse-soldiers, who always marched in front of the army, covering them like a cloak, reporting to their commander all the movements of the enemy, always hiding their own.

The morning after the battle, they pursued the conquered enemy; they did not leave them time to refresh themselves, and brought in prisoners by thousands. Hannibal was able to assume that the Romans were a blind enemy, but no one was more far-sighted than he. He knew every detail of the resources of the country through which he marched, the composition of the Roman forces, the lie of the land. He could always choose a field of battle, and ensure the execution of his plans of attack.

His favourite manœuvre was the turning movement, fatal to an immobile enemy. Then he attended carefully to the well-being of his soldiers, their food and their encampment. In a word, he had to the highest degree the qualities of a great soldier: science, far-sightedness, and decision.

Rome recovered because of her remarkable persistence. She

armed all her able-bodied men, and even slaves. Hannibal, the winner in the open field, was not able to seize the colonies; their garrisons were intact. Thanks to them, the Roman generals, taught by the war and returning to Fabius's tactics, enclosed the enemy in a true iron circle.

During this time, Hannibal, exhausted by his success, retired to Capua looking for help. The Latins, upheld by Rome, refused to rise against her; Carthage, jealous of his success, refused him reinforcements. He then applied to his brother Hasdrubal, who had remained in Spain; he allied himself with Philip of Macedon and with Syracuse. But Rome sent armies to Spain and Illyria, and took Syracuse after a famous siege, in which the learned Archimedes perished. Hannibal, in vain, redoubled his activity; his enfeebled army could not prevent the Romans from taking Capua. Hasdrubal out-manoeuvred the Romans, and hastened into Gaul with an army of Spaniards and Gauls; but he was stopped and killed on the banks of the Metaurus (207 B.C.). Then Hannibal shut himself up in the mountainous Calabrian region. The Romans, not daring to force him to battle, crossed into Africa. The expedition was commanded by the young Scipio, son of the commander defeated on the Trebia, who had been sent to conquer Spain. He won over the Numidians to his side and attacked Carthage, which, alarmed, recalled Hannibal. He left Italy, putting to death all those soldiers who refused to follow him. For fifteen years, he had held the Romans in check without having been conquered, and only his isolation had saved Rome from ruin.

Scipio and Hannibal measured swords at Zama (202 B.C.). But now Hannibal no longer had his veterans from Spain, and Scipio, allied with the Numidians, was superior in cavalry. The conquered Carthaginians had to make peace. They undertook to deliver their arms, elephants, and warships, not to make war without permission, and to pay 10,000 talents in fifty years. Carthage was no longer a great commercial city, and to keep her in this state, the Romans proclaimed the independence of the

Numidian king Massinissa, its ancient subject. Hannibal from the first advised the acceptance of these hard conditions. "Offer sacrifices to the gods," he said, "and pray them that the whole Roman people ratify the treaty that has been proposed to you."

The Romans still cherished a rabid hatred against their old enemy. Fearing their intrigues, Hannibal fled into Syria, near King Antiochus, whom he pushed into war against Rome. Antiochus defeated, Hannibal fled to Bithynia, but the Romans followed him there, and he poisoned himself in order not to fall alive into their hands (183 B.C.).

Fifty years after Zama, Carthage recovered her prosperity sufficiently to alarm Rome. Cato, the censor, who went to survey Africa, showed one day in the Senate some fresh figs and said: "The land which produced these figs is only three days from Rome," and he added, "I am of the opinion that Carthage must be destroyed." "*Delenda est Carthago.*" This was always the conclusion of all his speeches.

The occasion was scarcely delayed, and the Romans seized it with singular bad faith. To repress the brigandage of the Numidian king Massinissa, Carthage had been obliged to levy an army. Rome pretended that this was a violation of the treaty of 201 B.C., and sent an army to Africa. The Carthaginians offered reparation. The Romans demanded their arms, their war engines, and their ships. When they had delivered them, they were given the order to retire ten miles inland. This was in order to ruin their trade.

The entire city rose indignant at this perfidy. They demolished houses to pluck out the beams and constructed ships and war engines. The women gave their long hair to make cord. The patriotic spirit was such that for two years, the Romans were not able to force the walls. The blockade became more stringent under the direction of Scipio Aemilianus. He surrounded the city with a trench and closed the port with a mole. The famished Carthaginians made a passage by scaling the rock which sheltered the port. They were driven back, but they held out in spite of famine. At last, the Romans succeeded in gaining possession of the quays and penetrated into the city; this was a terrible assault, which lasted six days and nights. The defenders, taking refuge in the steep lanes which led up to the citadel of Byrsa, disputed after ground inch by inch. The corpses were so numerous that the besiegers were obliged to clear them away with a fork before advancing. Pressed on all sides, the 30,000 men shut up in the citadel with their leader Hasdrubal surrendered. But Hasdrubal's wife and 1,000 refugees retreated to the temple of Eshmun, which they set on fire, and threw themselves in the flames.

Carthage was rased to the ground, the site was declared accursed, and the territory turned into a Roman province.

On the strength of the Punic Wars, Rome seized Southern Gaul and Spain, from which Hannibal had drawn his forces. She made these conquests to crush the allies of Carthage and assure her own dominion.

First, the Romans conquered definitely the Cisalpine Gauls. Then, making the excuse of coming to help the Greeks of Massilia, they passed into Gaul, reduced the country between the Durance and the Rhone, and created a province. These conquests assured the route to Spain.

The struggle in Spain took nearly a century. It began in 218 B.C.. To cut Hannibal's communications, the Romans landed an army in Spain, which was destroyed. Scipio, the future Africanus, was then charged with the command, in spite of his youth. He defeated Hasdrubal and took New Carthage and Cadiz. By 206 B.C., the country was completely subdued. The Romans, who came as liberators, showed themselves to be hard masters; then the Spaniards wished to regain their independence. They rose and began against the Romans a long guerilla war. This insurrection had its hero, Viriathus, whose exploits were the terror of the Senate, who had him assassinated. All their courage broke up before the disciplined Roman army, and the taking of Numantia, the last citadel of the insurgents, brought about the submission of these fierce mountaineers.

Rome had fought Carthage for her very existence. After Zama, she made war for ambition and profit. The kingdoms of the East, the remains of Alexander's empire, softened by luxury and enfeebled by division, tempted her activity. This activity was exercised less by arms than by diplomacy, for the Roman forces were otherwise occupied. She intervened in the quarrels of these peoples, practising the policy of dividing in order to rule. She only made war when forced by circumstances or when there was an attempt to drive her from territory where she had taken root. Her conquest of the East was a commercial undertaking which she carried out methodically with the least possible expense.

The most formidable kingdom was Macedonia, whose king Philip, the ally of Hannibal, dreamed of renewing Alexander's empire. Rome hastened to declare herself the protector of Greece and Egypt. This resulted in a war in which Philip was beaten at Cynoscephala by the consul Flaminius (197 B.C.). The legion triumphed over the phalanx, Greece was declared free, and Macedonia submitted to a Roman protectorate. She wished to regain her independence under her new king, Perseus, but he was defeated at Pydna by Paulus Aemilius (168 B.C.), whose triumph, in which Perseus figured, was the most magnificent that had yet been seen.

Rome had freed Greece in order to rule her. The country was divided into political leagues, the Achaean League and the Aetolian League, which made relentless war on one another. It was a struggle of rich against poor, nobles against the people. A third party was formed, whose leader was Philopoemen, who wished for the independence of his country. Then Rome intervened and, supporting the aristocratic party, inaugurated a reign of terror. More than 150,000 persons were massacred. The democrats, fighting to the last, rose and were wiped out. Rome made some terrible examples. Corinth was destroyed like Carthage, and Greece was reduced to the position of a Roman province (146 B.C.).

During this time, Antiochus, the king of Syria, whose lands were in Asia Minor and on the Indus, had given asylum to Hannibal, and on his advice had come and attacked the Romans in Greece. He was defeated at Thermopylae, and crossed into Asia, where the Romans followed him. His army was annihilated by Scipio Africanus at Magnesia, near Mount Sipylus (190 B.C.). He had to submit to the protectorate of Rome, and the Asiatic coasts were divided among the allies of Rome.

Henceforward there was no longer a power in the ancient world which could hold up its head against Rome. She possessed the three Mediterranean peninsulas and had taken root in Africa and Asia; she was able to call the Mediterranean *"Mare Nostrum."*

CHAPTER XXII

THE PRIVATE LIFE OF ROME

ROMAN life until the first century remained the life of peasants, of surprising simplicity. We have evidence in stories which show us a dictator, Cincinnatus, working in his own fields, and a consul, Curius Dentatus, having wooden plates and dishes.

The Romans, even after they had become masters of the world, continued to live in the manner of their ancestors. They were farmers, soldiers, and politicians; they were neither merchants nor artists; they left both trade and the arts to foreigners and slaves. Most of them, even the rich, lived, like Cato, in the country in the midst of their slaves; they only came into the city for the elections and for lawsuits. They only thought of enriching themselves, and not of enjoying life. They managed affairs of State with as much regard for gain as their own affairs, and this activity kept them from luxury and corruption. They kept the tradition of old customs, a modest house, a united family, and a great regard for their dignity. When Rome became rich and powerful, she soon lost these old virtues; that is the time at which to study the private and public life of her citizens.

We saw that the square enclosure traced by Romulus round the Palatine had been replaced under Servius by a greater enclosure which shut in the seven hills. On the sides of the hills clustered irregularly built houses without order or plan, according to the needs or caprice of individuals. They were of two kinds: the house of the rich, domus, inhabited by a single family, and the house of three and four storeys, inhabited by numerous tenants. The storeys were constructed so that they projected towards one another in such a manner that the roofs of opposite houses nearly touched.

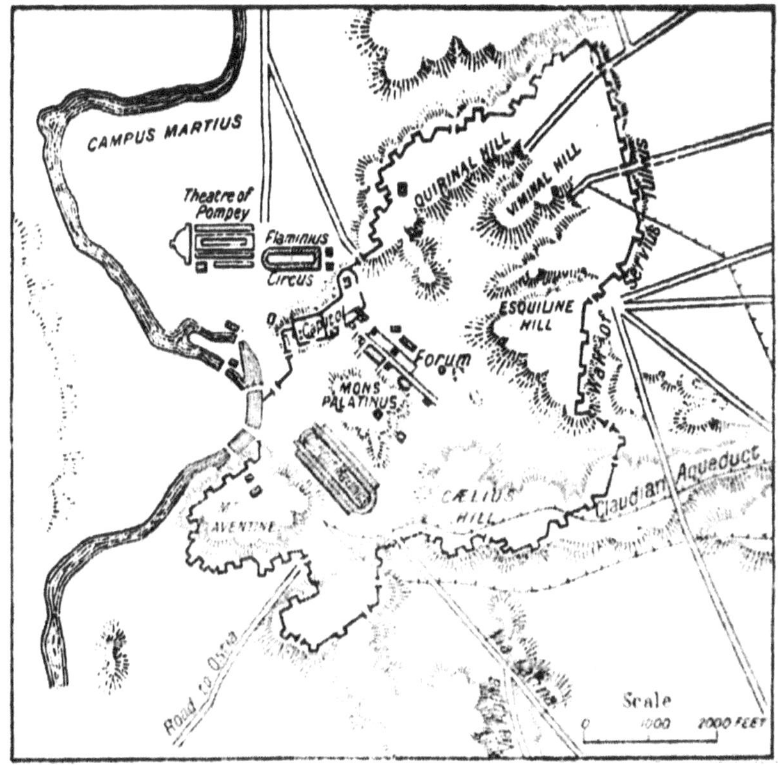

FIG. 82. - A plan of Rome.

The roads were alleys, twisting and dark, inaccessible for carriages. They were not lighted at night, and the body of *vigiles*, who were half policemen, half firemen, had great difficulty in preventing nocturnal robberies and fires.

The Romans lived very little in their houses; they preferred to crowd together in public places. These were the *Forum*, where were held the meetings of the Senate, the law courts, and the comitia; the *Capitol*, the religious centre of the city; the *Campus Martius*, situated outside the walls, the place for military reviews. On various raised places, monuments were erected which were the pride of Rome, for the Romans, like the Greeks, neglected private, and gave all their care to public architecture.

One peculiarity of this city was the care the administration

FIG. 83. - Early Latin hut, as it would have appeared.

took to secure a water supply. Numerous aqueducts brought water to the city from sources as far away as forty-five miles. A network of sewers rendered the different quarters healthy. Sewers were entirely a Roman invention.

The first Latins inhabited huts without windows, made of wattles and mud; the roof was pierced in the middle by a square opening. First, the Etruscans, then the Romans, built this hut in stone and called it *atrium*. This was a great square apartment without any other opening than the door; in the centre was a little basin, *impluvium*, which corresponded to the square opening in the roof through which came the daylight, but through which also fell the rain. In this apartment was the altar of the Lares, the hearth for cooking, the parents' bed raised on a platform. There they lived during the day, ate, and slept at night, the children and the slaves making their beds in the corners.

Little by little, the atrium was flanked by little rooms, *alæ*, and lengthened by an open room, *tablinum*, which was the workroom of the head of the family. A later innovation was due to Greek influence: the *peristylium* of the Greek house was added to the Roman, that is to say, an

FIG. 84. - An Etruscan house.

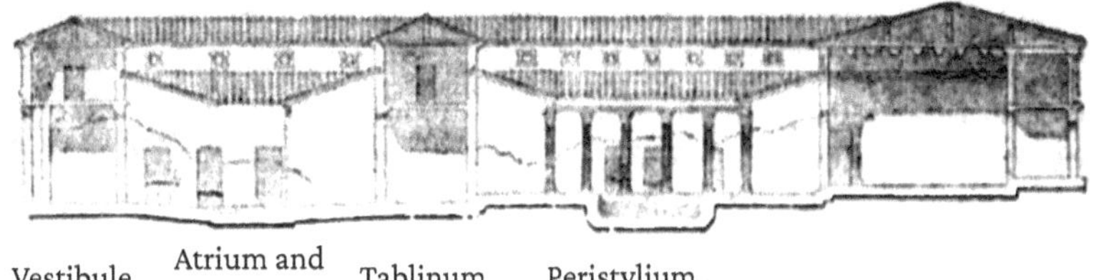

FIG. 85. - Section of a Roman house.

apartment which consisted of a colonnade opening onto a garden, and thus were constructed the houses such as have been found among the ruins of Pompeii. In this house, one entered by a wooden door, which opened inwards and gave admittance to a vestibule leading to the atrium. Behind the atrium came the tablinum, which was connected by lobbies with the private apartments set round about the peristylium. The vestibule, atrium, and tablinum were the public part of the house. There the rich Roman received his clients; there he displayed the portraits and busts of his illustrious ancestors. The additional rooms consisted of bedrooms and dining rooms, *triclinia*. The rooms for domestic purposes, kitchens, baths, and store-rooms, were relegated to the back of the house.

The Roman house was built of stone and brick, bound together by a cement which was celebrated for its solidity. The walls were covered with plaster and colour-washed. The house had few openings on the outside because they did not use windowpanes; all decorations were within. The outside walls were furnished with stalls and let to shopkeepers.

After the conquest of Greece, the inside decorations became rich and varied, even in small houses: the walls were covered with domestic or mythological pictures; there were many marble columns, paving of rare stones, mosaics. Tapestry and carpets completed the ornamentation, but the rooms were small and contained little furniture. The Roman house was a dwelling in a hot country, very different from our rooms full of furniture.

Roman costume was not very different from Greek. The man wore pants, *subligaculum*, and a long shirt called a tunic, *tunica*,

FIG. 86. - Portion of a frieze found in a house at Pompeii.

made with or without sleeves. Senators' tunics were edged with a wide purple border and called for that reason *laticlave*. Over the tunic, the Romans wore the *toga*, a great length of white cloth, cut in the shape of an ellipse, 14 feet in length and 9 feet wide. It was the distinctive garment of a citizen, and was forbidden to foreigners and slaves; it was an art to gather the folds correctly. Freeborn children also wore the toga, but striped with purple and called *protexta*. It gradually became the custom to wear under the tunic a close-fitting vest, *subucula*, and over it when traveling a cloak open at the sides, *panula*, and furnished with a hood, *cucullus*. These garments were first made of woollen cloth, but fashion soon introduced into Rome the lighter fabrics from Greece and the East.

The woman also wore a tunic and over it the *stola*, a long, straight robe with sleeves, caught in at the waist by a belt. When she went out she wrapped herself in the *palla*, a big cloak or shawl resembling the Greek himation. Roman women, who appeared a great deal in public, paid great attention to their toilette. They enclosed the waist with leather corsets; they bleached their hair or wore wigs; they used rouge and cosmetics, and covered themselves with jewellery of very delicate workmanship, of which we possess many specimens.

FIG. 87. - Roman women: a fresco from Pompeii.

Neither men nor women wore stockings; they put on in the street the buskin, *calceus*, a kind of high half-boot closed in except over the toes. Certain magistrates wore red calcei called *mullens*. In the house, they wore sandals. In the army, soldiers wore an iron-shod boot or *caliga*.

The Roman, in his own house, was absolute master of his family and his slaves. Paternal authority was very great, and for a long time the father had the right of life or death over his own.

In the city, he was, above all things, a citizen. He was not, like the Greek, engrossed in trade; he gave all his time to public affairs. If he were rich, he received his clients in the morning, listened to their requests, and distributed advice or assistance. Then he went to the Forum, took his seat in the Senate or in the law-court. If he were poor, he became the client of a rich patron, attended him in public, and gave him his vote in elections. Amusements were rare. In the afternoon, he played at a kind of three-cornered tennis, or went to the baths, which were the resort of the idle. A few religious processions, a few games in the circus, alone broke the monotony of the year. This life suited a race of rural proprietors, but the customs were soon altered and Rome became, under the empire, a city of pleasure.

The position of the woman was more important in Rome than in Greece. She also ruled her household, but with more authority than the Greek woman, because she was more closely associated with her husband's life. She took care of her house and spun the wool, but in reality, she did more. She shared in the honours bestowed on her husband, she appeared with him in public at functions and games, she was surrounded with respect, she was the lady, *matrona*. At home, she was not confined to her own apartments, but took part in meals and receptions. Her influence, although not recognised by law, was very great. Cato discovered it when he wished to put down by law luxury among women. The citizens did not dare to vote without consulting their wives, who attended the Assembly.

The Roman State rested on the family, and the family on marriage. When the patricians were the only citizens, there was only one form of marriage, the religious marriage, *confarreatio*. It consisted in the betrothed pair offering a cake of spelt before the flamen of Jupiter. Then the bride, clothed in white and veiled in red, was conducted with the sound of flutes and songs to the house of the bridegroom, which made her free of the threshold, and she was lifted over it in his arms to counterfeit a capture. She was then detached from the gods of her own family, and attached to those of her new home.

When the plebeians had won their equality, a civil marriage, *coemptio*, was gradually substituted for the religious marriage. It consisted of a fictitious sale performed before a magistrate. The bridegroom touched a balance with a piece of copper, which he then gave to the parents of his bride as the price of his wife.

Women had dowries, which were returned to them in case of divorce; and divorces, rare at the beginning, became more and more frequent as the old customs changed. In early times, the husband alone, by virtue of his right as head of the family, repudiated his wife. Later, the wife, in her turn, could demand separation. In the time of the empire, the philosopher Seneca said indignantly, "Noble ladies divorce in order to re-marry, and re-marry in order to divorce again."

The child received his name, that is to say, he was recognised by his father, a week after birth, on a day called *dies lustricus*. He was generally educated by his mother until he was old enough to go to school. He wore round his neck a little bag, or *bulla*, containing amulets to protect him against the Evil Eye, which he kept until he put off the toga praetexta and assumed the toga virilis. This coming-of-age ceremony took place before the altar of his Lares when he was seventeen, but he still remained under his father's control.

At school, he learnt to read, write, and count under the direction of stern masters who punished the least fault with the rod. The children of the wealthy had private tutors. Music and gymnastics were regarded only as accomplishments. After this elementary education, young Romans received a literary education, which included the study of the law of the Twelve Tables, the Greek poets, and Latin writers, for they aimed at becoming administrators and orators.

Slaves were very numerous in Rome; there were 900,000 in the city in the first century. They performed all domestic work and practised all

FIG. 88. - Slave working a wheel to quarry stone.

trades so completely that it was difficult for a freeman to gain a living. All citizens, even the poorest, possessed slaves, and there were rich proprietors who owned as many as 10,000 or 20,000. They bought them at a market where they were shown on a platform with a placard bearing their age, origin, and qualities. Once bought, they became the property of their masters, who worked them very hard, for the Romans had not the humane feelings of the Greeks. Cato recommended the sale, without hesitation, as of old scrap iron, of the old slave no longer able to work. Those who were employed in the town had a fairly easy time, particularly if they had some special talent as teachers, musicians, artists, or doctors.

The slaves who worked in the fields had a horrible existence. Compelled to do the heaviest work, they were badly fed, clothed in a simple tunic, shod with clogs, and exposed to all kinds of suffering under the superintendence of an overseer or *villicus*.

They were beaten with rods, they were hung by the neck in a forked stick, their feet put in fetters, they were shut up in an underground prison, *ergastulum*. The worst suffering was to turn the millstones to grind corn; if they were condemned to death, they were crucified.

This harsh treatment often resulted in insurrections. However, they were able to purchase their freedom by means of the peculium, the savings which the slave managed to gather together from his meagre salary. At other times, the master's caprice freed the slave. But the freedman could never become a citizen, nor could his son; his grandson alone could have all the rights of a freeman.

The Roman morning was given up to business; then they ate lightly. There were two meals in the morning, the first or *ientaculum* at rising, and the *prandium* at about eleven o'clock. The principal meal, at which the whole family and guests were present, was the *cena*, at about three o'clock. In early times, a porridge called *pulmentum* was eaten, the polenta or maize porridge of the Italians. But with the progress of luxury, this meal became very important and consisted of three courses of the most varied dishes. The Romans drank the famous products of Massicum and Falernum, rich wines which had to be diluted with water in a special vessel called the crater. This meal was laid in the triclinium, a dining-room furnished with three couches arranged in the shape of a horse-shoe round a table.

The sides of the walls were furnished with tripods and dressers to hold dishes. The couches were furnished with cushions and a rug, and held three diners, who ate while reclining on the left elbow. They took their food with their fingers, sometimes with a spoon, and they wiped their hands on a table napkin. They had already moved far from the rusticity of the early Romans, who ate sitting on stools; but the meals at which guests were present became still more elaborate, true feasts, at which jesters and women dancers appeared. Then was added an evening meal or supper, *comissatio*, which was little better than an orgy. This was lighted with candelabra furnished with candles, or with oil-lamps.

The worship of the dead was the religion of the family; that was why funerals were celebrated with so much pomp that they cost fortunes. The corpse, before it was laid out, was put in the

FIG. 89. - Tomb of Cecilia Metella.

hands of the slaves of the professional undertakers, who planted a cypress before the house, and set up a state bed for the body in the atrium. Then the body was carried to the tomb on a litter, preceded by trumpets, flutes, and female mourners. Behind the body walked the relations and friends of the deceased. If he was of good family, the procession was increased by the parading of all the ancestors' images. Then they stopped in the Forum, where someone pronounced a funeral oration. It was the custom to burn, not bury, the body. A funeral pyre was prepared, which the relations lit with a torch, and they then turned their backs. The ashes were collected in an urn, which was deposited in a tomb. Nine days afterward, the family celebrated the funeral repast, and, when they were able, gave gladiator shows to appease the manes of the dead. The tombs of the wealthy were built along the great roads, and particularly along the Appian Way; these were imposing monuments. The tombs of the poor were very simple. Many even had no tombs; they hired a place for their urns in special buildings constructed by contractors and called *columbarium*, because they were like pigeon-cotes.

Some of these monuments were formed of galleries dug out of the earth, which were later called catacombs. Whatever the

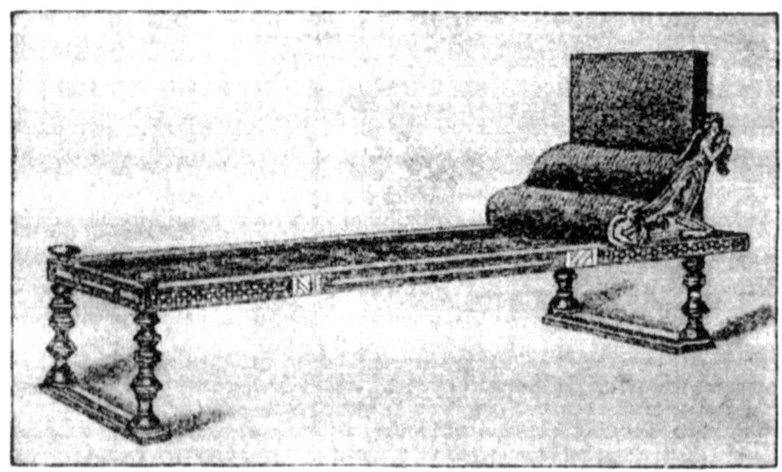

FIG. 90. - Bed with bronze fittings, found at Pompeii.

tomb was like, the dead man buried according to rites became a god, and had a right to a share of the worship of his descendants.

New manners were introduced into Rome after the conquests. The Romans became less attached to family and public duties. The reason was that many of the middle-class families had disappeared in the wars, and that others had enriched themselves inordinately by exploiting the conquered world. With wealth came the taste for luxuries imported from Greece and the East. Men laid out their fortunes in clothes, furniture, buildings, and receptions. They had innumerable slaves, litters to carry them in the streets, houses, works of art. Greek philosophy and literature found admirers and imitators in Rome, and this was a good thing. But these were the pleasures of the few; the majority of Romans, even the rich, were eager for coarse enjoyments, and Roman luxury had always the character of gross extravagance; it was the luxury of those who had newly acquired wealth. However, it must not be thought that it was general; the writers who condemned it were doubtless generalizing, and attributing to all what was true of some. It is certain that ancient customs disappeared with the ancient Romans, and that Rome at the end of republican times was no more than a great city where a certain number of millionaires fed and amused a parasitic people.

CHAPTER XXIII

THE PUBLIC LIFE OF ROME

Roman society retained to the last an aristocratic character. All citizens were equal by right, but they were not so in fact; there were three distinct classes. First, there were the aristocracy, who included the old aristocracy of birth and the new aristocracy of office. They all gave themselves up to political life and prohibited themselves from trading for money. They had the right of displaying the statues of their ancestors in their atria and at their funerals, and their sons, when they came of age, were made magistrates. They were rich, for they made a great profit on the administration of the provinces. After them came the knights, equites, who constituted a moneyed aristocracy, for they had the monopoly of trading and banking enterprises. The rest of the population were the *plebs urbana*, who for a long time were composed of small proprietors. But war and debts gradually ruined this middle class, and they migrated from the country to the town, where they swelled the ranks of the populace. They had, however, the title of citizens, and this title, which made them electors, was in theory a great privilege, since by their votes they were supposed to govern the world. Instead, they felt their misery, and it was not long before Rome was troubled by the hatred of the poor for the rich. All political activity in Rome was concentrated in the Forum. This was the name given to the rectangular space between the Palatine and the Capitol. This place, the name of which means market, was surrounded by trading booths which gradually gave place to monuments.

The meetings of the Senate, the law-courts, and the popular assemblies were held in the Forum. The Senate sat in a building

FIG. 91. — Rules of the Forum, showing the columns of the Temple of Saturn in the centre.

called the *Curia*, a large hall standing on an esplanade and furnished with wooden benches. Beside it was the *Basilica Emilia*, the law-courts. Several temples were erected in the neighborhood, among them that of Vesta and that of Castor and Pollux. The space itself was decorated with triumphal arches, statues, and monuments of every kind. The most famous was the pulpit for orations, rostrum, decorated with the beaks of ships taken from the enemy. All the Roman roads started from a golden pillar in the middle of the Forum, thus showing that there was the head of the Roman Empire.

The influence of the Senate preponderated in Rome. This assembly was composed of 300 to 600 members chosen by the censors from among those who had at least filled the office of questor. It met in the Curia or Senate-house, under the presidency of a consul or a praetor. The meetings were not public, but the door of the Curia remained open. The president read the words of the proposal under discussion and took the advice of senators, questioning them one after another. He who was by right questioned first was called *princeps senatus*. Speech was free, and a speaker could not be stopped.

The discussion ended, the vote was taken, which was not done by ballot nor by show of hands. The senators rose; some of them ranged themselves on the right, others on the left side of the hall, and then the number of people in each group was counted. The accepted proposal became a decree, called *Senatus consultum*. The tribunes of the plebs were present at these deliberations and could always stop them by their veto.

The Assemblies of the People, or comitia, elected all the magistrates and passed the laws. There were three types of assembly: *comitia curiata, comitia centuriata, and comitia tributa.*

The *comitia curiata* was a patrician assembly where the plebeians had no political rights. It was formed on the ancient religious division of the Curia, and it was retained for the *examination of religious questions. Only the senatorial families were able to take part.*

The comitia tributa was the original assembly of plebeians, composed of the city and country tribes, and presided over by the tribunes. Their decisions or plebiscites had the force of law. But when the poor plebeians had all migrated to Rome, there remained only rich citizens in the country tribes; on the other hand, the votes were counted by tribes and not by heads. As a result, the preponderating element were proprietors, that is to say, the rich men of the city. The vote of the tribes no longer expressed the demands of the poor.

The true people's assembly was the *comitia centuriata*, the assembly of the centuries which made up the army. Under the kings, it voted on peace or war. Under the republic, it elected the higher magistrates, such as the consul, and passed the laws.

It retained its military character for a long time. It met in the Campus Martius, outside the city, for armed forces were forbidden to enter Rome. The consuls called it, and took auspices as before a battle. The meeting was called by sounding a bugle; the red flag, as in time of battle, flew from the Capitol, and the consuls appeared as if to lead the army to battle. After sacrifice and prayer, the consul gave the reason for the assembly, gave the names of the persons who might be elected, and then voting took place. The vote was taken by centuries. The proceedings had to end before sunset and were postponed to another date if disturbed by a clap of thunder or an attack of epilepsy.

The manner of voting was curious. They first of all drew by lot a century, which voted alone, for it was believed that the gods showed their will in this way. Then all the other centuries voted at the same time. They lined up round an enclosure made of planks, a sheepfold with as many doors as there were centuries. The citizens entered one by one by the door into the enclosure by crossing a bridge of planks, and gave their votes to the scrutineers. They voted for a long time by the spoken voice, then they voted by a ballot dropped into an urn. The majority of each century settled the vote of the century.

In appearance, this assembly was composed of all the citizens, but in reality, the vote belonged to the wealthy classes. By the constitution of Servius, the whole people were divided according to wealth into seven classes and 193 centuries, of which this is the table: -

Knights (those who possessed a horse):   18 centuries
First class (rich foot-soldiers):   80 centuries
Second class (small proprietors):   26 centuries
Third class (small proprietors):   20 centuries
Fourth class (small proprietors):   22 centuries
Fifth class (small proprietors):   26 centuries
Populace (those who possessed nothing):   1 century

193

The 193 centuries constituted 193 votes, but the knights and the citizens in the first class determined ninety-eight, that is to say, the majority; so the rich were the true masters of the State.

The chief Roman magistrates were the consuls, censors, and prators, elected by the centuries; the questors, adiles, and tribunes, elected by the tribes. All the magistrates had the right to an ivory chair called *sella curulis*. We have seen the functions of the consuls and tribunes. Here are the characteristics of the other curule magistrates -

The censors, two in number, had special charge of the census, or numbering of the citizens, which took place every five years. They then prepared a list of the citizens, verified the state of their fortunes, and divided them into the different classes. It was their right to deprive an unworthy citizen of his rights or to place him in a lower class. It was they who chose the senators. Thus, they exercised a real moral control over the city, and their office was an object of great respect.

The prators had charge of the administration of justice; they were able to assist the consuls in the government.

The questors were financial officers; they administered the treasury and overlooked the accounts of the provinces and the army.

The adiles had charge of the streets, the monuments, and the public services. They also organized the games, for which they contributed money. Their hardest task was the provisioning of the city, for the State charged itself with providing Rome with corn and selling it at a low price.

The conquered country outside Italy was divided into seventeen provinces, of which ten were in Europe, five in Asia, and two in Africa. Each province was administered in the name of the Roman people by a governor, empowered to maintain order and levy taxes. Obey and pay — that was all Rome required of the conquered. These conditions fulfilled, they were free to govern themselves as they liked and to retain their customs and religions. The Roman republic, an aristocratic government, did not feel the obligation, as the empire did later, to rule the conquered peoples; they only saw domains to be exploited. It was enough that they were peaceful, and to obtain this peace they took care to divide them. Every city was not treated in the same way; some had privileges refused to others. They were not able to enter into negotiations with one another; in some cases, even marriage was forbidden between neighboring peoples. Citizens were not on the same footing: some were subjects without any rights; others had the Latin right, that is to say, the civil rights conceded to the Latins of Italy; some had the Roman right, that is to say, they were counted as true Roman citizens. All had a common duty — to submit to their governors.

The governor was a true monarch in his province. He was chosen from among the consuls and the prators leaving office; that was why he was called proconsul or proprator. Both had the same powers. Nominated by the Senate, they arrived in their province clothed in the *paludamentum* of a general, preceded by lictors, surrounded by an army of officials and attachés; they made a solemn entry into the cities. They exercised absolute power, *imperium*. They took what measures pleased them by their edicts, and they especially directed justice and administration. They had the right of life and death over all inhabitants except

Roman citizens. This office was very much sought after because it permitted the holders to remake their fortunes. As they had the right of requisitioning, and of billeting troops, they sold their goodwill to the subject cities. They robbed the cities and the temples of their treasures; in particular, they demanded money and works of art. A special tribunal was set up in Rome to judge their exactions; but the judges were friends who might imitate them some day, and they did not fail to buy their complicity or their silence. Some were honest, but many resembled Verres, the governor of Sicily, whom Cicero caused to be condemned after a celebrated trial lasting four months.

The inhabitants of the provinces bore heavy burdens. They had to maintain the governor, his retinue, and his army. They paid, in addition, a personal tax or *tributum*, a land tax, or *vectigal*, and customs, or *portoria*. The method of collection aggravated these burdens. The State did not collect its revenues itself. It farmed out this work to financial companies, who collected also for themselves and deducted big profits. These were the *publicani*, whose agents exacted from the provincials much more than the sums fixed by edict, and that with a thousand annoyances. The governors put armed force at their disposal, and the collection of the taxes often resembled the pillage of war.

Sometimes cities, overburdened with taxes, were unable to pay. Then they borrowed from the publicans, who lent at a very high rate of interest, as much as 40 percent. If they could not repay, the publicans called in military intervention. At Cyprus, a squadron blockaded the Senate, which was unable to pay, and five senators died of hunger. Nonetheless, there were confiscations and forced loans. "To satisfy the publicans without ruining the provincials," said Cicero, "requires a divine nature."

These exactions excited a terrible hatred, but it was remarkable that the provincials rarely tried to throw off the Roman yoke; instead, they sought to be the equals of the Romans. This was because Roman rule had its advantages. To the countries of the

West, it brought civilisation; to the East, peace. Roman avarice was the price of these benefits.

This greed for money in Rome eventually killed all the civic virtues of the ancient Romans. The city became nothing more than an electoral market, where the rich bought the electors and the poor sold their votes. It was of the utmost importance to be elected to the high offices of consul or praetor, which were followed by the lucrative government of a province. All manner of means were taken in order to succeed. The candidates' comitia bought en bloc the working men's corporations or isolated citizens. They also sought popularity by distributing food to the people, by celebrating public games, by rendering all kinds of services. Rome, untroubled by enemies from without, found her true enemy in this corruption, and the republic fell in the bloodstained troubles which resulted.

CHAPTER XXIV

INTERNAL TROUBLES

HER conquests had changed the conditions of private and public life in Rome. The patricians and the knights were immensely enriched by the spoils of the world, and the populace were impoverished. There was scarcely anyone in Rome but the rich and the poor, and extreme wealth and poverty do not make for civic integrity. The middle class of small peasant proprietors, whose virtues had shone so brightly, had gradually disappeared. The wars had taken each year one citizen in eight and had killed a great number. These same wars took others far from their lands, and when they returned, they fell into debt to meet the needs of their families. Also, agriculture was ruined by slave labour and the importation of corn at a low price from the provinces. It resulted in the unhappy peasants, overwhelmed with debt, selling their lands at a miserable price to their creditors and emigrating to Rome. These ruined peasants increased the always-growing number of citizens without resources, for freedmen had the rights of citizens in the third generation. This populace no longer held the traditions of ancient Rome. The greatness of the country and the upkeep of its dignity mattered little to them. Scipio said to them in a crowded Forum, "Listen, stepsons of Italy, former slaves whom I have brought to Rome, you will not frighten me because your arms are no longer hung with chains." This crowd had only appetites; they were ready to serve any ambitious man who would feed them.

This danger was not hidden from the statesmen, and they tried to find a remedy. Some, like the Gracchi, wished to reinstate a middle class who would consider independence dignified.

Others, the nobles, did not wish to give up their privileges and believed that they would be able to control the appetites of the people by force. It resulted in a series of struggles between the populace, who supported ambitious individuals, and the rich, who defended the Senate.

The Gracchi were the first to take the side of the people. They had less ambition than genuine love of reform. They had received from their mother Cornelia, the daughter of Scipio Africanus, a careful education and high ideals; so, in spite of being of patrician birth, they took up whole-heartedly the people's cause.

The elder Tiberius was neither a demagogue nor a revolutionary. He was a gentle, good man, an educated and delicate orator. He was moved by the misery of the poorer classes, who were a menace to Rome. "Wild beasts," said he, "have dens, and these men have not even a family tomb. They are called the masters of the world, and they have not even a clod of earth for their own." Nominated tribune in 134 B.C., he wished to give them this clod of earth, and he proposed an agrarian law — that is to say, a distribution of lands among the people.

The matter might appear easy, for Rome was the owner of vast lands taken from the conquered; this was the public land, *ager publicus*. But these lands had been for many generations leased to the rich, who cultivated them by means of slaves or fed sheep on them. Gradually, they had ceased to pay rent to the state, and these farms became in their hands real property, which they were in the habit of selling or transmitting to their heirs. They recognised the right of the state over these lands, but they managed in such a way that it was seldom exercised. Thus, they possessed great domains called *latifundia*. Any proposals having for their object the return of these usurped possessions were sure to rouse their anger and hostility.

Tiberius did not propose to rob the holders of public land entirely. He offered to leave them a part and to pay them an indemnity for the improvements they had carried out on the remainder. This remainder was to be divided among poor citizens at the rate

FIG. 92. - The Rostrum, from which Tiberius spoke.

of seven hectares per family. The tribune thought he could thus give back to the republic the small proprietors who had been her strength. He believed, like Cato, "that among labourers were born the strongest men, the bravest soldiers, and that those who were occupied in this work were never evil-disposed."

The rich placed the protection of their fortunes before the needs of the country. To combat the agrarian law, they engaged a tribune, Octavius, who interposed his veto to the appeal. Tiberius had him deposed, and the law was passed. Then his opponents tried to raise the people against him and spread the rumour that he aspired to become king. Tiberius, threatened with a judicial accusation, demanded a second tribuneship in order to remain inviolable. On the day of the election, the nobles provoked a disturbance in the Forum and caused a crowd of vagabonds and slaves to attack the friends of the tribune. Tiberius raised his hands above his head. A band of nobles, led by Scipio Nasica, declared that he demanded a crown and a kingdom, and under the pretext of saving the republic, they knocked him down with benches.

Ten years later, Caius Gracchus repeated his brother's projects. He had the same honesty, the same patriotic desire to regenerate Rome; moreover, he was a great orator and possessed a dauntless spirit. He resolved to break the power of the Senate, which was opposed to improving the lot of the poor.

He wished, first of all, to put an end to the misery of the populace. To do this, he caused measures to be passed for the distribution of lands and the foundation of colonies on the site of the cities destroyed at Carthage, Corinth, Tarentum, and Capua. For those who did not wish to work on the land and preferred a parasitic life in the city, he had passed a law of public assistance, *Lex Frumentaria*, which gave to every citizen each month five modii of corn at 6½ asses (3d.) a modus.

At the same time, he proposed to give the rights of citizenship to the Latin peoples, in order to renew the Roman population and balance the influence of the freedmen, who came from every corner of the world. For fear of senatorial opposition, he took away the right of sitting on juries and gave it to the knights, who had become their rivals. The wealthy class thus had divided interests, to the advantage of the popular party.

The threatened Senate played on the worst instincts of the crowd and practiced a policy of outbidding the reformers. They bought the tribune Drusus, who decreed free distributions of corn. Moreover, when the time came for voting on admitting the Latins to citizen rights, the consul said to the populace, "Do you think that when you have conferred the rights of citizenship upon the Latins you will have the same seats in the comitia, the games, and the public amusements?" Caius withdrew his law and left to found a colony at Carthage. On his return, he saw to what extent he had become unpopular. He wished to be re-elected tribune that he might propose a law which would strike a blow at the power of the Senate. He had to retire to Mons Aventinus, but he was followed by rioters and bowmen; he fled into a sacred wood, where he was killed by one of his slaves.

Three thousand of his supporters were massacred (123 B.C.). His name was cursed, and his mother was forbidden to wear mourning.

The Gracchi had perished as martyrs to the popular cause, and the people had not known how to defend them from the nobles' anger. They had dreamed of saving Rome by legal means, and their generous dream had been drowned in the blood of citizens.

Henceforward, there was no one in Rome but the nobles and the populace — the one having everything and not wishing to concede anything, the other wishing for its part in the pleasures of life, opposed to one another in desires and interests, and determined to resort to violent means to satisfy them. It was, in reality, the end of the republic, and the history of Rome becomes that of ambitious men, some of whom contended for power by force, like Sulla and Pompey, others, like Marius and Caesar, who raised themselves to the first place in the State by appearing to serve the democracy.

The Gracchi dead, the victorious nobility abolished their laws. They kept only the *lex frumentaria* to conciliate the people by feeding them. The Senate also occupied itself with the question of the *ager publicus*. It altered the laws of usufruct property (right by occupation) to include lands rented from the State, and the aristocracy ended by becoming masters of all the land.

This security of wealth engendered the greatest corruption. "Luxury and avarice," declared Cato, "killed the republic." Revolts broke out without being repressed. A barbarian, Jugurtha, flouted Rome by buying the magistrates and cried, "A city for sale, which only awaits a purchaser."

Jugurtha was the nephew of Micipsa, a king of Numidia, the ally and protégé of Rome. He had inherited a part of this kingdom, and he resolved to wrest the remainder from his cousins. At the request of one of them, the Senate intervened. But the commission they sent to Africa was bribed by Jugurtha, and they decided in his favor. He continued to enrich himself, and the Romans were obliged to make war. He even bribed the generals. Called to Rome to answer for himself, he bribed a tribune, who protected him. Then he returned to Africa and defeated a Roman army (118–109 B.C.).

The scandal was so great that Roman pride awoke, and the war was undertaken seriously. They sent to Africa an upright man,

Metellus, who defeated Jugurtha without being able to prevent him from retaining the land and harassing his army. It was then that Marius appeared.

Marius was one of Metellus' officers, an excellent soldier, and a protégé of the senatorial party. Conscious of his strength, he was ambitious enough to want to be elected consul and asked Metellus' permission to go to Rome. This was refused because of the jealousy between nobles and plebeians. Then Marius threw himself into the democratic party and excited it by his rough eloquence, through which he obtained the consulate with the mission of ending the war with Jugurtha.

Marius' first act was to reform the way in which the army was recruited by decreeing that henceforth the proletariat should be enrolled. This measure, good from a military point of view, since it increased the number of soldiers, contributed to the ruin of the republic. Since the populace who were enrolled remained in the army, where they were paid, they became professional soldiers who made war for the sake of the spoil. They were always devoted to the leaders who allowed them to plunder; they recognized no other authority, and the leaders, on their part, were all-powerful at the head of their armies. Rome no longer obeyed laws but ambitious men who had succeeded in making an army follow them.

Returning to Africa, Marius quelled his elusive enemy by following him ceaselessly with flying columns. At length, Jugurtha was given up by his own men to Sulla, Marius' lieutenant and successor in command, and led to Rome, where he perished in prison (104 B.C.). Marius held the consulship for many years in spite of the law, for he was given the command to stop the invasion of Cimbrian and Teutonic tribes which menaced Italy. These German invaders came from the shores of the Baltic and had marched through Europe with their wives, children, animals, and vehicles, covered with leather, to seek a country in which to settle. They laid waste to everything in their passage, and when they reached the banks of the Rhone, they destroyed several Roman armies. The Roman commanders were not warlike, and their soldiers were frightened by these giants, with their fair hair, ferocious appearance, and indomitable courage. Fortunately for Rome, the barbarians stopped to pillage Spain, and Marius had time to arrive and harden his army to war by making them submit to harsh discipline. The Teutons tried to enter Italy through modern Provence. Marius waited for them near Aix, and Roman tactics triumphed over barbarian courage (102 B.C.). The battle lasted for two days and was ended by an appalling massacre. The Cimbri, on their part, had crossed the Alps and were descending into the valley of the Adige. Marius met them near Vercellae and annihilated them (101 B.C.). The German women killed the fugitives and then killed themselves. More than 200,000 perished.

Drunk with his success, Marius, who had not as yet played a political part, intrigued for a sixth consulate and associated himself with the leaders of the popular party. He was elected and employed himself in satisfying the demands of his partisans. He gave each of his veterans twenty-five hectares of land in Africa, with power to sell it; the poor of Rome had land in Cisalpine Gaul, and each citizen had the right to forty measures of corn per month at a very low price. The Senate swore obedience to these laws and decreed the death of any who dared to question the sovereignty of the Roman people. This formula served to cover so many crimes that people detached themselves from Marius, and the senatorial party regained power.

They found a leader in Sulla, who succeeded in putting down the Italian revolts. Rome had been in great danger. The peoples of Italy, to whom all the ambitious leaders promised the rights of citizenship, were tired of being made a laughingstock and revolted. They furnished Rome with money and soldiers, and in exchange, they were treated like subjects. To cite an instance, a consul had the chief magistrate of an Italian town beaten with rods because the public baths were not evacuated quickly enough to please his wife, who wished to bathe. It was a terrible war, for the tactics and armaments of both sides were equal. Roman soldiers were struggling against Roman soldiers. The frightened

Senate divided its enemies, making concessions and giving the rights of citizenship to all those who remained loyal. The others, after an atrocious war, were reduced, thanks to the valor and skill of Sulla (90–89 B.C.). Saved from the peril, the Senate thought it advisable to show itself generous, and two years later, all the Italians were declared Roman citizens (87 B.C.).

Marius had not played a great part in this war; instead, Sulla, his old lieutenant in Africa and at Vercellae, had gained a great reputation. He was a man of good birth, who had been treated by Marius as he himself had been treated by Metellus. Brilliant and generous, he won the soldiers' affections by his generosity. The patricians also had confidence in him, and the Senate gave him, as a reward, the command of the army which was sent to Asia against King Mithradates. This was a great advantage, for this command enabled its holder to enrich himself and become the master of a permanent army.

Marius, who wanted the direction of this war, made friends with the tribunes, the leaders of the populace. After a riot, he was nominated in the place of Sulla by the vote of the people, who broke the Senate's decree. Sulla then raised his faithful army and gave the order to march on Rome. This was the first time such an attempt had been made. The officers refused to follow their chief, but the soldiers, in hope of pillage, attacked Marius' troops, defeated them, and entered Rome. Marius fled, and after hiding in the marshes around Minturnae, succeeded in reaching Africa. The conqueror Sulla abolished the democratic laws, re-established the power of the Senate, and left for Asia.

During Sulla's absence, Marius returned to Italy, and with the aid of the consul Cinna, raised an army of Italians and slaves with which he attacked Rome. The city was taken by starving it out, and during five days and nights, there followed a wholesale massacre of the nobles and their supporters. Thanks to the terror he exercised, Marius was seven times consul. He declared Sulla to be a public enemy and gave himself the command of the army in Asia. He was about to depart when he died (86 B.C.), leaving Rome in the hands of his friend Cinna and his son, the younger Marius, who governed for three years.

Then Sulla returned, after having conquered Mithradates in Greece and Asia Minor and securing an enormous booty which enabled him to give his soldiers a wage equal to nearly twelve shillings a day. He brought back an army enriched with spoils and confident in the valor of its general. Cinna tried to bar the way and raised six armies. Sulla defeated some and won over others, for his reputation for generosity gained him soldiers. During this civil war, the Italians rose again; he wiped out the revolts. Having taken Rome and pacified Italy, Sulla received from the Senate the title of dictator for life.

He then proceeded to liquidate the past by revenging himself on those whom he had banished and preparing the way for his reforms. His vengeance was terrible. He prepared a list of his enemies and permitted them to be killed; their goods were confiscated and sold, their children excluded forever from holding office. For six months, the soldiers cut throats and pillaged; Sulla's friends bought at a low price the property of the condemned. The names of the condemned were placarded — *proscriptio*; these executions gained the name of proscriptions.

To prevent anyone else from doing what he had done, Sulla wished to reorganize Rome and to give it a strong oligarchical constitution.

The Senate became the principal body in the State; the Assembly of the People was no longer sovereign. The tribunes no longer had the right of veto, and the consuls, deprived of the command of the army, had to resign themselves to being no more than civil magistrates. These laws met with no resistance; the power of the dictator was too great. His work completed (79 B.C.), Sulla resigned the dictatorship in order not to occupy a position contrary to the constitution and died the following year (78 B.C.). He had a magnificent funeral and was buried in the Campus Martius, which had not been used for this purpose since the time of the kings.

Sulla believed he had made an end of revolutions, but he had done it by seizing power by force. He thus destroyed respect for, and the power of, the laws which he tried to restore. Everyone who commanded a victorious army aspired to govern Rome, and the quarrels of the parties served as pretexts for them to realize their designs.

The first occasion did not delay in coming. The democratic party, wishing to abolish Sulla's laws, attached itself to a division of the army; their leader, the consul Lepidus, marshaled the troops and demanded from the Senate the restoration of all the rights of the tribunes. As the Senate resisted, they marched on Rome and were stopped at the Campus Martius by Pompeius. Rome was to find a new master.

Pompeius was noble, rich, and brave. He had supplied Sulla with three legions and had fought bravely at his side. Sulla dead, he undertook the defense of the Senate. But he was a mediocre general and a politician without ideas. He had exceptional luck, and his vanity prevented him from making well-arranged plans of action. He changed sides many times, according to his interest or fancy. His true strength was in his huge fortune, with which he bought many interests in such a way as to give him all the advantageous commands. He accumulated triumphs and riches, and his pride was less that of mastery than that of being called Pompeius Magnus. He succeeded in ending four wars which others had waged.

To reward their savior, the Senate sent him to Spain. Sertorius, a lieutenant of Marius, had revolted against Sulla after calling the Spaniards to independence, and had established a regular kingdom, which he governed with the assistance of a Senate nominated by himself.

A Roman army had pushed him hard for some time when Pompeius arrived. Sertorius was defeated at Saguntum. The Spaniards, discouraged and discontented at his severity, abandoned and assassinated him (72 B.C.). Pompeius was awarded a triumph.

Returning to Italy, he helped to put down a slave revolt commanded by an intelligent and energetic gladiator, Spartacus. The insurrection was nearly over, for the Roman general Crassus had enclosed Spartacus in the Calabrian peninsula. Crassus was the conqueror, while Pompeius wiped out the bands which ravaged the north of Italy. The repression was terrible. On the road from Capua to Rome, 6,000 slaves were crucified (71 B.C.).

Rome took breath again, but there were in Italy two victorious generals and two armies. Civil war would break out if they had opposing ambitions. But instead of fighting, Pompeius and Crassus agreed together to govern Rome, and they were nominated together for the consulship (70 B.C.). Pompeius, in agreement with Crassus, abandoned the aristocracy and favoured the democracy. They abolished the laws of Sulla, and the tribunes regained their old privileges. The Senate accepted everything, for the consuls' armies camped at the gates of Rome (70 B.C.). The tribunes, in their turn, rewarded Pompeius by giving him 500 ships and 120,000 men to clear the Mediterranean of the pirates that infested it. During the troubles, a crowd of adventurers had equipped fleets of light ships with which they pillaged ports, robbed temples, and preyed upon merchant ships. Their lairs were in Asia Minor, and they were able to possess real ships of war. Masters of the sea, they threatened Rome with famine, for she was only fed thanks to the supply of corn coming from Africa, Sicily, and Egypt. The low price of corn had made the Italians give up growing it, and the Romans, like the English nowadays, depended upon imported corn. In three months, Pompeius cleared the Mediterranean, and abundance returned to Rome. The Romans did not wait even until the end of the campaign to give him, by way of reward, the mission of pacifying Asia.

Western Asia had been entirely conquered through intrigue by Mithradates, king of Pontus, a little kingdom on the shores of the Black Sea. Rome had not had such a dangerous enemy since the time of Hannibal. Endowed with extraordinary vigour and general intelligence, Mithradates, the son of a barbarian and a Greek, an intrepid warrior and an unscrupulous despot, reigned through a policy of terror and bribery. He allied himself with neighbouring kings, extended his conquests on all sides of the Black Sea, and, having won over the Greeks to his cause, persuaded the whole Eastern world to revolt. A hundred thousand Romans were massacred in one night. He even crossed over to Greece, where Sulla defeated him at Athens, Chaeronea, and Orchomenus and imposed peace (84 B.C.).

Forced to return to Asia, he began his intrigues again. He created a new army, equipped like the Roman, sought allies, and conceived the plan of attacking Rome in Italy by marching through the Crimea and along the Danube. The Romans stopped him and sent against him Lucullus, who defeated his ally Tigranes, the king of Armenia, and took his capital, Tigranocerta (69 B.C.). He found forty million in gold there.

Pompeius arrived then to gather the fruits of the war. The coasts of the Black Sea were conquered, the Mithradates allies were bought, and the king of Pontus, abandoned by everyone, was killed by a soldier after having tried in vain to poison himself (63 B.C.).

The conqueror, Pompeius, overran Asia to pacify it, for the war had given the opportunity for all the allied or conquered kingdoms to make themselves independent. He met with no resistance except at Jerusalem, which was taken by assault. The kingdoms of Pontus and Bithynia formed one province, Syria another; Armenia became an allied kingdom, and the Euphrates was henceforth the boundary of the empire (63 B.C.).

During Pompeius' absence, Rome was troubled by agitators who entered politics at the head of armed bands. One of them, Catiline, organised a conspiracy, which forms a good illustration of the break-up of Roman morale. He was an ambitious noble who, without having political schemes, wished to obtain power to be able to satisfy his own and his friends' desires. All kinds of discontented persons, nobles, proscribed men, ruined veterans, adventurers, and even slaves entered into the plot.

One of the consuls that year was the orator Cicero, famous

through his speech against Verres. He was a new man, a provincial knight, but an honourable man in spite of indecision of character. Having discovered the plot, he wished to restore order by law. He arrested and executed the conspirators, except Catiline, who fled from Rome and was defeated and killed (63 B.C.). Cicero could take his oath that he had saved the republic.

All was over when Pompeius returned from Asia. Intoxicated by success, he believed himself all-powerful and disbanded his army on landing. He soon discovered that he had made a mistake. He was given nothing that he demanded, and the Senate refused to ratify his settlement of Asia. Discontented, he found his old colleague Crassus equally discontented. Their agreement was shared by a new ambitious man of the popular party, Caesar, already popular by reason of his gifts and who aimed at the consulship after having been elected Pontifex Maximus.

He was the nephew of Marius, the son-in-law of Cinna, the descendant of one of the most illustrious families in Rome, since he claimed Aeneas as an ancestor.

He had a maxim that it was better to be first in a village than second in Rome. His birth, extravagance, ambitious character, and high intelligence enabled him to aim at anything. Pompeius, Crassus, and Caesar formed an association called the *triumvirate*, which had for its object the control of the republic.

Things arranged themselves as they had planned. Caesar was nominated consul in 59 B.C., with the promise of the command of a province. Pompeius' acts were ratified, Crassus was given the command against the Parthians in Asia, which permitted him to renovate his fortune. The people had their share. They passed an agrarian law which gave lands to all citizens who had three children.

The Senate opposed the measure, but they passed it notwithstanding, and Cicero, the most eloquent of its opponents, was sent into exile. On leaving office, Caesar received the proconsulate of Cisalpine Gaul for five years with three legions. Transalpine Gaul and a fourth legion were added (58 B.C.). He soon began the con-

FIG. 93. - Julius Caesar.

quest of independent Gaul (see the following chapter).

Crassus, left to fight the Parthians, perished in an attempt to follow this nation of horsemen through the desert (53 B.C.). As for Pompeius, he was appointed to the command of the army in Spain, but he did not leave Rome.

Rome was again painted red with blood by the bands of idlers who supported an agitator named Clodius. The Senate, to make an end of these disorders, appointed Pompeius sole consul with full powers. He did not know how to stop them, but as Caesar, the conqueror of Gaul, wished to come to Rome to get his acts ratified and stand for the consulship, he tried to oppose his plans. Caesar then suggested that both should abdicate. Pompeius refused, and he obtained a vote which ordered Caesar to disband his army. Caesar was camping on the banks of the Rubicon, the boundary of his Cisalpine province; he decided to obtain by force what he could not obtain by legal means, so he crossed the Rubicon and marched on Rome.

There was not, as in former times, a struggle between two parties, but a struggle between two men. Pompeius, whose army was in Spain, had no means of opposing Caesar's veterans. He fled to Greece, and the Senate, through fear of the conqueror, accompanied him. Without loss of time, Caesar restored order in Rome and left for Spain to put himself at the head, as he said, of "this army without a general." He increased once more his military glory by taking Massilia after a celebrated siege.

That done, he crossed the Adriatic in the midst of winter without Pompeius' fleet trying to bar his passage. He had few troops with him, but they were men used to fatigue and accustomed to fighting. Pompeius' army was completely defeated at Pharsala (48 B.C.), and he fled to Egypt, where he was assassinated.

Before he returned to Rome, Caesar undertook the pacification of all the countries where armies devoted to the Senate and to Pompeius still held the field. First, he established himself in Egypt, where he gave the throne to the famous queen Cleopatra. After that, he passed into Africa, where he defeated Pompeius' sons at Thapsus (46 B.C.). He followed them into Spain and completed their defeat at Munda (45 B.C.).

Master of Rome and of the world, Caesar, as Sulla had been, was nominated dictator for life, and his decrees had the force of law. He did not take any new titles, but he absorbed all the higher magistracies and was, in truth, king without having the name. He reduced the Senate to the state of a consultative assembly and raised its numbers to 900 by allowing provincials to enter. He set about re-establishing order by excellent measures. He tried to relieve the city of the populace who encumbered it by distributing lands, undertaking great constructional works, and founding colonies. He introduced more justice into the administration and repressed the publicans' excesses.

Caesar's domination was well received, thanks to the sweetness of his character. He was a benevolent despot, but he was a tyrant in the eyes of the senators deposed from power. Some of them conspired against him under the pretext that he wished to take the title of king, and he was assassinated in full Senate by senators who believed that through his murder they could restore the old state of things. At the head of this plot was Brutus, Cato's nephew, whom historians have represented as an honourable and virtuous man, but who was under an obligation to Caesar, who had treated him like a son, and who forgot the dictator's kindnesses and struck him down with a dagger (44 B.C.).

CHAPTER XXV

THE CONQUEST OF GAUL

THE conquest of Gaul, which made Caesar's military reputation, was only an episode in the Roman civil wars. In making the Romans give him the proconsulate of Gaul, the future dictator was imitating all the ambitious men who had preceded him; he only sought to provoke a war in a new country where he would find an army, glory, and profit. Caesar did not know much about the enterprise he had undertaken; he only knew that a war against the Gauls would be popular in Rome, for the Romans had often had reason to fear them. But it was dangerous to attack this courageous people; he was obliged to use policy as well as force. The Gauls themselves, however, offered him an opportunity of interfering in their affairs.

The Gauls occupied all the country from the Apennines to the sea, with the Alps, Juras, and the Rhine as boundaries. The Romans had already formed two provinces: Cisalpine Gaul, or the valley of the Po, and Transalpine Gaul, which consisted of the coast of Gaul from the Alps to the Pyrenees and formed the way into Spain. The rest was independent.

In Caesar's day, the Gauls were divided into small communities, each of which had a fortified camp or oppidum. These peoples were torn by quarrels between rival chiefs. Added to these dissensions were the rivalries of confederations which were formed between several communities. The Gauls, rich from their lands, formidable because of their bravery, were reduced to impotence by these divisions. Far from thinking of uniting, they called in a stranger to take part in their quarrels. Thus the Sequani, fighting against the Edueni, demanded help from the Germans; so the

FIG. 94. - A Gallic horse-soldier.

Edueni asked it of the Romans.

Ariovistus came with his Germans to the assistance of the Sequani, who were established in Burgundy. He founded a kingdom and suppressed the neighbouring Gauls. At the same time, the great Gallic tribe of the Helvetii (Swiss) tried to leave the mountains and seek a less severe climate by the seaside. Gaul found itself threatened with an invasion which would overflow into the Roman province. This was an excellent excuse for Caesar to enter Gaul and to present himself as a saviour from the Helvetii, a deliverer from Ariovistus. Caesar first marched against the Helvetii, who had entered the Rhone valley. He cut them off to the north in the Saone valley, surprised them near Mâcon, annihilated them at Bibracte, and drove the remainder of the invaders back into Switzerland.

He next marched against Ariovistus; the Roman army trembled at the idea of attacking the German barbarians, who had such a terrible reputation, but Caesar rallied their courage and annihilated Ariovistus' army to the north of Besançon (58 B.C.).

Once having entered Gaul, Caesar wished to make it submit to him. It took him eight years and eight campaigns. He had good fortune in that the Gauls, except once in 52 B.C. under Vercingetorix, never perceived the danger at the same time and only fought in partial union.

The first of the coalitions, formed through the uneasiness the presence of the Romans caused, only included the tribes of the Belgae; even their neighbours, the Remi, took Caesar's part. He entrenched himself on the banks of the Aisne and resisted the coalition successfully. Then he took the offensive, made them submit one after the other, and ended the campaign by defeating the Nervii in the valley of the Sambre. The encounter was so fierce that Caesar had to fight in the first rank.

The following year, the whole of the west united under the leadership of the Veneti, a powerful maritime and commercial people. As Caesar had no fleet, he built ships on the Loire and manned them with oarsmen from Provençe. But the oared ships were ill-fitted for struggle against the sailing ships of the Veneti. He had the idea of making his triremes row through their fleet, cutting their cordage with scythes, and thus the Veneti were at his mercy.

At the same time, Aquitaine was conquered by his lieutenant, Crassus. It seemed that nearly the whole of Gaul accepted Roman rule (56 B.C.), and for two years peace reigned. Caesar spent these years in expeditions against the Germans and the Britons.

The Germans having crossed the Rhine, Caesar attacked and annihilated them. He then resolved to protect Gaul by reducing the people on the other side of the Rhine to submission. He crossed the river on a wooden bridge, built in ten days, obtained their submission, and formed alliances which enabled him to recruit cavalry (55 B.C.).

He then turned towards the Britons, who were of the same race and religion as the Gauls, and were concerned in plots against the Romans. He crossed the sea twice, and in his second expedition succeeded in penetrating into the heart of the country (54 B.C.).

This done, Caesar returned to winter in Gaul. He was fully confident of the submission of Gaul, for the aristocracy he had set up was resolutely faithful to Rome. Moreover, he had placed legions in the outlying districts. But the people, worked up by two patriotic chieftains, organised a great plot, and once again all the people of the north took up arms. A Roman legion was massacred; another was blockaded. However, the other Gauls did not take up arms and come to their assistance. Caesar called together his troops, relieved the legion in danger, and crushed one after another the revolting peoples. The repression was without mercy; all the rebels were either killed or sold as slaves (53 B.C.).

The Rising of the North was scarcely over before a new insurrection started. This time the whole of Gaul rose. The Gauls were weary of providing the conquerors with food and soldiers and of submitting to the pecuniary exactions of the publicans. The desire to free themselves made them sink all their differences, and Caesar was faced "with the extraordinary unity of the wish to regain liberty."

The hero of the war of independence was Vercingetorix. He was a chief of the Arverni, an ardent patriot, who had dreamed of a united country of Gaul, and of whom even Caesar said, "He armed not for his own interests, but to win liberty for all." He understood that to win, he must have a united effort, and he terrorized those who hesitated to follow him.

Vercingetorix wished to starve the Roman army by leaving a waste before it and destroying all the towns where they might find provisions. He made a mistake in yielding to the prayers of the inhabitants of Avaricum and sparing their town. It fell into Caesar's hands, and he found provisions for his army there. But Caesar failed completely when he tried to lay siege to Gergovia, the capital of the Arverni and the center of the resistance.

He was then in a very critical position and began to march toward the Transalpine province when Vercingetorix tried to bar his passage near Dijon. The German knights Caesar had enrolled in large numbers gave him the victory.

Vercingetorix was obliged to retreat to Alesia, where Caesar followed and blockaded him. Then began the memorable siege that ended the war. Caesar surrounded the town with an entrenchment of over nine miles. Then, fearing attack by a relieving army, he protected himself with another trench of over twelve miles. Every method of siege warfare—earthworks, siege-towers, and machines — was used. "All this," says the French historian Michelet, "was accomplished in less than five weeks by less than 60,000 men." Gaul was utterly broken. The desperate efforts of the besieged, reduced by a horrible famine, and those of 250,000 Gauls who attacked the Romans from outside, failed equally. The besieged, with despair, saw their friends turned by Caesar's cavalry, defeated, and dispersed. Vercingetorix, keeping alone a steady mind in the midst of universal despair, delivered himself up as the author of the war. He mounted his war-horse, clothed in his richest armor, and, having wheeled about in front of Caesar's tent, threw his sword, javelin, and helmet at the Roman's feet without saying a word.

Caesar kept his prisoner for five years and had him put to death on the day of his triumph. The fall of Alesia marked the end of the war. The rebels submitted one after the other. Only the city of Uxellodunum held out for several months; it was taken in its turn, and its defenders had their hands cut off (51 B.C.). Gaul was definitely conquered.

Caesar gained in these hard campaigns a reputation equal to that of Alexander or Hannibal. A fearless soldier, he always marched at the head of his troops. Endowed with remarkable intelligence and great decision of character, he knew how to make the best preparations for conquest.

This war was a war of skill, in which tactics and discipline triumphed over Gallic heroism. The Roman army owed its victory to its equipment, its machines, military formation, forced marches, and engineering feats. Nothing is more remarkable than the work undertaken by the Roman soldiers — the investment of Alesia, the bridge over the Rhine, the fleet built to oppose the Veneti. It seems as if the pickaxe and the trowel did more toward the conquest of Gaul than the sword.

The Gauls could only bring their bravery and their contempt of death to oppose all this science. But in spite of everything, their numbers should have enabled them to drive out the enemy; their lack of unity was their undoing.

As soon as they had made their submission, the Gauls adopted the civilization of their conquerors. They adopted Roman manners and clothes, and the most wealthy among them even adopted Latin speech. The Gallic aristocracy had already given themselves to Caesar; the people followed, and there was soon an entirely Gallic legion, called the "legion of the lark" because of its standard, under the pro-consul's command. On the whole, Roman domination was to the advantage of Gaul; it gave to a divided country internal peace, unity, and civilization. None of the other countries conquered by Rome submitted so completely to her influence; the Gauls became Gallo-Romans and quickly forgot their ancient state.

CHAPTER XXVI

THE RISE OF THE EMPIRE

CAESAR'S death threw Rome into great disorder. His murderers wished to re-establish the old constitution; when they had completed their crime, they left the Senate House and called the people to liberty.

But among the people, the well-to-do were tired of civil wars and fifty years of anarchy, and as for the poor, the method of counting votes had prevented them from ever taking a real share in the government. The people remembered with regret Caesar's good government, which had given order to Rome; nor did they hide their regrets. On their side, the Senators hesitated; they feared the appearance of some new master. They did not have to wait long. Antonius, an old officer of Caesar's, at that time consul, wished to profit by events. He was a brave officer of coarse appearance, famous in the wine shops for his great height, his soldier's uniform, and his reputation as a heavy drinker. He suddenly disclosed himself as an able politician.

He organized Caesar's funeral and there pronounced an oration to the dictator in the Forum, read a will that gave money to the people, and awoke general compassion by exposing the toga, bloodstained and pierced with twenty-eight dagger stabs that had entered Caesar's body. At the sight, the crowd rose against the murderers, and Brutus and his friends were forced to flee.

Antonius' plans were disturbed by the arrival in Rome of Octavius, Caesar's nephew and adopted son. He had come from Athens, where he was studying, in order to claim his uncle's inheritance. He was a young man of nineteen, small, lame, sickly, and shy; he spoke badly, lacked courage to the extent of being afraid of thunder and the dark, but under this puny exterior, he hid great political boldness. He played the part of a good young man who only sought knowledge, flattered the Senate, called Cicero his "father," kept Caesar's old soldiers in his pay, and soon found himself at the head of an army.

Cicero and the Senate believed that they had found in him the man who would rid them of Antonius, who had already left Rome in pursuit of Brutus. Cicero now pronounced his famous orations, the Philippics, declared Antonius an outlaw, and procured the command of the war against him for Octavius.

Octavius was the winner; he claimed the consulate as his due, which was at first refused him. At this point, Antonius, having secured the support of the governors of Gaul and Spain, returned to Italy at the head of an army. The two ambitious men realized that it was to their mutual interest to unite against the Senate, which favored Caesar's murderers.

They allied with Lepidus, governor of Narbonnese Gaul, and the three formed, for three years, a second triumvirate, which at a much later date was ratified by the people's votes. They divided the provinces among themselves and made the title of triumvir that of a new magistracy (43 B.C.).

The first care of the triumvirate was to proscribe their enemies. The proscriptions were announced on a placard worded thus: "If the perfidy of wicked men had not repaid kindness by hatred, if those whom Caesar in his clemency had saved, enriched, and loaded with honors after their ruin had not become his murderers, we also would have forgotten those whom we now declare public enemies. This is that which we command: that anyone who shall hide any of those whose names are given below, anyone who shall assist any of the proscribed to flee, shall be proscribed himself. If he shall be brought to us for reward, a free man shall receive 25,000 drachmas, a slave 1,000 and the rights of citizenship. The names of murderers and denouncers shall be kept secret."

Three hundred senators and 2,000 knights perished, among them Cicero, whom Octavius sacrificed to the wrath of Antonius.

After these massacres, Octavius and Antonius crossed the Adriatic to attack the legions Brutus and Cassius had collected in Macedonia. They defeated them in two days at Philippi, and Brutus committed suicide, crying, "Virtue, you are only a name!" (42 B.C.).

Antonius left for the East to punish Egypt, which had sent help to Brutus.

At the court of Queen Cleopatra, he forgot duty for pleasure, and Octavius had to subdue the West unaided. He had first to combat the intrigues of Antonius' wife Fulvia, who died just at the time that war was declared between the triumvirs.

Then he subdued Sextus Pompeius, son of the great Pompeius, who had collected a fleet and was master of the Mediterranean. He triumphed after two years' fighting, thanks to the military talent of his friend Agrippa (38–36 B.C.). Lepidus, the third triumvir, played an insignificant part in all these achievements; Octavius made him Pontifex Maximus. There remained the struggle between the two ambitious men.

After an unsuccessful expedition against the Parthians, Antonius had returned to Cleopatra at Alexandria, where he lived a lazy and licentious life.

He dreamed of an Eastern empire for his queen and gave some Asiatic lands to their son. Octavius easily exploited this attitude of mind to excite Roman indignation against Antonius; hiding his personal rivalry under the cover of national war, he decreed an expedition against "this woman who has planned the fall of the Capitol and the ruin of the empire." Antonius and Cleopatra awaited Octavius in Greece with a fleet and an army. Their fleet was defeated near Actium on the Adriatic, at the entrance of the Gulf of Arba, and Cleopatra fled, followed by Antonius.

Octavius pursued them to Egypt and defeated Antonius at Actium, near Alexandria (31 B.C.). Cleopatra tried in vain to negotiate with the conqueror. Antonius committed suicide, and believing that everything was lost, Cleopatra followed his example, employing the bite of an asp. Octavius was the sole master of the world, and the republic was at an end. Octavius, although in appearance he did not change the function of Roman institutions in order not to excite the same hatred as Julius Caesar, ruled without appearing to do so. He did not wish to accept the title of dictator; he allowed the Senate, the consuls, and the comitia to remain; he only accepted a new title from them. There was a desire to call him Romulus, the second founder of Rome, but they decided on the name of Augustus, which connected him with the sacred family of the founder. As Caesar, he held all offices, and he had full powers because he held all the offices. The first of his titles was always that of Imperator (victorious general), which indicated the origin of his power and gave him legal authority over the whole army. In addition, he was Tribune, which rendered him inviolable; Censor, which enabled him to nominate senators and watch over citizens; Pontifex Maximus, that is, head of the State religion; Princeps, or president of the Senate, that is, controller of their debates.

Augustus then had absolute power, but everything seemed to exist as it had always existed. The Senate made the laws, the comitia voted on them, and the magistrates executed them in the name of the people. The standards of the legions continued to bear the letters S.P.Q.R., the initials of the words which mean "The Senate and the Roman People." Augustus lived the life of an ordinary citizen, took part in voting, put up his friends for election, addressed the Senate in his turn, and lived on the Palatine in a modest house, open to all. He wished to restore order to Rome, and he set the example himself.

All this public life was only an appearance; in reality, Augustus directed everything. A private council really administered the empire; a guard called the Pretorian Guard, consisting of nine cohorts, maintained order in the city. At the head were the pretorian prefect, the emperor's principal agent, the prefect of the city, the prefect of the watch, and the *prefectus annona*, charged with the provisioning of Rome. An army of secretaries worked under the magistrates; the majority were freedmen whose loyalty was assured.

With order, prosperity reigned in Rome and the city became covered with monuments. Augustus boasted of finding a city of brick and leaving a city of marble. He reorganised the water supply by constructing aqueducts, for which he created a special corps of engineers. He also attempted to reform the morals of Rome, for corruption had become extreme. He wished to re-establish the old religious practices, and strove to restore the old family spirit and to fight the abuses of divorce and celibacy.

His collaborators were his friends, Agrippa, the conqueror of Antonius, and Mecenas, a man of culture who patronised letters and arts. In his circle were the historian Livy, the poets Virgil and Horace, and many others whose writings have given to this period the name of the Augustan age.

The provinces benefited a great deal by the establishment of the empire. Instead of being oppressed as they formerly were by the proconsuls, they were administered according to laws by officers who had fixed appointments and were called legates. They were appointed by the emperor and were answerable to him. The provinces had the right of electing assemblies which could petition the Emperor directly. Augustus made several journeys in order to investigate their needs; roads were made, great works undertaken and security assured. The conquered recognised the advantages of imperial rule and they spoke of the Pax Romana.

The provinces were protected by a line of natural frontiers: the Rhine, Danube, Euphrates, the deserts of Asia and Africa. On the other side lived barbarian peoples who were a perpetual danger to the empire. Augustus tried to make them respect the frontiers, and he organised a permanent army of twenty-three legions reinforced by a great number of auxiliaries. Settled in camps at each point of danger, they assured the peacefulness of the provinces. Augustus had only one serious loss, against the Germans between the Rhine and Danube, as we shall see later.

The emperor had no son by his wife Livia; his heirs were his grandsons, the children of his friend Agrippa and his daughter Julia. They died young and he had to adopt Tiberius, Livia's son by a former marriage. His last years were saddened by these deaths; he had also the unhappiness of exiling his daughter because of her misconduct, and of hearing of the disaster of the army of his legate Varus in Germany. He died at the age of sixty-six (A.D. 14) and was buried with great ceremony in the tomb named after him.

The dead emperor was treated as a god; ceremonies were instituted in his honour and a college of priests was founded to celebrate them. The worship of the emperor was called his apotheosis. All the magistrates, generals and assemblies had to pay homage to the emperor's memory; it became a token of fidelity to the imperial rule and also the moral link which united all parts of the empire in a common worship in addition to the diverse religions. Thus the founding of this new worship was an act of policy. The empire passed from Augustus to Tiberius without trouble. The people and the provinces were attached to the new rule, which gave them peace and abundance. Only the senators regretted their old privileges, but they were too corrupt and too degraded to shake off the imperial yoke. The army supported Tiberius, for he had had a command in Germany. Aged fifty-six, he appeared to take up power with reluctance; he refused all titles and honours, and wished to be only princeps. The Senate was associated with him in the government and had to ratify all his decisions. The provincial governors were chosen for merit and inspected rigorously.

But this good administration came suddenly to an end when Tiberius had seen perish Augustus' nephew Germanicus, the conqueror of Germany, and his son Drusus. He discovered that the murderer was his favourite Sejanus, who wished to exterminate the whole of Caesar's family in order to obtain the throne. The emperor conceived a violent hatred against all patricians; executions multiplied; he killed Sejanus and retired to the island of Capri, where he lived in superstitious fear, surrounded by diviners and astrologers. This lasted until his death (37 A.D.). The historian Tacitus gives a recital of his crimes, but his proscriptions affected the nobility alone; the rest of the empire, being well governed, was indifferent.

The empire fell to Caligula, Germanicus' son, so named because he wore soldier's boots. He began by being a good ruler, but afflicted with epilepsy from childhood, he became entirely mad. His reign was a succession of extravagances, debaucheries, and murders. One reads of him throwing money to the people in the circus, illuminating mountains, having himself worshipped in the place of Jupiter and nominating his horse as consul. The prefect of the pretorian guard delivered the world of this dangerous lunatic.

The prefect wanted to restore the republic, but the soldiers did not wish it. They discovered, hidden behind a curtain of the palace, Claudius, a brother of Germanicus, and made him emperor, receiving in return a big gratuity, the donatum. This was the first emperor chosen by soldiers for the reward of money. He was old, bald-headed, besotted with drunkenness, shut off from public business by his archaeological studies. He was weak and was governed by women and freedmen. Freedmen were the masters of Rome. One of them, Pallas, made him marry Germanicus' daughter Agrippina. She poisoned Claudius with a dish of mushrooms in order to gain the throne for her son Nero (54 A.D.).

Agrippina had hoped to rule in the name of her seventeen-year-old son. She was present at meetings of the Senate hidden behind a curtain, and she governed with the help of the philosopher Seneca and the general Burrhus, whom she had appointed tutors to the prince. But Nero, prompted by Narcissus, a freedman, soon grew tired of this tutelage. Agrippina, alarmed, supported Britannicus, Claudius' son. Nero had him poisoned at a banquet. It was Agrippina's turn four years later. He tried to drown her at a water fête, but she saved herself by swimming. Then he accused her of conspiring against him and had her strangled. The whole nobility showed "an extraordinary admiration for depravity";

Seneca himself wrote an eulogy of the crime. But this did not content this jealous, vain and hypocritical prince.

He repudiated his wife Octavia, condemned her to death, and gave himself up to all manner of debaucheries with his freedmen. He believed himself to be a great artist, and liked to perform in public to the applause of a crowd of hired admirers. He took part in chariot races, recited his own verses in the theatre, played the lyre, and made a tour in Greece, where he won 1800 wreaths. All this appeared infamous to the Roman mind and only worthy of a slave. One day Rome was devastated by a huge fire; rumour accused the emperor of the crime, and he ordered the first persecution of the Christians in order to create a diversion.

After thirteen years of his rule, the soldiers on the frontiers revolted, and Rome, where several conspiracies had been wiped out in blood, followed their example. Nero fled and then committed suicide, exclaiming, "What an artist perishes in me" (68 A.D.).

The revolted legions fought among themselves as to who should appoint an emperor, for the elected prince rewarded his soldiers liberally. The first to succeed were the soldiers from Spain, who elected their general Galba, aged seventy-three. He refused to give money to the Pretorian Guard in Rome, who in consequence set up in opposition to him Otho, a friend of Nero's. Galba was killed. Meanwhile, the legions from Gaul arrived with their general Vitellius. Otho was defeated and killed himself. Vitellius was not permitted to enjoy the fruits of victory for long; the Eastern army, superior to the others because of the continual fighting against the Parthians, arrived and elected in their turn their general, Vespasian. He won the battle of Cremona (69 A.D.), and peace returned to Rome with the new dynasty of the Flavians.

Vespasian, the son of a customs officer who had risen in the army through merit, was a middle-class emperor, hard-working and economical. He reorganised the finances, which were nearly bankrupt through Nero's follies, re-established discipline in the army, and put down revolts among the Germans and the Jews. He reformed the Senate and abolished the *lex maiestas*, by which so many had been proscribed. He died a natural death, making fun of the divine honours which were accorded to dead emperors. "I feel that I am becoming a god," he said (79 A.D.).

His son Titus, the conqueror of Jerusalem, only reigned two years, long enough to be called "the darling of mankind." He complained that he had lost a day if he had not found some good action to perform. The famous eruption of Vesuvius which destroyed the towns of Herculaneum and Pompeii took place during his reign (79 A.D.).

He was succeeded by his brother Domitian, who reigned just as wisely for thirteen years; the provinces had never been so well governed. Then in 93 A.D., he became like Nero, a cruel tyrant, who massacred men at random, drove the philosophers from Rome, persecuted the Christians, and perished by assassination (96 A.D.). His wife was privy to the plot.

The Senate gave the empire to one of its own members, Nerva. He founded the Antonine dynasty, but instead of regulating the succession by relationship, he introduced adoption, and thus secured a succession of excellent masters for the empire (96-98 A.D.).

Trajan, whom he had adopted, was a good general and a good administrator. He conquered the Dacians on the Danube and the Parthians on the Euphrates. He built the famous Trajan column in the Forum to commemorate his campaigns. He treated the Senate with the respect of old days and lived in great simplicity. "I will be to others," he said, "as I would, if I were a citizen, emperors should be to me." He undertook great works: the bridge across the Danube at the Iron Gates to reach Dacia, the Alcantara bridge in Spain, and Trajan's Forum in Rome. He took wise steps to encourage commerce, agriculture, art, and letters. Then he showed his humanity in instituting for the first time assistance from public funds for poor children, who were brought up at the prince's expense. Henceforth, the Senate adopted as a salutation to emperors, "May you be happier than Augustus, better than Trajan." He died in Asia (117 A.D.).

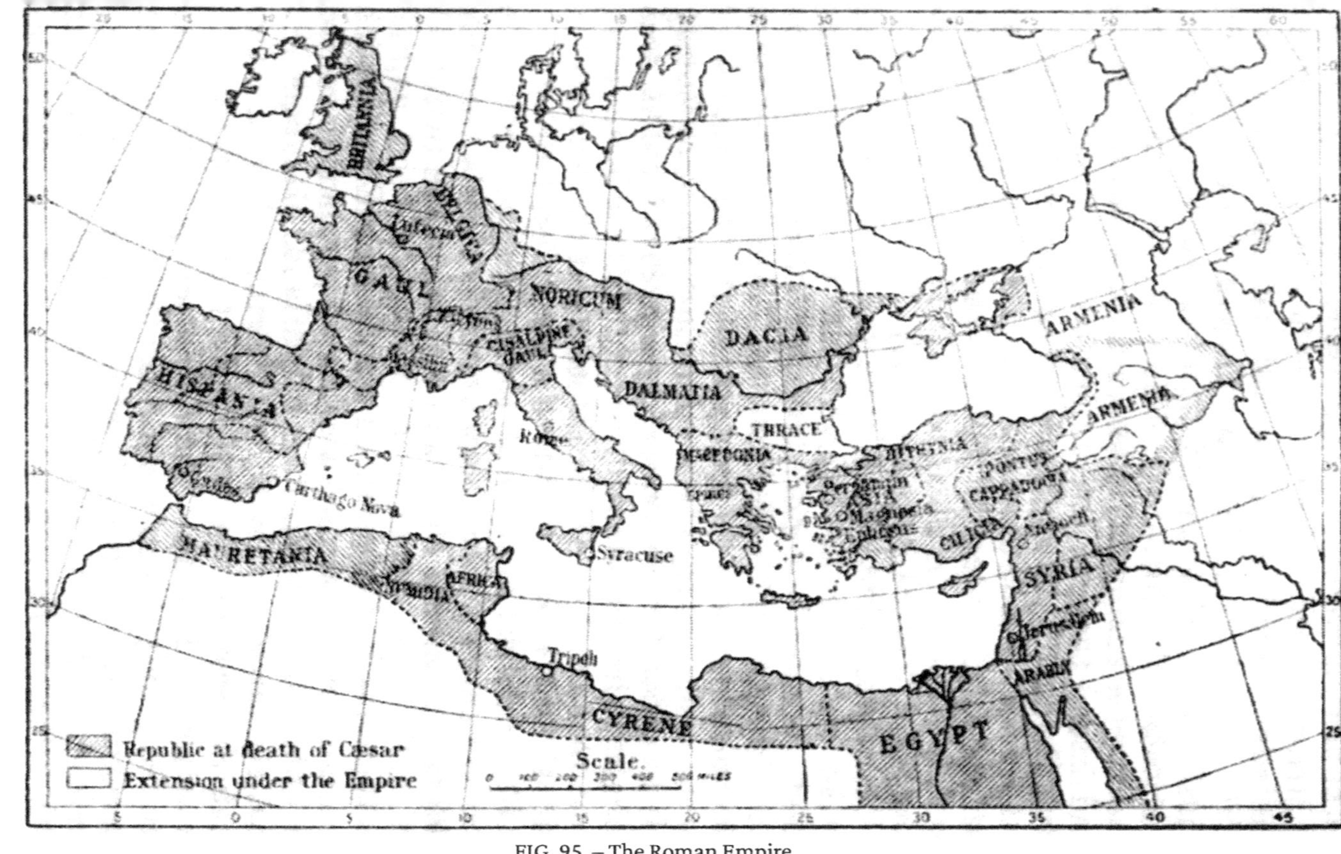

FIG. 95. – The Roman Empire.

His successor, Hadrian, was a peaceful emperor. An artist, a writer, an indefatigable traveller, he covered the whole Roman world with buildings, restoring ruins or constructing new monuments. Athens, where he lived, became "Hadrian's City," so numerous were his "improvements."

His principal claim to fame is that he organised the administration. Until his time, the work of the civil service was done by freedmen. He decreed that henceforth it should be given to free men and instituted the hierarchy. He collected and edited the laws made by the praetors during past centuries, and issued them in one unified code. Thus, he may truly be said to have organised the empire (117-138 A.D.).

Hadrian was succeeded by Antoninus Pius, so famous for his integrity that his name has been given to this whole series of emperors. He chose a worthy successor, Marcus Aurelius (161 A.D.).

Marcus Aurelius was a philosopher who continued to be one after he ascended the throne. He was good, humane, disinterested, and passed his leisure time in writing his Meditations, "wonderful sayings of ancient wisdom." He looked after the welfare of slaves and increased benevolent institutions. But by the irony of fate, this emperor, who loved books, was obliged to live in camps. He had to defend Rome from threatened danger on the Danube and the Euphrates, and died at Vienna whilst on a campaign (178 A.D.). He made the mistake of leaving the empire to his son Commodus, who became a bloodthirsty imbecile like Domitian and Nero, and was murdered in 192 A.D.

Augustus had surrounded the Roman Empire with a cordon of troops and a chain of permanent camps in order to keep out the barbarians. He believed that it was necessary to hold them at bay in order that the rest of the world might enjoy peace and prosperity. But this very prosperity made these people greedy for plunder, and they did not cease attacking the Roman frontiers. Thus, there were these wars of defence, not of conquest, lasting as long as the Roman Empire itself.

We have already seen that the Rhine, Danube, Euphrates,

and the deserts were the frontiers. They were not equally open to attack. The Sahara only contained, as it does today, a few plundering tribes; the sea protected Spain and the coasts of Gaul. The formidable enemies were the Germans on the Rhine and the Marcomanni on the Upper Danube, the Dacians on the Lower Danube, and the Parthians on the Euphrates.

Augustus, following Caesar's plans, thought that he would win the submission of the Germans. His general Drusus crossed the Rhine and conquered the country as far as the Elbe. But he was killed by an accident, and his successor, Varus, allowed himself to be surprised in the forest of Teutoburg by the German leader Arminius, and he and three legions were cut to pieces. It was said that Augustus, crazy with sorrow, never ceased to murmur, "Varus, give me back my legions."

Varus' disaster was revenged by Germanicus during the reign of Tiberius. He destroyed the confederation of the Cherusci and devastated the lands of the Batavi. The Germans remained quiet until the troubles which followed the death of Nero. At that period, the Batavian Civilis, with the help of the prophetess Velleda, tried to found a Gallic kingdom on the Rhine; it was, however, soon destroyed. Domitian was, in his turn, beaten on the Rhine (81-96 A.D.). Trajan tried to pacify the country soon after his accession; his armies were everywhere victorious, but in order to protect the weak part of the frontier, the region of the Rhine and the Upper Danube, he built a great entrenchment, like the great wall of China. It was composed of a ditch and a rampart consisting of an earth palisade. Behind the rampart, a stone wall studded with towers was erected. Behind this wall, there stretched a military road bordered by camps. A second wall and ditch completed the fortifications. The same type of fortification had been built by Hadrian in the north of England to resist the raids of the Picts and Scots.

During the reign of Marcus Aurelius, the Quades and the Marcomanni raided Greece and penetrated into Italy. Rome was in a panic. The emperor sold the imperial jewels to raise troops and took command of the expedition himself. He made several campaigns before he drove them back and was obliged to fortify strongly the city of Vienna in order to keep them at bay.

The Dacians, as fierce a people as the Germans, lived in the country across the Danube, the modern Transylvania and Roumania. They entered the empire during the reign of Domitian, who could not prevent them. Trajan marched against them. He began by building a road which followed the course of the Danube, of which there still remain traces beside the river in the celebrated pass of the Iron Gates. At the end of the pass, he built across the river a huge stone bridge to give him an entrance to Dacia. The war lasted five years (101-106 A.D.); the capital of Dacia was taken, their king was killed, and the land was made a Roman province. This province on the other side of the river was like a fortress populated with Roman colonists who have left traces of their name and language among the modern Roumanians.

The Parthian knights never ceased their attempts to cross the Euphrates. They were defeated first by Crassus, then by Antonius, but their boldness was never rebuffed by these checks. Vespasian, Trajan, and Marcus Aurelius had to send expeditions against them. Under cover of these wars, there were many revolts in the East. The most famous was that of the Jews; they were conquered by Titus after the celebrated siege, which was commemorated by his triumphal arch in Rome, and which led to the destruction of Jerusalem and the dispersal of the Jews.

Whilst the legions were fighting on the frontiers, the provinces, administered justly by the emperors, enjoyed the advantages of the Pax Romana.

CHAPTER XXVII

THE "PAX ROMANA"

IT is important to understand exactly what changes took place in the Roman world through the substitution of the imperial government for that of the republic. The new rule gave the provinces justice, peace, and prosperity; that is the reason why the conspiracies and revolutions which painted Rome red with blood were not repeated under the empire. The people continued to be as well governed under a Nero or a Domitian as they were under an Augustus or a Trajan, and they never wished to revolt.

The provinces were no longer only territory given over to pillage by the Senate to its members. Some, those inland, were still administered by the Senate; the others, those on the frontiers, were ruled by the emperor. But all the governors, whether of senatorial or imperial provinces, were civil servants with fixed appointments. The army was entirely dependent upon the emperor, and was paid from a special fund; the provinces no longer had to bear the charge.

Peace reigned everywhere, since the empire had made an end of the civil wars which had ruined the provinces, and the army, camped on the frontiers, kept the barbarians at bay. As a result, trade and agriculture flourished.

The emperors turned their attention to the maintenance of order, governing not for the benefit of a small clique, as the Senate had done, but for the general interest. Roman rights were given step by step to all the provinces, and Rome, instead of being the city mistress of a conquered world, became only the capital of the Roman Empire.

The emperors' absolute authority and the ideals they set

before them, obliged them to appoint men upon whose loyalty they could depend to supervise the administration of justice and the finances according to fixed rules. This was the origin of the legal codes and the civil service, and has been imitated in the administrative machinery of our modern states. These schemes, so important in the history of the world, date from the time of Hadrian. The earlier emperors had prepared the way, but it was he who organised. He also substituted for the caprice of praetors one law for all, the expression of the emperor's will. This was the Perpetual Edict. Henceforth, contracts between individuals or with the State were ruled by laws laid down exactly. Thus, the notion of right was introduced: public right and private right, which is the basis of modern constitutions. That is why the study of Roman law forms an important part of legal training.

The practice of regulating everything in the empire is shown in a curious way in the rules for workingmen's corporations. The emperors permitted men of the same trade to unite in associations to protect their interests, provided their associations were authorised by law. "Whoever," said a jurist of the period, "founds an illegal association is liable to the same penalties as those who, fully armed, attack others in the public places or the temples." These associations had their ritual, festivals, and officials, and took part in public processions with their banners; in fact, they resembled the modern trade unions. They had the right of appealing for justice for their members and insured the burial of their members by erecting their own burial places. But when the imperial government made itself responsible for the provisioning of Rome and the whole world, they supervised the corporations and would not allow the members to change their trade. Then imperial manufactories were founded, in which the workmen, once they had entered, were branded and had to remain for life.

We have seen that the Pax Romana was maintained by a continuous chain of fortresses on the frontiers. There was also an army in Spain, in Africa; at Antioch in Syria, two on the Rhine and four on the Danube. These armies consisted of legions and

FIG. 96. - A Roman aqueduct.

auxiliary cohorts which were generally employed far away from their homes; for example, in Africa there was a cohort of Germans and one of Syrians.

All these soldiers signed on for twenty years and received at demobilization a small estate. They lived in permanent camps, *castra stativa*, made of stone, and they dwelt, some of them in huts and some in houses. In the center of the camp, there was a building called the pretorium, which was occupied by the general. There was nearly always a Roman town, with its forum, triumphal arches, theatre, baths, and temples, in the neighborhood of the camp. During times of peace, the legions were employed in public works: they built roads, bridges, aqueducts, and entrenchments like Hadrian's Wall in England or Trajan's in Germany. Camp life was not as rough as it had been in earlier days: the legions had their personal property and their slave-orderlies; the officers and the non-commissioned officers had their clubs; the neighboring town offered them all the pleasures of Roman life.

To maintain their dominion over the world, the emperors built both fortifications and roads of extraordinary solidity. They were not simple earthworks, but the work of masons undertaken under the direction of military engineers.

The roads, like those of republican times, were built-up carriageways covered with tessellated pavement. They had footpaths and were sufficiently wide for the passage of two carriages. Augustus was the first to build them outside Italy; he made the road from Spain through the south of Gaul. Then the road from Illyria and Greece was built; later, those in Gaul and on the Danube. Little by little, all the countries of the empire were connected, so that neither rain nor winter could stop convoys. They were an instrument of domination, but they also aided trade. Moreover, they were an assistance to the administration, for the emperors could issue commands through couriers, who were always ready in relays; this was the first system of posts in Europe.

All the emperors were great builders, and the greater portion of their buildings were for the public good or to satisfy the needs of the populace. There were theatres, circuses, temples, basilicae or law courts, thermae or public baths, aqueducts, triumphal arches, and gateways.

Rome was covered with magnificent monuments, often of colossal proportions, which improved the city and also gave work to workmen. Augustus added a new forum to the old one, built the theatre of Marcellus, and the Pantheon, a temple intended to be dedicated to all the gods.

After the burning of Rome, Nero hoped to rebuild it on a regular plan, and he built a luxurious palace, which was called the Golden Palace.

The largest amphitheatre, the Coliseum, was built under Vespasian; it could contain 100,000 spectators. Titus built his triumphal arch, and Trajan leveled the space between the Capitol and the Quirinal, and there erected monuments, among them his statue and the well-known column which commemorated his victory over the Dacians. Hadrian built his own tomb, which is now the castle of S. Angelos; Caracalla built baths. A great many of these monuments are still standing and testify to the strength of Roman architecture. The provinces were as favored as the capital, and in them all, as far as the edges of the deserts, Roman ruins are to be found.

Architecture was the art in which the Romans excelled, and although it was inspired by the Greeks, it did not lack original- ity. It was distinguished by its useful character, its large propor-

FIG. 97. – The ruins of the Coliseum.

tions, and the employment of the arch, which the Romans had learned from the Etruscans. Their sewers were vaults; aqueducts, bridges, triumphal arches were arches or a succession of arches; the amphitheatres were arches built upon one another; the Pantheon was a cupola, that is to say, a spherical arch, and the sides were decorated with arches which were to become the arc-shaped windows of Roman-Gothic architecture. But the Romans borrowed from the Greeks their pillars, statues, and color decorations, and their works of art had not the originality and personal character of Greek work. Their architects and artists were often craftsmen who, once they had adopted a model, were able to copy it almost mechanically. This was very evident in their statues and mural paintings, which were usually of a trivial character and reproduced general forms easily copied; they were made by the dozen. They planned towns and monuments in much the same way as exhibition grounds are laid out today. They had to work quickly; but there were doubtless some builders and masons who were true artists.

In republican times, Rome had presented a picture of very active public life, and at the same time a simple and austere home life. Under the empire, there was no longer any civic life, since the will of the princeps replaced that of the Senate and people, and the Assemblies became merely ceremonies. No one listened to orations in the peaceful Forum.

On the other hand, corrupt morals broke up family life. In its place, there grew up an outdoor life of loafing and amusements. The emperors favored this movement, and were careful to feed and amuse the people in order to protect themselves from revolts. Their method of governing was: peace in the provinces; bread and games, *panem et circenses*, in Rome. The state of Roman society lent itself to their designs, for Rome was in reality only a city of beggars.

The nobility, so powerful in republican times, had nearly disappeared. They had been decimated by proscriptions, ruined by confiscations, and also they were no longer able to pillage the

FIG. 98. - Paquius Proculus and his wife: one of the paintings found at Pompeii.

provinces. They had given place to a new aristocracy of officials, many of whom were provincials and for the most part owed their wealth to the liberality and pensions of the princeps. The knights continued their lucrative methods of trading and money-lending, but they depended on the emperor, who was able to regulate their profits. Enormous fortunes were rarer in this period, and the increase of luxury diminished the number daily. When one reads of the prodigality of certain Romans, of their lengthy meals, their palatial houses, their crowd of slaves, it is only true of a small number, often freedmen who were the favorites of the emperors. The true extravagance, which was really very great, was public extravagance, which was paid for by the emperor to please the populace.

The people were very exacting. There were in Rome 300,000 citizens who were Roman only in name. These descendants of freedmen derived from their origin all the vices of slaves. The greater number of them did not work; no one regarded dependence as a disgrace. Those who practiced some trade, or had some means and education, did not hesitate to add to their resources by becoming the clients of rich men. Every morning they besieged their atriums, where they were given the *sportula*, that is to say, a little basket of provisions.

The others, the most degraded, lived on the imperial distribution of corn. The gifts of rich provincials were added to these doles, and the lives of the citizens were passed in idleness. To occupy their leisure, they were given shows and amusements.

The rich and elegant idlers made up for the lack of public life by the distractions of social life. They visited one another, invited one another to sumptuous banquets and festivities, at which women took part, for they had given up the austere morals of ancient times. When they traveled, they went to bathe in the sea or into the country. A fashionable literature, consisting of letters, slight verses, and impressions, sprang up in Rome; and people often met together to hear an author read his own works.

The common people congregated in the taverns (*popinae*), where they drank to the sound of Eastern music, and watched acrobats and dancers. The less rude drinkers frequented, like the Greeks, the shops where mulled drinks were sold. Many people used the promenades as meeting-places. These promenades were of two kinds: gardens and porticoes. The gardens covered both banks of the Tiber and the sides of the hills; there were a good many of them, for the great families and the emperors perpetuated their names by opening their grounds, which were named after them, to the public.

The porticoes were covered promenades, formed by colonnades arranged in either rounds or squares about a garden. One side was closed in by a wall, and the other open and supported by columns. There were twenty such porticoes in the Campus Martius; the columns were of rare marble, the ground was paved with rich mosaics, and the walls decorated with pictures and statues. They afforded shelter from rain and sunshine, and they were perfect places for conversation in the open air.

The most widespread taste was that for the *thermae* or public baths. There were 900 of them in the neighborhood of Rome, of which some, like the *thermae* of Caracalla, were of gigantic proportions. They contained hot, cold, and vapor baths. People generally began with a cold bath in a bath called the *frigidarium*, then went into a tepid room, the *tepidarium*, and then into a sweating room, the *caldarium*. They next gave themselves up to masseurs and depilators, who were very necessary to the Romans, for they wore their legs and arms bare. The baths were heated by furnaces in the basements. They did not go to the baths solely for the sake

FIG. 99. - A Roman theatre.

of bathing, but to meet their friends. There were reading-rooms, fencing-rooms, barbers, and even lecturers and singers.

The emperors assembled the people together for great festivities for which there were never-ending novelties. In the Roman year, there were sixty-five feasts; some of them, for example, the opening of the Colosseum, lasted for 100 days. During these feasts, spectacles were given in the theatre, circus, and amphitheatre. They began in the morning and lasted until sunset. These spectacles, at which the emperor presided, were made the occasion for distributing among the people presents, sweets, or wine.

In the theatres, of which the theatre of Pompey was the largest, comedies, tragedies, farces, and pantomimes were presented. The comedies were those Plautus and Terence had translated or copied from the Greek; they amused the Romans as late as the fourth century. Tragedies were less successful, for the audience had not a sufficiently refined taste, but they loved above all farces and pantomimes. The farces, called *Atellan* farces, were coarse pieces in one act, in which everyday subjects were mixed up with conventional persons, such as our Punch, Harlequin, and Pierrot, which we derive from Italian comedy.

The pantomime was performed in dumb show and with very great talent. Thus the Roman stage appealed to the eye rather than the mind.

Chariot races were held in the circus. The Circus Maximus held 300,000 spectators and consisted of tiers of seats surrounding an elongated track. The middle of the track or arena was decorated with a line of altars, obelisks, and statues, ending at its extremities by two golden posts. This was called the *Spina*; it was about three-quarters of a mile in circumference and had to be traversed seven times in the course of a race.

There were twenty-four races in a day, each consisting of four chariots drawn as a rule by four horses. The drivers wore different-colored liveries: blue, white, green, and red, according to the stables they represented; they were very popular and gained large sums of money. They had their backers, like the jockeys and professional sportsmen of today, and their supporters were not content with cheering them: they often fought for them, and there were even riots in the circus. The calling had its dangers, for the chariots might easily overturn when turning the corner-posts. The emperors gave great dignity to the races. They attended in state, with the magistrates, priests, statues of the gods, and competing charioteers marching in front of them.

The largest amphitheatre was the Coliseum. This was like the circuses, only the arena was round and devoid of the Spina. The gladiators gave their combats there. These combats had their origin in the human sacrifices made by the Etruscans at the funerals of great people to appease their ghosts. In the Roman world, these sacrifices were replaced by a fight between two slaves; under the empire, these became regularized as games at which as many as 500 pairs of gladiators would come to blows.

Some of the gladiators were men condemned to death, some were slaves or prisoners of war, sometimes even free men who were eager for advertisement. They were trained in special schools called *ludus gladiatorius*; to own a school of this

FIG. 100. - Gladiators.

kind was very profitable. They fought on foot, on horseback, and in chariots, in pairs or in groups. Generally, men differently armed were opposed to one another. There were the Samnites, men who fought nearly naked with a great square shield and a bent sword; the Mirmillones, armed like soldiers; Hoplites, covered with armor like medieval knights; the Thracians, distinguished by a helmet with great wings; and the Retiarians, armed only with a fishing-net and a trident. All who came to take part in the games were drawn up to start with before the emperor's throne and called, "*Ave, Caesar Imperator, morituri te salutant.*"

The dead bodies were removed from the arena by slaves, who drew them out with hooks. A man dressed as Mercury made sure they were dead by touching them with a red-hot iron, and those wounded too badly to recover were killed. These cruel games, which to our ideas seem horrible, were the delight of the Roman people.

Sometimes the arena was turned into a lake and naval fights were given. At other times gladiators called *Bestiarii* fought against wild beasts. Men condemned to death were often thrown to lions and tigers; this was usually the fate of the Christian martyrs. Sometimes the arena would be turned into a forest, where rare animals would be hunted. The emperors collected them to satisfy the bloodthirsty tastes of the populace; and the organization of the games received their greatest care. Augustus boasted of having had 3,500 animals killed in hunts of this description.

Our knowledge of a Roman city during the imperial period is not solely conjecture; we are able to see with our own eyes and touch with our hands the remains of this civilization in the ruins of Pompeii.

Pompeii was buried under the ashes of Vesuvius during the reign of Titus (79 A.D.). The details of this eruption were recounted by Pliny the Younger, and they remind one strangely of the destruction of the town of S. Pierre in Martinique in 1902 A.D. Men saw the same column of smoke, suffocating cloud, rain of cinders, and slag. The houses of the city were covered up for centuries and were excavated in the nineteenth century; and streets, fixtures, the furniture inside houses, ornaments, shops with their accessories, walls with inscriptions and placards, the bodies of men caught by the eruption, could all be seen. This city was a little seaside town with two theatres, one of which held 5,000 people. The wall-paintings, jewels, household and toilet utensils, and all kinds of familiar articles have been discovered in great numbers, and make it possible to reconstruct the private life of Italians of this period.

CHAPTER XXVIII

THE DECLINE OF ROME

THE death of Commodus was followed by a century of indescribable confusion. The period may be termed "military anarchy," for each army tried to nominate its own emperor. Between elections, there was continual fighting, and the emperor was he who survived the longest. There were, in consequence, twenty-five emperors in ninety-three years, and that is only counting the emperors who really reigned. But in the midst of this anarchy, the empire was broken up. Provinces revolted, the frontiers yielded to barbarian encroachments. A reorganization of the empire was necessary; this was undertaken by Diocletian.

The emperors were in the habit of giving their soldiers, on the day of their accession, a large gratuity, called the *donativium*. The election of an emperor was therefore a profitable undertaking for the army who supported him. The Pretorian Guard at Rome, and the armies in the provinces, wanted to gain these advantages at the same time; the empire, therefore, was in the hands of the soldiers. Thus a succession of the most extraordinary people occupied the imperial throne.

Commodus was succeeded by Pertinax, the son of a charcoal-burner. The Pretorians chose him, but they found his rule too severe and killed him at the end of eighty-seven days.

After that, the empire was put up to auction by the Pretorians. Two candidates offered themselves. The highest bidder gained the day, but he was murdered after a reign of sixty-six days, before he had paid the promised sum.

During this time, the armies from Brittany, Illyria, and Syria each nominated an emperor and marched on Rome. The Illyrian army, which guarded the Danubian frontier, was the nearest and was the best-trained. It had an African, Septimus Severus, at its head, who defeated his fellow-competitors and reigned alone. He was a very hard-working emperor, who took for his motto, *Laboremus*. He re-established order in the provinces and on the frontiers, defeated the Parthians and the Scots, and died pronouncing the following sentence, which gives a good idea of the age: "My son, please the soldiers and you can laugh at the rest." His son, Caracalla, followed his advice and gave himself up to dissipated living. He built, however, the great baths named after him, and signed the edict which gave Roman citizenship to all the subjects of the empire.

One of his cousins, Elagabalus, a Syrian priest aged fifty, reigned after him. He introduced into Rome the worship of Mithra, the sun-god. He wore women's clothes, surrounded himself with hairdressers and dancers, and even added women to the Senate to discuss fashions.

He was succeeded by a wise man, Alexander Severus, a philosophical and tolerant emperor, who placed in his oratory the images of Orpheus, Abraham, and Christ. He was assassinated by Maximinus, who took his place. Maximinus was an old Thracian soldier, part athlete, part glutton, who was able to eat thirty pounds of meat a day and to break the jawbone of a horse with a single blow. He did not even arrive in Rome, and the confusion was so great that there were at one time twenty-nine emperors (254–268 A.D.).

During these civil wars, the frontiers were guarded or neglected by poor troops. The barbarian auxiliaries were almost the only cavalry and formed half the army. The infantry was recruited from the population in the neighborhood. The soldiers were no longer trained and required a long procession of carts to carry their food, baggage, and even their arms. The barbarians profited by this confusion and began to invade the empire.

The Alemanni, a German people from the Upper Danube, passed into Switzerland, and from there into Italy, which they penetrated as far as Milan, plundering the land through which they passed.

The Franks, who lived on the lower course of the Rhine, crossed the river, plundered the whole of Gaul, and even penetrated into Spain.

The Goths came from the banks of the Vistula, crossed the Danube, and laid Thrace waste; they took 100,000 prisoners. They were paid to go away (251 A.D.). Some time later, they returned by sea and plundered the coasts of Greece and the Archipelago.

An independent empire, which lasted for nine years, was instituted in Gaul. On the Euphrates, the Parthians had been conquered by the Persians, who in their period of obscurity had retained the military keenness of the time of Cyrus. One of their kings, who was said to have been a descendant of Darius, began what proved to be a series of wars, lasting over several centuries, against the Romans. He marched into Syria, took Antioch, and then made the Emperor Valerian, who tried to stop him, a prisoner. He dragged the unhappy man about in his retinue and made him act as a footstool when he mounted his horse. The empire was saved by the Arab king of Palmyra, to whom another emperor, Gallienus, gave the title of "imperator."

These invasions, and the fact that the Romans treated with the barbarians, show the feebleness of the empire during this period.

The remedy arose out of the evil itself. The soldiers, perturbed by the barbarians' victories, sought energetic generals who would lead them against the menacing enemy. They found them in the Illyrian legions, which, recruited from the sturdy populations of the Balkans, formed the finest of the Roman armies. The generals, like the soldiers, were simple, brave peasants, who drove out the barbarians and re-established order in the empire. They were not Romans, and as they were born in Illyria, they were named the Illyrian emperors.

Such a man was Aurelian, nicknamed "The Iron-handed," who once declared: "I have gold for my friends and iron for my enemies" (270-275 A.D.). He defeated the Alemanni, the Franks, the queen of Palmyra, and the emperor of Gaul. Rome for a long time had not contemplated having to defend herself, but he surrounded the city with a gigantic rampart called Aurelian's Wall.

His successor, Probus (276-282 A.D.), lived with simplicity worthy of ancient Rome. It was told of him that the Persian ambassadors found him in his tent in the midst of feeding out of a porringer of pork and peas. He threatened to send them back to their own country as bare as his head, which was very bald, and he added: "If you are hungry, take from this dish; if not, depart." This peasant delivered Rome from the Vandals and the Franks.

Two years after his death, Diocletian, who altered entirely the organization of the empire, reigned. Diocletian was a Dalmatian, the son of a recorder. He had passed through the ranks and had become prefect of the Pretorian cohorts. Elected by the soldiers during the disturbances which followed the death of Probus, he resolved to divide the empire and to take for a colleague his companion in arms, Maximian.

The empire, with the addition of new provinces in the East, on the Danube, and in Brittany, covered an immense area very difficult to guard and to administer. In the center, there were perpetual revolts; on the frontiers, continual invasions, and it was difficult to deal with either because of the feebleness of the army. Thus, the division of the empire was a defensive as much as an administrative measure.

The two emperors took the title of Augusti and fixed their residences, Diocletian in the East at Nicomedia, Maximian in the West at Milan. Rome was abandoned as a capital, for it was important for the emperors to be nearer the threatened frontiers.

Even divided, the empire appeared to be too heavy a burden for the Augusti; they added two assistants, whom they intended to become their heirs and whom they called Caesars. They were Constantius, who had Trèves for his capital, and Galerius, who established himself at Sirmium on the Save. Thus, there were four rulers: two Augusti and two Caesars, with four capitals and four governments. This division was termed the Tetrarchy, that is to say, government by four.

At the same time, Diocletian changed the boundaries of the provinces and completely altered the character of the imperial dignity. That done, the two Augusti abdicated and Diocletian retired to Salona in Dalmatia to watch the working of his scheme.

It worked ill. The two Caesars became Augusti and appointed new Caesars. But they neglected to appoint Constantine, Constantius's son, who was elected Augustus by the soldiers. Galerius opposed him, and Maximian returned to the people with his son Maxentius. There followed a long period of civil wars, during which there were at one time six emperors.

The disorder ended with the victory of Constantine, who defeated Maxentius near Rome at the Pons Milvius (312 A.D.). Maxentius was drowned in trying to make his escape. There still remained an emperor in the East; he was defeated and killed in 324 A.D.

Constantine (306–337 A.D.) was then sole emperor and accomplished three things which changed completely the face of the empire and the world: (1) He recognized the Christian religion; (2) he founded a new capital, Constantinople; (3) he organized the imperial government. He has been judged very differently by his contemporaries. Many Christians, because he protected their faith, considered him almost as a saint; pagans looked upon him as a cruel tyrant. It is difficult to consider him a virtuous man, since he had his father-in-law, brother-in-law, son, and wife killed. He had hit upon a clever policy.

The son of a Christian mother, he knew that Christianity had increased in spite of Diocletian's persecutions. The Christian churches from East to West were in communication with one another, and their members formed a vast association of men and women devoted to the same cause.

Constantine had had to withstand formidable rivals. He resolved to win the support of the Christians, who were to be found in every part of the empire, and thanks to them, he won the Battle of the Pons Milvius. It was said that before this battle, a cross appeared to him in the sky bearing these words: *In hoc signo vinces*. He reproduced this cross and this inscription on a special standard called the Labarum. But even if he adhered from that time onward to the Christian faith, he was not baptized until he was on his deathbed. He always acted with great political prudence, and so he placed Christians and pagans on the same footing, kept the title of Pontifex Maximus, built temples as well as churches, and made religious liberty a principle of his government.

To reward the Christians for the help they had given him against Maxentius, Constantine restored all the rights which Diocletian's persecutors had taken away and permitted them to practice their religion freely. He made no distinction between Christians and pagans; they were equally eligible for office, and churches became, like the temples, places of refuge. The Edict of Milan (313 A.D.) confirmed this new principle of religious tolerance. Constantine said there:

"We have resolved to accord to Christians, as to others, the privilege of practicing the religion they prefer, so that the God who lives in the sky shall be as propitious and favorable to us as those gods who live in our dominions."

Constantine's respect for the Christian religion developed into protection when he had defeated his colleague in the East, who had tried to dethrone him by raising the pagans against him. The quarrel between the two emperors was really a struggle between the two religions, and Christianity triumphed.

The Christian conquerors were divided. Heresies arose; the most famous was that of the Arians, who denied that Christ was the equal of God the Father. These divisions alarmed the emperor, who feared trouble and wished for order in religion as in everything else. He convened a council at Nicaea, where an assembly of bishops stated definitely the articles of the Christian faith. He presided at the council, which ended in the publication of the Creed, which is called the Nicene Creed. The Arian heresy was condemned by name, and the emperor undertook to respect the true Christian doctrine, which was termed Orthodox. He sought out heretics and punished them severely; the cities which cast out their idols received special privileges (325 A.D.).

Constantine wished to give the empire a new capital and founded Constantinople on the site of the ancient Byzantium. His reasons were partly political, partly religious. He wanted the seat of the empire to be nearer the Danube and the Euphrates, threatened respectively by the Goths and the Persians. He wished also that the new religion should triumph in a new town without being inconvenienced by being constantly reminded of the old gods.

The site was well chosen, at the meeting place of the European and Asiatic worlds, on an easily defended peninsula, near a marvelous port — the Golden Horn. The city was built in the Roman fashion with aqueducts, thermae, palaces, forums, a hippodrome, Christian churches, and pagan temples.

Constantine invited Italian nobles there, brought there by force the inhabitants of the neighborhood, organized libraries, and set up works of art taken from Greece. A special fleet, the Alexandrian fleet, was chartered to bring the necessary corn from Egypt to feed the people. The city developed rapidly; it became the mart for the trade of the East, and its wealth, as well as its power, enabled it to resist all invasions for eleven centuries (330–1453 A.D.).

Constantine completed Diocletian's work of organizing the imperial monarchy. The assemblies, as well as the Senate, which had existed only in name, were now abolished, and there were only an emperor, an administration, and subjects.

The emperor was from that time onwards master (*dominus*), and he was surrounded with all the pomp of Eastern sovereigns. He wore a purple robe, with a crown of gold; gold dust was thrown under his feet, and his subjects addressed him on their knees. His person and everything that belonged to him was sacred. The emperor had under his orders a number of people who constituted the imperial household. They included five ministers who directed all the military and civil services. The two principal ministers were the Grand Chamberlain and the Grand Chancellor.

The empire was divided into four prefectures, subdivided into dioceses; each diocese contained many provinces, and each province many cities. The prefectures were administered by prefects, the dioceses by vicars, and the provinces by rectors.

The military commanders were inferior to the civil officials; the highest grades were those of dukes and counts. The army scarcely resembled that which had conquered the world. The legions contained only 1,500 men, and the troops on the frontiers, less well paid than those in the center, were composed mainly of barbarians who were called federates. They incorporated bands of the invaders, and in this way the barbarians slowly trickled into the empire, which was badly prepared for defense. Soldiers deserted in numbers, and it became the custom to brand them to prevent them from leaving the flag.

Constantine, at his death, divided the empire between his three sons, and civil war began again. Three great events stand out during this troubled time: an attempt to restore paganism, the installation of certain barbarians within the empire, and the definite triumph of Christianity, which became the State religion.

The attempt to restore paganism was the work of the emperor Julian, Constantine's nephew, who had been brought up as a Christian. He had lived for some time in Athens to study literature and Greek philosophy. When the civil wars made him emperor, he abjured Christianity, adopted the worship of Mithra, rebuilt the abandoned temples, and restored all the ceremonies of the ancient religion. Christians named him the Apostate; he did not attempt persecution. He said himself: "I am determined to use softness and humanity in dealing with all Galileans." But he tried to ruin their influence; he excluded them from public offices and forbade them to teach profane letters, saying: "Be content to believe and cease wanting to learn." His attempt was not lasting, for he died in an expedition against the Persians (360–363 A.D.).

Julian died without heirs. The empire was once more the prey of soldiers of fortune: Valentinian, Valens, and, much later, Theodosius (379 A.D.). The last-named was a Spaniard, a good soldier, whose first care was to reorganize the army and repel an invasion of the Visigoths, who had penetrated into the Balkan peninsula. After defeating them, he took them into the pay of the empire, and thus, at one moment, 40,000 barbarians entered the Roman army and installed themselves in the frontier provinces. This prepared the way for further invasions.

Theodosius was converted to Christianity as the result of an illness (380 A.D.). He published an edict which made the judgments of the Council of Nicaea the law of the State. Taking the part of the Orthodox against the Arians, he ordered by this edict, signed at Salonica, "that all his subjects should live in the religion which the holy apostle Peter had taught the Romans." The Council of Constantinople condemned all heretics and closed their churches.

In 391 A.D., the emperor began to move against the pagans. He made visits to the heathen temples punishable, and in 392 A.D., he forbade the worship of idols. These measures were taken by Theodosius as the result of an event which shows clearly that a new power, that of the clergy, had arisen. The people of certain Eastern towns were indignant at the favor the emperor showed the Christians.

There were several revolts, and one of them was put down with great cruelty at Salonica (390 A.D.). The emperor ordered his Gothic soldiers to surround the circus during a performance, and 7,000 persons were massacred. This horrible action aroused universal indignation. When the emperor presented himself at Milan Cathedral, the bishop Ambrose forbade him to enter until he had expiated his crime. Theodosius submitted and did penance.

Before his death (395 A.D.), Theodosius divided the empire between his two sons. The elder, Arcadius, was to rule the East; the younger, Honorius, the West. The empire of the West lasted less than a century (476 A.D.); that of the East lasted until 1453 A.D., when the Turks took Constantinople. The division of 395 A.D. marks the end of the history of the Roman Empire.